REQUIEM

FOR THE

DEVIL

A Novel

Jeri Smith-Ready

iPUBLISH.com
at Time Warner Books

Song lyrics in chapter 6 by Gregory Miller and Jeri Smith-Ready.

For information address Warner Books, 1271 Avenue of the Americas, New York, NY 10020.

Ⓦ A Time Warner Company

ISBN 0-7595-5007-7

First edition: April 2001

Visit our Web site at www.iPublish.com

Table of Contents

To my husband Christian,
and to the memory of my father

Acknowledgments

The mythical framework of *Requiem* is derived from that of John Milton's *Paradise Lost*, to which I consider this novel one of many possible sequels. Other sources include historian Jeffrey Burton Russell's *Mephistopheles: The Devil in the Modern World*, Genevieve and Tom Morgan's *The Devil: A Visual Guide to the Demonic, Evil, Scurrilous, and Bad*, and all the bad Hollywood devil movies that left one good story untold.

Thanks first to my parents and family, for a lifetime of encouragement. Thanks also to author Catherine Asaro, my mentor and friend, for showing me the way; to Warner Aspect editor-in-chief Betsy Mitchell, for passing my manuscript to iPublish.com; to Barry Gerber, for the original concept; to Rob Staeger and Cecilia Ready, for their invaluable editorial feedback; to Beth Venart, for her creative insights that helped form the characters and their destinies; to Gregory Miller, for the song that betrayed his gender's most guarded secrets; to Li-Su Javedan, for offering support instead of sympathy when I faced setbacks; to Adrian Ready, for the 1:30 A.M. phone call; to Anne Griffith Liebeskind and Tom Liebeskind, for their inspiration. Thanks especially to my editor, Paul Witcover, for opening the door. I'd offer him my first-born child in return, but he already has it.

My deepest gratitude will always belong to my husband, Christian Ready. He has inspired and proven the central truth of this book: that love is infinite in its power and patience.

I

Liber Scriptus Proferetur

S ome days it's good to be the Devil. November 7, 1997, began as one of those days, and ended as something quite different.

". . . so I was going to fly out to Stanford for her homecoming dance, but the night before I was supposed to leave, she told me she had another date and didn't want to see me anymore. We've been together almost two years."

The boy sitting next to me at the coffee shop counter fingered the W on his blue George Washington University baseball cap. I sneaked a glance at my watch and realized I was late for a conference call with a "freely elected" South American dictator. This diversion had been too tempting to resist, though.

"I can't sleep anymore, I can't eat," he said. "My grades are in the toilet. I'll probably flunk out this semester."

"Have you thought about getting professional help?" I asked him.

"Yeah, I saw a psychiatrist. He gave me some antidepressants that didn't work, so I stopped taking them."

I could smell the young man's despair—sweet and acrid, like a candle just blown out. He needed direction. I had one for him.

"Could it be that your girlfriend just doesn't realize how much you love her?"

"How can she, when she's totally cut me off? She changed her phone number, her e-mail address, she sends back my letters without opening them." He pinched the bridge of his nose. "It's like she's dead."

"Maybe you need to send her a message she can't ignore."

His bloodshot green eyes met mine, then he glanced over his shoulder toward the window. "I wanted to go into that church across the street, but it's been so long since I went to mass I figured God wouldn't recognize me. So I sat here and asked Him for some kind of sign." He looked at me again. "That's when you showed up. I figured you were my sign. That's why I told you all that stuff, even though I don't know who the hell you are."

"You looked troubled."

"Yeah, and you asked me what was wrong, and that was cool. Most people don't even notice." The boy sat silent and rubbed his stubbled chin, then suddenly reached for his bookbag and pulled out a bottle of pills. "I kept these. I've got three weeks' worth left. You think . . . I mean, do you think that's enough?"

"Enough for what?"

"Enough . . . to send a message." His thumb fidgeted with the edge of the childproof cap.

"I don't know much about that sort of thing," I said. "However, I do know that women are all die hard romantics."

"Yeah. My girlfriend loved that *Romeo and Juliet* movie—you know, the one with the kid from *Titanic*?" He stopped fidgeting and looked at me. "Hey, you think if she knew I was—I mean, if she thought I was . . ."

He had his own momentum. Time for me to go.

"Sorry to cut this short," I said, "but I've got to get to the office." I paid for my coffee and bought a bottle of spring water while the boy cradled the pills and gazed dreamily through the wall. "I hope everything works out," I said to him.

"Thanks for listening to me, man. You've helped me a lot." He was calm now, and when he shook my hand, his grip was firm.

"I'm sure she'll get the message." I turned and walked out, leaving the spring water on the counter.

Later that day, Beelzebub and Mephistopheles called to tell me they were on the prowl for soft young female flesh. On a Friday night in Georgetown, that meant a trip to the Attic. The meat market dance club scene was beginning to bore me, but I decided to indulge them once more.

While waiting for them to arrive, I wrote another movement of my latest piano concerto. Now that the busy Halloween season was over, it was time to find another composer to torture. I planned to track down a starving unknown musician playing in a dilapidated bar, infect their mind with one of my melodies, then watch them never sleep again. They would go mad and eventually self-destruct, but not before releasing into the world a work of great beauty and terror, a work that would rock the foundations of humanity's faith.

"Are you ready yet or what?"

Beelzebub leaned against the doorjamb, his head cocked.

"You're late," I said.

"You're surprised." He bounced over to straddle the piano bench, facing me.

"Where's Mephistopheles?"

"He's out preening himself in front of the mirror in your

foyer." He pronounced "foyer" with an exaggerated French accent. "He thinks he may have a piece of lint on his jacket." Before I could close the piano cover, Beelzebub knocked out a double-time version of "Chopsticks" on the minor keys.

"I love that tune." He smoothed a stray lock of blond hair under his baseball cap, worn backwards at an angle.

I glanced at his baggy pants and denim jacket. "You look like you're about twelve years old in that outfit."

"Hey, it's the style. It's what all the frat boy assholes are wearing these days."

I knew he intended "frat boy assholes" as a term of endearment. He was, after all, their king.

We walked into the foyer to find Mephistopheles. His face was inches away from the full-length mirror, and he seemed to be examining his teeth.

"Are my nose hairs getting too long?" he asked me.

I shouldered my way in front of him to comb my hair. "Fine, thanks, and you?"

"Huh? Oh, sorry, Lucifer. And how is Your Most Unholy Highness this fine evening?" Mephistopheles bowed and kissed the toe of my boot. I smiled at his sarcasm-coated respect. Sincere groveling has no place in my regime.

"Hey, Lou," Beelzebub said, "I know I ask this every time we go out, but—"

"No, you may not be taller than me, even for one night." I looked at Mephistopheles. "New outfit?"

"You know it," he said. Mephistopheles burned clothes after wearing them once. Even his face changed subtly with the caprices of fashion. Over the past twenty years, his skin had grown darker, his nose broader, and his hair coarser. "Sort of a reverse Michael Jackson," he would say.

We left my apartment and went down to the lobby. While the valet fetched my car, we walked outside my building to wait.

"I trust you had productive days," I said.

Beelzebub took a coin out of his pocket. "I deflated a Third World country's currency." He melted the coin in his hand. "Bangladesh, I think it was. Or maybe Barbados. I get them mixed up."

"I hacked my way into the Defense Department's research and development files," Mephistopheles said. "Rearranged some of the blueprints for a new missile delivery system. Now it's not quite as accident-proof."

"Not bad," I said. "I inspired a suicide this morning."

"Shit!" Beelzebub shoved my arm. "You lucky little snake, you."

"It's like these people fall into your lap," Mephistopheles said. "I wish I could get me a sweet hands-on project like that. I look everywhere, and damn if I can find them."

"That's why you can't find them," I said. "Stop looking, and despair will find you when you least expect it. Just like love."

We all shared a belly laugh at the concept. Beelzebub started singing a spoof of the Motown hit "You Can't Hurry Love." Mephistopheles sang backup.

You can't hurry woe
No, you just have to wait
Gloom will come easy
and soon their hope will suffocate. . . .

I parked the car seven blocks away from the club. Even our powers were not such that we could get a decent parking space on Dupont Circle on a Friday night.

The crowd parted subconsciously as we strode down the sidewalk. Outside a shoe store, a group of window-shopping young women turned and stared at us with a faint glimmer of

familiarity. I smiled at the tall brunette, the one I'd enter-
tained months ago.

"July, wasn't it?" Mephistopheles asked.

"July Fourth," Beelzebub said. "We met them that day on
the Mall and then fucked during the fireworks. On your balcony, right, Lou? Man, what a view that was. I love this city."

As we walked past them, the women only blinked at us, as if
they didn't remember our liaison, which of course they didn't.
After a casual incursion into the life of a human, we would leave
him or her only with a vague disturbing fascination, but no
memory.

We came upon a sandwich board outside an alley. On the
board was a handwritten poster that read, PLAYING TONIGHT
AT THE GROTTO: "THE GOSPEL ACCORDING TO THE BLUES." An
arrow pointed into the alley.

"Wait," I said.

Beelzebub hopped from foot to foot.

"Lou, come on. We're late already. Right now my tongue
should be down the throat of some drunk girl who can't
remember her own name."

"Go ahead. I'll catch up." I left them behind and strode
down the alley. I stopped in front of the Grotto's door, my
hand an inch from the knob.

Beelzebub appeared at my side. "What's up?"

"I don't know. This place . . . there's something odd here . . .
maybe the musician I'm looking for."

"You're such a wack job sometimes, I swear." Beelzebub
turned the knob. "Let's just go in, okay?" He pulled the door
open and waited for me to enter.

The smoky, shabby bar was only about a quarter full. I
moved inside and edged around the cigarette machine to get a
better view of the place.

We were the youngest-looking inhabitants of the bar by at least ten years. Two of the burly men next to the decrepit pool table leaned on their cues and glowered at us. No one else turned to look our way. Early rhythm and blues squeaked from the tinny speakers in the ceiling. A flickering black-and-white television on the edge of the bar displayed a silent, grainy image of a hockey game. A neon BEER sign glowed in the window.

"How did this dive land in this neighborhood?" Beelzebub said.

"I don't know," I said, "but I think I like it." I sat down at the bar and ordered a whiskey from the gruff, muscular bartender. Beelzebub and Mephistopheles stood behind me.

"Think they got any microbrews here?" Beelzebub asked.

"Doubt it," Mephistopheles said.

"What a waste of time."

"Shhh. Bub, let's just hang out 'til Lou figures out what he's here for. I trust his instincts, even if they are coming between me and a nice piece."

"There aren't even any women here, did you notice that?" Beelzebub tugged at my shirt. "I said, did you notice that?"

I pushed his hand off my sleeve. "Shut up and go away."

"What?"

"You heard me," I said. "Go cast your lines into the slut pool at the Attic. I'm not in the mood."

"You're kidding, right?" Mephistopheles said. I glared at him, and he backed away, holding up his hands. "Okay. It's cool. We outta here."

Beelzebub followed him, shaking his head. "We'll be back to get you later, bud."

"Whatever." I slouched over my drink, which was all the company I wanted. A cymbal rang on the far corner of the bar as the blues band began its set. I stayed where I was so I could hear, but not see, the piano player. Whoever it was, was good. Not much technical prowess, but there was a rawness of emotion, with a touch of torment. A squeaking, purring harmonica played a few bars, then stopped. It was time to take a peek. I moved to the end of the bar just as the singer stepped into the light.

I stared at her for the entire first verse before realizing I hadn't blinked. She didn't open her own eyes until after the first chorus. When she did, she looked straight at me. She smiled for half a second, then slid back into her world of voice.

Not a single note was on key, but she sang like she didn't care. Her conviction was so potent that it seemed as if the musicians were the ones who were tone-deaf. Every inch of her body believed in the music.

Cold water splashed onto my fingers. I looked down and saw that my hand was trembling so violently that the ice in my drink had leapt out of the glass. I placed the glass on the small table in front of me and sank into the chair, never taking my eyes off of her. The piano player was long forgotten.

When the song was over, she cast a grim smile at her band and tucked her chin-length black hair behind her ears. Tepid applause trickled through the room, and I stood up to clap, tipping my table but catching it before it fell over.

She looked at me, then at the rest of the inattentive bar, and back at me again. The band began to play an even slower, more hypnotic song. The world's most perceptive bartender set another whiskey in front of me, along with a large glass of ice water. I handed him fifty dollars.

Her almond-colored eyes lay under thin, arched eyebrows. Her angular face looked as if it had been carved by hand while all other faces had been hacked out of some generic human mold. A long-sleeved velvet dress cleaved to her thin body and was a deep, delicious red that made my eyeballs feel drunk. I fought to remember who I was and to maintain an aloofness appropriate to the second most powerful being in the universe.

I wasn't successful.

When she stepped off the stage after the set, I pretended to study the graffiti carved into the table.

"I can't believe they let you in here."

I looked up. She stood before me, her right fist planted on her hip.

"What?"

"You must have a really good fake ID," she said. "Either that or a note from your mom."

"Do you always introduce yourself by insulting people?"

"It's a defense mechanism." She slumped into the chair across from me and rested her chin on her knuckles. "Thanks for paying attention while I sang. Most people are too embarrassed to actually look at me."

"It was easy. You were good."

"It wasn't one of my better performances." She winced. "Actually, it was one of my better performances. That's the problem." She chuckled and fluttered her hand. "Oh well, it's fun, in a sick, sad sort of way."

I beckoned the bartender, who was now in my thrall. He appeared in a moment. "Would you like a drink?" I asked her.

"Shot of Jameson's. Thanks."

"My name's Louis." I extended my hand. She took it. Her fingers were long and strong and soft.

"Hi, Louis. I've never seen you here before."

"I never knew this place existed before tonight. I was on my way somewhere else with some friends when it caught my eye."

"Where were you going?"

"The Attic."

"Never heard of it."

"It's one of those preppy sleazeball dance clubs," I said. "Not really your type of place, I imagine."

"Doubt it. Call me impudent, but you don't strike me as a preppy sleazeball."

"That's why I'm here and not there."

She looked around. "Guess what? You don't exactly fit in here, either. Then again, neither do I."

"So tell me where we'd fit in, and let's go there."

"Nah, I'd rather stay here and stand out." Her drink arrived, and she grabbed it. "Oh, thank God. This is just what I need after making an ass of myself onstage." She held up her glass. "What should we drink to?"

"Let's drink to . . ." *to the long night of blistering sex ahead of us* ". . . to spontaneous changes in plans."

"Hear, hear." She downed her shot in a gulp. "Louis, it's been nice talking to you, but I gotta go."

I nearly snarfed my whiskey.

"Go? It's early yet."

She stood up. "Maybe for you, but I've been up since five A.M."

"Can I see you again?"

"I don't think so. I try not to date younger men."

"I'm older than I look."

"Yes, I'm sure you are, and you're probably mature for your age, but even men my age aren't mature enough, and that's old enough to be president."

I had wanted to win her over the modern way, by being charming and sweet and of course stunningly attractive, but there was no time for that. I touched her hand and stared into her eyes.

"Please." I gazed past her retinas into her mind and searched until I found the right neuron to trigger. "I'd really like to see you again. I think we'd have a nice time together."

Her face turned blank for a moment, then she blinked. "Um . . . okay."

"What's your phone number?" I could find it myself in her memory, but I didn't want to poke around too much. She pulled her hand away.

"No, let's just meet somewhere. Sunday. How about by the Reflecting Pool? One-thirty okay?"

"I'll be there." She turned to leave. "Hey," I said, "you never told me your name."

"If I decide to show up Sunday, I'll tell you then." She waved as she walked out the back exit.

A spurt of giggles shot from the front door behind me. I turned to see Beelzebub and Mephistopheles enter with three young women.

"Hey, bud," said Beelzebub, "I know you were busy doing whatever, so I brought you your very own friend to keep you company. Say hi to Trish. Trish, this is Lou. He's a little fucked in the head tonight, but I guarantee he's worth the trouble."

A short red-haired woman in a tight green sweater staggered forward. "Wow, you told me he was cute," she said, "but I thought you meant like in a good-personality-type kinda way. Hi."

"Hello," I said.

"So, like, what's your major?"

It didn't usually matter that a woman was annoying, as long as she was weak-minded enough to bend to my will, which this one obviously was.

"Don't take this personally," I said to her, "but I don't want you."

"Huh?"

"Believe me, these two will occupy you more than you could ever imagine." I turned to leave. Beelzebub caught my shoulder.

"What the hell are you doing, Lou? We went to all this trouble to find a girl for you."

"I appreciate the thought, but I said I don't want her, and I meant it." I pulled my car keys from my pocket. "Here. Take the car. Don't crash it. Good night."

I left the bar and turned down the street toward home.

2

In Quo Totum Continetur

Unprecedented. Absolutely unprecedented.

I sat in my library, surrounded by stacks of books, hundreds of thousands, millions of words, centuries of human knowledge. On all sides of me stood walls of poetry, drama, astronomy, psychology, none of it worth the pulp on which it was written as far as helping me solve this mystery.

"Dammit!" I threw down my pen in disgust. It bounced off the top legal pad, which was filled beyond the margins with notes and equations. The midmorning sun trickled through the window, performing a slow waltz for the dust motes.

My mind would not let go of her song. Even as the rational portion of my consciousness focused on the written words, the faint, pulsing part of me continued to play the music and her voice in the background. At times it would get louder, and the pages would blur as I slipped into memory, then fantasy, playing the past off the future.

During one of these reveries, Beelzebub's head appeared over a wall of books.

"Dude, you okay?"

"What?"

"I knocked," he said, "but I guess you didn't hear me."

"You didn't knock, Beelzebub. You never knock."

"Okay, but I was walking really loud." He held up my keys and jangled them. "In your parking space and in one piece. Who says I can't perform miracles, huh?" He dropped the keys on the table and pawed through a stack of books.

"Keats . . . Shakespeare . . . Kepler . . . Freud? What kind of research are you doing, Lou?"

"I'm not sure yet."

Beelzebub picked up one of the three legal pads filled with scribbles.

"After all this, you're not sure yet? Have you been up all night in here?"

"Yes, why?"

"Man, you missed a great party. Trish took us back to her sorority house."

"No kidding."

"Yeah, you know that circus trick with all the clowns in the Volkswagen?"

"Uh-huh."

"Well, they had this hot tub . . ."

"You must be exhausted."

"All in a night's work." He fondled the cover of *Antony and Cleopatra*.

"Have you ever read that?" I said.

He snorted. "What do you think?"

"I think that before the advent of *Sports Illustrated*, you didn't read anything but road signs."

"Okay, just to prove to you that I'm not so stupid, I'll read it right now."

"Good. Have fun."

He sat down, propped his feet on the table, and turned to page one. I moved the rolling ladder left of the fireplace, climbed it, and searched for the first volume of Newton's *Principia Mathematica*. Within a minute, I heard pages flipping behind me. I turned to see Beelzebub looking for the last page before the appendices.

"They all die in the end," I said.

"Oh. Oh, good." He tossed the book back onto the pile. I resumed my search. He began whistling a recent dance club tune and drumming on the table to accompany himself.

"Do you want to help me or not?" I said.

"Yeah, sure."

"Go get me a bagel. And some French roast coffee from that place across the street."

"What am I, your intern?"

I glared at him. "Last night I let you have my car and an extra half a woman, and you won't even get me a bagel?"

"Oh, yeah . . . sorry. You want fries with that?"

"Go."

After he left, I climbed down the ladder and moved to the living room. If the answer to my dilemma lay not in words, perhaps it hid in music. I sat at the piano and played.

Ten minutes later, Beelzebub appeared next to me. My fingers rested for the first time since he'd left.

"What the hell was that?" he said.

"I don't know." I played a few more bars. "It just came to me."

"It sounds weird. Different."

"I know. It's in the key of C. I've never written anything in the key of C before." I continued, my fingers never approaching the black keys.

"Okay, Lou, step away from the piano now. You're freaking me out."

I closed the key cover and stared at my hands. "Me, too."

3

Tantus Labor Non Sit Cassus

T he sky was a sharp slate blue when I entered the Mall on Sunday afternoon. The feeble November sun pierced a flimsy layer of clouds.

I found her on a bench near the Lincoln Memorial end of the Reflecting Pool. She was reading the latest issue of the left-wing journal *The Nation*, her knees pulled up to provide both a shelf for the journal and a barrier against the breeze. I wanted to preserve this picture of her, absorbed and unselfconscious, so I waited before approaching her. Every half-minute or so she would tuck the same loose strand of black hair behind her left ear. I watched her until the need to have her eyes on me grew too strong to wait any longer.

"Now I've met both people in this town who still read that magazine," I said.

She looked up. "I think the other one moved to a commune outside Poughkeepsie last week. Maybe he'll send us a postcard."

I returned her smile.

"Hi."

"Hi." She gestured to the bench. "Sit down?" I did. She studied my face and furrowed her brow. "Don't take this the wrong way, but you look a lot older today than you did the other night."

"When I go out at night I prefer to be filmed through gauze, like an aging movie star." Actually, I had added a few tiny lines at the corners of my eyes and mouth, enough to place me plausibly on the edge of thirty.

"You should stick with reality. It looks good on you." She raised the zipper of her jacket another inch. "But you probably hear that a lot."

"Hear what a lot?"

"What did you say your name was?"

"Lou." I reached for her hand. "Louis Carvalho. And you are?"

She hesitated, then grasped my hand. "Gianna. Gianna O'Keefe. Spelled like three syllables, pronounced like two."

"Gianna. That's an interesting name."

"Yes. I'm part of a set."

"How so?"

"I have three older brothers—Matthew, Marc, and Luke."

"Ah, I see."

"Yes, when I turned out to be a girl, my parents couldn't decide what would be worse for me—feeling left out or feeling ridiculous. They chose ridiculous. Now we're chronically Catholic and chronically cute. A fucking circus act."

"At least you're not bitter about it."

"Right. Sorry." Gianna rolled up her paper. "I get torqued up when I read about what those imbeciles on Capitol Hill are doing this week. But I probably haven't known you long enough to talk politics."

"You obviously haven't lived in D.C. very long if you think two and a half minutes is too soon to talk politics."

"I've lived here long enough. That's the problem with this city. It either chews you up and spits you out, or it gets inside you and changes you until you're as shallow as the rest of them. Either way you're devoured."

"Yes, but it's the weekend now," I took the paper from her hands, "and you know what weekends are for?"

"No, what?"

"For fattening up."

"Excuse me?"

"So that when the bastards start to nibble away at you," I said, "there'll be more of you left over afterwards."

Gianna took back her *Nation*. "Left over for what?"

"For whatever you like."

"For whatever I like." She placed the magazine inside her jacket and looked around. "I like ice cream. Let's get some."

As we meandered down the sidewalk, I stole glances at her face. Her intensity streamed from every pore. I had a sense that she was restraining this power somewhat; perhaps it had frightened others.

"You're right," she said. "It's Sunday afternoon, and I'm still not wound down from the week. I suppose it's a lost cause by this point."

"It's never too late to relax. And if today's not enough, you'll just have to take a vacation, starting now."

"A vacation? That's impossible."

"It's not," I said. "Think about it. It is entirely possible that in two hours, we could be on a plane bound for Bermuda."

She stopped. "You're kidding."

"I'm just saying that it's possible, that the only barriers to doing it are the ones we choose to erect."

"We just met."

"Then we'll just get ice cream."

We walked on in silence. A few minutes later she said, "I kinda wish I'd said yes."

"Yes to what?"

"To your Bermuda idea."

"The offer stands."

"No, it wouldn't be the same," she said. "A spontaneous proposition deserves a spontaneous response."

"You gave me a spontaneous response when you said no."

We reached the ice cream shop, which was empty except for a couple of coffee drinkers hunched over steaming Styrofoam cups.

"Let's split something," she said. "You pick two flavors. I like them all."

I turned to the boy behind the counter.

"Except one," Gianna added.

It was a test I could pass without the slightest peek into her mind.

"Give us two scoops of anything but vanilla," I told the boy.

Gianna leaned against the freezer. "Very impressive."

"I could tell you're the anti-vanilla type."

"Why not, with so many more interesting options?" she said. "I used to go out with a guy who always ordered vanilla. It wasn't just ice cream. We'd go to the finest Italian restaurants in South Philly, and he'd order spaghetti and meatballs."

"I can't imagine that relationship lasted very long."

"No, only about nine years."

"Here you go, sir, chocolate peanut butter and pistachio."

I looked at Gianna. "Now that's a bowl of anti-vanilla."

We sat outside at a tiny round white metal table, mostly out of the wind but in view of the huddled passersby who paused to stare at us before shivering and scurrying on. I allowed myself to feel the full force of the cold air, because sitting near Gianna made complete humanity and all its sensations alluring. Engrossed in her every gesture, I was forgetting who I was.

"Jesus loves you."

A short, saggy-faced woman with huge glasses and a plaid scarf shoved a lime green flyer into Gianna's reluctant hands. As she moved inside the ice cream shop, the woman nodded and repeated, "Jesus loves you."

"Then how come he never calls?" Gianna said, only loudly enough for me to hear. "Sorry. Hope I didn't offend you."

"Your irreverence is refreshing," I said.

"I spend all week watching every word I say, so my nastiness gets a little pent up." She read the flyer. "'Charles Darwin—the real father of Communism.' No wonder these people don't believe in evolution. It obviously hasn't worked in their favor." She crumpled the paper in her hands. "Sometimes religion can be so absurd, you know?"

"Yes, I know."

"What about you?" she asked.

"What about me?"

"What religion are you? I'm only asking because if I tell my mom we had sort of a date, she'll want to know if you're Catholic."

"I'm not really any religion."

"Are you an atheist?"

"Far from it. I believe in a supreme being. It's just that the things I believe about him don't fit into any religion that I can stomach."

"Oh. That's cool. At least you think about it. Lots of people inherit their religion and never even consider it." Gianna scraped the bottom of the ice cream cup with her spoon. It squeaked, and she cringed. "I think it'd be better for people to be born with no religion at all and then later choose one, or more than one, that they feel most at home with."

"You think you'd still want to be Catholic?"

"Definitely. It's a very cool religion, as long as you can ignore the Pope." She licked the back of her spoon. "I don't think God much cares what religion anybody follows, as long as we're basically good, which just about everyone is."

"You've got pistachio ice cream in your hair." I drew my fingers across the rogue strand and wiped it clean. She glanced in the direction of my hand.

"Yeah, well, you've got . . . you've got some on your . . ." Gianna touched my face near the corner of my nose. Her fingers were cold, and I had a sudden urge to put them in my mouth, and in other warm places.

She jerked her hand back and shivered. "I'm going back inside to get coffee. Want some?"

"Okay, I'll—"

"No, you stay. I'll take care of it." She rushed into the shop without looking back.

"General, long time no see, sir."

I turned to see Moloch, commander of my defeated army, dressed in his usual crisp fatigues with boots so shiny you could see your soul in them. He was saluting me.

"Moloch," I said. "It's been a while. At ease, please." He maintained his position. Without standing, I returned his salute. It seemed to satisfy him.

"Sir, we need to talk, if I may." Moloch pulled a map from one of his thirty-two pockets and began to unfold it.

"Actually, Colonel, I'm in the middle of something here."

"Yes, sir, but I thought you should know right away. I may have discovered a back door to Heaven."

"What, another one?" I glanced back at the ice cream shop. Gianna was still in line.

"We're positive this one's real, sir. I'm still working on the numbers, but I think that with all the recent recruits, the stolen Russian fighter jets, and the element of surprise on our side, we could make another stab at taking back the Celestial City."

"Right. Look, Moloch," I patted his thick arm, "you keep working on that, but not a single movement without my permission."

"Never, sir. We'll speak again soon, I hope."

"Certainly. Call my secretary and have her book us a couple of hours."

"Will do, sir." Moloch saluted me and retreated just as Gianna came out of the ice cream shop.

"Who was that?" she asked.

"Some Vietnam vet, just left the memorial. Wanted to educate me on the MIAs. They're having a special ceremony Tuesday for Veterans Day."

"Oh." She handed me a cup of coffee. "Why did he salute you?"

"Habit, I guess. Are you feeling fatter yet?"

"Huh? Oh, that." She blew on her coffee, then smiled and looked at me. "You want fat? I'll take you to a place that floats in fat."

We stood eye-to-eye on the escalator descending into the Metro station.

"So we've talked about politics and religion already," she said. "Now for the icky stuff. What do you do?"

"I have my own firm, a combination think tank–consulting firm. We do government consulting, mainly in economics."

She stepped back one escalator step and looked down at me. "Wait . . . you're *that* Carvalho, of the Carvalho Group?"

"You've heard of us."

"Are you kidding? You put out some pretty innovative stuff. It's hard to figure out where you stand politically."

"I like it that way. Gives us a wider potential client base."

"Ah, a mercenary," she said.

We reached the platform and sat on a smooth granite bench to wait for the train.

"What about you?" I asked.

"I'm a lobbyist."

"Speaking of mercenaries . . ."

"No, I'm on the side of the good guys," she said. "Of course, everyone claims to be a good guy."

"I don't."

"Congratulations."

"So what slice of American pie do you represent?"

"The people I fight for don't get any pie," she said, "unless you count the stale crumbs. I'm an advocate for the poor."

"Then you're a brave woman. Compassion is a scarce commodity these days."

"True, it's not the trendiest of jobs, or the most lucrative." The smooth silver train slid into the station. The rush of wind through the tunnel blew Gianna's hair into a black corona around her head.

"This time of year," she said, "people's consciences gnaw at them. They give away truckloads of canned goods and quote Dickens and wring their hands over the 'less fortunate.'" We boarded the Metro and took seats perpendicular to each other. "But God forbid anyone should address why they're poor in the first place, or try to change the structures that keep them poor. Then the 'less fortunate' turn into 'welfare queens' and 'derelicts.' But if I were a lobbyist whoring on behalf of some transnational corporation, I'd never hear the word 'derelict.'"

"So when it comes to taking care of poor people," I said, "if Mother Teresa is the Hallmark card, then you're the electric bill."

Gianna laughed. "I'm going to put that observation on a poster in our office." She propped her feet on the edge of my seat, folded her arms in front of her chest, and examined me. It felt good. "Louis Carvalho, in the flesh. Brilliant, handsome, and probably very wealthy. What's it like to be on top of the world?"

"Excuse me?"

"Sorry," she said. "I have a psychological disorder that prevents me from keeping thoughts inside my head where they belong. Are you married?"

"Would I be here with you if I were married?"

"Sure. You'd be a jerk, though, and I'm trying to rule out that possibility."

"No, I'm not married."

"Ever been?"

"No," I said, "not even close."

"Why not?"

"No one ever asked me. What about you?"

"Countless times," she said.

"Married or asked?"

"Asked. But all the times don't really count, because it was always the same person."

"Mr. Vanilla?"

"How'd you guess?" The train slowed into another station. "Here's our stop."

"Where are you taking me?"

"To the world's greatest chicken," she said.

The world's greatest chicken apparently roosted in a joint called the Squabhouse, where the grease seemed to ooze from the wood paneling itself. We sat at a tiny window table.

The waitress arrived with menus. I scanned the beer list, dismayed at the choices. "I guess I'll have a glass of—"

"We don't got glasses."

"Sorry?"

"We only serve beer by the pitcher," the waitress said. "Then you drink it out of a cup."

"It's okay," Gianna said. "We'll have a pitcher of light beer." After the waitress left, Gianna said, "All things in moderation, right?"

She was right about the chicken, and there was nothing moderate about it. It tasted like it had been smothered in manna and fried in the sweat of angels.

After several minutes, I broke the silence of unbridled ravenousness. "This is incredible."

"Isn't it? I love eating chicken with my bare hands. It makes me want to snarl at people, even more than usual." She licked the grease off her fingers and picked up her cup of beer. "So you like this place? You're not mad I made you slum?"

"Of course not." I scarfed another onion ring. "You can't eat ambience."

"I'll drink to that." We tapped plastic cups in a toast. My mobile phone rang.

"Just a second." I reached inside my jacket for the phone. "Yes?"

"Hey, it's me," Mephistopheles said.

"Go ahead, Malcolm."

"Oh, you're with someone."

"Yes, I'm on a date. Get to the point." Gianna split the last onion ring and left half of it in the basket.

"Sorry, Lou. I'm at the home of one of our minions. One of the humans. A lawyer."

"Let me guess: he wants to renegotiate his contract."

"Bingo. He says we tricked him into agreeing to indefinite terms."

"Did you remind him about Article II?"

"You mean the one about free will?"

"That's the one." I watched Gianna eat the remaining onion ring half.

"We reviewed the whole agreement in detail," Mephistopheles said. "He wants to talk to you."

"I'm busy right now. Have him send me a memo."

"Please, Lou, as a favor to me, would you get him off my back?"

I sighed. "Fine. Put him on."

"Thanks. His name's John Vaughn. So if you're on a date, we shouldn't wait for you tonight?"

"What's tonight?"

"Sunday. Movie night at Bub's."

"Oh, yeah. No, don't wait for me." I stood up and said to Gianna, "You'll have to excuse me for a moment." I stepped out onto the sidewalk.

"Hello?" a man's voice said on the phone.

"Yes?"

"How are you this evening, sir?"

"Extremely occupied, Mr. Vaughn. Now state your complaint in twenty words or less."

"It's not exactly a complaint. More of a request. I'd like to get out of our contract early."

"Very funny. What do you really want?"

The other end of the phone was silent for a moment. "I—"

"Mr. Vaughn, haven't we given you more money, power, and respect than you could possibly deserve?"

"Yes, but—"

"And in return, you've served us well. I think both parties are benefiting from the arrangement, don't you agree?"

"Actually, I think the time is approaching when this party will cease to benefit. I'd like to file a habeas corpus on my behalf, and—"

"A what?!" I glanced back at the restaurant window, waved and smiled at Gianna, then turned my back. "Listen to me, you pathetic little prick, I know what this is all about. You're getting older, staring death in the face, and you're looking for a little salvation insurance."

"I—"

"The only way out of our employment is to be terminated."

"How do I get—"

"Don't ask. Look, for your sake, let's both pretend this conversation never happened. Good night, Mr. Vaughn." I hung up.

Gianna was finishing the last drumstick when I re-entered the Squabhouse.

"Sorry about that," I said. "One of our clients didn't understand the terms of our agreement, and my account exec was having trouble setting him straight."

"It's okay. It's too bad they have to bother you on the weekend, though."

"If you want peace, never own your own business." I looked at the empty plates and cups on the table. "So first we had dessert, now we've had dinner. Shall we complete the cycle and go have cocktails?"

"We just drank a pitcher of beer," she said. "Any more and I'll be unconscious."

"Hors d'oeuvres, then?"

"I'm stuffed."

"Soup? A couple of crackers? What about . . . anything?"

She looked at her watch. "I really need to get home soon. I've got to get up early tomorrow."

"Oh. I see."

"I'd like to see you again, though. Can I call you?"

"I'd like that." I gave her my card.

"How about Friday?"

"How about tomorrow?"

"A Monday night date?"

"We'll defy Monday and have a great time," I said. "I was thinking of the Holy Trinity—drinks, dinner, and dancing."

"Well, Tuesday is Veterans Day, so things at the office will be slow. I could go in late." She bit her lip, then shook her head. "No, I really need to catch up on some paperwork."

"Paperwork?"

"And filing."

"Filing?!"

"I'm kidding," she said. "It's interesting to see how far your ego will stretch to accommodate someone else's wishes."

"What did I do to deserve that comment?"

"Nothing yet. I just have this feeling you're the kind of guy who needs to be kept in check."

"Look, Gianna," I said, "I appreciate your candor and the fact that you feel comfortable enough around me to express every thought that enters your head. But I am not any kind of guy. I am like no one you've ever met before. So don't dump your emotional baggage in front of me and expect me to tiptoe around it."

She stared at me for a moment, then cleared her throat. "Okay."

The waitress arrived with the check, which I paid. "Keep the change." I turned to Gianna. "Okay what?"

"Okay nothing. You're right. I shouldn't attack you like that without cause." She stood and let me help her into her coat. "I'll wait until I have cause. Then I'll attack you."

I turned her to face me. "Expect to be attacked in return."

Her eyes sparked, and the inches between us crackled.

"I can't wait." She uttered a soft little hiss and moved out of my grip. "Let's get out of here."

We walked back to the Metro station in silence. When we boarded the train, I sat next to her. She didn't protest, but averted her eyes. There was something between us that hadn't been there before—something that both separated and connected us.

Finally she pulled out my business card. "I'll come by your office around seven tomorrow night. How's that sound?"

"Great. Seven. That sounds . . . good."

"Okay, then. Good." The train slowed. She stood up. "This is my station."

"Let me walk you home," I said.

"No, don't. I prefer quick good nights. Fewer decisions that way." The train stopped, and the doors opened. "Good night, Louis. I had a brilliant time today."

"Gianna." She stepped onto the platform. I caught her hand and brought it to my lips. As I kissed her fingertips, our minds clicked onto an image so powerful and sensuous that it shocked us both. Our eyes flew open and met. Two chimes signaled the doors' closing. Gianna almost stepped forward, then pulled her hand out of mine a moment before the doors sealed shut.

As the train moved away from the station, I steadied myself and watched her disappear. My view turned to tunnel wall.

"You make a beautiful couple."

I turned to see an elderly black woman in a gray wool coat. Other than a teenager listening to a Walkman stereo, she and I were the only ones remaining in the car.

"Thank you," I said. "This was our first date."

"There's gonna be many more, I can tell."

"Really?" I sat in the seat in front of her.

"Mmm-hmm. Ain't many young men these days know what a fine kiss on the hand can do to a girl. Give her butterflies to keep her up all night."

"I hope she gets some sleep. We're going out tomorrow night, too."

"Oh, she'll have plenty energy, no matter what. You both will. That's the way it is with new love."

My hands went cold. "What?"

"I said, that's the way it is with—"

"I heard you." I stood up and backed away. "It's not like that. It's not like that at all."

She shook her head and let out a throaty cackle. "That's what you think." Her laughter grew louder, erupted into coughs, then faded back into a soft chuckle. "That's what you think."

Just then, the train pulled into another station. I sprang off and ran up the escalator out into the night.

Insane woman, I thought. What does she know? Certainly I find Gianna intoxicating; perhaps I'm even infatuated with her presence. But love? I could no more feel love than a moth could fly to the moon.

I glanced up at the street sign and realized I was less than a mile away from a guaranteed antidote.

Ten minutes later, I knocked on Beelzebub's door. When he opened it, he was wearing a toga.

"Hey, Lou, come on in!"

"Am I late?"

"No, you're just in time. We're getting ready to watch *Caligula*. Wanna join us?"

"Maybe." I followed him down the hall to the living room.

"Yo, Lou!" Mephistopheles's attire matched Beelzebub's. "Sorry I forgot to tell you on the phone to bring your own toga." He handed me a beer. "How was your date?"

"You had a date?" Beelzebub jumped onto the sofa. "All right, story time!"

Mephistopheles muted the television. "Yeah, Lou, regale us with your wondrous tales of whoopee."

"There's nothing to tell," I said.

"No way," Beelzebub said. "Lucifer the Lustpuppy has an everyday, ordinary screw? Say it ain't so."

"No, I mean, there was no sex. But we had a pretty good time." They looked at me blankly. "I'm seeing her again tomorrow night." Their jaws dropped as if choreographed.

"You got a second date?" Mephistopheles said.

"Yes."

"What for?"

"I had a second date once," Beelzebub said. "Just as an experiment. Same deal as you. I didn't score on the first try for some reason, so I decided to have another go at it."

"Did it work?" I said.

"I lost interest by the end of the night. I think I let you have her instead, come to think of it. Remember, tall muscular blonde chick, about three years ago? She kinda had fat knees."

"Doesn't ring a bell."

"I guess I wasn't missing anything then." Beelzebub bounced down onto the cushion and leaned back on the large sofa pillow. "So are you gonna hang out with us tonight or what?"

"I haven't decided yet."

"Come on, Lou," Mephistopheles said. "We're only gonna ask you twice."

"Yeah, we're not in the mood to beg tonight."

"I didn't bring a toga," I said.

"No problem." Beelzebub stood up, removed his toga with one nimble maneuver, and held it towards me. "You can wear mine." He was, of course, naked underneath.

I hesitated for a moment, then thought of the old woman on the Metro, with her sly insights and presumptuous laughter.

I yanked the toga out of his hand. "Get me another beer."

4

Quando Coeli Movendi
Sunt et Terra

Nothing dispels dangerous delusions like a night of debauchery, I thought as I prepared for my second date with Gianna. Now when I looked at myself in the mirror, fastening my gold cufflinks, I saw a man in control.

"I'm only going to say this once."

I turned to see Gianna standing in my office doorway. She looked as if she had always stood there. Her black velvet dress clung to her arms, breasts, and waist before flaring below her hips and swishing above her knees. Her hair was pulled up away from her face, save for a wisp on either side caressing her jaw and cheek. She smoldered with a dangerous elegance.

"You're probably already aware of it," she said, "and I don't want to be in the business of feeding your ego, but you are the most beautiful man I have ever seen."

I stared at her, paralyzed by her radiant beauty, her self-possession. The inexplicable urge to fall to my knees at her feet swept over me. Then I realized she was waiting for my reaction.

I blinked. "Sorry, what did you say?"

She wrinkled her nose and said nothing.

"Gianna, you look . . ." I took a step toward her, then another. "You look . . ." For once, I was at a complete loss for words. "Here, this is for you." From my desk I picked up a white rose, the petals of which were edged with deep red, and presented it to her.

"It's beautiful," she said. "You can't find roses this color just anywhere." She held it to her face and inhaled, then smiled coyly. "Am I to assume from this, monsieur, that your feelings toward me are essentially pure with just a tinge of passion?"

"They didn't have any roses that were red with a tinge of white."

"Oh." She gestured with the rose. "This is a negative image then?"

"It may be backwards, but there's nothing negative about it, I assure you."

We gazed at each other for a moment, and I almost kissed her then, but instead offered her my arm. "Shall we away then?"

"Yes, let's away." She inserted her hand through the crook of my arm, and with her touch I felt the power that had fallen away when she walked in the room return tenfold.

On our elevator trip to the garage I felt a ridiculous need to make small talk.

"Did you have any trouble finding your way here?"

"I took a cab."

"Oh, of course." I couldn't stop staring at her. I reached to touch her hand, but the doors opened first. Gianna took a few steps into the parking garage and gasped.

"Wow, look at that! It's an E-type Jaguar, early sixties, I

think." She crept near it to look inside. "This is one of the world's coolest cars. Not too flashy, you know, a real class act, but so sleek, it's almost terrifying. And black, too. God, I would kill to drive something like this."

The car's alarm disengaged with a loud *doit!* when I pressed the button on my keychain. Gianna sprang back like a startled cat. I held up the keys.

"Whom exactly would you kill to drive it?"

Her eyes widened. "This is yours?" I nodded. "Then pick a victim," she said. "We'll drive to jail in style."

I dropped the keys into her open palm and crossed to the passenger side. She didn't move, only cradled the keys.

I opened the door. "You coming?"

"You sure you trust me to drive this thing?"

"Sure," I said. "Besides, if you wreck it, I can always replace it with one of the two others in the world just like it." I got in the car.

Gianna opened the door and sat in the driver's seat.

"Ohhh," she said. "It just feels like power. The way the seat's shaped, the steering wheel, the gear shift—oh, look at that dashboard." Her hands skimmed over the instruments like a water bug over a pond. She pulled them back as if she had been burned. "Let's get something straight here. I am not impressed with . . . impressed by . . . with . . . material things. Wow."

"It has an engine, too, which will go a long way towards getting us to where we're going."

"Right . . . right. Okay." She turned the key in the ignition. The car roared to life. "Oh, my God. You do have a lot of faith in me, don't you?"

"Not faith—confidence."

"Good. Let's go." She put the car in reverse, then looked at me. "Where are we going, anyway?"

"We have dinner reservations at the Four Seasons at eight-thirty, but I thought we'd hit that little martini bar around the corner first."

"The Four Seasons? Again, wow." She began to back out of the parking space again, then stopped. "Um, since we both earn a salary, I think we should—"

"Relax," I said. "It's my treat tonight." She started to protest. "In exchange for your services as a chauffeur."

"It's a deal. Just sit back and enjoy the ride, sir."

"I already am."

We left the Jaguar at the Four Seasons. Gianna placed her hand on the car's roof in a silent thank-you-goodbye before joining me on the sidewalk.

"That was incredible," she said. "A completely frivolous expense, of course."

"Of course."

"I mean, one payment on that thing could feed a family of four for two months."

"If they had steak every night."

"So officially I feel tainted and offended."

"Get used to it. I have."

"I'm sure," she said.

"Martinis?"

"Okay." She took my arm again, and we walked to the next block and into the martini bar. The magenta-haired hostess put down her cigar and showed us to a table by the window, which stretched along an entire wall. Each tiny black table was trimmed with a strip of neon. Ours was red.

"Wow." Gianna ran her finger along the glowing line. "How do you think they get that in there?" She looked up at me. "That was a really stupid question, wasn't it? I should begin drinking as soon as possible to justify my idiotic remarks." A waitress arrived, and Gianna placed her order. "Bring me something red, to match the table."

"Cinnamon martini okay?"

"Right." Gianna looked at me and made a frightened face.

"How about you, sir?"

"Let me try the blue one." The waitress left. I turned to Gianna. "So when's your next performance?"

"A long time, thank God, to give this town a break from that absurd form of torture. See, the other members of that band are my three brothers, and they all live out of town. Okay, here's the lineup. Pretend you're interested. Marcus, he's the oldest one, he's thirty-eight, a social worker up in Baltimore. He's the only one of us with any musical talent."

"The piano player."

"You noticed. Matthew and Luke, they're twins, thirty-seven. They run an animal shelter outside of Philadelphia— that's where I'm from, by the way. It's one of those humane shelters where they keep them forever, kind of like a nursing home for animals. Matt and Luke are kind of weird, like they share a brain or something. They finish each other's sentences, for instance, and they married another set of identical twins in a double wedding five years ago. They don't have any kids yet, because they're devoted to their business.

"And then there's me. I'm thirty-five, and also married to my career. It's funny, the only one of us who wants children is Marc, and he's gay."

"Do your parents know?"

"They know, but they pretend they don't," she said. "At least they've stopped asking him when he's going to get married."

"So when you turned down countless proposals from Mr. Vanilla . . ."

"My folks were . . . concerned, to say the least, about their dwindling chances for grandchildren. They didn't understand. Not until later, anyway."

"Why? What happened later?"

The waitress arrived with our martinis. Gianna took a sip and changed the subject. "What about you? Family?"

I thought of Beelzebub. "I have one brother, younger. That's all."

"Your parents are dead?"

"Not exactly," I said.

"What do you mean?"

"I never had a mother—that is, I never knew her."

"Oh, I'm sorry."

"It's okay. Bob—my brother—and I were raised by our father." I rolled the olive against the inside of my glass. "He was a father and mother to us. Things were good until . . ."

She leaned closer. "Until what?"

"As an adolescent, I was . . . you might say I was the rebellious type."

"I can imagine." Gianna's mocking smile faded. "I'm sorry. Go on."

"There came a time when I . . . when I did something that so infuriated my father that he cast me out of his home. My brother chose to follow me. Our father hasn't spoken to us since."

"No kidding. Where is he now? Your father, I mean."

"He could be dead for all I know."

"How terrible," she said. "But what could you have—I mean, what did you do to make him so angry? You don't have to answer that."

"It's okay." I stared past her at the black-and-white-checkered wall across the room. "I just . . . I just didn't want to be like him. Or rather, I did want to be like him, wanted to *be* him even, but there was already one of him." I looked at her. "Do you follow me?"

"I think so." Gianna rested her chin in her hand and squinted at me.

"Let's just say he didn't appreciate my outlook. The family wasn't big enough for both of us."

"What about your brother?"

"Bob was an opportunist. He cast his lot with the one he thought would prevail in the end. It was his mistake, one I shouldn't have let him make. I'll never live that down."

"I don't get it," Gianna said. "A lot of fathers aren't crazy about how their children turn out. But that doesn't mean they have a right to banish them like that. Your dad sounds like a tyrant, if you don't mind my saying."

"I don't mind at all." I smiled at her and drained the last of my martini. "I also don't mind not living in his shadow anymore. My brother and I have made good lives for ourselves on our own. He works for me now. Hopefully you'll meet him someday."

"I'd like that."

"Bob's a bit startling," I said.

"Like you?"

"No, more like you."

"Oh. Neat." She shuffled her glass on her cocktail napkin. "Do you miss him? Your dad, I mean?" She looked at my face, then at her watch. "Whoa, emotional land mine. Let's go eat."

I loved the way Gianna held a glass of wine in between sips, as though it were an extension of herself. Her thin wrist bent as far as it would go, curving the glass back towards her body, where it almost touched her shoulder.

"It may surprise you," she said, "that being a public defender was a thankless job. The people I represented for the most part didn't seem to care whether they went to jail or not. Their time on the outside was more like a vacation than a way of life. Then of course there was the sneering DA on her crusade to rid Philadelphia's streets of every last scumbag."

"So you thought lobbying for the poor in a Republican Congress would be less frustrating," I said.

"I wanted to affect the big picture. The individual faces were too painful, so I abandoned them."

"Abandoned them? You may help more people with one law passed or prevented than you did during your entire stint as a lawyer."

"That's the theory, anyway." Gianna swished her bread through the escargots' remaining garlic butter. Her self-righteousness had faded into humility, and I decided to reverse the flow.

"Doesn't it burn you up to know that you're giving so much to society when other people just take?"

"Sometimes," she said. "But that just means I need to do more to compensate for those who can't contribute."

"I'm not talking about the poor. I'm talking about rich ass-holes like me, who won't leave this world any better than they found it and will probably make it a little worse. How do you feel about taking up our slack?"

She swallowed her mouthful of bread. "Is this a trick question?"

"No. I'm just amazed that people like you are willing to essentially give out interest-free loans with no payment-due date. We'll never repay you—or society."

Gianna studied me for a moment, then shrugged. "I'm not worried about you. I just do what I need to do to let me sleep at night. I try not to judge others." I raised my eyebrows.

"Okay," she said. "I am very judgmental, and I condemn all of you rich assholes for not doing more."

"That's better."

"At least you're honest," she said. "There's not a sanctimonious bone in your body, I can tell. Unlike most of the people I work with." She took a sip of water. "Unlike me."

"I bet that even with all you do, Gianna, you still can't sleep at night." She frowned and glanced away.

"Oh, look," she said, "it's three of the Ways and Means Committee members and that lady from the Brookings Institution. I went to policy school with her."

I turned to look at the entering group. They saw us and waved before sitting at a table halfway across the restaurant.

"I wonder what they're talking about," Gianna said.

"At the moment, probably us."

"No, you think?" She gasped. "Jesus God, I forgot it's Monday. They might think this is a business meeting."

"So?"

"My organization can't afford the likes of you. We're supposed to be grassroots. It'll ruin our image."

"Fine," I said. "Give me your hand."

"What?"

"I'll prove to them this isn't business. Give me your hand."

"No." She put her hands under the table out of reach.

"Look, Gianna, obviously appearances are as important to you as they are to everyone else in this town."

"That's not true. I don't care what they think," she said. "Now if you'll excuse me, I have to powder my nose."

"Of course." I stood to excuse her. As she passed me, I touched her elbow. "Gianna?"

She turned. "Yes?"

I kissed her on the cheek, not too quickly. "Nothing. Have a good powder."

After dinner we danced.

In motion she was more intoxicating than any wine. The blood rushed to my head as she spun around me, and for a few moments, the world revolved around some point between us, where gravity ceased its battle. I could taste her sweat in the air.

Then we moved together, our gazes locked as tightly as our grasp, guiding each other with eyes and hips. Strand by strand her hair fell free, until it slithered over her face like a thousand black snakes.

Holding her close was a relay point, where one desire rested only to launch another, stronger one. If I could not have her tonight, the consequences to the natural world would be blistering. I imagined the Tidal Basin cherry trees lighting like match sticks in the first hours of my frustration conflagration.

At 2 A.M., the dance club's cruel house lights ushered us out into the night. We walked to the parking lot swooning.

Gianna lifted her hair off the nape of her neck to cool herself. "I don't have to tell you that was wonderful."

"You don't have to," I said, "but go ahead anyway."

She laughed and let her hair fall in her eyes. "You're a magnificent dancer, Louis."

"So are you." I held up the keys to the Jaguar. "Would you like to drive again?"

"No, thanks. I'm still too hazy from the drinking and dancing. I'd probably put us in the Potomac."

"You don't live near the Potomac."

"But you do." Gianna opened the car door and looked at me. "Let's go see your swanky little flat."

I nodded and got in the car. My throat tightened. This was

real, this was actually going to happen. As I adjusted the seat to accommodate my body's proportions, I thought how they compared to hers, how her legs and arms were surprisingly long, and I imagined how they would feel wrapped around me.

"Are we going or not?"

I realized I had become briefly frozen in fantasy. I looked at her.

"Yes." I jerked the car into gear and screeched out of the parking lot. The car tore through the now-quiet back streets of Georgetown, barely slowing for stop signs. Out of the corner of my eye I saw Gianna tighten her grip on the door handle. "Sorry," I said. "I don't usually drive like this."

"Right."

By the time we pulled into the circle in front of my building in Foggy Bottom, I was able to take several deep breaths to rein in my slavering lust—at least to the point where I could help Gianna out of the car without yanking her arm off. The doorman nodded to us as we entered the building.

"That guy just gave you a look," Gianna said when we were in the lobby.

"What guy?"

"The doorman. He gave you a knowing look."

"Did he? I didn't notice."

"You must bring a lot of women here."

"Actually, I don't. That's probably why Charles gave me a look." It was true. It was usually less complicated to have sex with a woman at her place, then leave while she slept. Sleeping people provide much less resistance to memory wipes.

We entered the elevator, and I inserted a small key next to the top button, which read "P," and pressed it. Gianna wore a mask of casualness.

The twelve floors seemed to crawl by as the tension in the elevator grew. I tried to avoid rocking on my heels, tapping my feet, or spinning my keys, any sign that might reveal my impatience—or perhaps nervousness.

At last we reached my apartment door. My fingers flew over the security keypad, entering a complex series of codes.

"It's quite a fortress," Gianna said.

"Paranoia is one of the side effects of being fabulously wealthy." I opened the door, turned on the foyer light, and let her step through ahead of me. "But I find that it's worth it."

We entered the hallway, which was still dim in spite of the overhead light. I removed our coats and hung them in the closet, then led her into the living room. Gianna let out a low whistle of admiration.

"Look at that view." She swept to the floor-to-ceiling window that overlooked the balcony. "This is incredible. It's like I could reach out and touch the Washington Monument, even though it must be what, a mile away?"

"Almost." I joined her at the window and placed my hand lightly on her neck, at the edge of where her hair fell. She turned to me.

"Look, I don't trust rich people," she said. "Either they inherited the money, which means they're spoiled, or they earned it, which means they're ruthless."

My gaze matched hers. "I earned it. Trust me."

"Hmm." She looked away and caught sight of the piano behind us. "Louis, you didn't tell me you played."

"It was a surprise."

"Would you play something for me?"

"Perhaps later." I took her hand.

"What's in there?" She pointed toward the dark library.

"That," I led her into the library and turned on the light, "is where I worship."

Her reaction to the towers of volumes filled me with an almost crippling passion.

"Wow." She broke away from me and ran her hands along the shelves. "I think I just died and went to Heaven."

"You might say that knowledge is my religion." I caressed the worn edges of an early Euripides collection. "And this is my shrine."

Gianna spun in a circle and craned her neck. "I almost expect to see clouds covering the top shelves, like they go on forever. It looks like you've read all these books, too."

"Of course," I said. "Why else would I have them?"

"To impress people."

"I don't care to impress anyone. I just like to be surrounded by thoughts. See, Gianna, I believe that the human brain is potentially the single most powerful force on earth. The tragedy is that so many people let their minds atrophy. They mire themselves in mediocrity and forget what truly amazing beings they can become. But I can tell you're not one of those people."

"No, I'm not."

"And that's why you wouldn't marry Mr. Vanilla, even though he would have made you moderately happy."

"There's nothing wrong with being moderately happy."

"Nothing wrong at all. It's good enough for ordinary people."

Gianna looked down at the table between us and spied my papers and stacks of books left over from the other night. "What are you working on here?"

"A small research project. Just a passing fancy."

Gianna examined the titles of the volumes. "Very eclectic mix of sources, I must say."

"It's a complex topic. Many layers to peel away. I may never find the answers I'm looking for, but I think the search will be very rewarding."

She looked up at me, then flinched.

"What is it?" I asked.

"Nothing." She laughed a little. "It's just that I keep forgetting what huge eyes you have."

"Mmm. The better to . . . well, you know." I slid around the end of the table to her side.

"Of course. The better to seduce me with." She turned to the shelf behind her and straightened a Henry Miller novel. "But you can forget about that, mister, because it is I who will seduce you—when the time is right, of course."

"I see." I sat on the edge of the table and propped one foot on a chair. "Yes, the smoothest seductions of all are those where the one being seduced believes that she herself is the seducer."

Gianna turned to face me and opened her mouth to retort. We stared at each other in silence. Our smirks faded. The game was over.

I rushed to her. She filled her hands with my hair as I pressed my lips into her mouth. After the first succession of reckless, gasping kisses, we fell onto the table, scattering the books and papers I no longer needed.

Gianna began clawing at my clothes, and I took her hand to lead her to the bedroom. She pulled me back.

"No," she said. "Right here. Now."

"No, I want . . . I want it to be perfect."

"It's not going to be perfect, it's going to be now!"

I blinked once, then crawled on top of her.

The urgency of our lust would have made the casual observer (if an observer could have been casual) believe in the imminence of Armageddon. Our bodies raged together, fused by a point of furious energy that swiftly grew to swallow us whole.

I collapsed onto her body and rested my forehead between her breasts. My breath heaved into the silk of her dress.

"I was so tired of not doing that," Gianna said. She stroked my shoulders with her long fingers. "So what do we do now?"

"Now . . ." I stood and offered my hand. "Now we get to show off. Maybe even remove some of our clothing."

She grabbed my hand, and I pulled her into my arms and lifted her off her feet.

"Wow," she said. "Officially, I have to mention that this is patronizing and demeaning and somewhat cavemannish."

"Uh-huh."

"But I like it."

"Good." I carried her across the living room into the dark bedroom and laid her on the bed. "Just a moment." I lit candles on either side. They cast a warm, weak glow into the darkness.

"Speaking of caves . . ." Gianna rubbed her arms.

"Are you cold?"

"I am now." Her voice was smaller than I'd heard it before.

"I'll build a fire."

"You have a fireplace in your bedroom?" She sat up.

"In fact, I do." I knelt in front of the fireplace, opened the glass and iron doors, and lit the fire. When I turned to her again, her eyes were fixed on an object atop my bureau.

"What is that?" she whispered.

"You mean this?" I took the long, tattered black feather, the one keepsake from my dark angelic existence, off its perch and handed it to her. She caressed the edges of it with quavering fingers.

"Lou, this is magnificent. What kind of bird did it come from?"

"From a rare breed of . . . condor, in the Amazon Basin."

"It must be four feet long, and look at the way it arches at the end. I've never seen anything like it."

"The birds get very large down there."

"It stirs the imagination," she said. "Like it could be a feather from the wings of Icarus, scorched by the sun."

"Except Icarus's wings didn't scorch. The wax holding them together melted, or so the legend says."

"In any case, it looks like it could almost be that ancient." She handed it back to me. "Here. I'm afraid I'll break it."

"It is quite old." I placed the feather back on top of the dresser. "I've had it since I was a . . . since I was very young."

"Your father gave it to you, didn't he?"

I hesitated a moment, then adjusted the feather in its place. "Yes, in a sense, he did."

She looked at me with a strange mixture of curiosity and understanding, as if on a subconscious level she knew exactly what I was all about.

"Nice fire," she said.

"Thanks." I closed the fireplace screen.

"You seem to have a natural talent for that."

"More like lots of practice."

"I'll bet. Especially here, right?"

I moved to her and pressed my fingers against her mouth. "Shh. No more sarcasm, Gianna. It doesn't go with the candle-light."

"I know, but I can't help—"

Her words disappeared into our first soft kiss. Lips that minutes ago had ravished and bruised now caressed each other with a trembling delicacy. She sighed, and I drank in her warm breath.

"Louis, I think you should know, I have intimacy issues."

"So do I, but we seem to be working through them." I kissed her again, deeply.

"I suppose this is more constructive than psychotherapy." Her hands were at my throat, unfastening my tie. She pulled it slowly, and it slithered off my neck. After she had removed my shirt, she slid her hands over my bare shoulders and gasped.

"Your skin," she said. "It's so warm . . . so warm." She pressed her cheek against my neck.

"Are you still cold?"

"Cold enough to want to be covered with you."

I took her in my arms and pressed her body against mine until she burned as I did. We explored each other with hands, lips, tongues, until anything less than total union seemed like torture.

From the moment it began, I knew something was different. Gianna's body had a fullness that could only be felt from the inside. Every movement, every quiver, sent shocks of bliss through my entire being.

I clung to her, closed my eyes, and felt myself rise to terrifying heights, heights from which I'd only fallen before. A tempest began to rage inside my head. Gianna must have felt my distress, for she took control of the rhythm and coaxed me to give up the struggle. My slow surrender erased the boundaries between us. Her sensations and emotions spilled over onto mine until I wasn't sure who was feeling what.

Sweat and tears mixed in salty streams that coursed over our faces and necks. I melded my mouth with hers and breathed in her moans. A blinding light filled my mind, and I nearly tore myself away from her, but instead released my fear in a final, frantic cry.

We separated, and the thunderstorm in my head faded into a distant rumble. I stared at the ceiling, to a point far past it.

"That was . . . beyond . . . " she said, "beyond . . . well, simply beyond." She placed her hand on my shoulder. "Louis, are you still there?"

I blinked, then turned to her suddenly. I pushed back her hair, which was pasted to her forehead with sweat, and grasped her face between my palms.

"Who are you?" I hissed.

"That's the oddest thing anyone's ever said to me after sex."

"But who are you?" I peered into her eyes. "Where did you come from, and why are you so different?"

"Different?"

"The way it felt with you, the way I feel right now, I've never felt before."

"You're scaring me a little, Lou."

"Not half as much as you're scaring me."

Gianna sighed and pulled my hand from her face. "Then I should go."

"No."

"Okay."

I slid my arm around her waist. "I want you to stay and sleep in with me in the morning. Then we'll eat breakfast and spend the day out together. Unless it rains, in which case we'll spend the day in together, maybe right here."

"Let's pray for rain." She nestled in closer to me, her face tucked into my throat. "I should go into the office in the afternoon, though."

"I think that's a very bad idea. It's a federal holiday, and you're not being patriotic."

"Lou, I can't lose a whole day of work."

"Yes, you can. I'll show you how easy it is." I turned over, picked up the phone from my night stand, and dialed my office. "Good morning, Daphne, this is Lou. I won't be in today." I hung up. "See? Now you try." I handed her the phone. "Call your secretary and tell her—"

"I don't have a secretary. I have an assistant, and his name is Leo."

"How progressive. Call him."

She began to dial, then stopped. "He'll know by the voice mail signature that I called at four in the morning, and not from my apartment."

"So?"

"People will talk."

"And you'd like that."

"True." She redialed and waited while the other line rang. "Hi, Leo, this is Gianna. I won't . . . uh . . . I won't be in today. I've got this . . . thing I have to do and I . . . I just won't be in, okay? If you could, please reschedule my three o'clock with the senator and tell her I'm terribly sorry. Thanks. See you Wednesday." Gianna handed the phone to me and rolled onto her back.

"You canceled an appointment with a senator?" I said.

"Hey, it's just a job, right?"

"You're catching on." My fingers glided down her arm and intertwined with hers. "Come to think of it, I think I was supposed to meet with someone from the White House tomorrow. Oh, well." I brought her hand to my lips and kissed the inside of her wrist.

"Oh, well." She turned to me and slid the length of her thigh against mine. "I'm not tired yet, are you? Good."

I almost couldn't bear to be inside her again, feared the blinding flashes of light and roaring crescendos that would come without warning, each more intense than the last. But I craved her, and this craving knew no fear, and it would not flee in the face of such a small death.

5

De Poenis Inferni

I woke slowly and lazily, a waking fit for a federal holiday. My arms were full of Gianna, and my face was buried in her hair. I breathed in her scent, let it fill my head, and sighed.

Contentment suddenly spiked into panic. Every muscle tensed, and I fought the urge to run, to throw her out the door, the window—anything to separate us.

What was I doing? Why was she still here? This entire experience was deviant from the beginning.

I could tell her that I had lots of work to do and that I'd call her sometime, a line that usually resulted in frustrated tears and slammed doors. That image didn't appeal to me, but the alternative was worse.

Gianna stretched, pulled my hand from around her waist, and kissed my fingertips.

"Good morning," I whispered. She did not respond. That tiny gesture of tenderness had taken place in her sleep, an unconscious token of affection. Something inside me rolled over and played dead.

One more day with her can't hurt, I thought. Perhaps even one more day and night.

I got out of bed, pulled on my robe, and walked into the living room. The sky was heavy with clouds. I went out onto the balcony to clear my head in the chilly air.

Rather than clearing, though, my thoughts returned to the previous night and became stuck in honey-soaked memories of Gianna's body. There was something open and uncharted about her that begged to be explored. I'd never fled from a mystery before, and the pieces to this puzzle lay scattered inside her mind. I had to gather them, to find the answer to a question I hadn't yet conceived.

I returned inside, sat down at the piano, and began to play in muted tones.

A few minutes later, I felt a hand on my shoulder and stopped playing. Gianna sat beside me on the bench, and I was awed at how her beauty actually increased in daylight.

"Morning becomes you," I said.

"You, too." She placed her hand on the piano. "You play very nicely."

"I was just puttering. I didn't want to wake you."

"I'm awake now, so stop puttering and play something for real."

"Maybe later," I said. "Right now I'm far too serene to play much of anything with the intensity it deserves." I trickled a Chopin prelude. "This is a rare mood for me, so you might want to take a picture."

"I am." She listened until I had finished. "I know you're not showing off, but that was perfect."

"Such as it is." I looked at her. "Isn't that my shirt?"

"Yes. I couldn't bear the thought of squishing myself back into that cocktail dress. I hope you don't mind."

"Not at all," I said. "I find you very sexy in my clothes, partly because of my own narcissism."

She lifted the collar to her face. "It smells like you, too."

"I think you smell like me now, and I you." With my arm around her waist, I pressed my lips into her neck and caressed her body through the soft fabric of the shirt.

"So much for morning-after awkwardness," she said.

"I can't imagine ever feeling awkward with you again, Gianna." I brushed a curl off her face. "I feel like we've seen inside each other, even if only a glimpse."

Gianna looked startled, then pulled away and moved toward the kitchen.

"Got any coffee?" she asked.

"Beans are in the freezer." She disappeared, completing her sudden departure. The way to lure her back was under my nose.

The piano jumped to life as I charged into the third movement from Beethoven's "Moonlight Sonata." By the time I reached the end of the first bar, I could see Gianna out of the corner of my eye, standing in the kitchen doorway.

After a stormy seven minutes, the last note faded into the air like a ghost. I looked up at her and shrugged. "You asked me to play something for real."

"Louis . . . that was amazing." She crept toward me. "How did you do that, with so little warm-up?"

"My hands have been warm all night," I said.

She sat next to me. "Why aren't you a professional?"

"I don't want the attention. Of millions, that is. I'll take yours, though."

"You've got it," she said. "Play something else."

"Like what?"

"Like anything. No, wait—more Beethoven. I'm a sucker for a tragic hero."

"What about a tragic anti-hero?"

"What's the difference?"

"We shall see." My hands hovered over the keys. "Okay, I'll play the Allegro from the Fifth Concerto, but you have to sing the orchestral parts. In German."

"I don't know German."

"Me neither," I said. "Just make it up."

"Okay, go."

Poor Ludwig. His life was never easy, and that morning one of his finest masterpieces was as sloppily butchered as a squirming pig. I bet he never rolled over like that for Chuck Berry.

After breakfast, I drove Gianna to her apartment on Connecticut Avenue. As we got out of the elevator on her floor, she said, "I should warn you, it's very tiny. But it suits my needs just fine."

"That's all that matters, right?"

"Don't patronize me."

"If you have apartment envy now, that's between you and your home. It's not my fault."

Gianna opened her door and pushed ahead of me to turn on the light.

Tiny didn't begin to describe her home, an efficiency apartment with a kitchen, bathroom, walk-through closet, and a combination living room/bedroom, which was divided into functions by a dressing screen.

"I'd give you a tour, but you just had it," Gianna said.

"It's intriguing," I said. "There's something very sexy and

distracting about your bed always being in sight like that. How do you ever get any work done?"

"I'm usually alone. Except for Antigone."

"Who?"

"There you are!" Gianna lifted a rumpled cover from her unmade bed to reveal a fat black cat curled into a tight sleep ball. "Poor Tig, all tuckered out after a night of sitting around." She picked up the cat and kissed it behind the ear. "Antigone O'Keefe, I want you to meet—"

The cat saw me and howled like a treed mountain lion, its ears flattened against its head. It clawed its way out of Gianna's arms, then crouched on the floor, uncertain whether to attack or flee.

"Jesus God, Lou, I'm sorry. She's never acted this way before, I swear."

"It's okay," I said. "She just woke up, and I'm a stranger who happens to be very tall." I knelt down in front of the sofa and stared into the cat's eyes. It stopped in mid-snarl, pricked its ears, and gazed back at me. In another moment, Antigone was on her back at my feet, paws in the air, purring. I scratched her stomach.

"That was weird," Gianna said. "What are you, a snake charmer?"

"No, just a good despooker."

"Lucky you. She doesn't even let me scratch her belly."

"Jealous?"

"Not yet. You two make friends while I go change my clothes."

I sat on the floor and stroked Antigone under her chin, where a small triangle of white formed a bib. Her plush fur made me long for animal companionship. I had long ago given up having pets, as I had a tendency to eat them when I was in a bad mood.

The day rolled by like a bad video montage from Hollywood's latest romantic comedy. Museums, fountains, and cafés filled with our goofy laughter and sloppy kisses. A week ago, if I had observed two people acting the way we did that day and night, I'd have placed a gruesome tragedy in their path to shatter their smug, happy little existence.

But I had a blast, anyway.

The next morning, I drove Gianna to her office on K Street. After several lingering goodbye kisses, I said, "Sorry you had to miss your appointment with the senator."

"I lied. There was no appointment with a senator. Not yesterday, anyway."

"I see."

"And you didn't really have a meeting scheduled at the White House, did you?"

"Actually, I did," I said.

"No kidding?"

"Would I lie to you?" She hesitated. "It's okay," I said. "It's not like it was with the president. That's not until next week. So when can I see you again?"

"How about Friday? My other band's playing at the Shack at ten."

"Your other band?"

"See, there's still much to learn about me," she said.

"What kind of band?"

"The kind of band that plays at the Shack."

"Sounds intriguing," I said.

"It's more my speed, or rather more in line with my talent, or lack thereof. Bring your brother and a couple of friends. We'll hang out after the show."

"You may regret that invitation."

"Nah," she said. "We could use some new groupies." She looked at the clock on the dashboard. "I'd better go now."

"Until Friday then." I kissed her hand.

"Until Friday."

W e didn't wait until Friday. I arrived at her office that day at five o'clock with another red-and-white rose. She feigned surprise, then spent the next two nights with me.

6

Ad Te Omnis Caro Veniet

Friday night Mephistopheles met me outside the Shack around nine-thirty. Beelzebub was amusing himself by making screeching imps out of wet leaves and dropping them into the sewer system. When he saw me, he brushed off his hands and came over.

"This place rocks," he said to me.

"You've been here before?"

"We've been everywhere before," Mephistopheles said.

Our eyes followed a pair of leather-skirted postpubescents as they sauntered past the bouncer, who winked at them, unaware he was being ignored. Beelzebub started to follow them inside. I held him back.

"Think you can remain unattached until after the show, Bub?"

"If I have to, I guess." He looked at his watch. "Where's Belial, anyway?"

"If I were any closer, I'd be up your ass."

Beelzebub turned to face Belial, who had crept up to stand behind him. "If you were up my ass, I doubt I'd notice."

Belial put his arm around Beelzebub's shoulder. "I know this great little dark alley where we could find out."

"Gentlemen," I said, "let's go inside."

Belial joined me on the way in. "And how is life treating you? Splendidly, unless the grapevine lies."

"What do you mean?"

"My carrier pigeon tells me that you've spent the whole week with this particular inamorata." He stopped to buy a pack of cigarettes from the vending machine.

"It's been a good week."

"Why?"

"I enjoy her," I said. Belial's slick green eyes studied me. "I think you'll see why."

"I can't wait. Anyway, Lou, I've been working on the ad campaign for our new HMO." As Hell's smoothest and most colorful liar, Belial was the ideal marketing/public relations director. "The motif will be sleeping children. After all, kids are cutest and least intrusive when they're asleep—it conjures up images of good health, peace of mind, quiet time alone with one's spouse, maybe even the prospect of a connubial bonk or two before the rugrat wakes up wanting to know why Daddy's wearing a harness and Mommy's wielding a riding crop."

"I like it. It says we care."

Beelzebub and Mephistopheles had gone ahead of us and gotten a table in the center of the crowded room, right behind and above the mosh pit.

"Nice view," I said.

Mephistopheles pulled over a few extra chairs. "For some reason the people who were sitting here when we arrived decided to leave."

"Yeah, funny how that worked out. They paid for our first round of drinks, too." Beelzebub moved to my side of the table. "I get to sit next to you and make lewd remarks about your woman during the show."

"Be careful," I said. "By the way, I told her you were my brother."

"Why?"

"You are my brother."

"I know, but I never got to be in real life before." He offered me a cigarette, which I declined. "Did you tell her about dear old Dad?"

"I told her we're not as close to him as we used to be."

"Hey, how come I don't get to be your brother?" Mephistopheles asked.

"Have you looked in the mirror lately, homey?" Belial said. "You *are* a brother."

A waitress with black sequins pasted across her forehead brought our drinks as the music from the overhead speakers faded. Dim blue lights illuminated the stage. The crowd in the mosh pit hooted and cheered as four women walked on stage and picked up their instruments for a last-minute sound check. I could barely make out Gianna in the shadows holding one of the guitars. She seemed taller than I remembered, even though I was looking down at her.

The drummer counted off, then the stage erupted in light and noise. Gianna commanded the front spotlight, looking as though she were born there. Stretched over her lean, muscular torso was a black tank top, over which draped a long dark gray vest. She wore tight black leggings that accentuated her lithe build, with ankle-high suede boots to match. The obligatory heavy dark makeup encircled her eyes, giving her that back-from-the-grave sparkle. I admired the panache with which she carried the cliché.

I was in the shower this morning
When it suddenly occurred to me.
There was a nugget of wisdom and yearning
To be able to stand when I pee.
And I stood in the shower contemplating
That masculine fixation with masturbating,
A subject about which they're so obsessive,
Why are they all so fucking possessive?
I want a dick for a day.
I want a dick for a day.
I'll use it, abuse it,
And then I'll throw it away,
And then I'll throw it away.

Her arm muscles rippled as she sawed away at the guitar. I became entranced with the rhythm of her stroke and didn't hear Beelzebub calling my name until he shook my shoulder.

"I can see why you wanted a second date," he said. "So when are you going to share?"

"Share?"

"Though she's not really my type. I prefer them blond and dumb like me, but—"

"I'm not going to share," I said. "Don't even think about it."

"Lou, what happened to your generosity?"

"I never had any." I finished Beelzebub's drink and tried to focus my attention back on the stage.

Envying that daily decision,
Do I go with boxers or briefs?
That right-leg-vs.-left-leg division,
Either way, it all ends in grief.
I just do not understand it
That self-involvement, bird-in-hand bit.

Anyway, it's overrated,
Better off to be castrated.
I want a dick for a day.
I want a dick for a day.
I'll use it, abuse it,
And then I'll throw it away,
And then I'll throw it away.

"Does she have a sister?" Beelzebub said.

"No."

"How about a mother?"

"Do you mind?" I said. "I'm trying to watch the show."

"Aunt, cousin, anything?"

"Shut up."

I could behave just like a man then
Bragging about how well it's hung
Lying to myself all the time, when
The truth is that girls prefer tongue.
Silly princes, silly palace,
What's so charming 'bout a phallus?
Try it once, and that'll do it.
Penis envy? I say 'Screw it!'
I want a dick for a day.
I want a dick for a day.
I'll use it, abuse it,
And then I'll throw it away,
And then I'll throw it away.
Give me a dick for a day.
So I can throw it away!

The song ended with a screech of guitar strings. Gianna
pushed back her hair and gave the crowd a surly smile.

"Hey, how's it goin'? We're Public Humiliation, the politically correct punk rockers. It's good to be back opening up for Riot Kittens again. For those of you who've been following us . . ." Several dozen people screamed. ". . . both of you, I have some pretty big news. I learned a new chord. I like to call it . . . F, and it goes a little something like this." She bashed out the chord and let the clamor die away before she continued.

"You'd be amazed how many songs don't use F. Especially songs we write. We have a new one, though, tonight, featuring this wonderful chord."

The band slammed into the next song, which had a slower grind to it than the first.

Gianna stepped aside and let the lead guitarist take the front spotlight. This woman had long flame-colored hair and flashing hazel eyes. Her tonsil-ripping screech contrasted with Gianna's guttural growl, and though she was short, she looked powerful enough to lodge one of her combat boots in someone's skull with a single kick.

Mephistopheles leaned across the table towards me. "It's a good thing we're not threatened by strong women, huh?"

While the redhead "sang" a song about pesticide-induced two-headed children, Gianna scanned the crowd until she found me. I tipped my glass to her, and she winked at me over the mosh pit's colliding bodies.

"Remember, gentlemen," I said after the show was over, "this should be a night to remember, not a night to forget. Don't do anything evil to these women unless they specifically request it."

"Why not?" Belial asked.

"Because Lou's got a girlfriend," Mephistopheles said with a mocking lilt, "and he thinks we'll embarrass him so she won't bring him home to meet her momma."

"She's not my girlfriend, and I have no interest in meeting her mother, other than mere curiosity, but I might like to see her again. So if you would try to recall the art of the graceful one-night stand, I'd be very much obliged."

"What's that one line you came up with?" Beelzebub asked Belial. "'This night has been so perfect . . .'"

"'This night has been so perfect, I can't bear to ruin the precious memory of it by making you see me again, because I fear I'll only disappoint you.' Was that it?"

"Yeah, but you know, that line never works for me. They always say, 'Oh no, you could never disappoint me,' and then I end up panicking and saying something like 'I'd rather saw off my dick with a plastic knife than stick it inside your clammy little body again.'"

"Ouch, that'll work." Mephistopheles crossed his legs. "But it's not as subtle."

"The trick with the 'perfect night' line," Belial said, "is that you have to say it with commitment, with charm."

Beelzebub shook his head. "I use up all my charm to get them into bed. There's none left over afterwards." The three of us shared a smirk.

"You do have an admirable assortment of pickup lines, Bub." I picked up my fourth whiskey.

Mephistopheles hooted. "My favorite one is 'I wish I were *you*, so I'd get to fuck *me*.'"

We roared and banged our glasses together in a raucous salute. "If that line works," I said, "you know you have an enthusiastic night on your hands."

"Dude, I think you have an enthusiastic night on your hands." Beelzebub nodded past me. "Here she comes."

Gianna waded through a pack of sycophants to reach our table.

"Hi," I said. "You were—"

She cut me off with a ferocious kiss. Six demon eyes probed us with their gazes.

When she pulled away, I said, "You just broke the hearts of two dozen leather-clad lesbians."

"That was the secondary motive." Gianna took a shot of whiskey from the sequin-faced waitress, who looked at her longingly out of the corner of her eye while she picked up our empty glasses. Gianna placed hers on the waitress's tray. "Thanks, Dariah. Bring me two more, would you please?"

"Your wish, Gianna," Dariah said. "Another round for everyone else?"

"Yeah, can we get some beers, too?" Beelzebub held up his glass. "This whiskey's making me thirsty."

I stood up. "Gianna, let me introduce—"

"No, don't tell me." She examined each of my companions, then extended her hand towards Belial. "You must be Bob."

Beelzebub cackled. "Sorry, that would be me."

Gianna glanced between the two of us. "You two are brothers? You don't look a thing alike."

"We're half-brothers," I said.

"Right," Beelzebub said. "Half brothers, half something else." He rose to his feet and took her hand. "It's a pleasure to meet someone with such power."

"Oh . . . why, thank you." She smiled at him. He held onto her hand a half-second longer than I would have liked.

"And these are our friends Malcolm and Bill," I said.

They each shook her hand and gazed at her with a lustful curiosity that would have knocked most women off their feet. Gianna blinked a few times, then sat down.

"So what'd you think, honestly?" she said to me.

"I thought you were incredible."

"If you didn't know me, what would you think?"

"If I didn't know you, I'd want to."

"Fair enough." She leaned close to me. "My friends will be pleased with your friends, I believe. They'll be along in a minute." She turned to Beelzebub. "Excuse me." She reached into his shirt pocket and pulled out his pack of cigarettes. "May I?"

"Absolutely." As he lit her cigarette, his eyes moved rapidly over hers as if he were reading between the lines of her irises. I gave him a swift telepathic kick in the groin. He winced and looked away from her.

"Looks like the groupie agency came through for us big this time, eh, Gianna?"

The other three members of the band stood at the end of the table. Gianna stood to make the introductions. I grasped Beelzebub's arm.

"Keep your eyes off her mind," I said.

"You wouldn't respect me if I didn't at least try."

Gianna's friends joined us at the table. Ellen, the red-haired guitarist, had a voice as sweet offstage as it was acidic onstage. Lisa Anne was tall and wiry, her hair blond and spiky with dark roots. I recognized her as the bass guitarist. Veronica the drummer had wary gray eyes and long, coarse black hair. Like Gianna, they were all high on themselves and ready to party.

"You girls have some catching up to do," Mephistopheles said after everyone was seated. "We're all pretty heavily distilled already."

"Just keep the beer and the Jack Daniel's flowing, and we'll fix that soon enough." Ellen pounded the table. "And don't call us girls, by the way. We hate that."

"Yeah, you see any frilly pink lace at this table?" Lisa Anne said.

"I for one am wearing a very demure pair of white panties with little bunnies on them," Veronica said with a straight face. "Does that count?"

"So what should we call you, then?" Beelzebub tilted his head towards Ellen at a devastating angle. "Man-hating castrating bitches?"

"Works for us." Ellen raised her glass to Gianna and met Beelzebub's admiring gaze as she downed the shot of whiskey. He turned to me a few moments later and mouthed the word "Wow."

"I'm curious, then," I said. "Do you consider yourselves feminists?"

"All the way, feministas!" Ellen said. The women clanked their half-empty beer mugs together. "Do you have a problem with that?"

"Not at all," I said. "But by acting like men, aren't you dishonoring the female?" Everyone squinted at me as if I had just dropped an open bag of ants onto a picnic table. "It seems like a case of identifying with your oppressor to the point where you imitate him. The actions you hate the most in men are the very ones you perpetuate."

The women looked at each other, then Ellen said to Gianna, "I don't recall giving the men permission to speak, do you?"

We all laughed. Gianna patted my hand. "Next thing you know, they'll be wanting to vote."

"Okay, brief sociopolitical tirade, then we party." Lisa Anne pointed her cocktail straw at me. "Louis, you can laugh off our insults because you know that you're still the one with the power. You can afford to indulge us, as long as we don't come close to taking that power away."

"That's why we gotta be nasty," Veronica said. "To show any weakness would be to lose ground. Gotta keep that pendulum swinging our way as long as possible."

Gianna set her glass down. "I think that eventually, maybe not in our lifetimes, but someday, men and women will treat each other as true equals and stop this power struggle. But it won't happen overnight, and as long as there's a battle to be fought, we'll fight it."

"With the most potent weapon at our disposal," Ellen said.

"Which is?"

"Overstatement!" the women chimed in ragged unison. Their glasses slammed together again and contributed to the expanding puddle of booze on the center of the table.

"Now with all due respect, Mr. Cerebral," Lisa Anne said to me, "shut up and get wasted."

"I'm doing my best."

"You'll have to be patient." Mephistopheles curled his arm around the back of Lisa Anne's chair. "It takes about a dozen drinks before Lou starts to loosen up."

"Yeah, too bad he passes out after the eleventh one," Belial said.

"I know what you need." Gianna took my hand. "We'll be right back." She dragged me towards the back of the bar and through an unmarked door. She locked the door behind us and led me down a short flight of stairs into a small, dimly lit room.

"Who would've thought a place like this would have a wine cellar?" I said.

"The lady who owns this place, a friend of mine, also owns the posh restaurant above the bar. That place is closed this time of night, so no one should interrupt us."

"Was there something you wanted to show me?" I asked her as she knelt before me and unbuttoned my pants.

"Don't be coy, Louis. You're not very good at it."

"A rare Beaujolais? Your favorite Pinot Grigio? Perhaps a Cabernet Sau—ohhhhh . . ." I steadied myself against the wine rack, my fingers scrambling over the rough wood for a secure handhold. They finally came to rest in her hair, which was sticky with sweat and hair spray. My groans blended with the pulse of the bass guitar above our heads. She wasted no time making me come, and I was grateful, since my legs were lique-fying and I feared my shudders would cause the wine rack to topple on us at any moment.

Gianna stood up and examined my face. "A definite improvement," she said.

I clutched her shoulder. "I need to go sit down before my knees break the floor."

I arrived back at our table alone and slumped in my chair.

"You look much more relaxed," Beelzebub said.

"Bub, I have found the perfect woman."

"It's hard to argue with you there, bro. Where'd you go?"

"The wine cellar."

"Ah. So what's the verdict? Is '97 a good vintage?"

After a minute, Gianna joined us again. In our absence, the other six had gotten nicely acquainted and were involved in a lively game of "Truth or Dare." The irony of three telepathic men who led lives of complete falsehood playing this game was not lost on me. My admiration for my compadres grew as I watched them spontaneously weave complex details of their "lives" into cohesive stories.

"—and that was only two days after I got out of the Iraqi POW camp," Belial concluded.

Veronica squeezed his elbow. "Okay, Bill, your turn to ask now."

"I was going to dare Gianna to do something, but judging by the goofy look on Lou's face, I have a feeling she just did it." Belial turned to me. "So let's hear a truth from Louis."

"What if I'd rather have a dare?"

"Then I'll just dare you to tell the truth about something."

"Cheater," I said.

"Tell us, Lou, before this week, how many times have you gone out with the same woman twice?"

"You mean in a row?"

"Right. In the same year, even."

I smiled and stared through my beer at the bottom of my glass. "Never."

The women gasped.

"You're kidding me," Gianna said. I shook my head without looking at her.

"And you're how old?" Veronica asked.

"I don't believe it's your turn to ask questions," I said.

"It's my turn!" Ellen waved her hand over her head. "And while we're in the business of embarrassing the lustbirds at the end of the table, Gianna, why don't you share with everyone what you told me before the set tonight?"

"What are you talking about?" Gianna said.

"You remember, you told me what it's like to fuck Louis."

The table hissed with surprise and anticipation.

"Please, Gianna." Ellen folded her hands in mock prayer. "It was so cool, you have to share it."

"No way I'm repeating it." Gianna picked up another cigarette and lit it without looking at anyone. "No way."

"Come on, it's the rules."

"Gianna," Beelzebub said, "if you don't tell us, then when it's my turn I'm going to ask Ellen what you said, and you know she won't do it justice."

"See, there's no way out," Mephistopheles said. "Tell us what you said."

The others began to chant: "Truth, truth, truth, truth, truth—"

"All right! Just shut up." Gianna took another drag and fixed her eyes on the table. "I said that . . . having sex with—"

"You said 'fucking,'" Ellen said.

"Whatever . . . it's like being a cheerleader at Armageddon."

"What's that supposed to mean?" Beelzebub said.

"Shhh." Ellen put two fingers over his lips. "Let her finish."

"Like being caught in a maelstrom," Gianna continued, "a great battle between good and evil and not knowing which side I'm on or which side is winning and not really caring. I've never felt so close to death . . ." she raised her eyes to meet mine, ". . . or so close to life."

We all stared at her, and the table's silence seemed to permeate the entire establishment.

"Yeah, they all say that," Beelzebub said.

The rest of them burst into laughter at his comment, but I kept staring at Gianna and wondering how many indecency laws I was about to break.

"I think that's game," Mephistopheles said, "unless anyone thinks they can top that."

Beelzebub stood up. "How 'bout we take this party back to my place? We can walk from here."

In haste we paid the bill and stumbled out of the Shack. Gianna and I lagged behind the others, who had paired off and were laughing and bouncing off each other in the first playful stages of lust. Beelzebub put his arm around Ellen and whispered something in her ear. She erupted in the cheeriest chortle I'd heard this century and swayed her body into his as they walked along.

"Ellen's shitfaced," Gianna said to me.

"They'll have a good time tonight." I put my hands in my pockets. "So . . . a cheerleader at Armageddon, huh?"

"Never had a second date before, huh?"

"No, I haven't—hadn't, rather, until you. By the way, you were amazing tonight."

"Nothing I haven't done for you before."

"No, I don't mean in the wine cellar," I said. "I mean

onstage. You were . . . you were . . . shit, the whiskey is making me stupid. Elated, but stupid. You were great."

We neared an intersection. "You know," Gianna said, "if we take this side street, we could be at my place in ten minutes."

"Is that a fact?"

"Five minutes if we run."

Our friends got not even an extra glance as we took off down the side street, leaping towards Gianna's apartment building. We were breathless in her lobby, but our panting slowed while we waited for the elevator. The doors closed behind us. We attacked each other with mouths and hands.

When we reached her apartment, Gianna fumbled with her keys, and I almost smashed in the door in my impatience.

The sex was scrambling and howling, more like a battle than a union, each of us pawing and clawing for dominance, with no clear victor in the end, only two gasping, exhausted lovers pretending not to notice the atmospheric changes.

Gianna tilted her head back and blew her bangs off her forehead.

"This has been lots of fun," she said. "This week, I mean."

"I'm glad you've enjoyed it." I watched a drop of sweat creep from her skin onto mine. "I certainly have."

She lifted herself off of me and reached for her shirt. "So maybe we should quit while we're ahead."

"Quit what?"

"Quit this." Gianna gestured to the space between us. "Quit seeing each other."

A door is opening, one I should probably dash through and slam behind me.

"Are you sure?" I said.

She hesitated. I could smell her fear. It was contagious.

"Gianna, I don't understand this desire to stop doing something that feels so good."

"Of course you don't." She continued to dress. "You've never been in a relationship before. Never felt the dull agony of disappointment."

"You think you'll disappoint me?"

"No."

"Oh. I get it." My pride was already out the door, in the car, keys in the ignition. I sat up to follow it, but stopped short. "What makes you think I'll let you down? Tell me your vision of how I disillusion you. Do I commit some atrocious betrayal, or do I just start to smell bad?"

"Lou, don't—"

"If you don't like me, just tell me, and I'll leave." I moved onto the couch next to her and brushed my fingers against her hair. "But I think you do like me. Maybe you like me a little too much for your own comfort."

"That's not—"

"Maybe you can't stop thinking about me during your long, tedious days." My hand traveled down the center of her body, from her neck to her navel. "Maybe you stare at the pages in front of you, but you can't erase the memory of the previous night. You close your eyes, and you see my face, my body, you feel my hands on your skin, bringing parts of you back to life you thought had died forever." I slid my hand between her legs. She grabbed my wrist, but didn't move it away.

"Louis, I can't keep seeing you just for the sex. That's not a good enough reason."

I kissed her jawline in front of her ear. "Then let me stay until you find a better reason."

"I'm afraid that I will," she said.

"You're afraid?" My fingers twitched. "Fear excites me."

Her breath quickened. "Even your own fear?"

"Especially my own. If my fear doesn't paralyze and consume me, then it can lead the way to strange and beautiful new worlds." I let my hand heat up a few degrees. "Like the one inside your mind."

Her chuckle mixed with a gasp of desire. "That's a scary one."

"I want to know you, Gianna. I want to know what else you fear. I want to know what makes you laugh and what makes you cry, what makes you want to kill and what makes you want to die."

Her grip on my wrist loosened. "Your voice."

"Go on. Tell me."

"Your voice, it crawls under my skin and heats everything until I feel like I'll burst into flames if I can't get you next to me."

"And this burning," I traced the inside of her thigh with the barest edge of my fingertip, "do you fear it?"

Her hand slid up my arm to my shoulder, and she looked straight into my eyes. "No," she said. "It makes me feel alive. But I don't know how much longer I can live with it."

"Please don't make me leave, Gianna," I whispered into her mouth.

"No." She shivered, then pulled my body tight against hers. "Don't leave, Louis. Not tonight."

Sometimes I'm too persuasive for my own good, I thought. Then I stopped thinking about missed opportunities. Then I stopped thinking at all.

7

Sed Tu Bonus Fac Benigne

A bleating telephone jarred me out of sleep. Gianna groaned and disentangled her limbs from mine before stumbling out of bed to reach the phone.

"Hello?" Her voice was low and hoarse. "Hey, girlfriend, how's it goin'? Sorry we ran out on you last night. It was kind of an emergency. How'd it go? . . . That good, huh?" She laughed and walked into the living area. "You're a maniac. No, of course I won't tell him you said that . . . of course I'm lying. Are you gonna see him again? . . . Oh, thank God. It would be too incestuous and freaky for you to date Lou's brother."

She lowered her voice and moved into the kitchen. "Actually, I kind of changed my mind about that . . . Yeah, he's here . . . Shut up! Do not even mention the 'b' word. I've only known him a week . . . Yeah, what a week, but still, Ellen, come on. Let's not jump the gun here."

Antigone leapt onto the bed, curled her body around my

head, and began to purr. The sound blotted out Gianna's voice for a moment.

"Well . . . yeah, I suppose, happier than I've been . . . since I can remember. I'm sure it's temporary." She yelped. "Sorry, I just looked at myself in the mirror. Girl, I'm getting too old for this shit. I should be making scrambled eggs and watching cartoons with my two-point-three children in some suburban Cape Cod with aluminum siding. Huh? . . . I don't know, maybe out golfing or at a Lions Club meeting or something. I don't see a guy in that picture. . . . I know, I know. In that respect, this universe beats that parallel one by a mile. Hey, my head hurts too much to get philosophical. I'll call you later. Go back to sleep . . . Uh-huh. You rock, too, sweetie. 'Night."

Gianna hung up the phone. "Well, Louis, it looks like you've got a new girlfriend."

I flipped over to gape at her. "What?!"

"Antigone. She worships you already." Gianna climbed into bed and stroked the cat's back. "It took her months to get this close to me. She was a stray, you know."

"A tragic heroine?" I said.

"Something like that. You know, Ellen said your brother is the most edible man she's ever met. Promise you won't tell him."

"Trust me, he already knows. They're not dating now, are they?"

"Hell, no," Gianna said. "Perfect one-night-stand material, according to Ellen. Cute, young, and quite the sprinter. Wham, bam, thank you, sir. Everyone's happy this morning. After all, we all got incredibly laid last night. What's not to like?"

I should have had more faith in Beelzebub. He could leave a decent impression if he tried.

"Speaking of perfect," Gianna traced my right pectoral muscle with her fingertip, "I believe I've taken a complete inventory of your body. . . ."

"Is everything there?"

"Almost everything."

"What do you mean?"

"I mean there's nothing wrong with you," she said. "No scars, no birthmarks, not so much as a freckle or an extra hair."

"You should see me on the inside. It's pretty gross."

"Seriously, though, it's bizarre."

"Are you complimenting me or telling me I'm a freak?"

"Both, I guess." She grinned. "Are you sure you're not an alien?"

"Damn, my cover's blown. Okay, I am actually an alien. My mission is to travel from planet to planet, fornicating endlessly with the single most beautiful native specimen I can find."

Gianna snuggled in close to me. "Endlessly?"

"I think I made the right choice for Earth. It was between you and this walrus I saw. Where I come from, tusks are very sexy." I kissed her shoulder and ran my hand over her hip. She caressed my back, then stopped.

"That's odd," she said.

"What?"

"Turn around."

"Why?"

"Please, just turn around and let me look at your back."

I obliged her. "What is it? Did you find the imperfection you were looking for?"

"No, that's the problem," she said.

"What do you mean?"

"Last night I could have sworn I scratched your back hard enough to make it bleed." She touched the skin over my ribs. "This morning there's no marks, not a trace."

I didn't panic. "I don't remember that."

"Bullshit. It drove you wild. You could barely control yourself."

"I guess I have a vague memory." That "vague memory" was awakening a fierce arousal again, but I feigned indifference. "I guess you didn't do it as hard as you thought you did. Plus, I take lots of vitamin E. Keeps me looking perfect." I reached up to trace the mascara smudge down her cheek. "You, however, look like one of those refugees they show on the evening news."

"Thanks a lot."

"It's very compelling. Makes me want to shower you with money or U.N. peacekeepers. So what do you want to do today?"

She grabbed her pillow and hugged it to her chest. "Wanna watch cartoons? I'll make scrambled eggs."

"Make mine over easy, and you've got a date."

"Cool." She gave me a quick kiss. "First, though, I'm going to whip out the makeup remover and rejoin the ranks of the living."

Gianna was halfway to the bathroom when her phone rang. She trotted back to it and picked it up.

"Hello? . . . Hello? . . . Who is this? Is this—?" Her face hardened, and she slammed the receiver back into its cradle.

"Who was that?"

She looked at the silent phone and tugged on her bangs. "Um . . . I might as well tell you. That was Adam, my ex. You remember, Mr. Vanilla?"

"How could you tell?"

"Sigh through the nose," she said.

"Excuse me?"

"When he calls, he doesn't say anything. He just sighs, through his nose, like this." She inhaled, then exhaled through her nostrils.

"I see," I said. "Then he's called you before?"

"Yes, a few times."

"How many times is a few?"

"In the last six months, since we broke up . . ." she looked to the ceiling and counted on her fingers ". . . forty-six times."

"Forty-six times? He's stalking you, Gianna. Where does he live? I'll break his—"

"No, you won't break anything, Louis. Take it easy. The calls are tapering off, anyway. This is the first time he's phoned in over a week."

"You've hardly been home in the last week. You've been shacking up with me, remember?"

"It doesn't matter whether I'm here or not. He'll leave a sigh through the nose on my answering machine."

The phone rang again. I reached for it, and Gianna smacked my hand away. "I can answer my own phone, okay? Hello? Hey, Marion, what's up?" She covered the mouthpiece and whispered to me, "It's my boss."

I found my shirt behind the couch and put it on.

"No, no, it's okay, I was awake," Gianna said into the phone. "Yeah . . . right. I know the one. God, do I ever know that bill. It's been in subcommittee ever since I got here. So what—wait, me? When? Jesus God. Shit. No, I'd love to do it, are you kidding? I've got to start preparing like, two weeks ago." She looked at her watch. "I'll be there in an hour. Thanks, Marion. I swear I won't let you down."

Gianna hung up the phone. "Yes!" She pumped her fists in the air. "Guess what I'm doing next week? I'm testifying before Congress on the biggest bill of the session, HR 4875—you know, the so-called War on Crime Bill."

"I'm familiar with it."

"It's in the Judiciary Committee's Subcommittee on Crime. The hearing's on Friday. Marion wants me to be an expert witness. I'm gonna kick ass."

"I'm sure you will."

Gianna paused in her jubilation. "I'm sorry, Lou, but I

don't think I'll have time to see you this week. I'll be working on my testimony night and day. Maybe after the session's over we can get together again."

The word "maybe" crawled into my ear and gnawed at my brain.

"We don't have to go out." I moved closer to her. "I could help you—bring takeout to your office for dinner, drive you to work," I ran my fingers through her hair, "give you a way to release your tension at the end of the day."

"Mmm, it does sound nice, and I appreciate the offer, but I never get any sleep around you."

"I'll be good."

"I won't." She took my hand off her and squeezed it. "I promise I'll see you before Thanksgiving, okay?"

"Okay." I gathered the rest of my clothes and began to put them on.

"Besides," she said, "these two weeks will give you a chance to catch up on your own work."

My own work. My own work included a report supporting the same bill Gianna was fighting against.

"In the interests of full disclosure," I said, "I think I should tell you . . ."

She turned and looked at me, her eyes gleaming with excitement. "Tell me what?"

Maybe she wouldn't find out. Better yet, maybe I could use her own arguments against her.

"Tell me what?" she said again.

"That . . . that you're the most wonderful person I've ever met."

She stared at me without speaking, then slowly sank into the chair next to her. I finished tying my shoes, then stood to leave.

"Bye now." I kissed her on the forehead and walked out.

8

Ne Cadant in Obscurum

M onday morning I arrived early at the office to work on the War Against Crime report. Obviously, a reduction in violence was not among my goals and objectives for this or any other year. I had conceived of many methods for humans to increase crime while appearing to fight it. The War Against Crime bill contained most of these methods—at least the ones acceptable to a democratic society.

When my secretary arrived, she brought me my mail and a fresh cup of coffee.

"Good morning, Daphne. How was your weekend?"

"Smashing, Mr. Lucifer. And yours?"

"Very good, thanks."

"I can tell. You've been so much less gloomy this last week. It's a refreshing change, I must say."

Daphne had been my secretary for seventeen years, since the day I recruited her straight out of community college. The college's career services department had given me the person-

ality test results of each member of the graduating class. I
wanted someone who exhibited no moral values whatsoever
except one: loyalty. Within a year I had bought her allegiance
with money, respect, and the occasional night of unforgettable
sex. After she married, her sexual fidelity transferred itself to
her husband, but when it came to important matters, matters
of business, Daphne was with me until death.

She picked up the dictation tapes on the side of my desk
and started to walk out.

"Hold on." I poured the coffee into a glass mug, then raised my
laser pointer and shone it through the mug. Daphne sighed. A
faint red dot wavered back and forth on the wall. "What happened
to the coffee I made this morning?" I asked her.

She curled her lip. "There's not enough creamer in the
world to make your coffee drinkable."

"I don't take cream, so I'm not interested in that observation. Please find me a stronger cup, something not so
translucent."

Daphne took my coffee cup, tossed her auburn hair over
her shoulder, and left without a word. I returned to the chart I
was constructing. I had to choose the scale and time frames
that would make the rise in crime look most alarming.

The intercom buzzed. "Mr. Carvalho, Ms. O'Keefe is here
to see you."

An involuntary grin passed over my face. "Great. Send her
in." I closed the program to hide my work, then stood to greet
Gianna.

She entered, then leaned back against the closed door.
"Hi," she said.

"Hi. This is a nice surprise." I crossed the room halfway
towards her.

"Yeah, I was just, uh, leaving work." She pushed her rumpled
hair back from her face and let her gaze travel over my office.

"You've been up all night?"

She nodded. "I'm pretty tired, but . . . I'm also really wired." She looked straight at me and tilted her head. "Really, really wired."

"Oh. Okay, then." I moved toward her. Her eyes feasted on my face and body. I reached behind her to lock the door, then stopped. "Wait a minute." I opened the door and poked my head out.

"Daphne . . . ah, I don't have any appointments for the next hour . . ." I looked back at Gianna, who had already kicked her shoes off and was sitting on the edge of my desk, swinging her legs like a schoolgirl, "or hour and a half, do I?"

Daphne gave me a patronizing glare. "Let me guess. No interruptions."

"You read my mind." I lowered my voice. "But buzz me at ten-thirty, so I can wrap this up before the subcommittee chair gets here at eleven."

"Right." She rolled her eyes. "Wouldn't that be awkward?"

I locked my office door and joined Gianna at my desk. "I'm glad you decided to drop by."

"Uh-huh." She pulled my head down to meet hers. Though it had been scarcely forty-eight hours since I'd been with her, I kissed her like a thirsty man at a well, and sank into her soft embrace.

❋

"I feel so cheap, so used."

"Sorry." Gianna pulled on her stockings. "But I need to go home and sleep for a few hours before heading back to the office."

"How's your testimony coming?" I straightened the knot on my tie and combed my hair in the mirror.

"Brilliant. I'll have those fascists crying in their coffee."

"What do you have so far?"

"It all depends on which years' statistics you compare. If you compare today's crime rates to those of fifteen years ago, it looks like it's skyrocketed, and everyone panics and starts building prisons and throwing children into them. But compared to a few years ago, the FBI's numbers show that crime, particularly violent crime, has actually fallen."

"But the public is afraid," I said. "You're not going to win any support by telling them that it's all in their heads."

"I know that. The other half of the equation is to show that prevention is the key to stopping crime, and I'm not talking preachy public service announcements. I'm talking about getting at the root of criminal behavior."

"Which is?"

"Poverty."

I covered my mouth to hold back my laughter.

"What's so funny?" she said.

"Nothing."

"You have a different theory?"

"You mean, for instance, that all humans are inherently evil? That's more than a theory. It's a fact."

"You don't believe that," she said.

"I do."

"Why?"

"Why does anyone believe anything? Because from my point of view it's true."

Gianna finished buttoning her blouse. "They say that one's worldview is a reflection of one's own self-image." She looked at me. "Do you believe you're inherently evil?"

I met her gaze for a few moments, then turned away without answering her. She followed me.

"I think sometimes that you hate yourself," she said. "You try to hide it under your vanity and arrogance, but they only magnify it." She slid her warm hand under my arm. "You're not evil."

I tensed. "How do you know I'm not evil?"

Gianna didn't blink or flinch. "Because on rare occasions," she said, "I can see inside of you." Her voice stooped to a whisper. "And I know who you really are, underneath your mask."

"No, you don't, Gianna. If you really could see . . ." I brushed her hand off my arm and turned away. "You should go now. I have a meeting to prepare for." I returned to my desk and began to shuffle through a stack of papers.

"There's a light in your eyes, Louis. You've probably never seen it. But I've seen it."

She was out the door before I could respond. After a few moments, I moved to the mirror and examined my eyes.

Nothing. Even the light spilling from the window was sucked deep into my pupils instead of reflecting off their surfaces. Like two miniature black holes, my eyes consumed every particle of light and hope that dared approach me.

9

Tremens Factus Sum Ego et Timeo

" . . . To summarize, Mr. Chairman, our research indicates that increased penalties for juvenile offenders, including prosecution as adults, incarceration with adults, and lowered minimum ages for the death penalty, have resulted and will continue to result in higher rates of violent crime, as well as higher rates of recidivism."

I sat in my boardroom, watching Gianna's testimony on one of the congressional access channels. Her evidence was solid, her analysis was thorough, and she presented her case well, like the brilliant lawyer she must have been. I had taken three full pages of notes during the testimony. Her views were fascinating—ludicrous, but fascinating.

"Furthermore," Gianna continued, "the shift in juvenile justice philosophy from an emphasis on rehabilitation to an emphasis on punishment represents a dangerous revision of attitude. If our solution to the problem of juvenile crime is to shut these kids away and pretend they don't exist, then our nation will lose one of its most valuable resources—its youth. Any steps to reduce juvenile violence should be taken in a way that increases, rather than decreases, their chance to become full, contributing members of society. Young lives, representing the future of America, are at stake. I urge you to vote against this bill as it exists. Thank you."

The camera angle shifted to the chairman, who was watching Gianna with his chin in his palm. He cleared his throat before replying.

"Yes, very nicely stated, Ms., um, O'Keefe. However, this committee has employed an outside research firm to provide analysis of the issue, and from this report it looks like, rather than being too hard on these juveniles when we send them to prison, we're coddling them."

Here it comes. I began to twirl my pencil between my fingers.

"Coddling them, sir?" Gianna said. "With all due respect, have you ever been in prison?"

A guffaw broke from the throat of the congresswoman sitting next to the chairman. She beamed at Gianna.

"No, ma'am, I'm happy to report that I have never been incarcerated," the chairman said. "Anyway, this report shows that the average length of institutionalization for violent juveniles is 353 days. Doesn't it bother you, Ms. O'Keefe, that a teenager who commits cold-blooded murder could be back in our neighborhoods in less than a year?"

Gianna frowned and tapped her pen against her notepad. "Mr. Chairman, may I see that report?"

"Certainly." A page passed my report to Gianna. The pencil in my hand spun faster.

Gianna pulled a pair of glasses from her pocket and put them on. I knew she didn't need them but rather was using them as a stalling tactic to grant her more time to examine the report before reacting. She scanned the introduction, then flipped to the figures. Her brow creased, then she glanced at the foot of the page for the source of the report.

Gianna froze. My pencil snapped.

Her eyes widened for a moment, and she took half a sharp breath before returning to the same cool composure she'd kept during her entire testimony.

"Do you need more time before you respond, Ms. O'Keefe?" asked the chairman.

"No," she said, "I'm ready."

I left the VCR to record. On my way out of the office I grabbed my coat and said to Daphne, "I'm going over to the Hill. I might be back later."

I arrived at the Rayburn House Office Building in five minutes and waited across the street outside the North Entrance. Soon Gianna appeared through the bronze-etched doors, accompanied by a tall, smiling man with light brown hair and tiny glasses. When she reached the landing, she spied me. She barely broke stride, but continued down the stairs to the sidewalk, where she continued her conversation with the man.

He seemed to be trying to convince her to go somewhere. Gianna was shaking her head and gesturing vaguely at the Capitol Building behind me. Then a short black woman in a green suit came out of the building and joined the other two. Their argument stopped, and a minute later Gianna ended the conversation with a nod and a tight smile. Her colleagues waved goodbye to her and walked west towards South Capitol Street. Gianna turned to face me.

"I'm sorry," I shouted across Independence Avenue.

"You should be," she shouted back.

She moved up the street towards the crosswalk at New Jersey Avenue. I followed her on my side.

"I had a job to do," I said.

"I understand that."

"I had the job before I ever knew you were working on this bill, before I even met you." I trotted across to meet her on the median strip. She continued walking past me. "But I should have told you."

"Oh, yes," she said, "you definitely should have told me. Why didn't you?"

"I didn't want to upset you."

"Right. And I'm not upset now. After all, I was only just nearly humiliated in front of a congressional subcommittee while being simulcast on C-Span. And there was so little at stake: my job, my reputation, not to mention the millions of lives affected by this bill."

"How did it go?"

"I shredded your argument like confetti," she said.

"I see."

"Those figures were for all juvenile violent crimes put together. You didn't weight the numbers for the seriousness of the crime. The majority of those convictions were simple assault, so of course that will dramatically lower the average time served. It's like throwing two oranges in a bushel of apples and then claiming that oranges are red."

"I know."

"What do you mean, you know?"

"That's the flaw I wanted you to notice."

She stopped. "What are you talking about?"

"I'm not saying it was a free gift. My report was logically tight, tight enough to fool my client the chairman. But not so tight that someone as brilliant as you couldn't poke holes in it."

Gianna pointed her briefcase at me. "Are you saying you threw the fight?"

"Very carefully, yes."

"Why?"

"Because it meant more to you than it did to me."

"So?"

"Gianna, you know that the truth is infinitely malleable, and that anyone can manipulate the data to fit his or her version of the truth. I didn't care as much about my truth as you did about yours. So I wanted you to have your way, if you were good enough to deserve it, which obviously you are."

"I don't get it." She started walking past the steps of the Capitol. "People around here don't do things like that unless they want something from you. What do you want from me, Louis?"

"To begin with, I want you not to be mad at me."

"I'm still mad at you for not telling me. But I suppose that could have been seen as a conflict of interest. Even now, seeing us together, people might suspect."

I gestured behind us. "Who was that man you were talking to outside the Rayburn Building?"

Gianna shrugged and looked away. "Just a colleague of mine. You know, what you did could hurt your reputation as a consultant."

"They'll have forgotten about it by next week. All I have to do is analyze some issue in a clever way that feeds their belief system. Toss them another bone." I slipped my arm around her waist. "Besides, I can always find another profession if this one doesn't work out."

"You've always got your music," she said.

"You'd rather date a poor musician than a rich consultant, wouldn't you?"

"I do prefer macaroni and cheese to filet mignon."

"All right, then." I pulled her behind a hedge and kissed her nose. "Tonight we'll eat macaroni and cheese out of a box, sitting on the floor, and I'll play for you as long as you want, whatever you want, and you can dream your wildest fantasies about shacking up with me in a cramped, drafty sixth-floor walk-up studio apartment, washing my two shirts by hand and hanging them out to dry on a line in the alleyway overlooking a decrepit pizza parlor, the proprietor of which gives us his leftover garlic bread at the end of the day because he feels sorry for us, and sometimes in the summer we make love on the fire escape because we've no air conditioning, and there's nothing in our apartment but one frying pan, two forks, a used mattress, and a $100,000 Bösendorfer baby grand."

"I'll be there at eight."

✳

"I assume you want to eat it out of the pot," I said to Gianna as she entered my living room.

"Just give me a fork and a paper napkin, and I'm good to go." She held up a brown paper bag. "I even brought cheap beer."

"What better way to celebrate your victory for the vermin?"

"Since I've already had a few beers with my colleagues, I'll forget you said that."

I took off her coat just as the kitchen timer rang.

"Here, I'll hang it up," she said. "You get that."

I went to the kitchen, drained the tiny macaroni, and added the baby-aspirin-colored cheese powder, along with milk and butter.

"You realize, of course," I carried the pot of orange ooze out to the living room, "that this is only fun because we can afford better."

"Of course." Gianna and I sat on the floor between the chair and the sofa. "I've seen too much poverty to romanticize it."

"But you believe there's a nobility in poverty, don't you?" I popped the beer's top with a short hiss. "A nobility in the suffering of the poor?"

"Are you kidding? No, poverty has a way of trampling the humanity out of people—a lot of people, anyway. I don't think I could rise above it, personally. I'd be one of those kids popping a complete stranger because he looked at me funny."

"No, you wouldn't."

"Louis, I'm full of rage now, and I'm a thirty-five-year-old woman. I can't imagine what I'd be like as fourteen-year-old boy with brand-new testosterone coursing through my system and nothing to look forward to in life. Joining a gang and hurting people, it's the only way for them to get even a shred of power. People need power, and if they don't get it, they take it. How can society shit on these kids and then expect them to follow its rules?"

"You have a point, I suppose."

"Maybe I don't understand them as well as I think I do." She took a sip of her beer and ran her finger through the wet ring it left on the coffee table's glass top. "I can only guess what goes on in their heads. But when I look at these kids, on the one hand they seem like such monsters, yet I think, hey, that could be me." She looked at me. "You know what I mean?"

"I do."

"So no, I don't think there's a nobility in being poor. Some poor people have more dignity than others. And a few, in their own way, are just as decadent as some rich people. But take you, for example."

"Uh-oh."

"No, listen. You're obviously incredibly wealthy, but it doesn't show. You're not ostentatious." Gianna speared several pieces of glow-in-the-dark pasta on her fork. "It would take someone with a knowledgeable eye to look at you and realize that what looks like a nice two-thousand-dollar suit is actually a seven-thousand-dollar suit."

"Have you been stealing my credit card receipts?"

"It's still decadent to spend so much on one item of clothing, but at least you're not obscene."

"You want obscene?" I said. "You should see my diamond-encrusted mini-briefs."

"I'd like that."

"I'm saving them for a special occasion. For when I get to sleep with the Queen Mother."

"See, I knew you had a thing for older women." She took a long chug of beer.

I watched her against the backdrop of my abode and reveled in the feeling of uncommon and absolute contentment, one of the rare moments when I wasn't yearning to flatten myself on top of her, heaving and grunting like a rutting bull elk.

She noticed the dopey look on my face and said, "So what do you think about all this?"

"All what?"

"We're heading into double digits, with the number of dates."

"Mmm, something like that."

"And since you've never had more than one date with anyone before . . ."

"No, not in a row," I said.

"What do you think?"

"I think . . ." I dropped my fork into the empty pot. "I think it's time for me to hide behind the piano."

"Cool." Gianna settled on the sofa and gazed at me over the back of it as I sat on the bench and lifted the smooth wooden key cover into the body of the instrument.

"What would you like me to play?"

"I'd like you to play the violin that's hidden in your coat closet," she said.

"Ahh . . . that thing."

"You do play it, don't you?"

"I used to. It's been years." Ever since the Charlie Daniels Band recorded "The Devil Went Down to Georgia," playing the violin seemed too painfully stereotypical.

"Will you play it for me?"

I looked down at the piano keys and stroked the smooth, comforting surface of middle C.

"Certainly," I said. "Go get it."

Gianna leapt up from the couch and dashed into the hallway. She returned and presented me with the case in both hands, reverentially, as if it held Excalibur itself. I set it on the table and opened it slowly.

"Jesus God," she said, "it's a fucking Stradivarius."

I picked up the bow and the block of rosin. As I drew it across the bow, the rosin's weak, piney scent filled my head with memories so intense I had to turn away from Gianna for a moment to catch my breath. While the piano was a dear friend and confidante, my violin was more like a lover that had been caressed and obsessed-over once too often. I wasn't sure if it would even talk to me now, much less sing. I picked it up.

"It's beautiful," Gianna whispered.

"You mean it's pretty. Its true beauty can't be seen, only heard and felt."

"Still, it's gorgeous."

"I hope . . ."

"What?"

"Nothing." I lifted the violin to my chin.

There was no question as to what I would play. Bach's Violin Sonata in E Major was the most breathtaking solo piece

I had ever encountered, and I knew that if I could pull it off, Gianna would never leave me. For a moment I pondered whether that was a good thing or not, then closed my eyes.

The bow wavered in the air an inch above the strings for a moment and made a few practice strokes. I opened my eyes and began.

The notes gushed like a waterfall, and my mind emptied as I chased them across and up and down the strings, eight, sixteen per second, at some moments creating the illusion of two violins singing together, their voices intertwining in a duet of mad rapture.

Halfway through the second minute of this headlong pursuit, the sweat collected on my forehead and threatened to obliterate my view. My fingers and arms remembered every twist of this intimate dance. I allowed my eyes to close, shutting the salt water both inside and outside. The music stretched forth.

A minute later, I stabbed the climactic note, paused, then tumbled back into the few remaining, cascading measures. The final note came abruptly. The silence hissed with the missing sound and Gianna's soft gasp.

I opened my eyes and lowered the violin to my side. Gianna rose, slack-jawed, from the chair into which she had sunk, and approached me. She took my face between her palms and kissed me. Then she slid her arms around my neck and leaned her forehead against my chin.

"That was . . ." She gasped. "That was the most . . ." Gianna threaded her fingers into my hair and kissed me again, this time with an urgency that was becoming familiar and precious to me.

When we made love that evening, the thunder and lightning returned to crash inside my head, for the first time since our first night together. Afterwards, I lay trembling in her arms while she spoke to me.

"I felt a million different feelings while you were playing," she said. "Mainly helplessness. It seemed like the music had grabbed me and was carrying me wherever it wanted to, and if it had led me right over the side of the balcony I would have gone." She stroked the curve of my shoulder. "I'm not sure if I can bear to hear it again."

She feels helpless. Her touch immobilized me. Odd, strong words of tenderness leapt into my throat. I swallowed them just in time.

"You are amazing," she said. "You must let the rest of the world know how talented you are."

"No, not now."

"Louis, look at me." She shifted to stare into my eyes. "You make beauty. How many other people can say that? There are artists of all kinds out there lying to themselves that what they create is art, is beauty." She touched my cheek. "You have some kind of weird gift, a genius that comes so easily that you don't appreciate it. I won't rest until you share it with someone besides me."

"I'm happy doing what I do."

"You're happy being an intellectual prostitute?"

"I'm not an intellectual prostitute," I said. "It only seems that way."

"You're letting other people use your mind for their own agendas."

"So I make money off of stupid people who have too much power. What's wrong with that?"

"Don't you believe in anything?"

"I'd like to," I said. "But for now, I figure it's better to be empty than to be full of shit."

"Hey." She poked my chest. "You're lucky I'm too dazzled by you right now to take that personally."

I was right. The sonata had hooked her. What was I thinking?

"I didn't mean you, necessarily," I said.

"Yes, you did. Go ahead, say it. I'm close-minded and self-righteous. Say it."

"It wouldn't hurt for you to reexamine your beliefs once every decade or so."

"I can't, don't you see?" She lay back down and gestured at the ceiling. "Too many liberals are willing to make too many concessions. They want to be fair, open-minded. There's nothing wrong with that, of course. They're good people. They're also wimps. I don't want to be fair anymore. I want to win. Soldiers don't question the motives or the tactics of a war. They just fight. It's their job."

"And you're a soldier?"

"I prefer the term warrior," she said. "More inspiring."

"Couldn't you be court-martialed for sleeping with the enemy?"

"There's more to you than your money, Louis. You'd be beautiful in rags." Gianna stretched and yawned. "Speaking of sleeping, I've had a rather vigorous day and would like to end it within the next few minutes."

I kissed her goodnight, then went back to the living room to clean up. I stroked the Stradivarius once more before replacing it in the closet to continue its exile. After the dishes were put away, it was barely eleven o'clock, and though I wasn't tired, I returned to bed.

I have slept beside thousands of women during my existence, yet always resisted the urge to observe them in their slumber, to witness their transitory peace, a reminder of the tranquility I lacked. But Gianna mesmerized me even as she slept. Many nights that first month I would lie awake for hours, marveling at the angles of her face and listening to her quiet breathing. I would cast my hand over her arms an inch above her skin to feel the vibrations of her nerves and the radiance of her heat.

Often mere observation would turn into exploration, and she would awaken in an advanced state of arousal. That night, however, I was content only to watch her sleep and feel her resonate beside me.

10

Flammis Acribus Addictis

Gianna returned to her parents' house for Thanksgiving that weekend, leaving me with some much-needed time alone. I didn't see Beelzebub or the others until Thanksgiving Day. He had planned a Pilgrim-style orgy, but due to its inherent incongruity, his vision never materialized, so our Thanksgiving was much like that of other Americans, consisting mainly of turkey, football, and falling asleep on the couch under the mighty grip of L-tryptophan.

The following day I held a cabinet meeting in my office to discuss my latest project. Beelzebub, Mephistopheles, Moloch, and Belial attended.

"You've all seen those Web sites featuring a camera focused on the inside of someone's apartment that takes a new picture every thirty seconds or so." I turned on the projector. A home page with a pink and yellow background showed up on the screen. "The most famous and meticulously narcissistic of these is CandiCam, produced by, directed by, and starring Candi Kane—presumably not her real name."

I clicked on the camera icon to bring up the latest photo from CandiCam.

"Cool, she's having sex with her boyfriend," Beelzebub said.

"Check it out," Mephistopheles said. "On the left side of the screen. The dog's watching."

"I heard the dog has his own Web site," Belial said.

"Shh." I used my laser pointer to indicate an object in the corner of the camera lens. "Watch the green armchair." I narrowed my eyes and concentrated on the chair for about fifteen seconds.

"Sir, what should we be looking for?" Moloch asked.

I reloaded the page to get the new image.

"Holy shit," Mephistopheles said. "The fucking chair's on fire!"

I snickered. "Hopefully this time they'll smell the smoke before anything else starts to burn."

"This time?" Belial said. "You've done this before?"

"Of course. I had to practice before showing you. This is the third piece of furniture to spontaneously combust in Candi's apartment this week. But now that I've demonstrated it to you, I can leave her alone."

I reloaded the page again. Frozen by the camera's frame, a naked Candi was pointing a fire extinguisher at the armchair. I turned to my comrades.

"What do you think?"

"How'd you do that?" Beelzebub asked. "Do you know where she lives?"

"The answer to both questions is, I have no idea." I leaned back in my chair. "I just think about things catching on fire, and *poof!* they do."

"Lucifer, you become more godlike every day," Belial said.

"Ah, you flatter me, Belial. That's why I like you." I stood up. "I got the idea after reading an article about a group of doctors who have been performing double-blind studies on the healing power of prayer. They've finally figured out that energy can flow a great distance to help someone who doesn't even know he's being touched. I've been converting negative energy into heat for thousands of years, and I've taught you to do the same. So I thought I'd try sending some heat through another dimension, and as you can see, it worked."

"The potential uses for this power are endless," Moloch said.

"You could tie up police forces around the country investigating arson rings," Beelzebub said. "Or ruin people's ski vacations."

"Or destroy a year's worth of vaccines," Belial said.

"Or make entire towns smell really bad by heating up their cemeteries."

"Or watch live news broadcasts and incinerate the anchors' desks."

"Or," Beelzebub lifted his arms over his head, "you could evaporate Liechtenstein from the comfort of your own living room!" He and Belial high-fived each other from across the table.

"Let's not get carried away," I said, "This power is limited, not to mention very draining. To destroy an entire nation, even one as tiny as Liechtenstein, would require hundreds of us with the same power, and we'd probably be shattered for months afterward."

"Can you teach us how to do that?" Beelzebub said.

"There's nothing to teach. You can either do it, or you can't." I nodded to the screen. "Why don't you give it a try? All of you. See if you can set Candi's coffee table on fire, or even just the papers on top of it."

The four of them knit their brows and leaned forward in deep concentration. The projection screen burst into flames.

"Stop!" I said, but it was too late. The screen was already a pile of ashes. "You're all thinking in only three dimensions, and your mistake just cost us about two thousand dollars."

"Sorry," they all mumbled.

"Can we try again?" Beelzebub asked.

"No. Not with my equipment."

"Can you be sure it was all of us who did that?" Belial said. "Perhaps one or more of us actually succeeded."

"Let's see, shall we?" I turned the laptop computer to face the others and reloaded the Web page. It revealed Candi and her boyfriend sitting on the couch fondling each other. "I guess not." My brows pinched together to express my regret, but inside I was grinning, my superiority reaffirmed. "Oh, well. Let me know if you have any success. This meeting's adjourned, if no one has any further business."

"Good day, sir." Moloch saluted and left the room.

"Hey, let's go practice that trick down at the electronics store," Beelzebub said. "That way if we set something on fire, we won't have to pay for it."

"Excellent idea," Belial said. "Mephisto, will you be joining us?"

Mephistopheles, who had been silent and pensive since my demonstration, shook his head. "No, I need to talk to Lucifer about something. You go ahead."

The other two sauntered out of the boardroom. I pressed the button on the intercom.

"Daphne, would you have Maintenance come in here and clean up this mess in the boardroom? Tell them we had a short circuit."

"What happened?" she said. "I heard something pop."

"Never mind. Please order a new projection screen, too."

I disconnected the computer and began to pack up the

equipment. Mephistopheles drew near to me and said in a low voice, "Lou, this power of yours fits in perfectly with my new plan."

"What new plan?"

"A plan for radical misery on a monumental scale."

"Really?" I snapped the locks on the laptop case. "Sounds like an occasion for lunch."

We went to a local pub, mediocre enough to be unhaunted by Christmas shoppers, and sat in a dark booth near the back of the tavern.

"I've been working on something, Lou. Something big."

"You have?" With his attention to detail and keen strategic mind, when Mephistopheles says he's been working on something, it usually means he's got it planned from start to finish. "Tell me about it."

"Living as a minority has taught me many things, things I only suspected before."

"Such as?"

"Ever wonder why the police don't care when one black man shoots another?"

"No," I said, "but then again, I don't know why they care when anyone shoots anyone."

"They don't care because they know," he leaned closer to me, "that if the brothers ever stopped poppin' each other and decided to turn their guns on the real enemy . . ."

The corners of my eyes twitched. "What are you suggesting, Mephistopheles?"

"A new rebellion. Lucifer, our inner cities are filled with rage. This society has no idea what kind of powder keg it's sitting on. If we could channel that energy, if violence could unite them instead of ripping them apart, think of the power, think of the potential for bloodshed and chaos."

"Are we talking riots here? Like in L.A.?"

"No, not riots," Mephistopheles said. "More organized, more strategic. A mobilized corps of pissed-off niggas. A Million Man March that actually has a million men. No stopping to break windows and loot storefronts—just marching and killing. They'll advance out of Anacostia and Harlem and Compton, into the suburbs, into the countryside. Meanwhile, I will have crippled law enforcement's communication and tracking systems, setting them back a few technological decades."

"Wait a minute. When they get to the countryside, they'll run up against those civilian militias. They've got some heavy artillery, too."

"That's when the real fun begins, brother." Half of his mouth curled into a smile as he waited for my reaction.

"You mean . . ."

"Uh-huh."

"War." I savored the word as it blew past my lips.

"War, Lucifer. Another American Civil War, only this one won't be nearly so civil as the last one. We're talkin' Uzis and nines, not muskets and bayonets."

"Shit. Let me buy you another drink." I motioned to the waiter.

"It's what the white man has feared for years, black men putting down their crack pipes, picking up their guns, and getting the revenge they've deserved for centuries. We'll make Selma, Alabama, look like fucking Woodstock."

"There's just one problem," I said.

"What's that?"

"I look white."

"What are you worried about? You're immortal."

"I know, but it still hurts when I get shot."

"Don't worry," Mephistopheles said. "You'll be protected. So will most of the white power establishment, though there will be selected assassinations. You see, Lou, the final chapter is what makes this truly evil. The Man's still got the police, the National Guard, and if necessary, the entire military-industrial complex on his side. They'll crush this rebellion within days, weeks at the most, and once the violence is stopped, the oppression will be worse than ever."

He paused while the waiter delivered our new beers, then continued: "Forget affirmative action, forget friendly dialogues on race relations. Membership in the KKK will skyrocket."

"And all the latent racism inside civilized people will bubble to the surface again," I said. "People of all colors will feel justified in their hatred. Brilliant." I lifted my glass to him, and he tapped his own against it.

"This country will never be the same," he said.

I set my beer down suddenly without drinking it.

"Do you realize, this could even destabilize the world economy," I said. "If America approached something like martial law, even if only for a short time, businesses around the world would take a hit." I gripped his arm. "To have this kind of effect, your rebellion has to be enormous, and organized down to the last detail."

"Exactly. It needs a leader with a brilliant strategic mind, someone with enough looks and charisma to make them stop their squabbling and keep their eyes on the big prize. Someone who can make millions of men want to kill and die for him."

"You, for instance?"

"Got somebody better in mind?"

"I can't think of a more perfect candidate," I said. "What will you call yourself—Malcolm Y?"

"Very funny. I've been developing this project for years. Finish your beer, and I'll show you."

Mephistopheles occupied the basement floor of a former hotel near Woodley Park. His home was a series of mazes, each leading to another segment of his life. We walked past a row of cubicles containing graveyards of computer parts to a large wooden door in the corner. He punched a long series of codes onto the keypad. The door clicked open, and we entered.

The office was windowless, with white cinder-block walls. Mephistopheles turned on the desktop computer. After further elaborate security clearances, he shifted the monitor to face me.

"Check it out," he said.

Displayed on the screen was the introduction to what looked like a war strategy simulation package. His logo, a red M with a long pitchforked third tail, sat in the center.

The scenarios he showed me made my skin crawl with anticipation. No one would be safe, even in the gated communities that had become so popular among the frightened rich.

Mephistopheles pushed his chair back from the desk. "Would you like to play?"

My fingertips tingled. For the next two hours I explored his scheme's possibilities and even made a few improvements on it. He explained to me his intricate system of networked backups, in case this office ever met with an unfortunate fate.

"You need a theme song," I said. "I'll work on that this weekend. When can you get this plan rolling?"

"The sooner the better. Churches are starting to bring hope to the inner cities, making these people think that You-Know-Who is somehow gonna save them."

"How cruel."

"Speaking of churches," Mephistopheles said, "that's where your awesome pyrokinetic powers come in."

"What do you mean?"

"I figure if you torch a few strategic places of worship, a couple of black churches one day, a couple of white ones the next day, it might help stir the frenzy a little more."

"I don't know, Mephistopheles. Burning churches is pretty in-his-face. I don't want to do anything stupid."

"You won't get in trouble. It'll just be a few here and there."

The image did please me. "All right. Just a few." I exited the program and turned to him. "I want a project time line Monday morning."

"No problem." His grin widened. "You look excited."

"I am. This is genius, Mephistopheles, absolute profound evil. If I could, I'd promote you, but if you were any higher, you'd be me."

"And there's only one you."

"Seriously, though . . . don't ever tell Beelzebub this, but if anything were to happen to me, I'd want you in charge."

"Nothing will ever happen to you," Mephistopheles said. "But thanks."

"No . . . thank you."

I returned home later to find a message from Gianna on my voice mail. She had left her number at her parents' house, so I fixed myself a drink, reclined on the sofa, and called her back. She answered on the first ring.

"O'Keefe's Discount House of Kitsch. May I have your order, please?"

"Hi, I'd like fourteen of those windup unicorn carousels. The ones that play 'Mack the Knife.'"

"Damn, you're quick, Lou."

"How was your day?"

"Ugh. My mom dragged me out shopping on Black Friday. We spent two whole hours looking at curtains, goddammit, curtains! The guys got to go to the football game with Dad. It's the worst example of gender discrimination I've seen in this family since they wouldn't let me wear pants to First Communion."

"Poor thing."

"There were some pretty good sales, though." There was a crunching noise. "Sorry. We're having a party tonight, and I'm cutting up carrots for the veggie plate. One of them accidentally got in my mouth."

My phone beeped to signal a call on the other line.

"Do you have to get that?" she asked.

"No, the voice mail will pick up the message." I propped my feet up on the back of the couch. "So when are you coming home?"

"I'm leaving early Sunday morning to beat the train crush. Would you be a hero and pick me up at Union Station at noon?"

"Sure. I was thinking—" The phone beeped again.

"You sure you don't want to get that?"

"Yes, I'm sure," I said.

"Okay. So you were thinking what?" she said with her mouth full.

"Mmm. I was thinking I was wishing I was one of those carrots."

"Oh, wow." Her voice lowered. "I've got several of them right here in front of me."

"Are you alone?"

"Uh-huh. Ooh, here's a really big one."

"Yeah?"

"Yeah. I've got it in my hand right now."

"Yeah?"

"And you'll never guess where I'm putting it," she said.

I swallowed. "Where?"

"Right underneath my . . . chef's knife." A loud chop came through the phone.

"Ow! Gianna, you have no idea how much that hurts."

"The power of your imagination is maybe a little too strong, then. Sorry." She giggled. "I couldn't bear the thought of you all frustrated on my account. Trust me, it's better this way."

"I disagree."

"I miss you."

"I miss you, too," I heard myself say.

"I better go get ready for the party. See you Sunday?"

"See you then." I hung up and retrieved my two messages. The first one contained Beelzebub's frantic voice.

"Lou, it's me. Call me on my cell phone right away. As in now!"

I sat up. The second message was also from him.

"Lou, for fuck's sake, pick up! I know you're on the other line. This is an emergency. Call me!"

I hung up the phone, but it rang again before I could dial.

"Lou, it's me," Mephistopheles said. "Something's happened to Belial."

"What happened?"

"I'm not sure," he said. "Beelzebub just called and said something about the shopping mall and setting people on fire and Belial becoming somebody else."

"What the hell is that supposed to mean?"

"I'm telling you all I know. Bub's on his way over to pick me up, then we're coming to your place." A car horn honked several times in the background. "That's him. See you in a few minutes." He hung up.

I stared at the phone in my hands and felt like I'd just seen the first pebble in a landslide bounce past me.

I I

Confutatis Maledictis

Ten minutes later, my front door slammed open. Mephistopheles led a quaking Beelzebub into my living room.

"What happened?" I said.

Beelzebub paced back and forth, his head twitching. "Aw, fuck, man, I don't know. One minute we were just playin' around with the food people, next thing I know he's crying and goin' off on how he's a demon from Hell and shit . . ." He clutched his hair in his fists. "This is crazy, this is so incredibly, royally fucked up."

"Here." I handed him a shot of whiskey, which he downed, then let the glass fall on the floor. It bounced once on the Oriental rug before rolling under the sofa.

"Sit down and tell me what happened," I said.

"I can't. I can't sit down, I—I think I'm gonna be sick." He dashed into the hallway bathroom.

"I could use a drink." Mephistopheles headed for the bar.

"Did he tell you anything?"

"No, he was like this the whole drive over. I couldn't hear a word under all his howling. He just kept rambling on about shopping and killing and the truth."

"The truth? What do you mean, the truth?"

Beelzebub coughed behind us. He leaned against the wall in the doorway, his face gray. "Belial told them the truth."

"What are you talking about?" I said. "Here, sit down and start from the beginning."

Beelzebub obeyed. He sat in silence for a moment on the couch's middle cushion, then pulled his knees up to his chest. Mephistopheles and I stood on either side of him behind the sofa and waited for him to begin.

"We were in the department store, in the electronics section, trying to do that trick you showed us." Beelzebub clutched the toes of his sneakers. "We were watching the local news. They were broadcasting live from one of the other malls, doing a Christmas shopping story, I guess. We knew where they were coming from, so we figured we could nail it pretty easy." He stopped a moment to chew his thumb, then continued.

"First he tried . . . tried to set this doll display behind the reporter on fire. It didn't work, but I think he might have just missed by a little, because a fire alarm started going off in the background. So I decided to give it a shot." He closed his eyes. "I blew up the television."

Mephistopheles clicked his tongue and shook his head. "Geez, Bub—" I held up my hand to silence him.

"Go on," I said to Beelzebub.

"We got out of the store and went to the food court. I was pretty pissed off that I couldn't do it right, and pissed that he got closer than I did. So I'm lookin' around for things to set on fire."

"In the mall?" Mephistopheles said. "While you were standing right there?"

"I just wanted to see something burn, you know? Anyway, I'm not that dumb, I figured out a way to make it look like an accident."

"How?"

"There was a cheese-steak place with a guy frying up stuff on this big griddle. I decided to flame the poor bastard and make it look like a grease fire. I told Belial what I was gonna do, and he laughed. But then he . . . he . . ." Beelzebub cringed and wrapped his arms around his knees.

I slid around the sofa to sit beside him. "He what, Bub? What did he do?"

"He stopped laughing. He stopped laughing, and his face got all loose, and he told me not to do it. I laughed at him, 'cuz I thought he was joking. But he said it again, 'Don't do it, Bub,' he said, and I said, 'Fuck off. I don't take orders from you,' and I did it.

"It was . . . so cool. The flames just leapt up from the grill right into the guy's face. His hair caught on fire, and he started screaming. Then Belial starts screaming, too. He rips off his jacket, you know, that awesome leather one, and get this—he jumps over the counter and grabs the guy, who's running around like an idiot. He throws him on the ground and puts the fire out with his jacket."

"Wait a minute," Mephistopheles said. "Are you saying Belial saved this guy's life?"

Beelzebub nodded slowly, still not looking at us. "He even called the ambulance. There was a woman there who was an off-duty paramedic, and she gave the guy first aid. Everyone was gathering around Belial, patting him on the back for doing such a . . . such a . . . good deed."

The three of us hung our heads at these words.

I headed for the bar. "That's bizarre."

"It gets worse," Beelzebub said.

I stopped and turned to him. "Worse?"

"Much worse." Beelzebub took a deep breath. "Someone mentioned to Belial how fast he reacted, as if he knew it was going to happen. So Belial says, 'I did know it was going to happen.' At this point I got ready to run. But he says, 'I knew because I did it.'"

"Oh, shit," Mephistopheles said.

"Yeah. And it got real quiet all of a sudden. All you could hear was the lame music playing over the speakers. I remember that part, 'cuz it was a crappy version of a song I used to like back in the seventies."

"Anyway . . ."

"Anyway, he yells, 'My name is Belial, duke of Hell, and I could incinerate you all if I wanted to.' Some people kinda laughed a little, but everyone got real nervous. Then he goes, 'But not anymore. A few moments ago, I saw a new light, and it illuminated my . . . my . . .' wrongdoings? No, that's not the word he used. 'It illuminated my . . .'"

"Sins?"

"No, that wasn't it."

"Transgressions?" Mephistopheles said.

"No, not that either. 'It illuminated my . . .' Shit, what was the word? It sounded really good."

"Iniquities?" I said.

"That's it! 'It illuminated my iniquities.'" Beelzebub stood and faced us. "Then he gets up on the counter, waves his finger towards me and says, 'I renounce you, every one of you.' Of course, everyone thinks he's crazy, so I just play along and look around like, 'Who's he talking to?' Then he looks at the crowd, and he says . . . he says . . ." Beelzebub glanced at me, then turned his face away.

"What?" I grabbed his shoulders. "What did he say?"

"I . . . I can't repeat it."

"Tell me, dammit!" I shook Beelzebub and forced him to look at me. "Tell me what he said!"

"He said . . ." Beelzebub stared at my face, then lowered his eyes. "He said, 'I renounce Satan and all his works.'"

My fingers went numb. "He called me . . . that name?" I dropped my hands from Beelzebub's shoulders and turned away.

"Yeah. Sorry. And then he said—"

"I don't want to hear it."

"He said, 'I hereby repent and throw myself on the mercy of . . .'—well, you know who."

"On the mercy of—"

"Did he actually say the name?" Mephistopheles asked.

"Yeah," Beelzebub said in a voice breathy with what sounded like admiration. "He said it, all right."

"And what happened?"

"Nothing. I mean, nothing like what you'd expect. Everyone started backing away real slow. Someone must have called security, because these three mall cops came running and dragged him off the counter. He didn't even resist. They took him to an office and locked the door, locked him inside while they called the police. That was when I . . . I got the hell out of there." Beelzebub collapsed in the chair and ran his fingers through his hair. "I should have stayed, I know. But I panicked. I didn't want to get dragged into it. And Belial's always been able to talk his way out of anything. I figured he'd be okay."

"This has got to be a joke," Mephistopheles said.

"You're right," I said. "Like the time he became a priest and did all those exorcisms just to disprove the gospel."

"Yeah, or the time he delivered all that food to those famine victims, and it turned out to be rancid."

"I'm telling you guys," Beelzebub said, "this was no joke. You should have seen his face. He looked like one of those, what do you call them, born-again Christians. He looked—he looked happy."

The phone rang. I picked it up. "Hello?"

"Hello, may I please speak to Louis Carvalho?"

"Speaking."

"Good afternoon, Mr. Carvalho. This is Sergeant Russert down at the Tenth Precinct. Sorry to bother you, but there's someone here who says he works for you. His driver's license identifies him as William Hearst, but he says he's . . . what did you say your name was?"

"Belial!" said a voice in the background. "Duke and governor of the southern quadrant of Hell. I'll write it down for you if you like."

"Yes, uh, anyway," Russert said, "we're taking him to the local hospital for an emergency psychiatric evaluation. He hasn't done anything wrong—on the contrary, he saved someone's life." He lowered his voice. "But he's raving like a maniac, and frankly we're afraid he'll hurt himself or someone else."

"How awful," I said. "He did work for me until just recently."

"Let me talk to him!" Belial said.

"Would it be okay if I put him on the phone?" Russert asked me. "You don't have to speak to him if you don't want to."

"Put him on." I gestured to Beelzebub and Mephistopheles.

"Congratulations, Lucifer! You're the proud recipient of my one phone call."

"Uh . . . Bill, is that you?"

"No, it's Belial! Have you forgotten one of your favorite Hell's angels already?"

"Bill, what happened?"

"I had an epiphany," he said. "Hey, is Beelzebub there, too?"

"Uh, Bob's here, if that's who you mean. So's Malcolm."

"Whatever. Put me on speakerphone so you can all hear this."

Reluctantly, I hit the speaker button and returned the phone to its cradle. "Okay, go ahead."

"You remember how Saul of Tarsus had a conversion on the road to Damascus? I had one, too, except mine was in front of the Sizzle Steak. I can't explain it. Even I can't find the words to describe it." His voice lost its characteristic smoothness. "Lou, I'm sorry. But I can't serve you anymore. I can't bear the killing and the cheating and the lying. Especially the lying. That's why I have to tell everyone who I really am, and who you really are. Maybe then God will forgive me."

"You're crazy," I whispered.

"That's what they tell me. So I wouldn't worry if I were you. No one believes in us anymore. As long as no one believes, you'll be safe."

"Don't do this to yourself," I said. "They'll lock you up."

"It's okay. I've been imprisoned by my pride for ten billion years. The flimsy walls of a funny farm are nothing compared to that."

"Tell them this is a joke."

"It's not a joke, Lucifer. I can't lie anymore."

"Do it!"

"Don't bother giving me an order. I quit." He hung up.

The room was silent except for the dial tone coming from the speaker. My back was to Beelzebub and Mephistopheles as I stood in front of the phone. I could feel them staring at me, waiting for my reaction. It seemed as if our future rested on the strength of my composure.

I pressed the phone line to silence the speaker, took a deep breath, and turned to them.

"We'd better get started," I said.

"Started with what?" Beelzebub asked.

"Cleanup. We need to disown him before he drags us down with him. Mephistopheles, change William Hearst's medical records to show an extensive family history of schizophrenia. You can use the terminal in my library."

"Right. Good idea." Mephistopheles dashed into the other room.

"Beelzebub, I need you to recruit Belial's replacement."

"Replacement?"

"We need someone to head marketing and public relations. Maybe someone from Belial's crew, someone who learned from him. It can be a human, for all I care. PR people aren't exactly loaded with moral misgivings. Until then, I'll take care of the media." I stopped pacing. "The media. I almost forgot." I grabbed the remote control and turned on the television. "His little episode might make the evening news."

Mephistopheles appeared in the library doorway. "Hey, Lou, what about Belial's health benefits? Should we maintain them or cut him off?"

I paused. Without health insurance, Belial would be placed in a bleak state-run mental institution instead of a posh private psychiatric hospital. My choice meant the difference between giving Belial a prison sentence or a vacation.

"Cut him off."

"Whatever you say, Lou."

"I mean everything. Evaporate all his accounts, all his holdings. He no longer exists to us."

My brothers gaped at me.

"Do it," I said.

Mephistopheles nodded silently and turned to enter the library.

"And I want a complete media watch for the next two weeks. Monitor the newspapers, Internet newsgroups, Web sites, anything that mentions this incident. If anyone on this planet speaks, writes, or even thinks about it, I want to know."

"Okay, boss," Mephistopheles said.

The local news broadcast began. The theme music blared over a wide camera shot of the Potomac Mall.

"Uh-oh," Beelzebub said. "That's where the dolls were."

"The Christmas shopping season got off to a blazing start today at two local malls," the newscaster's voice-over said. "Good evening, I'm Marianne Wilkinson."

"And I'm Rob Chandler. Welcome to Channel 11 news at six."

"Two freak fires occurred within minutes of each other in the metropolitan area today. First we take you to Potomac Mall, where a blaze began to rage around three o'clock. It began in this store, Ye Olde Christmas Shoppe. Our correspondent Mickey Seaver is with the manager now. Mickey?"

"Thanks, Marianne. I'm standing here with Tom Wilson, the manager of Ye Olde Christmas Shoppe. Tom, can you tell us what happened?"

The manager, a short, chubby guy in a too-tight navy turtleneck, glanced at the camera. "Yeah, I was in the storeroom trying to dig up more of those talking Christmas trees—they're a big hit this year, and we have them at a real reasonable price—when suddenly I hear a sound like whoosh!" He threw his arms above his head. "I come out into the store and our huge nativity scene display was on fire, just like that, like someone had thrown gasoline on it and lit a match."

"How perfect," Beelzebub said.

The camera closed in on the smouldering, charred remains of a large ceramic nativity scene.

"Do you realize how hot that flame had to be to burn ceramic?" Mephistopheles said. "Belial's an idiot to turn his back on that kind of power."

"Firefighters arrived on the scene within minutes," continued the correspondent. "No permanent damage to the store occurred, and the store's owners say they hope to reopen on

Sunday, with a new and even bigger nativity display. In the meantime, the Montgomery County Police Department has dispatched its arson squad to sift through the evidence of this bizarre event. I'm Mickey Seaver, in Potomac."

"Thanks, Mickey." Rob Chandler turned to the camera. "And we'll be sure to keep you up to date on the investigation as it unfolds. In a seemingly unrelated story, a nearly deadly grease fire erupted at the Sizzle Steak in the Lafayette Mall downtown."

The news program depicted the incident and Belial's heroic act in much the same manner as Beelzebub had, but without all the whimpering. The correspondent tried to tie in some bullshit about the Christmas spirit overtaking this "angel," de-emphasizing his apparent psychosis, but the newscasters couldn't resist a quip or two at Belial's expense.

"Nothing like a good Black Friday sale to bring out the humanitarian in a decent demon, huh, Rob?"

"Yep. Those low, low prices'll give anyone second thoughts about being evil."

I glanced at Beelzebub and Mephistopheles, then gestured at the newscasters.

"Have them killed."

12

De Profundo Lacu

On Sunday morning, I had to circle the Union Station parking garage five times before I found a space. I arrived at the gate, red-and-white rose in hand, just as Gianna's train was pulling into the station.

She staggered down the hallway, her travel bag slung over her shoulder. A tired smile passed over her face when she saw me.

"I am so glad to see you," she said. I kissed her and offered her the flower. "Thank you."

I took her bag from her shoulder, and we began to wind our way through the crowd and out of the station. "How was your trip?" I asked.

"Excruciating. I had to stand the whole way from Philadelphia because there weren't enough seats, and all the assholes from New York wouldn't get up for any of us. Then this annoying little kid kept running up and down the aisles like a wild dog. He did this for about an hour, then he threw up all over the floor. He spent the rest of the trip crying, probably because he knew how much everyone wanted to kill him."

"Sounds magical," I said.

"How was your weekend? Anything exciting happen?"

"Oh . . . nothing much. The usual."

"I'm afraid to ask what the usual is."

"My car's over here."

Once we were winding through the streets of Washington towards her apartment, I said, "Gianna, I was thinking . . . let's take a trip together, just you and me."

"You mean like a vacation?"

"Yes. Wherever you'd like to go, I'll take you. Anywhere in the world."

"Anywhere?"

"Anywhere."

"I want to go to the Grand Canyon," she said.

"The Grand Canyon? Not Paris or Rome or Istanbul? Somewhere exotic like that?"

"What could be more exotic than the Grand Canyon? That's where I want to go."

"Then we'll go," I said. "Let's leave tonight."

"No way. I'm too tired."

"Tomorrow morning, then."

"What's the rush?"

"No rush. Let's just be spontaneous. If you dare, that is."

"I get it. Testing my sense of adventure," she said. "Okay, let's do it. Can we stop by my office? I just need to organize my desk."

"Your desk is probably already organized. This is a ploy for you to do work, work that can wait until you get back." I couldn't risk her reading about Belial's episode in the newspaper. Maybe she would accept the schizophrenia story, but it could lead to questions and more lies. "If you really want, I'll take you to your office, but you look like you could use a hot bath and a massage."

She leaned back against the headrest. "I'd be a masochist to choose work at this moment, wouldn't I?"

"Whatever your pleasure, darling."

"Take me home," she said.

"Good choice. I'll call my pilot and make the arrangements."

"No. We are not taking your plane."

"Why not?"

"It's so . . . you know . . ."

"Rich?"

"Lou, I'm not comfortable with doing something so wasteful. I know it sounds insane, and any other woman would probably tell me to shut up and let my gorgeous wealthy boyfriend sweep me off to Paris or wherever he wants to go in his private jet, but please respect my feelings about this."

"Then we'll at least fly first class. I'm not cramming these legs into a coach seat for five hours."

"Okay." Gianna clapped her feet together. "Wow, it just hit me. I'm going to the Grand Canyon! This is so cool." She cleared her throat. "You are aware, of course, that taking a trip together is a pretty serious thing in a relationship."

"No, actually, I wasn't aware of that. All I was aware of is the fact that I want to spend lots of time with you far away from our everyday lives, to offer you new and exciting experiences, and for us to get to know each other at a more profound level. I guess you might call that serious."

"Sounds good to me." Gianna tapped her fingers on her knee. "Did I just refer to you as my boyfriend a minute ago?"

"Yes, you did."

"Oh." Out of the corner of my eye, I could see her studying my face for a reaction.

I reached for her hand. "You're my first girlfriend."

"That's a scary responsibility."

"You have no idea."

Every time the flight attendant brought us something, Gianna would glance back at the curtain separating the cabins.

"What's wrong?" I said finally.

"How come we get served first?"

"Because we're in first class. If we weren't served first, it would be false advertising, or at least heavy irony."

"And we get real knives and forks," she said, "not those disposable ones. Nothing on our trays is wrapped in plastic."

"Wrapped in plastic?"

"Haven't you ever flown coach? Never mind, I don't want to know. But why do we get special treatment? We're not any better than the people back there."

"We paid more."

"So?"

"So you get what you pay for. It's a choice. Those people in coach chose to save their money for something else."

"Yeah, like food or rent."

"Gianna, why can't you just enjoy it?" I put my fork down, took her hand, and kissed it. "When will you realize that you deserve the best?"

She drew her fingertip across my cheek. "I already have that."

The flight attendant placed a headset on each of our trays. "The movie will be starting in five minutes," he said. "Can I get you anything else?"

How about some fucking privacy? I shook my head at him and sighed. If we were on my jet, Gianna and I would be having sex right now.

The in-flight movie served its purpose in passing the time and limiting my awareness of being boxed in a crate with 144 strangers. The film was some kind of tragic love story, or perhaps a comedy, I don't remember, but one scene in particular struck me:

The lead couple was standing on a balcony by the sea with the sunset behind them. They bantered for a few minutes about the difficulties of modern relationships, then the man suddenly cut her off in mid-sentence by saying, "I love you." She melted into his arms, and within moments they toppled onto the closest bed, tearing at each other's clothes. At this point, to maintain appropriateness for an airline audience, the film cut to the following scene, with the couple on the balcony again, this time eating breakfast.

I glanced at Gianna, whose eyes were riveted on the screen, then turned my attention back to the film.

✤

"I can't believe I'm letting you do this to me."

Gianna sat blindfolded in the passenger seat as I drove into the Grand Canyon National Park's West Rim Drive.

"I wanted you to have the most intense experience possible, Gianna. Now would be a good time to tell me if you have a weak heart."

"As if I could survive going out with you for a month if I had a weak heart."

"We're almost there," I said.

"Is it still snowing?"

"A little. Don't peek. You'll regret it."

I pulled into the turnoff for the Abyss, in my opinion the most breathtaking view accessible by vehicle on the canyon's South Rim. I helped her out of the car, and we stood in the empty parking lot.

"There's ice and lots of rocks," I said, "so it would be better if I just carried you."

"Oh, for God's sake . . ."

"What are you complaining about? This is the moment you've been waiting for all your life."

"That's the problem," she said. "With all this buildup, it can't possibly be that great."

"Trust me, it will be. Here, climb on my back."

I carried her along the path to the overlook. When we reached the edge, I let her down and guided her to the railing in front of me. "Ready?"

She clutched the railing and nodded. I took off her blindfold. She squinted, then her eyes widened as they adjusted to the light. Her knees started to buckle, and I wrapped my arms around her waist to steady her.

"Jesus God . . . it's so . . . it's . . ."

"Don't even try," I said. "Words are too feeble. Just look."

She put her knuckles to her mouth. "This isn't real. How can this be real?" We stood there for at least a quarter of an hour before Gianna said, "I need to sit down."

I led her to another vista a few yards away that offered a slightly different angle of the Abyss. We sat on a flat boulder. Gianna gazed out and down at the canyon.

"Beautiful doesn't begin to describe it. A flower is beautiful. But this is beautiful the way that a person is beautiful—terrifying with its jagged edges, yet seductive with its crevices that hide so many secrets." She put her hand to her throat. "Wow, where did that come from? I'm waxing weird all of a sudden." She turned to me. "Thank you for bringing me here. You've given me a tremendous gift."

"It's the least I could do, Gianna, in return for what you've shown me."

"What do you mean?"

"For the first time, I—"

"Wow! Check it out!"

We turned to see a young couple with small twin boys in matching orange coats. The kids pushed each other as they ran down the trail, each trying to get to the edge first.

"Hey, watch out!" the father called. "I'm not climbing down to pick up your dead bodies if you fall."

"Jack . . ." his wife said. "Good morning," she said to us as they passed. "Chilly weather, huh?"

Gianna smiled and nodded to the couple, then turned back to me when they had moved on. "So what were you saying?"

"Nothing."

We sat in silence for a few minutes, then the boys careened past us on their way back to the car. They leapt and batted at the falling snowflakes. Their parents shuffled behind.

"Can you buckle them in while I take one more look?" the woman asked her husband. She moved to the edge of the next boulder and faced into the Abyss. "This place deserves more reverence than those boys will ever possess. It's one of God's masterpieces." She zipped up her jacket. "You two have a good day. Enjoy your solitude while you still have it."

Gianna gazed into the canyon as if she were peering not into the creation, but into the face of the creator himself.

"She's right," Gianna said. "You could cure a lot of atheists by bringing them here."

I picked up a tiny shale fragment and chucked it over the edge.

"But I don't think God created the Grand Canyon," she said. "The Earth created it. But you could think of it as a temple, except it makes all manmade temples look vulgar and reaching. Perhaps the Earth created the Grand Canyon in praise of God."

"Or, perhaps, in fear," I said.

Gianna turned and looked at me with that same curious, understanding gaze I'd seen when I showed her the feather from my wings. She touched my hand.

"I love you," I heard myself say.

She blinked hard. "What?"

"I love you, Gianna," I said again, this time with all my breath. "I've never said that to anyone before." Her eyes darted away from my face. "I've never even thought it until just this moment, but it sounds right. It sounds more honest than anything I've ever—"

"How dare you?" she said.

My mouth hung open, empty and dry.

"How dare you ruin a perfect moment like this by saying that? Louis, I just got out of a nine-year relationship. The last thing I need right now is for someone to love me. I don't want to sink into that quicksand again. I can't!"

"Gianna, this is me we're talking about here, not some loser who doesn't have a clue about what you need."

"That's not the point. I'm just not ready."

"*You're* not ready? You think I was prepared for this? Believe me, if I'd known I'd end up feeling this way about you, I would have run screaming the moment I first saw you." She turned away and hid her face in her arms. "You love me, too, Gianna. Admit it."

"No, I don't."

"Look at me when you say that."

"No! I don't take orders from you. I'll do what I want, and if I don't want to love you—"

I grabbed her and turned her to face me. "Gianna, tell me you love me, or I'll throw you into the canyon."

"What?"

"I'm not kidding. I hate hypocrites."

"Are you insane?"

"I am now." I dragged her to the edge of the boulder until we were teetering halfway into the air. She shrieked and latched one hand onto my shirt and one hand in my hair.

"I'll take you down with me, I swear," she said. "We'll both die."

"That's the idea. Now tell me you love me."

"Fuck you."

I shifted us forward another inch. "Any last wishes?" I said.

"Yes, I wish you wouldn't kill me."

"I'll consider it, if you consider telling me the truth."

"You're a fucking maniac, Louis."

"And that's why you love me."

"No!" We slipped another inch. "Aren't you afraid?!"

"If being in love is a ten on the terror scale, then being pulverized on the floor of the Grand Canyon is about a two-point-four."

"Please, Louis. I don't want to die. Not now."

Her eyes begged my mercy. I shifted us back from the edge of the boulder to safety and let go of her. She clutched at the rock and gasped for breath.

"Sorry," I said.

"You son of a bitch. I can't believe you just did that."

"I'm sorry. I got carried away. Let's forget about the whole issue, okay?" She nodded, still short of breath. I stood and helped her up, then began to walk back to the car.

"Louis?"

"Yes?" I turned to her. She punched me. I spun and fell onto the icy gravel. While I lay there, my jaw throbbing, Gianna fished the keys out of my coat pocket, climbed in the car, and drove away.

13

Culpa Rubet Vultus Meus

The snow fell harder during the hour it took me to walk the four miles back to the Grand Canyon Village. I found our car outside the lodge near the restaurant entrance. I gathered all the dignity a soggy man could carry, and entered.

She was sitting by the window looking out over the canyon, though it was impossible to see farther than a hundred feet. The clouds had shuffled in and covered most of the canyon walls. I approached her table. She turned and saw me, then gestured to an empty coffee cup at the seat across from her. I sat down and wiped my hair away from my face so as not to drip ice water in the coffee she was pouring me.

"Thank you," I said.

She refilled her own cup. "So, Louis, what did you learn in relationship school today?"

"Not to almost kill you?"

"Very good." She tore open a pack of sugar and snapped

the contents into her coffee. "That was an important lesson. There'll be a quiz later."

"You were never in any real danger, you know." I took a sip of coffee. "Of course I wouldn't have let you fall." She didn't answer. "So what did you learn?" I said.

Her eyes flashed. "What?"

"I said, what did you learn, Gianna, in relationship school today?"

She glared at me over her cup, then set it down with a clatter, as if she'd lost the strength to hold it up.

"I learned that I need to go back to kindergarten, because none of this is making sense anymore."

My smile came too quickly to thwart.

"Don't give me that look," she said. "This is not funny."

I picked up my water glass and clinked it against hers. "We rock each other's world, don't we?"

"And you probably think that's a good thing."

"Sure," I said. "Conflict begets growth."

"No, conflict begets more conflict. What's wrong with a little peace?"

"Peace is overrated."

"You only say that because you've never felt it."

A cold drop of water trickled from my temple to my jaw and plopped onto the table. "Sometimes you see me so clearly, Gianna, it's like you . . ." I stood up. "Come with me."

"Where?"

I held out my still-clammy hand to her. "To look for peace."

※

Gianna built a fire in our room while I changed into warm dry clothes. Then I stretched out on the bed, surrounded by softness.

"Come here," I said.

"Lou, I'm really not in the mood."

"It's not what you think."

She sighed and sat on the edge of the bed.

"Take off your shoes and lie down," I said.

"Fine. Whatever." She lay beside me with her back to me. I slid my arm around her waist and laid my cheek on her hair. "Now what?"

"Nothing," I said. "Nothing at all."

"Oh." She hesitated, then placed her hand over mine. Her fingertips rested on my knuckles.

We lay together in silence for many minutes, while the logs in the fire shifted and hissed, and the snow skipped across our balcony. Our breathing synchronized and lulled me into a place somewhere between peace and sleep.

Finally Gianna stirred a little and spoke.

"Lou, if I had told you I loved you out there on the cliff, would you have believed me? Or would you have considered it a confession given under duress?"

I thought for a moment. "I don't know."

"You wouldn't have believed me," she said. "Even afterwards, if I'd sworn that I loved you, you would have always wondered if I were just piling one lie on top of another."

"Perhaps."

"That's the real reason why I wouldn't say it. Because it wouldn't have been a lie." She turned to me. My stomach tightened.

"Whether it's because you're a maniac," she said, "or because you make me feel like one, I don't know." She moved her mouth close to mine, and I inhaled her next words. "I love you."

As she kissed me, my brains felt like they had broken loose from my skull and were sloshing around inside my head. I pulled away from her and sat up.

"What's wrong?" she said.

"I . . . I suddenly don't feel well. I think I need to . . . take a walk."

"You're kidding me."

"No . . . not a walk. I need . . ." I stood and lurched into the bathroom, where my stomach convulsed its contents into the toilet. I continued to vomit long after there was anything to offer besides panic.

As I sponged my face with cold water, I studied my reflection in the mirror. Somehow I had thought love would ennoble my appearance. Instead I looked pallid and confused.

When I returned to our room, Gianna was sitting cross-legged in the middle of the bed.

"Sorry," I said.

"I doubt I'll forget this day any time soon."

"It's just that . . . no one's ever said that to me before, and I wasn't expecting it to . . . I didn't expect my reaction to be . . ."

"You didn't think it would make you puke."

"I know this looks bad."

"No one's ever told you they loved you before?" she said. I shook my head. She covered her face with her hands. "Oh, why didn't I check your emotional baggage at Customs?"

"It's a heavy load. This is just the beginning."

She got off the bed and opened the tiny refrigerator. "Want some ginger ale?"

"No, I think I really do need to take a walk now."

Gianna crossed her arms in front of her chest and nodded, not looking at me. "Okay. Have a good walk."

I put on my boots. "I'll be back soon."

"Right."

I turned to leave.

"Louis?"

"Yes?"

"You forgot your coat."

"I'm leaving it here so you know I'm coming back."

"I have no doubt you're coming back, but thanks."

"It's okay," I said. "I don't need it, anyway. The sun's coming out."

Besides, my body felt like it was on fire. Snow melted in a six-foot diameter around me as I crossed the lodge's parking lot to the closest overlook. The metal railing was ecstatically cold, and I leaned my forehead against it.

A raven squawked above my head. Its heavy wings thumped the air to my right as it alighted on the railing. I turned my head to admire it. The feathers on its thick throat rippled in the breeze like fur as the bird peered back at me. We stared at each other for a minute, then it took off with a leap and a rush of wings. A black feather fell to the pavement at my feet as the raven circled once overhead, then flew into the canyon.

As my eyes followed the bird, I noticed a moving figure on the wall of a section of the South Rim that jutted outward to my left. It was over a mile away, but I could tell it was human, and alone. The hiker strode along the trail without stumbling, probably whistling a happy, confident little tune.

The raven returned to the railing next to me, this time only a foot from my shoulder. It cocked its head at me as if it were waiting, expecting.

"Go beg some potato chips off the tourists," I said. "I don't have any food for you."

The bird shuffled back and forth a few steps, its talons scraping the steel railing. I looked at the hiker again, then glanced around to make sure I was alone.

"Pretty stupid to hike by oneself like that," I said to the raven. "One could get hurt." The hiker headed into a switchback that led him underneath a snow-covered cliff. "After all, with the sun coming out, a large chunk of ice might just melt enough to fall on one, mightn't it?" The excess heat was leaving my body already. My mind grew calm. I turned to the raven.

"What the hell. It would be a tragic waste to come to the Grand Canyon and not throw anyone in. Besides, you need lunch." *And I need to feel like me again.*

I focused my attention on the ledge above the hiker. "Just a small one first." A baseball-size nugget of ice broke from the cliff and tumbled to the trail in front of the hiker. He stopped and looked up briefly, then continued his ascent. A larger fragment fell in front of him again, cracking on the trail and spinning off into the canyon. He repeated his previous movements, but this time his pace quickened.

"That's it, little one. Ponder the possibilities for a few moments." Another ice slab crashed behind him, and he began to run. I glanced at the raven, who seemed to be watching the spectacle with his own midnight blue eyes.

The hiker scrambled up the path. When he reached a narrow, treacherous portion of the trail, a chunk of ice the size of a bowling ball fell from the cliff and grazed his head. He staggered, then toppled over the edge. The raven hollered a triumphant caw and took flight.

My lips twitched. Then I noticed that the hiker was clinging to a juniper bush a few feet below the trail where he had fallen.

"Tenacious little bugger, aren't you?" I focused on the ice bank one last time.

"What are you staring at?"

I started with a gut-wrenching shudder and whirled to face Gianna.

"What?"

"I said, what are you staring at?" She tucked her pine green scarf under her chin and peered in the direction of the hiker.

"Nothing." I stepped between her and the railing, forgetting for a moment that she couldn't possibly see the hiker from this distance. "I was just staring."

"You looked like you were focusing on something pretty hard."

I looked into the canyon and gestured at the raven, who was surfing the wind, spiraling towards a late breakfast.

"Ravens are the most beautiful birds," she said. "You know why?"

"Why?"

"Some of the northwestern native tribes believe that the Raven brought light to a world of darkness. One story says that he was originally the brightest of all the birds and had wings like rainbows, but that carrying the sun in his beak burned his feathers to black." She leaned against the railing and watched the bird descend. "To me, the raven's darkness is like a symbol of a tragic nobility, of one who would sacrifice his own beauty in the name of truth."

I bent down to pick up the raven's fallen feather and presented it to Gianna.

"Wow," she said. "What a souvenir. Not as exotic as your condor feather, of course."

"This one's in better shape."

"Yeah. Anyway, I brought you your coat, and I'm going to grab lunch now. I wanted to let you know where I was, so you didn't think I'd run away again."

"Thanks." I took my coat from her and put it on, in need of extra warmth now. "I think I'll join you."

"You actually feel like eating?"

I put my arm around her shoulder and kissed her temple. "I'm starving."

Before we left the overlook, I peeked into the canyon. My hapless hiker had pulled himself back onto the trail, where he lay face down, panting and praising whatever god he believed in, for surely he believed that something other than coincidence had saved his puny life. I watched Gianna caress the soft fibers of the feather and thought that perhaps coincidence was an insufficient god.

14

Quantus Tremor Est Futurus

"A toast . . . to a day that will live in infamy."

Gianna and I clinked our champagne glasses together. We sat at the table in our room and looked out over the dark canyon. Stars carpeted the sky, bright enough to view through the thick window. A single candle burned on the table between us, and a fire crackled in the fireplace. I had never felt such ecstatic contentment.

I set my glass down. "Gianna, I want to tell you . . ."

"Tell me what?"

"I want to tell you the most romantic, eloquent things you've ever heard in your life, I want to say words that will make you wilt with joy, but when I look at you, I lose all my ability to . . . to . . ."

"To what?"

"Speak."

She laughed. "That's already the most romantic, eloquent

thing I've ever heard." She caressed my cheek. "How's your jaw? Still sore?"

"It's a gentle reminder to be a good boy."

"Let's not get carried away. If I was looking for a good boy, you'd be quite a disappointment."

I turned my head to kiss the inside of her fingers, at the soft place where they met her palm. She closed her eyes.

"I remember the first time you kissed my hand," she said. "On the Metro. I thought I was going to collapse on the platform right then. I almost got back on the train with you."

"I know."

"I'm glad I didn't, though."

"Why?" My lips moved down to her wrist.

"I liked the suspense," she said. "It gave me time to think about what it might be like. What did you do that night after our first date?"

My mouth hesitated for a moment. "I hung out with some friends." I neglected to mention that after that raucous evening with Beelzebub and Mephistopheles, I could barely remember her name.

"I went to bed early that night, for all the good it did me. Sleep eluded me, as it seems to have done almost every night for the last month."

"You must be exhausted." My hand swirled over her knee and began to travel up her thigh. "Perhaps we should go to bed early tonight."

Gianna took both my hands in hers and led me to sit on the bed next to her.

"Do you believe that I love you?" I said.

"I believe that you believe that you love me, and that's good enough for right now. Some day you'll convince me that it's true."

"How can I convince you?"

"Not by what you say, but by the choices you make. You'll know when the time comes, when you're faced with a pivotal decision and realize that love leaves you only one choice." She wrapped her arms around my neck. "But until then, I'll savor your confessions in all their naive sweetness."

I held her as tightly as I could without breaking her. "I love you, Gianna. Someday I'll prove it to you, but for now, just listen to the words." I repeated the phrase as I caressed her body, but in a corner of my mind I was thinking of the hiker I had almost killed, and of all the other choices I would face that could make a liar out of me.

In my dream I held an engraved invitation. My fingers traced the smooth gold lettering until the strange, blurry letters congealed into words:

Lucifer,
Please come home.
All is forgiven.
Love, Dad

"This is a joke, right?" I said to St. Peter, who had materialized in front of me, a white feather pen tucked behind his ear. We appeared to be standing (or hovering) on the outskirts of the Orion Nebula.

Peter sighed. "Hang on a second." He licked his forefinger and paged backwards through a tiny black book. He stopped when he reached the first entry. "It figures. It's on the last page I look. Huh. It says 'eternal damnation' in your entry, but it's crossed out. Let me see that."

I handed Peter my invitation, which he examined. "It's His handwriting, all right." He shrugged. "Okay, let's go."

"Wait a minute."

"'Wait a minute?'" he said. "Do you have any idea how long a minute is around here?"

"I have to ask you, is this forever?"

He scratched his chalk-white beard. "Forever is a relative term, Lucifer, you know that."

"I mean, I can never go back? To my life?"

"Why would you want to do that?"

"There are so many things I haven't done, projects I haven't finished."

"Oy," he said, "if I had an atom for every time someone said that, I could build my own wormhole."

"But I'm not—"

"'I wish I'd spent more time with the kids,' 'I wish I'd told my wife I loved her,' 'I wish I'd swum naked in the Hudson Bay,' 'I wish—'"

"Listen to me, Peter, I'm not like them. I'm not dead. I'm here of my own free will, and I can leave if I want, right?"

He held up his palms and tilted his head. "You always do what you want, Lucifer. Now is no different. But this offer could expire any moment. You know how capricious He can be."

I rifled my memory and came up with only one project that could not remain unfinished: the demise of country-western music.

"Can you hang on for just a moment?" I snatched my invitation and turned to leave. A whooshing sound came from behind me. Peter held up the black book, now in flames. He shook his head.

"You're all lost now," he said. "All of you rebels. No more second chances." He tossed the book to me. I caught it and held it in my hands as it burned. It flipped open, and I watched my name and those of my comrades curl and disintegrate with the pages they inhabited.

Then I fell again, this time into nothingness, forgotten and forsaken forever.

✷

"Lucifer."

I opened my eyes. Gianna's murmur had come from behind me. I lay on my right side, my back to the window.

"What?" I whispered.

"Lucifer."

I sat straight up like a twanged catapult and stared at her. How did she know? Had I been calling out my own name in my sleep again?

"What did you say?!"

"Didn't mean to scare you." She shifted on the window seat to face me. "I was just looking up at the morning star and thinking how they used to call it Lucifer, before they knew it was Venus."

Hearing Gianna speak my name, my one true name, sent a hot surge of blood to my ears.

"Kind of interesting, don't you think?" she said. "Considering how the surface of Venus is much like what most people imagine Hell to be like—hot and sulfuric."

The barest light of dawn cast a ghostly glow over her face and made her look as if she might shimmer into another dimension.

"It's actually quite cold," I said, more loudly than I'd intended.

"Let me guess. You've been there."

I slid out of bed and joined her on the window seat. "Which—Hell or Venus?"

"Both, likely." Gianna brushed the hair from my eyes. "You do have that 'Hell-and-back' look about you. Maybe someday I'll find out what happened to make you so—"

I kissed her quickly, then moved behind her and pulled her to lean against me. We gazed at the brilliant disk of Venus.

"Did you know that the name Lucifer means 'bearer of light'?" I began to unbutton her nightshirt. "They say that before he fell he was the most glorious of all the angels in Heaven."

"Mmm, and obviously the stupidest, too."

My fingers paused a moment in their journey, then continued.

"I mean, to rebel against God?" she said. "What are the chances of defeating an omniscient, omnipotent Creator? You'd have to be pretty ignorant to wage a losing battle like that."

"Or really bored." I ran my hands across her stomach and between her breasts.

"Exactly. Anyway, it's an intriguing myth, but I don't buy it."

"You don't believe in the Devil?" I brushed my teeth against the nape of her neck, and she arched her back against me.

"No more than I believe in Santa Claus or the Bogeyman."

"Why not?"

"Because the kind of God I believe in wouldn't allow such a terrible creature to exist."

"Oh." I halted my seduction attempt. "But then how do you explain evil?"

"I'm not so simple-minded that I have to personify it in the form of the Devil. Evil comes from within humans. We're doing a fine job on our own without help from some horny little pipsqueak from a flaming cave."

"But if this god of yours is supposed to be all-powerful and all-good, then how can evil exist?"

Gianna turned to face me. "Then one must choose between logic and faith. Logic says that God has to be either omnipotent or benevolent, and empirical evidence shows us that He's not both, because the world is such a craphole. Faith, on the other hand, says to just shut up and believe that we're too small to unravel the mystery of God's plan."

"And which do you choose?" I said. "Logic or faith?"

"I haven't decided yet." She planted small kisses on my throat and jaw.

"Do you think logic and faith can be reconciled?"

"Philosophers have been performing intellectual gymnastics for centuries trying to do that. But I don't think it's possible, not in my experience, not for more than a moment. I don't worry that my personal struggles of conscience will get me in trouble, though. They say God loves the doubters, because we're the ones who are seeking, we're the ones who care enough to question." Gianna stroked my ribs with the back of her fingers. "I love a good naked theological debate." She tapped my mouth. "What about you, Louis? Do you believe in the Devil?"

I stared at the ceiling while I answered her. "I used to believe. Lately I'm not so sure."

"Good. I say that the fewer people believe in him, the less power he'll have."

"On the contrary," I looked her in the eye again, "Baudelaire once said that the Devil's cleverest wile is to convince people that he does not exist."

"And what does Baudelaire know? Poets, they put a few words together in cute ways and they think they speak for everyone."

"What if there really is a Devil? What would you do if you met him?"

"My dad asked me that question once," she said. "He's a theology professor at Villanova, did I ever tell you?"

"And what was your answer?"

"I told him that if I ever met the Devil, I'd spit on him to show him I wasn't afraid. He seemed to like that response."

"I see. So what would you really do?"

"I probably would spit on him." Gianna chuckled. "Then I'd let him take me out and show me a good time."

"You mean like this?" I pulled her shirt back over her shoulders and used it to restrain her arms behind her. With my other hand I explored every crevice of her body until she writhed and moaned with pleasure. When I could feel that she was near orgasm, I pulled away. She glared at me.

"I can see why you believe in the Devil," she said. "Obviously you've met."

"Devil? What Devil? He doesn't exist, remember?" I leaned forward and grazed her belly with a single soft kiss. "Not unless you want him to."

"I don't need the Devil when I've got you." She curled her finger at me. "Now come back here and finish—"

"I'm feeling so sleepy all of a sudden. Must be the altitude." I yawned, moved back to the bed, and lifted the covers.

"Louis."

"Yes?" She didn't answer. "Did you want something?"

"You know what I want."

"I forget." I lay on the bed. "Why don't you explain it to me?"

"Fine." She stood to approach me.

"No. From over there, tell me. I don't want you to whisper it. I want you to be proud of your desires."

"I am." She sat back on the window seat and crossed her legs beneath her. "Okay . . ."

"And no clumsy metaphors. The more explicit, the better."

"You got it." Gianna took a deep breath, then began. The words she used, the pictures she painted, were so graphic that my eyes started to water. By the time she had finished her masterpiece of erotica, I was covered in sweat.

"There," she said. "I know it's a tall order, but how about it?"

I cleared my throat so that my voice wouldn't squeak. "Okay."

"Cool." She pounced on me. Her imagination proved to be a skillful scriptwriter, and I the ideal casting choice, at least until she said, "Sometimes I think maybe you are the Devil."

I froze and looked up at her. Her back was pressed against the wall, and her legs wrapped around me as I knelt below her. I saw that she was joking, so I decided to play along.

"What if I were?" I said. "Would you still love me?"

Gianna leaned her head back against the wall and smiled. "I'd still want to fuck you, that's for sure, but that ain't got nothin' to do with love." Her fingers tightened on my shoulder blades, and her breath came a little faster. "But since you're not the Devil, I do love you."

My blood cooled, and I felt myself shrink inside of her. She noticed immediately.

"What's wrong?" she said.

"I don't know." I lifted her off me and turned away to sit on the edge of the bed.

"Was it something I said?"

"No, I don't think—"

"It was something I said, wasn't it?" Her voice went up an octave. "Are you going to have some biological mishap every time I tell you I love you? First you throw up, then you lose your—"

"Gianna, I'm sorry." I went to the window. The sun had obliterated the light of the morning star.

"You can't even look at me, can you?" she said.

"There's nothing I want more than to hear you say you love me. It just takes getting used to." I turned to her. "Let's try again. This time, no theology."

"Okay, sorry. I just thought the whole Devil thing was working for us, like an erotic fantasy."

"Only to a point," I said.

"We'll take it easy on the religious icons from now on. Come back to bed."

Before I joined her again, I shut the blinds against the approaching morning and returned the room to darkness.

15

Repraesentet Eas in Lucem Sanctam

The trouble with going on vacation to escape troubles is that when one's vacation is over, the troubles are still there. The most one can hope for is a new, less troubling perspective on them.

Back at my office the next week, I was examining with reduced enthusiasm Mephistopheles's latest report on his Million Man Massacre, as he had come to call it. I had just finished the section on suburban mall blockades when Beelzebub entered.

"Hey, Lou. How was your vacation?"

"Brilliant, thank you. The canyon is always breathtaking, particularly in the snow. Thanks for keeping an eye on operations while I was gone."

"Not a problem. But your secretary's not as accommodating as she used to be."

"Leave Daphne alone. She's married."

"I know," he said, "but that just makes her more—"

"Paws off, Bub. Last warning."

"Okay, okay."

"How's the new PR director working out?"

"All right, I guess. I think she considers herself some kind of artiste. She wants to redo all our promotional materials. She practically threw up on our logo, said it was puerile, whatever that means."

"Get rid of her and hire one of our other choices. This time, no humans."

"Done." Beelzebub made a note on his pad, then closed it. "Speaking of PR directors, I was thinking of going over to Belial's old place and taking a look around. I wanted to wait until you got back from your trip so you could come with me."

"Belial who?"

"Come on, Lucifer. I thought maybe we might get a clue as to why he . . . you know . . . converted."

"Don't use that word! He has not . . . I don't know what he did, but it's not that."

"I tell you what. You sit here in denial, and meanwhile I'll go try to solve this mystery. That way we'll both be satisfied." He stood and moved towards the door.

"Wait." I reached for my coat.

Like all of our residences, Belial's Georgetown brick row home held no clues that pointed to his true identity. He even displayed several photos of a phony family on his oak mantelpiece. There was a picture of his mother and father posing with a Beefeater guard at the Tower of London, a photo of his twin sister graduating from Harvard, and a yellowing picture that was supposed to depict him as a child with his first puppy, a fluffy white Samoyed. The grinning boy in the photo wore yellow bell bottoms and a *Saturday Night Fever* T-shirt.

"He still had beer in his fridge." Beelzebub handed me a bottle. "Shame to let it go to waste."

I nodded, then set the beer down without opening it.

The orchids in Belial's greenhouse had withered almost to the point of death in the week and a half since his departure. Their fragrant rot made me choke, so I opened a window and offered the flowers a quick demise.

Beelzebub appeared at the doorway. "There's one very hungry python up there."

I followed him upstairs to the study, where a ten-foot brown-and-black snake curled listlessly around its tree limb. A cage on the other side of the room held two dead white rats, the smaller one mostly eaten by the larger.

"What should we do with it?" Beelzebub gestured to the snake.

"Give it some more rats."

"I saw a little dog next door. Maybe I'll—"

"Rats, Bub, rats."

I wandered into Belial's bedroom. His own long black feather hung over the headboard. I sat in a tall rocking chair facing the four-poster bed.

Beelzebub stopped in the doorway. We shared a momentary mournful glance. He crossed to the wardrobe, opened it, and ran his hand over the row of tailored shirts.

"He sure had a lot of cool ties," Beelzebub said.

"I doubt he'd mind if you took some of them."

"No, I'll leave them here, for when he . . . you know . . ." Beelzebub sighed and closed the wardrobe.

"Look." I crossed to Belial's bureau and picked up the only authentic photograph in the house—taken about six years ago at Devil's Den on the Gettysburg battlefield. I was seated on one of the massive boulders, flanked by Mephistopheles and Belial, with Beelzebub at my feet, the four of us creating a kind of diabolical diamond. It was the first time we had visited the site together since the battle itself, which had been a magnificent display of the human capacity for self-sacrifice. Little Round Top loomed in the background of the photo. Mephistopheles was whiter then, and Belial was sporting a tawny goatee that made him look older and wilier than he did the last time I saw him.

"I remember that trip," Beelzebub said beside my shoulder. "We scared the bejesus out of those kids playing on the rocks. Remember, when we made ourselves transparent and pretended we were Civil War ghosts?"

"I remember." I scanned Belial's bedroom for a sign, a clue. "Anything look out of place to you, Bub?"

"Nothing. It's creepy. It's like he died or something."

"I think he did die."

"Lou, don't say that. He'll come back."

I looked down at the photo in my hand, then placed it back on the bureau.

"I'll get him back." I nearly tore the door off its hinges on my way out of Belial's abandoned home.

The state psychiatric hospital was not the dreary prison I had expected. In fact, it was clean and bright, though the brightness served mainly to accentuate the sparseness and sterility of its halls.

The head nurse, a short man with an ironic face, prematurely gray hair, and biceps the size of telephone poles, led me down one of these hallways toward the recreation room.

"Your cousin William has an interesting twist on an old hallucination," the nurse said. "Instead of hearing the voices of demons inside his head, he actually believes he is a demon. Not only that, he also believes that God spoke to him and asked him to renounce his wicked ways. I'm telling you this so you won't be alarmed. He scared quite a few of the other patients at first, but he's so benign in nature that they came to like him right away."

"He's benign?" I said with a touch of disgust.

"Completely. In fact, I wish there were more people as nice as him out there." He pointed to the walls. "But he's very devoted to his delusion. The drugs haven't dispelled his faith yet, but it's only been a little over a week, so we're still hopeful." We reached a door at the end of the hallway, and the nurse slid his identification badge through the security card reader. The light above the door changed from yellow to green, and the lock clicked. The nurse placed his hand on the doorknob and paused a moment. "I just want you to be prepared: your cousin's probably not the man you used to know."

We entered the recreation area. About a dozen patients wandered through the large room. Some watched television, some watched the walls, some watched those watching the television and the walls.

"Where is he?" I said.

"Right over there." The nurse pointed to the far wall. "See him? He's playing chess with a catatonic."

I wouldn't have recognized Belial if he'd been standing a foot in front of me wearing an enormous name tag. Dressed in a fog-gray sweatsuit, white tube socks and tan bedroom slippers, Belial rested his stubbled chin on his knuckles, examining his opponent's face. His usual meticulously styled sandy hair lay in a tousled heap on his head. On the outside, he nearly blended into his barren background.

Except for the radiance. A faint but unmistakable glow emanated from Belial's face. Could the humans could see it or only sense it? I turned to the nurse.

"Don't worry," he said. "No one in this room is dangerous, least of all your cousin. Are you ready?"

"I think so." We crossed the room toward Belial. He turned his head to see me, and his face lit up even more.

"Lucifer!" Belial jumped up so fast, his plastic chair fell backwards and clattered to the floor. The catatonic didn't flinch. "What a surprise! I thought you'd abandoned me, too." He beamed at the nurse. "You won't believe who this is." He pinched my arm. "It's the Prince of Darkness himself, in the flesh."

"Now, Bill, remember what we discussed," the nurse said. "When you start talking like that, it scares the other residents, and I know you don't want to do that."

Belial cast an anxious glance over his fellow patients. "Sorry. I don't want to rattle any of my new friends, but seeing my evil ex-taskmaster stroll into this abode of absolution was quite a shock, as you might imagine."

"Would it be possible for us to speak in private?" I asked the nurse.

He indicated a nearby doorway. "I was just about to show you to the visitation room. Follow me." The three of us walked toward the door.

"Visitation room." Belial squinted and scratched his face. "That makes you my first visitator. Visitator. Vis-i-ta-tor." He rolled the syllables over his tongue. "The word makes sense. It sounds like a potato that can see, and potatoes do have eyes."

The nurse opened the door and ushered us in. The visitation room was divided into a lounge area with a large window on one wall and an observation room on the other side of the window.

"I'll be out here," the nurse said. "I can see you through the window, but I won't be able to hear you. This is as private as it gets around here, I'm afraid."

"That's all right," I said. Belial and I entered the other room and sat facing each other on chairs that were even less comfortable than they appeared. Belial folded his hands in his lap and stared at the floor to my right.

"You're here to kill me, aren't you?" he said.

"What are you talking about? You know I can't—"

"I've betrayed you. I've renounced you. What else can you do but destroy me?"

"Belial, listen—"

"I don't mind if you destroy me." He lifted his eyes to meet mine. "Either way I'm going back to Heaven."

"What?!" I glanced at the nurse through the window, then shifted to a chair next to Belial, my back to the observation room. "What do you mean, going back to Heaven? You can't go back."

"Says who?"

"Says . . . you know who."

"Apparently He's changed His mind."

"He doesn't change his mind, ever."

"Not true," Belial said. "You're forgetting Abraham in the land of Moriah when he was prepared to sacrifice Isaac. You're forgetting when Moses convinced Him to let the rest of the Israelites escape before the ground swallowed up Korah, Dathan, and—"

"Those are humans, Belial. Humans can get grace. We can't."

"Maybe you can't. But I just did."

"You're insane."

Belial blinked, then roared with laughter.

"What's so funny?"

"You think I'm insane, and they think I'm insane," he jerked his thumb in the nurse's direction, "but for opposite reasons. That is pure comedy." His laughter faded into a bright smile. "I saved someone's life, you know."

"Yes. So I heard."

"Aren't you the least bit curious about the experience?"

"'Curious' doesn't exactly—"

"I'll tell you what it was like," he said. "For a few moments, as I was putting out the fire on that man's head, I forgot I existed. Have you ever felt that way, so deep inside another person's soul that your own presence just evaporates?"

I thought about the episodes of almost unbearable intimacy I shared with Gianna, the moments when her breath was the only rhythm I heard or felt.

"Once I realized what I'd done," he said, "the feeling was indescribable. Saving a life . . . the rush . . . it was even better than the kill thrill." His eyes gleamed. "I can't wait to do it again."

"How long do you plan to continue this charade?"

"Until I'm called upon to do something else. Right now I need to rest during this time of transition."

"Transition to what?"

Belial began to answer me, then furrowed his brow and stared at the corner of the ceiling for a few moments. Finally he shook his head. "You wouldn't understand."

"Try me," I said.

He tapped his forefinger against his lips while he thought, then turned to me. "He spoke to me, Lucifer. God spoke to me."

I sat back in my chair, reeling as if he'd slapped me.

"I'm sorry," he said. "I won't say His name in front of you again. I just wanted you to see that I could utter it without heavenly retribution, that I'm free of that commandment now."

"But how—"

"I don't know. I spend most of my time here wondering why, why He chose me out of all of us." Belial grinned. "At first I thought maybe He needed a good public relations director, what with these fundamentalists running around offending everybody. But eventually I stopped wondering why, and just accepted it for the undeserved gift that it was."

"What gift?" I said. "I don't understand."

"Of course you don't. It's not yours to understand."

"Belial, he didn't speak to you. Even if he did, it was a lie. He's manipulating you, can't you see that?"

"I'm the master of mendacity. Don't you think I'd know a lie if I heard one?"

"Not if it sounded like what you always wanted to hear."

"What *I* always wanted to hear?" Belial leaned forward with a patronizing smile. "Let me get this straight. You're telling me that all this time *I've* thirsted for redemption, that *I've* longed to hear our Father speak to me with tender words of forgiveness, that *I've* dreamed of returning to Heaven and falling into His waiting arms . . ." He gestured at his surroundings. "In this institution, we call that 'projection.'"

"What are you talking about?"

"None of us missed Heaven much, missed His holy presence. We had you, after all—our own smaller but infinitely more entertaining deity. And you pretend you don't miss it either, that you don't care, but we can all see it."

"Don't you dare—"

"Not to worry, Lucifer, we wouldn't dream of dishonoring you by discussing it among ourselves. But we see your torment, your grief, your regret."

"I have no regrets."

He touched my knee softly. "I'm sorry, I truly am. I'm sorry you'll never share my experience."

I brushed away his hand. "I don't want your pity, Belial. I want your loyalty."

"You can't have it anymore. I renounced you, remember?"

"Then unrenounce me!" I gripped the arms of the chair. "Please . . ."

"Don't beg, Lucifer. It's unbecoming behavior for a prince such as yourself."

My left hand wanted to fly to his throat to smother his smug words. Instead, I collected the muscles of my face until they formed a stony facade. Then I stood and looked through him as I spoke:

"I came here to help you. It seems I am too late. Goodbye."

16

Et ab Hoedis Me Sequestra

"That is some fucked-up crazy shit, Lucifer."

"No kidding."

Mephistopheles rolled down the window on the passenger side of my Mercedes. "Mind if I smoke?"

"I sure as hell do. Stink up your own leather seats, Mr. My-DeVille's-in-the-Shop-Again. What is it with you and American cars? Can't you put ethnic trim on a BMW?"

"Not the same." He rolled the window back up. "So should we assume that Belial's never coming back?"

"These days, I never use the word 'never.'"

"Right. Hey, did you get a chance to look at my report?"

"Actually, I did, and I was thinking maybe you should . . . you know . . ."

"What?"

I scratched my head and tried to figure out how to suggest postponing the Million Man Massacre without looking suspicious. I came up empty.

"I think you should tell your people not to be taken alive," I said. "If they're caught, they should shoot themselves rather than be arrested."

"Yeah, that's brilliant." Mephistopheles pulled a small notepad out of his jacket. "I'll say that they're better off dead than being held captive by the Man again. 'Death before slavery'—that could be our motto."

"Also, I think you should martyr yourself. Try to fake your own assassination around the time the Massacre starts to break down." These thoughts came so easily.

"That's perfect!" He scribbled faster. "I'll inspire them from beyond the grave, inspire them to keep fighting, keep killing."

"You'll be a hero, Mephistopheles, an icon."

"An icon." He pulled down the passenger's-side visor and examined his image in the mirror. The bright red taillights from the car in front of us cast a crimson glow over Mephistopheles's smooth skin. "This face'll be on a trading card someday."

"Maybe even a coin," I said.

"You think?"

"I know some people in the Treasury Department." I pulled into Gianna's parking lot. "We'll discuss it more later. Remember what I said about tonight."

"Right. Pretend I'm Christmas shopping. Buy stuff for myself and mumble about how much my Uncle Sammy is going to love it." He stepped out of the car and lit a cigarette.

I walked into Gianna's building to meet her and nearly collided with her inside the front door.

"Hey!" she said.

"Hey, yourself." I pulled a red-and-white rose from inside my jacket. "Getting tired of these yet?"

"Never." She kissed me. "Thanks so much for taking me shopping. Christmas is one time it sucks not to have a car."

"My pleasure. Perhaps you can clue me in as to what it's all about. The shopping, I mean, not Christmas." I followed her out the door. "I invited Bob and Malcolm along, too."

"Cool. Where's Bill?"

"On vacation. One of those spa getaways, I believe, where they pamper your cares away."

"Sounds great," she said. "Hey, Malc."

"Hey," Mephistopheles purred as he opened the car door for her.

Next we picked up Beelzebub.

"Hi, honey." He kissed her on the cheek. She laughed.

"Watch it, mister," she said. "Remember I'm a castrating bitch."

"My favorite kind."

"Where should we go?" I said.

Gianna looked at her Christmas list. "How about Lafayette Mall?"

"NO!!" Beelzebub grabbed the back of my seat. "I mean, no, I've been there, and they don't have what I'm looking for. Can we go somewhere else?"

"Yeah, I hear they overcook their cheese steaks, too," Mephistopheles said. Beelzebub punched him in the arm, beginning a backseat wrestling match that I could tell was about to mutate into something less combative.

"I hate malls," I said. "Why don't we just go down to Dupont Circle?"

"Ugh, you're the one who has to park the car, so okay." Gianna leaned closer to me. "Should we find dates for them?"

I glanced in my rearview mirror to see one of Mephistopheles's hands on Beelzebub's knee. I couldn't see where his other hand was.

"No, not tonight," I said.

Gianna glanced into the back of the car. "Oh!" She sat back

in her seat. "Never mind, then." A minute later, she said, "That reminds me. I'm having dinner with my brother Marc next Sunday. Would you like to come?"

"What reminds you?" I said.

"Huh?"

"What reminded you of him?"

"Um, nothing. Never mind. So would you like to join us?"

"Sure," I said. "Hang on." I accelerated towards the oncoming stoplight, then slammed on my brakes. The occupants of the backseat crashed forward.

"Ow!" Beelzebub rubbed his forehead. "What was that for?"

"Just letting you know we're almost there, so you can get dressed," I said.

"Bite me. I am dressed."

"If you guys were back here, you'd be doing the same thing," Mephistopheles said.

I glared at him in the rearview mirror. "There's such a thing as propriety."

"Propriety, right." Beelzebub's head appeared between us. "So, Gianna, tell me, when you blew him in the wine cellar at the Shack, was your pinky extended?"

"That would be a waste of a damn useful pinky," she replied.

"I adore this woman," Beelzebub said to me. "Are you sure you don't want to share me with her?"

"You mean share her with you?"

"Whatever." He turned to Gianna. "Pronouns are such a bitch."

I parked the car, and we began to window-shop. While Gianna and Mephistopheles were drooling over boots, Beelzebub sidled up to me.

"I think she likes me."

"I think you amuse her."

"I've got a great idea," he said. "Tell her I'm not really your brother."

"Why?"

"'Cuz then maybe the three of us could, you know . . ."

"No!" The other two turned their heads to look at us, then went inside the shoe store. I lowered my voice. "Are you out of your fucking skull?"

"What's the big deal? I think she'd like it. I know I'd like it."

"I don't care what you'd like," I said. "It's not worth freaking her out and admitting that I lied to her. Besides, it doesn't interest me in the least."

"Oh, right."

"It doesn't."

"Whatever you say." Beelzebub moved a few feet away and studied a Salvador Dali-esque wall clock through the store window. "You're doomed, you know."

"Doomed?"

"Yeah, now that I've mentioned it, you won't be able to get the thought out of your head. You'll probably dream about it tonight." He tapped the window. "I'm going to buy that clock."

I watched him disappear into the store.

"Bastard."

While Beelzebub and Mephistopheles carried the hideous clock back to my car, Gianna and I continued to shop. Half in jest, she bought me a glass snow globe with a Christmas tree inside it, to "inject some cheer" into my apparently dismal office. On M Street, we paused outside a funky jewelry store.

"I didn't realize Bob and Malcolm were . . . you know . . ."

"They're not," I said.

"Not what?"

"A couple. They just like a change of pace once in a while."

"Don't we all?"

"What?"

"Wow, look at that." Gianna stepped away from me and pressed her nose against the glass.

"Which one?"

"That one, in the back row there. All the way to the left." She pointed to a small silver cross on a chain. Behind the intersection of the cross, two thin pieces of silver entwined to form a circle.

"What's so special about that one?" I said.

"I don't know, it just grabs me. I'm not usually one for wearing crosses or crucifixes. I find it kind of macabre, especially considering how I feel about capital punishment." She held her hand up against the cold window. "But that one is simple. It's hopeful. I love it." I placed my hand over hers and felt her vibrate with excitement.

"Hey, you guys wanna grab a drink or two or six?" Mephistopheles said behind us.

We went to the Wisteria, a gothic vegetarian bar and restaurant, the kind of place where you can get something pierced for free with your fifth drink, which tended to involve an obscure liquor pureed with a fruit or vegetable.

Gianna finished her first schnapps and celery juice. "I should have known I'd get no shopping done with this crew."

"Hard to believe I'd want to put a damper on the Christmas spirit, eh?" I said.

"Speaking of which," Gianna glanced over her shoulder at Mephistopheles and Beelzebub, who were using bar garnishes to make the vegetables on their plate look like terrified animals, "and if you say no, I'll never bring it up again, but would you consider maybe coming home with me for Christmas, you know, to meet my family?"

I blinked hard, then examined my wheat-grass whiskey sour. "What do they put in these drinks?"

"We'll just stay the two nights," she said, "and leave the day after Christmas."

"Then I'm not hallucinating. You're actually inviting me to spend Christmas with you and your family."

"I know it sounds strange, but—"

"You have no idea." I shook my head and began to chuckle. "You cannot begin to comprehend what a ludicrous proposition that is." My laughter became more uncontrollable, and finally I had to rest my forehead on the cushy vinyl edge of the bar until the giggles subsided.

"You're right. It was a stupid idea," Gianna said. "Forget I mentioned it."

"No, no." I lifted my head and leered at her. "You know what? It's too absurd not to try. I'll do it."

"You will?"

"You may regret it," I said. "In fact, I'm sure you'll regret it." I waved over the androgynous bartender. "Another round here. Bring us something seasonal."

Gianna wrapped her arms around my neck and kissed me. "I promise you it will be a unique experience."

"Considering I've never celebrated Christmas, and my entire family consists of that bizarre child over there making cocktail-onion goats, I'm quite certain you're right."

"Um, Bob's not coming with us, okay? Just you."

"Of course," I said. "In fact, I think I'll wait to tell him my plans until he's calmed down a bit."

Gianna turned to look at my friends just as Mephistopheles's roasted eggplant T. rex swatted Beelzebub's goat with its parsley tail. A feeble shriek came from Beelzebub's hand as he lobbed the miniature goat behind the bar, where it rolled under a keg of barley beer.

"Does he ever calm down?" she said.

The bartender arrived with two glasses of what tasted like a cranberry-nutmeg Manhattan. As he or she retreated, I noticed the little goat stagger out from under the keg before it disintegrated in a tiny flame.

17

Redemisti Crucem Passus

The following Sunday, while Gianna attended mass, I roamed the rainy streets of Georgetown and Dupont Circle to collect her Christmas gifts.

At one boutique, I laid a few thousand dollars' worth of dresses on the counter. A short, middle-aged red-haired woman behind me in line whistled in admiration.

"Is that all for one person?" she asked me.

"Yes, for my girlfriend."

"Wow, I'd love to see what she's getting you."

"What do you mean?"

"I mean, I'm sure she's getting you lots of nice stuff."

"I doubt it," I said. "She doesn't have the kind of money I do."

"Oh." The woman shifted her packages to her other arm and straightened her glasses. "Is this your first Christmas together?"

"Yes, why?"

"Then you should be careful not to overgift."

"Overgift?"

"Sir, will that be cash or charge?" said the cashier.

"Hang on." I turned back to the nosy woman. "What does 'overgift' mean?"

"If you get her disproportionately expensive gifts, then she might be embarrassed."

"Sir, cash or charge?"

"I said, hang on." I silenced the cashier with a snarl. "Let me get this straight: if I shower her with beautiful, expensive gifts, she'll actually be unhappy?"

"She might," said the next woman in line, a svelte young blonde. "But I wouldn't mind, personally."

"I'm sure she'll love all these dresses." The cashier no doubt sensed an impending loss of commission.

"I never thought it would be so complicated." I turned to the woman behind me. "What would you recommend?"

"If I were you, and I wish I were," she said, "I'd get one of these dresses, and then maybe something romantic, like a piece of jewelry. Something sentimental."

"Yeah, jewelry," the blonde murmured.

"We have jewelry here!" The cashier's voice went up an octave as she pointed to the case at the end of the counter.

"Never mind." From the pile on the counter I pulled one of the dresses, a strapless blue velvet gown with a matching jacket. "I'll just take this."

The cashier glared at the woman behind me, so I said, "Put her stuff on my bill, too."

"Wow, thanks," said the short woman. "You really are full of the Christmas spirit, aren't you?"

"Don't push it."

I stared past my reflection in the jewelry store window at the tiny silver cross and wondered what the hell I was thinking, spending Christmas with a bunch of Catholics. I pondered the fine line between healthy curiosity and blind stupidity.

"Admiring your handiwork?"

I turned to see Beelzebub standing behind me. He twirled his black umbrella once before closing it with a flourish.

"You mean our handiwork." I studied the cross again. "Getting him crucified was our greatest triumph—and our greatest mistake. Look what we started." I gestured to the green garland entwined with red lights framing the store window. "A religious industry."

"I keep telling you we should start spending December in Beijing or something. You get so gloomy this time of year, surrounded by all the 'Happy Birthday Jesus' crap."

"What kills me about this holiday—and Easter even more so," I said, "is that it reminds me that no matter what I do, no matter what atrocity I commit, it turns out to be part of his plan. It's like I'm not really free at all. No one is."

"You're free, Lou. We're all free. He's just one step ahead of us—if not more. After all, he's . . . who he is, and we're not. Not even you, dude."

"Maybe if I weren't so powerful," I said, "I wouldn't miss all the power I don't have."

"Sucks to be second best, doesn't it?" He held out his palm from under the awning. "Hey, it's stopped raining. Wanna go down to the Vietnam Vets Memorial and make helicopter noises?"

"Not really."

"Okay, then how 'bout lunch?"

Beelzebub ate all of his french fries in descending order of size before reaching for his hamburger. As I ate my Greek salad, I watched him pop off the bun lid, grab the ketchup squirter, and go to work. His tawny eyebrows knitted together, and he chewed his lower lip as he meticulously drew a face on the burger's surface. When he was finished, he spun his plate to show me Edvard Munch's "The Scream" crudely rendered in ketchup. His teeth flashed in a brilliant smile.

"That's very nice," I said. "I'll stick it on the fridge for the whole family to see, right next to your report card."

He giggled a little, then smashed the top of the bun down on the patty with a strangled noise. His head bobbed back and forth to a silent tune as he bit into the burger.

Beelzebub's delight in life's simple pleasures gave him an air of innocence that was perhaps his greatest weapon. He abused this power, the way a cuter-than-average toddler learns to manipulate with a smile or a pout.

The boyish charm could also disintegrate into demonic fury faster than you could say—

"What the fuck?!"

"What's wrong?" I said.

"I asked for medium well." He flung the burger onto his plate. "This is oozing blood. I could get salmonella!"

"E. coli, you mean. And you can't get it, no more than any other disease."

"Those dickheads in the kitchen don't know that. And it wasn't what I ordered."

"Calm down," I said. "Just send it back."

"I already drew on it!"

"So have them cook you another one."

"I want this one!" He slumped in the booth and folded his arms across his chest. "Can you fix it for me?"

"Fix it yourself."

"My aim's not so good. I might set the table on fire."

I set my fork on the table with a clang. "Fine." I stared at the burger.

"Should I get out of the way?"

"Shh." In a moment the burger sizzled and steamed. Beelzebub picked it up.

"Perfect. Thanks."

"I didn't cultivate this power so I could perform parlor tricks," I said.

Beelzebub resumed his head bob while he chewed. "My brother is so coo-ool, my brother is so coo-ool," he sang. "So when do you want to take off for Vegas?"

"Ah," I sipped my iced tea, "I've been meaning to talk to you about that. You see—"

"I was hoping we could stay at that circus casino this year, have some fun with the sideshow geeks, maybe get the elephants to stampede over the clowns—"

"I'm not going to Vegas with you."

His milk shake halted on the way to his mouth.

"How come?" he said.

"I'm going home with Gianna." He gaped at me, expressionless. "To her parents' house," I said. "For Christmas."

Beelzebub blinked twice, then shrieked with laughter. Several nearby diners turned to watch him pound the table and point at me.

"You almost had me there for a second, Lou. Man, I feel stupid. I believed you. You're good, really good." He looked at me and burst into a fresh spate of cackles. "The look on your face, even now, dead straight. I'm tellin' ya, it's priceless." He wiped his eyes and shook his head. "You kill me, man."

"I'm not joking," I said.

He laughed again, but not as hard as before. "You are, too. Knock it off now."

"I'm serious. I know it sounds ridiculous, but it's true."

His wide blue eyes studied my face. "Shit. You're not kidding, are you?"

"No."

"You're spending Christmas with your girlfriend and her family." I nodded. "Let me rephrase that," he said. "You're *celebrating* Christmas with your girlfriend and her family."

"I won't be celebrating it, but I'll be there."

"Why?"

"Call it an experiment, an infiltration, if you will. I want to experience this phenomenon firsthand, try to figure out what makes it so appealing to these humans."

"The more you know about it, the more you can hurt it."

"Exactly."

He pressed his finger down on the tines of his fork and rocked it on the table like a seesaw. "It's an interesting idea, Lou, but I still don't like it. You could get sick."

"I'll try to stay out of churches."

"How will you explain that to her family?"

"I haven't figured that out yet."

Beelzebub poked the remnants of his burger and scowled.

"What's wrong?" I said.

"What happens if . . . what happens if you like it?"

"Like what?"

"You know . . . Christmas."

"Why would I?"

"I don't know," he said. "You see all those TV shows where people get changed by the Christmas spirit, whatever the fuck that is."

"Mmm, yes. I can see the *TV Guide* synopsis now:

'Curmudgeonly old Devil, trapped by a blizzard with a puppy and an orphan, discovers the true meaning of Christmas.'"

He grinned. "It could happen."

"I'll be careful." I watched him turn his attention back to his appetite. "Bub, you and I haven't hung out, just the two of us, in quite a while. What do you say we—"

"Yeah! When? Tonight?"

"No."

"Tomorrow night?"

"How about Tuesday?" I said.

"Tuesday's great. Tuesday's great. Cool. Tuesday, then."

I glanced at my watch. "I have to go meet Gianna now. I'll see you at my office tomorrow morning."

Beelzebub peered at my sides as I stood.

"What are you looking at?" I said.

"I can't wait to see your scars."

"What scars?"

"From the spurs. Or does she use electrodes to keep you in line?"

My stare penetrated his eyes like ice picks.

"Sorry." He wiped his mouth. "Um, thanks for fixing my burger for me. It's really good."

I continued to glare at him.

"Hey, lunch is on me, okay?" he said.

I left without another word for my brother.

18

Inter Oves Locum Praesta

The setting sun bounced pink off the downtown Baltimore office buildings. Soon the same buildings formed walls of glass and steel around us as we drove eastward through the city streets. Thanks to its sizable Jewish population, Charm City's Christmas garnishes were more subdued than most. Here was a town where my retinas could rest.

I eased the Jaguar into a tight space on a Fells Point side street near Halloran's Crab House. Before we turned the corner, Gianna looked back at the car.

"Aren't you afraid to leave something that valuable on the street like that?" she asked.

"It's got a good security system."

The line to Halloran's stretched onto the sidewalk. A few minutes later, just before we crammed ourselves inside the door, a man hurtled down the street shrieking and clutching his charred, withered hand.

"What the hell was that?" Gianna said.

I shrugged. "He must have tried to steal the Jag." She laughed, confirming my suspicion that sometimes the best way to lie is to tell the truth.

Inside the restaurant, the savory stench of dead crabs and Old Bay seasoning swam into my nostrils, and my mouth watered at the thought of ripping open their defiant little bodies and scooping out handfuls of sweet, slippery flesh. Unfortunately, health department regulations required the crabs to be thoroughly cooked; when it came to eating animals, even the sharp ones, I preferred them raw and kicking.

"Jesus God, I'm famished." Gianna rubbed her belly and winced. "If Marc and Rick don't show up on time, let's start without them." She took my hand. "Are you nervous, meeting family for the first time?"

"No. Should I be?"

"Marc's cool. You'll like him. That's why I wanted you to meet him first, so you'd have another ally during Christmas."

"Why would I need an—?"

"There he is." She waved through the glass door at a dark-haired man in an Orioles cap sauntering across the street. "I guess Rick's meeting us here." She bit her lip. "He'd better be."

Marc fought a gust of wind to swing open the door. Gianna left our place in line and hugged him at the threshold. When they turned to join me, their physical similarity almost knocked me over. Her brother was taller, with shorter hair, but he had the same quick brown eyes and sharp cheekbones.

"Marcus, this is Louis Carvalho. Lou, Marc." We shook hands, and I mumbled a nondescript greeting, but couldn't keep my eyes from floating between their faces.

"You're that one guy who applauded for us that night at the Grotto," Marc said. "I've been wanting to thank you."

"I assure you, my applause was sincere. You're very talented."

"Notice he's only looking at you when he says that," Gianna said to Marc. "So I guess Rick's meeting us here?"

"Nope," Marc said.

"Why not?"

"We had a bit of an argument."

"Again?"

"And I told him to go fuck himself. Instead, he went and fucked somebody else."

"Oh, Marc, I'm sorry," Gianna said.

"It's one thing to be literal-minded, but to be inaccurately literal-minded is more than I can tolerate." Marc put his arm around Gianna's shoulders. "Don't worry, sis, this way you can be the only one bringing a new boyfriend home for Christmas."

"Were you that serious?" Gianna asked him.

"Maybe. He was good meet-the-folks material. Decent job. Clean-cut. Hardly any tattoos. He was even a practicing Catholic, if you can believe that."

"Shit. Hey, there's this guy in my office you might—"

"Don't even think about it, Gianna." Marc removed his baseball cap and twirled it on his finger. "Dating's getting to be too exhausting, anyway. I think I'll go back to hanging around bus stations and playgrounds."

"O'Keefe, party of four?" the hostess hollered.

We sat down at a table by the window. It was pockmarked with mallet blows that had missed their crustaceous targets. I sat across from Gianna, who sat next to her brother. "It's striking how much you two look alike," I said.

"Thanks for not mentioning that he looks younger than I do," Gianna said. She turned to Marc. "You should see Lou's brother Bob. They look nothing alike."

"How unfortunate for Bob." Marcus popped his eyebrows up at me. I accepted the compliment with a smile.

A waitress with enormous hair arrived at our table and took our order, then I asked Marc about the nature of his work.

"I work with the local domestic violence agency," he said. "Mainly I counsel batterers. I try to teach them how to handle their rage."

"Does it work?"

"Hardly ever," Marc said. "The recovery rate for abusers is pretty low. Even if they manage to stop hitting, they usually continue the emotional abuse." Our pitcher of beer arrived, and Marc poured us each a mug. "In my professional opinion, society'd be better off locking up these bastards like vicious dogs before they kill someone."

"Sounds like a depressing job," I said.

"Not always. It's worth it for the few that turn themselves around. Most batterers watched their own dads beat their moms, so when someone breaks the cycle, I feel like I've saved more than one life, like when their kids grow up, they'll be different." A sardonic grin crossed his face. "Almost makes up for turning on the news to see one of my clients arrested for bludgeoning his girlfriend with a golf club."

"It's not your fault, you know that." Gianna laid her hand on his forearm.

"If I can't blame myself for the failures," Marc said, "how can I take credit for the successes?"

"You could humble yourself a little and just decide that it's God working through you to help these people."

"So you think God works through me to let these guys kill the women who love them?"

"No, of course not—"

"Then who, Gianna?"

She glanced at me. "I think Louis and I had a version of this conversation at the Grand Canyon."

"And how did you resolve it?"

"By having sex," I said.

Marc laughed. "See, that's why Thomas Aquinas and the rest of those monks came to so many conclusions. You'll never get any treatises written as long as she's around."

"Who is the wiser," she said, "the philosopher, or the philosopher's whore?"

"And which one of us is which?" I said.

"You know," Gianna said to me, "sometimes you're sweeter than a big puddle of antifreeze." She stood up. "I've got to pee before the crabs come. Be right back."

I watched her retreat, then turned to Marcus. "So you're my practice run, before the big event."

"You'll do fine," he said. "Our family shouldn't inspire fear. Shock and alarm, maybe, but not fear."

"I think I can handle that."

"Sorry I was so obnoxious when we first met. I did it on purpose to make sure you could deal with me."

"Did I pass the test?"

"A-plus," he said. "You didn't even flinch when I flirted with you."

"Very little makes me flinch."

"Anyway, it's important to Gianna that I like the men she dates. Especially after her last boyfriend."

"You mean Adam?"

"Adam, the nine-year virus. We used to be good buddies until Gianna told him I was gay. After that, he never looked me in the eye again. My very expensive and time-consuming psychology degree told me that it was his issue, not mine, but I decided to hate him anyway. I tormented the poor bastard almost to seizures—a skill acquired from being the oldest of four children."

"He's been calling her at home," I said.

"Sigh through the nose?"

"Exactly."

Marc peeked over his shoulder towards the ladies room, then turned back to me. "Gianna would kill me if she knew I told you, but please watch out for this guy. She thinks I'm overreacting, but the situation is more serious than she realizes. Did you know he's been sending her flowers?"

"No, I didn't know that."

"Flowers, cards, little gifts. At least he was as of a month or so ago. He may have stopped, or maybe she just stopped telling me so I wouldn't worry."

"She never mentioned it to me."

"She makes out like it's no big deal, but this is turning into a textbook stalking case. As far as I know, he hasn't been threatening, just pathetic, but that can change."

"Here she comes."

"I just wanted you to be aware."

"Thanks."

Gianna reached the table along with the waitress, who set a large tray of steamed crabs in front of us. We dug in, and I imagined Adam's head under my mallet, cracking with the same gratifying brittleness of the dead crab's shell.

19

Sanctus Michael

"Morning."

"Hey. Sorry I'm late." Beelzebub set a bag of bagels and two cups of coffee on my office's conference table. "I go to the coffee shop, and they don't have any french roast. 'That's not one of our specials today,' the girl says. So I tweaked a few of her brain cells to change her mind. It wasn't easy, since there wasn't a lot to work with, if you know what I mean."

"So while you were in her head, did you—"

"Yeah, we're goin' out tonight. Her name's Betty or Betsy or something like that, I forget. No, wait. Ruth." He handed me my coffee and bagel.

"Ah yes, Ruth. The one with the nose ring, right?"

"Right." He picked up the snow globe and eyed it like a museum artifact. "Something tells me that's not all she has pierced." He shook the globe, shrugged, and placed it back on my desk. I moved it away from the edge.

"So what have you got for me this week?"

"Good news, bro." Beelzebub opened his briefcase and pulled out a red presentation folder. "Third quarter financial statement. Read it and weep with joy."

I perused the document. If these numbers were real, Beelzebub was still a financial wizard. For all his excesses in his personal life, on the job he was as parsimonious as Ebenezer Scrooge. I couldn't have asked for a better CFO.

"Nice work," I said.

"Thanks." He shifted in his chair. "But with profit margins like this, it's getting harder to explain why we won't sell shares."

"We are not going public," I said. "I won't kowtow to a bunch of whiny stockholders. Before we know it, we'll have a board of directors who'll want us to write a mission statement and adopt Total Quality Management."

"It means we're getting noticed, though." He took a sip of coffee and cleared his throat. "Maybe it's time we move on."

"Leave Washington? And go where?"

"I was thinkin' Tahiti. We could take a little vacation, thirty or forty years, me and you and Mephistopheles. All we'd need is a mobile phone and a laptop with a modem, and we could still control all our minions around the world." He leaned forward. "Think about it, Lou—sippin' piña coladas with our toes in the sand, surrounded by a smorgasbord of scrumptious humans."

"Sounds great."

"Yeah?"

"Yeah. Send me a postcard."

"But, Lou—"

"Things are too good here right now. We're gaining so much power and influence, and we're doing it slowly, inconspicuously."

"Oh, yeah?" Beelzebub pulled a scrap of paper from his shirt pocket. "Daphne asked me to give you this phone mes-

sage." I reached for it, but he pulled it away and read from it.
"It's from *Washingtonian* magazine, calling about their 'Most
Eligible Bachelor' issue."

"Ah, yes."

"They want to know when you're available for a photo
shoot for their COVER!"

"It's good publicity for the firm."

"This is not being inconspicuous!"

"You're just mad because they didn't ask you." I pulled the
message out of his hand. "I've decided not to do it, anyway."

"Please say it's not because you're no longer eligible."

"What else do you have for me today?" I said.

Beelzebub sighed. "Invoices. Need your signature."

He handed me a small stack of papers. I only needed to
sign off on the projects for which the others wanted no
responsibility.

"Are we turning into farmers now?" I held up an invoice
from a tractor supply company. "What do we need with three
tons of fertilizer?"

"Duh, dude."

"Oh, right, the . . . thing. Of course." My pen lingered
above the invoice for a few moments. "Hand me a napkin,
would you?"

"Sure."

While his back was turned, I placed the unsigned invoice
back in the stack of bills, which I then handed to him.
"Speaking of combustibles, how are things in Hell?"

"It's swingin'. Mammon just built a new sauna in the west
wing of Pandemonium. Lou, you really should visit once in a
while. The demons miss you. A lot of the new associates have
never even met you."

"I like it here."

"Especially now, right?"

"What's that supposed to mean?"

Beelzebub didn't reply, but pulled an accordion folder from his briefcase. "We need to talk famines. Now luckily we're going to get some help from El Niño this year, but Mother Nature always leaves lots of room for improvement. So I'm planning to ship a boatload of locusts to both Australia and South America to destroy the few crops that actually grow there this year."

"But—"

"I know what you're thinking: international aid to the rescue, right? But I've thought of that, too. I had Mephistopheles create a computer virus to infect the food banks' inventory systems. By the time they get them up and running again, all the food and money will be diverted either to us or Saddam Hussein."

I put my bagel down. "You know . . . I think maybe we should wait to move on this." I flipped a page on my legal pad. "Let's table this discussion for our next meeting, shall we? What's next on the agenda?"

"Lou, we can't table the famine item. Sure, we have some time on the Northern Hemisphere famines, but it's already early summer in these places." He held up the files. "We've got to get our agents in place soon, or—"

"I said no, Bub." I grabbed the folders from his hand. "No new famines."

"What's the matter with you? Are you suddenly having a pang of conscience?"

"Don't use that word around me." I placed the folders in my desk drawer. "I have my reasons."

"Yeah, you have one reason. A reason with a pretty little face and legs up to her eyeballs."

I slammed the drawer shut. "Don't bring Gianna into this. This has nothing to do with her."

"Oh, really? Ever since you started 'dating' her, or whatever you call it, I hardly even recognize you."

"Why? I haven't changed."

"You haven't changed?!" He sprang to his feet and grabbed the snow globe. "What is this cheerful little piece of shit?"

"It was a gift." I snatched the globe out of his hand and held onto it. "So what? I'm still the Devil. Now I'm just the Devil with a snow globe."

"Lucifer—"

"I thought this was a business meeting."

"Lucifer, you're going to her mom's house for Christmas!"

I stood and loomed over him. "I told you that was an experiment. Why do you question me?"

"Why do I question you? Because that's the way you raised us, to doubt all authority, even you. To keep us strong, you said, there could be no blind faith, no mindless obedience like those idiots in Heaven." He pointed at me. "You know who you're starting to remind me of?"

"Don't say it!"

We stared at each other for a long, tense moment, then Beelzebub smiled and looked away.

"No, I take it back," he said. "You're a much better dresser." He gathered up his papers and replaced them in his briefcase. "I'd better go now, if we're finished here. Look, it's okay about the famines. There's always next year, and anyway, El Niño . . . whatever."

"Thanks for the financial report. You've done well. Looks nice, too."

"Yeah, we got a new color printer in our office. Too bad the reports will have to be vaporized." He put on his coat. "We're still on for tomorrow night, right?"

"Of course," I said.

"I was thinking . . . instead of going out, why don't we just hang out at your place? I'll bring a pizza, we'll sit around and get drunk . . . you know, the usual."

I caught a faint whiff of innuendo. "The usual."

"Right."

I turned my attention back to the papers in front of me. "Right. See you at seven, then?"

"Great." When he was at the door, he turned and said, "I'll also bring the entertainment."

After he was gone, I tried to compose a letter to the chairman of the Senate Judiciary Committee. Federal judicial appointments had been dragging lately due to political temper tantrums, and there were several judges I needed to have in place by early spring. Beelzebub's hostility towards Gianna troubled me, though, and I needed to find a way to defuse it. To clear my head for deep thought, I played with my executive toy.

My office door opened. Mesmerized by the swinging skulls, I didn't look up, assuming it was Beelzebub. Daphne would have escorted anyone else.

"Forget something?" I said.

There was no reply. I looked up to see a man with translucent skin and iridescent hair towering over the center of my carpet.

"You . . ."

He curled a thin lip at me and seemed to grow a few inches taller. I flailed for my precious sarcasm.

"You," I said with a snarl, "do not have an appointment."

"I was just passing through and thought I'd—"

"You're never just passing through, Michael. What do you want?"

The intercom buzzed, and Daphne's voice squawked, "Mr. Lucifer, the Archangel Michael is here to see you."

I glanced at the speaker, then back at my guest. "Yes. Thank you, Daphne."

"Should I bring in coffee?" she said.

"Is it fresh?"

"I just made a new pot."

"Then never mind," I said. Michael rolled his eyes. The intercom clicked off. "It's the little extras that make a gracious host."

"And it's the little insults that wither what's left of your soul."

"Uh-huh. What do you want from me?"

"You mean, what can I command of you that you can laugh at and do the opposite of?"

"Am I that predictable?" I said. "Okay, this time I'll wait until you leave to laugh. I promise. Please, have a seat." I wanted to grill him about Belial's alleged conversion, but decided to wait until he broached the subject.

Michael moved as one who is not accustomed to gravity's pull. He examined the seat of the chair before sitting in it, then picked several pieces of invisible lint off his immaculate platinum-colored suit. I rapped the end of my pen against my desk blotter.

"Look, Mikey, I'm not getting any younger here. Shouldn't you be out bringing good tidings of great joy or whatever it is you do this time of year? I know I'm a very busy little angel myself."

"That's not what I hear, Satan."

I stood and tried to shatter his crystal gray eyes with my stare. "When you are in my office, you will not call me by that name."

He shrugged and examined his fingernails. "I don't have to call you anything at all." He spoke with a vague Oxbridge accent, as if he'd been watching *Masterpiece Theatre* to brush up on his humanity. "Do you think I enjoy visiting you, in your den of iniquity on this fetid little planet? I would not approach you if it were not God's very specific command."

"It must really be important for him to make you slum like this." I slithered to his side of the desk. His nose wrinkled. "How long has it been since you deigned to walk among the mortals? Five hundred, six hundred years? A lot's changed since then." I leaned against his chair. "I know this great little place on 14th Street where you can get your halo shined, if you know what I—"

"It's about Gianna," he said.

My sneer disappeared. I straightened up.

"Who?"

"You know who," Michael said. "The woman you've been spending time with."

I picked up my Rolodex and flipped through it, trying not to let my hands shake. "Let's see . . . Gianna, Gianna, Gianna— oh, yes, here she is. What about her?"

"Stay away from her."

Beelzebub entered the office. "Hey, Lou, you forgot to sign this invoice for the fertilizer." He spied Michael and stopped short. "Oops."

"Fertilizer?" Michael said. "Taking up farming, are we?"

"Hey, if it isn't Michael the Magnificent. How are you?" Beelzebub extended his hand. Michael didn't take it. "Can't fool you twice, can I? Ever since that time I gave you my own special brand of cooties."

"They don't call you Lord of the Flies for nothing, Beelzebub," Michael said.

"It's been a long time since I've been called Lord of any- thing." Beelzebub glanced at me out of the corner of his eye. "So, Michael, what brings you here? You're not here to kick our asses again, are you?"

"Let's hope it doesn't come to that," Michael said in my direction.

"Right." Beelzebub waited a moment for an explanation. "So why are you here?"

"It's a matter that doesn't concern you," Michael said. "It's between me and your commander."

"Who? My command—oh, right." Beelzebub stood at attention and shouted Marine-style, "Permission to speak freely, sir!"

"Granted."

"Why didn't you tell me Tinker Bell was coming?"

"I didn't know." I guided him toward the door. "You should go now."

"And leave you alone with him? It's not safe."

"I can handle it."

"What about this invoice?" Beelzebub said.

"Sign it yourself."

"No way my name's going on it," he whispered. "You're the only one who can stroke the FBI out of an investigation."

"Bring it tomorrow night, then." I opened the door.

"Fine." Beelzebub waved at Michael. "Hey, Merry Christmas, Michael. See you at Armageddon."

I closed the door behind him.

"It's a shame," Michael said. "He used to be such a delightful little cherub."

"He still is."

"What does he think of your girlfriend?"

"What girlfriend?"

"Don't insult me," Michael said. "We know everything. We see everything."

"You watch us?" For some reason, my mind flashed to the old woman on the Metro after our first date. "Why are you spying on me? You never cared about my personal life before. Why now?"

"You never had a personal life before. What you had was a . . . a series of brief physical encounters."

"'A series of brief physical encounters.' You make it sound

so clinical. But considering your paltry sexual experience, that's not surprising."

"Every day I bask in the glory of the Lord. Nothing on earth can compare to that."

"You know what, brother?" I perched on the table. "I've experienced the rapture of Heaven and the rapture of fucking, and given the choice—"

"This woman means more to you than the others. Don't deny it."

"What makes you so sure?" I said. "Maybe I just like the way she tastes."

"Word is you're spending Christmas with her family."

"So?"

"With your allergies?"

"It's an experiment."

"Does she know you're the Devil?"

"Not yet."

"Then you plan to tell her?"

"Eventually," I said. "Maybe."

"When?" He stood and approached me. "After it's too late for her? After you possess her soul?"

"No, that's not what this is all about! You have no idea—"

"Then what? Are you saying you actually have feelings for this woman?"

"No! Well, yes, but—look . . ." I slid off the table and backed away from him towards the window. "I don't see why it's any of your business."

"I care about her, too, Lucifer," he said. "He cares."

"Why? Why after centuries of silence, do you approach me now with this? I started wars, incubated plagues, crashed stock markets, and got no response from you or What's-His-Face. Now you come to me in an uproar over one human being. Why? What makes her so special?"

"You tell me." His stony features softened, and he peered at me as if he were trying to see inside me. "I mean it. Tell me. What is it about her?"

I studied his perfect face for an ulterior motive, but found only curiosity. "I don't know, Michael, I—it's just that I've never known such . . ."

"Such what?" His voice dropped half an octave. "Such joy? Such . . . love?"

I turned away from him to the window. "I'm not supposed to feel those things."

"No, you're not. But you do, and I want to know why." He moved next to me now, his face reflecting the blue sky outside.

"You wouldn't understand," I said softly.

"Why not?"

I placed my hand before me on the cold windowpane. "You don't spend enough time with them. You couldn't possibly understand what it's like to be loved by a human."

"Humans love me."

"I'm not talking about worship, having icons and prayers and rituals in your honor. I've had plenty of that, too, and it's worthless." I turned to face him. "The kind of love I'm talking about, Michael, is between two bodies, two souls who let the world slip away when they're in each other's arms." My voice became a husky whisper. "Humans don't kiss the way angels do. They have smells and tastes like you can't imagine."

Michael swallowed. "I can imagine."

"You want this, too. Why wouldn't you? Why should I, the most wretched of creatures, be part of the holiest union this world can offer, and not you?" Our faces were a few inches apart; my voice caressed his name. "Michael . . . don't you want a piece of this joy? Something tangible, something earthly, something to make you feel a little more . . . real?"

He couldn't rip his milky gaze from my eyes.

"Yes."

I patted his shoulder and turned away. "Nah, you just want to get laid."

"How dare you," he snarled, "you miserable little weasel."

"Not so miserable these days."

"I'll say this again, and you'd better listen. If you care about Gianna at all—and you know you do—then let her go."

"Or what?"

"Are you willing to risk everything for this woman? Are you willing to risk going to war again?"

"War? Oh my, is hers the face that launched a thousand angels?"

"We are many more than a thousand now," he said. "We've been recruiting."

"So have we." I sneered at him. "And I was paraphrasing Christopher Marlowe, you illiterate simpleton."

"I know you were. I know the story, and I know the ending. Don't assume Gianna will be as lucky as Doctor Faustus was." His eyes dumped disdain on me. "Bargaining with the Devil is one thing. Falling in love with him is quite another story."

"Get out of my office!"

"Gladly." Michael turned to leave. "I almost forgot. Do you have any messages for me to take back?"

"Messages?"

"Yes. I am required to ask."

"No kidding. Messages, let's see . . . Why, yes, as a matter of fact." I went to my desk and began to scribble on a legal pad. "Let's see, a memo from the executive offices of Eternal Damnation, Inc." I tore off the top sheet, which read "BITE ME," and handed it to Michael. "There."

He read the message and crumpled the paper in his hand. "You are so small. I don't know why He makes me bother with you."

I sat down and put my feet on the desk. "Maybe because he still likes me best."

"But I'm the one going back to Heaven." Michael dropped my message on the floor. "Where will you sleep tonight . . . Satan?" He headed for the door. I stood.

"You're a lackey, Michael! A lackey, and that's all you'll ever be. But not me! I've got my own lackeys—thousands of them! And they all—hey, don't you dematerialize in front of me, you sonofa—" He was gone.

I collapsed back into my chair and spun around. A gnawing pain lurked behind my right eye. I covered my face with my hands to blot out all light, but it was too late. Red circles began to dance sambas on the backs of my eyelids. I pulled the thick, forest-green curtains over the tall windows before opening my office door.

When Daphne saw my face, she stood up quickly.

"Are you all right?" she said. "I tried to stall Michael, but one moment he was standing in front of me, and then he was gone, and when—"

I held up my hand to silence her. "Please, Daphne, I have a headache," I whispered.

"Oh. One of *those* headaches?"

I nodded, and my neck creaked.

Daphne flinched. "I'll cancel your appointments and hold your calls. And I'll order a truckload of ice."

"You're an angel, Daphne."

"You don't have to insult me just because you're sick."

I would have given her a huge smile, if doing so wouldn't have split my skull in two.

20

Salva Me, Fons Pietatis

"Louis, you look like hell."

"How appropriate."

I brushed my lips against Gianna's cheek on my way into her apartment.

"What's wrong?" she said.

"Nothing, just . . ." I held my hand to the right side of my head and winced. "Bad day at the office."

"Headache?"

"Like a vise. Like a flaming vise."

"I know the feeling," she said. "Here, sit down." Gianna went into the kitchen and came back with an ice pack and a dish towel. She sat on the end of the sofa and placed a pillow in her lap. "Lie down." I obeyed. She wrapped the ice in a towel, placed it on my forehead, and held her hands on top of it. "Do you want to tell me about it?"

"No," I said. "I'd rather just forget it."

"Even better." She slid her fingers under my neck and held

them against the base of my skull. They were cool and soothing. Shivers of comfort spread through my head and shoulders.

"While you're back there," I said, "would you mind jabbing a syringe full of morphine into my brain?"

"Ugh, one of those headaches. It feels like your head is on fire. Try to relax."

The heat from my swollen capillaries dissipated into her fingertips. "Don't take this the wrong way," I said, "but you would have made an excellent nun."

"Thanks, but I doubt that. I'm not very good at celibacy. Or silence, for that matter."

I opened my eyes and gazed up at her upside down face. "But your love is so palpable, so healing, I shouldn't be the only one to benefit."

"Does this mean I can date other men?"

"I have a migraine. Don't take anything I say seriously."

"Damn." She cooled her fingers on the ice pack again and trickled them against my scalp. I sighed. In the midst of my serenity, I remembered Michael's threat, and the way his lip had curled as he uttered it.

"But seriously, Gianna, I don't deserve you."

"You deserve me, and much worse."

"I'm not joking. I don't want to bring you down."

"Why would you—Lou, you're not making any sense."

"I'm afraid you'll become like me. You're so good, it would be a tragic waste."

"Thanks for your concern for my soul," she said, "but don't worry about me. Worry about your own soul."

"There's not much of that left to worry about."

"You have a migraine. I'm not taking anything you say seriously, remember?"

"Gianna, I'm trying to warn you—"

"Shut up and go to sleep." She covered my eyes with her

hands. I fell silent, lulled by her sweet, cool darkness, and within minutes drifted off into a fitful slumber.

"A sshole!"

I opened my eyes.

"Excuse me?" I said.

"Sorry. I didn't mean to wake you." Gianna pointed to the television set, which mumbled at a low volume. "He won't even quit for Christmas."

"Who?"

"Senator Scrooge."

"You mean—"

"Don't say his name under my roof. Even at home he takes every chance to grandstand. Look, they're tearing down a community center to build a new prison."

I turned on my side away from the television and wrapped my arm around her leg. The throbbing in my head had faded into a faint pulse. My body felt like someone had stuck a faucet into it, turned it on, and let my life force drip onto the floor.

A commercial began, and Gianna muted the volume. After a few moments, she said, "Is it evil to wish that someone would die and make the world a better place?"

"You're asking me?"

"Never mind." She smoothed my hair back from my face. "Go back to sleep."

I awoke later to the smell of Chinese food. Gianna hovered above me holding a teapot.

"Feeling better?" she said. I nodded, groggy. "Have something to eat and some tea. You'll be good as new."

I slid off the couch onto the floor next to the coffee table, where Gianna had set up dinner. My nearly numb fingers tried to wrap themselves around the chopsticks.

"Want a fork?" Gianna said.

"No, I'll get it under control. It'll just take a minute."

"It's been months since I've had a migraine." She knocked on the table's wooden leg. "I remember the way I'd feel when it was over, like I'd gone through a firestorm and come out the other side. It was a triumphant, almost heroic feeling, not so much one of conquest, but endurance."

"Uh-huh."

"What a rush, to be free of pain after such a battle. Practically a high all its own, though I wouldn't wish it on anyone."

"Not even the senator?"

"Please, I'm eating. Let's talk about something pleasant."

I put down the chopsticks and picked up my cup of tea. "You mean like what it feels like to have a headache? Pleasant like that?"

"Geez, sorry. I thought you said you were feeling better."

"I'm very tired." I tried to smile at her. "Thank you for taking care of me. I'm not accustomed to that."

"Then get accustomed to it."

"Yes, ma'am." I picked up the chopsticks again and shifted the kung pao chicken around on my plate, trying to conjure up some hunger. "Remember, tomorrow night I won't see you. Bob and I are hanging out, doing the brotherhood male bonding thing, I suppose."

"Sounds like fun," she said.

"He's looking forward to it."

"And you're not?"

"I don't know. I guess so."

"I was thinking," she said, "Bob is bi, right?"

I scoffed. "Bob's not bisexual, he's . . . omnisexual. If he could have sex with himself, he'd never leave his apartment except to buy more beer. He's a maniac."

"Then this is definitely the worst idea I've ever had."

"What's that?"

"I was thinking maybe we should introduce him to Marcus."

"What?!" One of my chopsticks twanged out of my grip and hit the wall. "No. No. No. No. No. Absolutely not."

"Why?"

"Because my brother is a very, very bad man."

"Come on," she said. "He can't be any worse than you."

"Believe me, he is." I retrieved my rogue chopstick.

"Okay, okay, forget I mentioned it," she said. "It probably wouldn't work out, anyway. Despite what he said the other night, I think Marc is looking for another relationship, and your brother would probably appear too frivolous."

"No, he wouldn't, that's the problem. Bob can alter his manner and his personality to suit whomever he's seducing. He knows exactly what they need at any given moment and how to give it to them." I cracked open a fortune cookie. "He's amazing."

"Then it's a good thing you two are brothers, right?"

I looked up from my fortune, which read YOU ARE HONEST IN ALL YOUR DEALINGS. "Sorry, what?"

"I said it's a good thing he's your brother."

I reached for my teacup. "Right."

21

Ne Absorbeat Eas Tartarus

"You're early."

"I thought you said seven o'clock." Beelzebub stood in my foyer holding a shopping bag in one hand and a covered box in the other.

"I did."

"And it's quarter after seven now."

"I know. For you, that's early."

"Just trying to keep you on your toes." He moved past me towards the kitchen. I noticed the cologne he was wearing and was flooded with a familiar, unwelcome rush of anticipation.

"What's in there?" I said.

Beelzebub placed the box on the kitchen table and pulled the cover off with the flair of a magician. Inside the box, which was actually a small cage, flapped a small black chicken.

"Dinner."

"I thought you were bringing pizza."

"I had a hankerin' for fresh chicken." The hen pecked at the sides of the cage with a methodical casualness.

"Where'd you find a live one?"

"I bought it off some Satanists," he said. "I told them who it was for, and they let me have it half-price."

"You're shitting me."

"I shit you not." He raised his left hand to swear.

"Did they believe you?"

"I'm not sure. I think they were hedging their bets, though, just in case I was telling the truth."

I pulled the cleaver out of its wooden block next to the stove and a knife sharpener out of the drawer.

Beelzebub picked up the shopping bag and took out its contents. "I brought a six-pack for me and a bottle of Glenfiddich for you."

"Thanks." I drew the blade quickly up and down the shaft of the sharpener. It threw glints of light against the kitchen wall. The hen looked at me and grew quiet and still.

He poured me a drink and opened a beer. "So that was weird seeing Michael again yesterday, huh?"

"Yes, it was."

"Let me guess. He wasn't there to talk about the good old days." Beelzebub retrieved a butcher's apron from my broom closet and approached me with it.

"No, not exactly."

"Was it about Belial?"

"No."

He placed the apron around my neck, then moved behind me and tied it, his knuckles brushing my back.

"What do I have to do to get you to tell me?" he said.

"Tell you what?"

"What Michael wanted."

I stopped sharpening. The blade's last shrill echoes faded.

"Did you think if you only brought me pizza and cheap scotch I wouldn't tell you?"

Beelzebub sat at the table and poked his finger inside the cage. "You'll tell me if you want to, whether I bribe you or not."

I laid the cleaver on the table in front of him and replaced the sharpener in the drawer. The chicken turned around once in her cage.

"Michael . . . had a message for me."

"A message? You mean, from—"

"Yes, so he claimed." I placed an iron basting pan under a wooden chopping block on the table.

"What kind of message?"

"A warning." I reached for the cage, and the hen squawked to life, beating her wings against the thin bars. Little black feathers floated to the table and floor.

"A warning? Shit, what did we do now?" Beelzebub said. "Have we started too many civil wars again?"

"Nothing like that this time." I laid my hand upon the chicken and caught her wide yellow eye with my gaze. She lay still again, her tiny heart slamming against her breast.

"So what was it? Tell me."

I lifted the hen and cradled her against my chest.

"He wants what you want, Beelzebub. He wants me to leave Gianna."

"I never said I wanted you to leave her. I don't care what you do with her."

"You don't?" I scratched the chicken's head and stroked its back. Beelzebub looked at it, then at the chopping block.

"No, I don't, I just—"

I picked up the cleaver.

"You just what?"

"Nothing," he said.

"See, I think that Michael and his boss are scared." I began to pace the kitchen floor, flipping the cleaver, blade over handle, and catching it. "I think they worry that if, hypothetically speaking, of course, I were to discover love, the key to their domain—it would make me stronger."

"I—"

"You, on the other hand, Beelzebub, are afraid that love would make me weak."

"I don't—"

"Too weak, perhaps, to do this." I flipped the cleaver once more, caught it overhanded, and brought the blade down on the outstretched neck of the hen. She gurgled once, and her blood poured down the chopping block into the pan.

I dipped my finger in the warm liquid, leaned close to Beelzebub, and spread the blood on his lips.

"What other tests have you got planned for me?" I whispered into his open mouth.

"That wasn't a test." He licked his lips. "It was a gift."

I removed my apron and placed it on the table in front of him. "Then pluck the gift."

He stood and folded the apron in half before tying it around his hips. Then he removed his shirt and laid it over the chair.

"It's new," he said. "I'd hate to get it dirty."

I swilled the rest of my whiskey and reached for the bottle. "I'll be in the other room."

"How do you want this fixed?"

"Blackened."

"As you wish . . . commander."

His loaded smirk rose above his smooth bare shoulder. I left my glass on the counter and carried the bottle with me into the living room.

A nearly full moon was rising over the skyline outside my window. I went out to the balcony.

I needed a game plan for the evening, needed to decide now what would happen when the inevitable moment arrived. It wasn't so much a choice between Gianna and Beelzebub; I could have them both, and keep them both, with little effort. It was more a choice between me and myself, between parts of me I wanted to feel were in control. Whatever my decision, it couldn't be made out of fear.

I took another swig of scotch. It would be easier just to get very drunk and let events unfold themselves. But sooner or later sobriety would return to taunt me.

Whatever I want will happen, I reminded myself. But what did I want?

I'll start with an order of complete freedom, please, leave off the tomato and the consequences. And a bottle of anything to accompany it.

"Hey, don't get too loaded on that stuff."

Beelzebub stepped onto the balcony and closed the sliding glass door behind him. He had put his shirt back on.

"Why not?"

"Because," he reached into his pocket, "I have something better." He unwrapped the foil from a small brown block.

"Is that what I think it is?"

"It ain't a chocolate bar."

I took it out of his hand with the reverence of communion. "Where did you find hash in this city? It's not exactly the most fashionable drug these days."

"Actually, I've been saving it since my trip to London in October. Remember, Lou, when we lived there, the nights we'd sit in St. James Park and drink and smoke and—"

"Yes." I inhaled the sweet, woody fragrance. "Beelzebub, what are you up to?"

"What do you mean?"

"Am I missing something? What's the occasion here tonight?"

"No occasion." He hoisted himself onto the top railing of the balcony. "It's been a long time since we hung out, just the two of us."

"We had lunch two days ago."

"I mean, like this." Beelzebub tilted his head back and let the chill breeze stream through his hair for a minute. "Besides, I thought I'd give you a night to remember before you took off for the little town of Bethlehem."

"You mean," I crept towards him, "sort of an anti-holiness inoculation?"

"Yeah, something like that."

I placed my hands on the railing, one on either side of him. A mere breath from me would have propelled him into twelve stories of cold air and eventually an uncooperative sidewalk. He took his hands off the railing and crossed his arms in front of him.

"Nice evening, huh?"

"Gravity doesn't care how much you flirt with it," I said. "It still does its job."

"I'd survive the fall."

"But you'd be a mess for a little while, and we'd have so much explaining to do to the witnesses, so many memories to cleanse. Tedious work."

"It would put a damper on the evening, wouldn't it?"

"Quite." With a swift move, I slid my arm around his waist and pulled him off the railing. Before setting him down, I turned so that I was between him and the wide open city.

"Nice to know you still care." Beelzebub pulled the hash out of my shirt pocket and held it up. "Now or later?"

"Always now," I said. "Always now."

"How's the chicken look so far?"

"Looks good," I said. "Smells great. I just put the rice on, so we have about forty-five minutes."

"Perfect." Beelzebub sat cross-legged on my living room floor next to the coffee table, intent on his work. On a folded piece of paper in front of him lay a small pile of tobacco next to an empty cigarette with the filter torn off. With a small knife he shredded tiny pieces of the hashish into the tobacco. Humming the latest post-grunge hit, he fashioned a new filter from a tightly rolled strip of cigarette box and inserted it into the shell of the original cigarette, which was then refilled with the pile of chemically enhanced tobacco.

He held his finished work towards me. "Do you want to do the honors?"

"Outside." I moved toward the balcony door.

"It's freezing out there."

"I won't have my apartment smelling like smoke," I said. "Don't worry, after a few hits of that, we won't feel the cold."

On the balcony, we settled into a couple of lounge chairs, side by side facing each other. He handed me the hash-laced cigarette. I put it in my mouth and lit it with my fingertip.

The first drag lingered in my lungs long and sweet, as did the second. By the time I passed the burning stick back to Beelzebub, my face was beginning to thicken and tingle.

"How is it?" he asked as he took it from me. I just stared at him. "You're quiet. That's a very good sign." He closed his eyes and took a deep drag. When he finally exhaled, he barked and pumped his fist in the air. "Yes! I done good, bro. I done real good."

"That you have."

"Man, it's been too long since you and I got high together."
He settled deeper into his chair. "You sure I can't get you to try
heroin again?"

"I can't stand being that relaxed." I took another hit.

"You just don't like heroin because it's trendy. Gotta be different, you."

"If I'm not different, then who's going to be?"

He blinked at me a few times. "What?"

"What?"

"What did you mean by that?"

"By what?"

"What you said."

"When?"

"I don't know," he said. "Give me that."

While Beelzebub puffed away, I stretched my arms back
over my head and listened to my skin sing. "Sometimes it is so
good to be human."

"It's always good to be human," he said. "You think those
assholes in Heaven ever have this much fun?"

I shivered. "Fun isn't everything."

"Yes, fun IS everything, Lou. It has to be, because it's all
we've got. Here, have some more of this before you get gloomy
on me." He passed back the cigarette and returned to his deep
slouch. After a few moments he said, "Dude, I can't feel my
face."

I leaned forward and whacked his cheek hard with my free
hand. "How about now?"

He didn't reply, only stared at the skyline. The drug slithered through the spaces between my brain cells and forged
new lines of communication. A minute, or perhaps ten of
them, passed.

"Did you just hit me?" he said.

"Hit you?"

"Yeah, just now."

"I'm not sure. I think I wanted to."

"Oh." He scratched his face. "Why?"

"I don't remember. Here, I'll make it up to you. Finish this."

"You're a pal."

After he had finished, he pulled out a regular cigarette. "You want one?"

"No, thanks," I said.

"You sure? Between the carbon monoxide and the nicotine, it totally intensifies the experience."

"I know, but I'm perfectly happy exactly as I am right this second."

"I'm glad." He gazed at me over his glowing cigarette.

The wind ripped harder over the balcony now. We were both quaking from the cold, but made no move to go inside. The chill was more of an intellectual perception, anyway, as my skin now felt like it was several inches away from the surface of my body. I rolled up my sleeves to enhance the sensation.

"Lucifer, what do you wanna be when you grow up?"

"I want to be the Devil."

This remark sent Beelzebub into peals of laughter until tears squeezed out of his eyes. He nudged me with his foot.

"You already are the Devil, man. Which sucks for us, because I want to be God."

I stared at him and felt the world wobble. "What did you just say?"

"Yeah, I said his name, Goddammit, I say it all the time these days, just never around you. I say, 'Thank God it's Friday,' and I scream out 'Oh, God!' when I'm fucking someone or getting fucked, and you know what happens?"

"What?" I shrunk back in the chair.

"Nothing! Precisely dick, that's what."

An intense attack of paranoia gripped my body. I slid out of the chair, crawled to the wall, and huddled there with my back to the building.

"Yo, man, don't bug out on me," Beelzebub said. "I was just joking. About the 'Oh, God!' part, anyway."

"You were?"

"No." He threw back his head and cackled at the moon, a spurt of laughter that slid into an unknown high-pitched melody. "Ohhh, shit, my high is so high, so high." Beelzebub eased into a supine position on the chaise lounge and stabbed at the sky with his cigarette.

"Lucifer, your fear is a prison, man, a fucking prison, with bars of cold hard wasted energy, and you feel lucky 'cuz sometimes you get recess, a chance to break some rules and write graffiti on the prison walls and sneak back inside like you've done something bad." He lobbed his cigarette over the edge of the balcony. It arced like a meteor out of sight. "Flames and smoke and terror and all the nasty smells of Hell, I love it, if I love anything. I'm bad 'cuz I wanna be, but with you it's always looking over your shoulder hoping you'll get some recognition, but who cares, you gotta do it for yourself, 'cuz like Belial said, no one believes in us anymore."

Beelzebub stood and slapped the top of the chair, speaking like a preacher at a revival meeting: "Strip off that fear, boy, or it'll weigh you down, drown you like concrete boots when you try to plunge into freedom, freedom from the God that ain't there, the God that doesn't care." He peered over the edge of the balcony. "Look at them down there, our precious humble little ants, shuffling their days and nights into their pasts, squandering their hours, leading gray, subterranean existences in the hope of salvation, as if practicing for the eternal boredom of Heaven. They forget how to want, after years of telling themselves that wanting is evil, or that wanting makes them miserable, and if only they could stanch the mad flow of desire and find peace, maybe they could sleep at night, but there's no sleep in the world as deep as mine, and I want, I want, I want all the time . . ."

Beyond the drone of Beelzebub's voice, I thought I heard crickets chirping. My mind grasped on to this sound and clung to it for several minutes before I remembered that it was December, when all the crickets are on vacation.

". . . just stiff ghosts of themselves, passing their years going to Labor Day sales at the mall and putting together jigsaw puzzles of kittens playing with yarn and inventing ghastly new recipes involving Jell-O brand gelatin and taking them to the church picnic, and always with these vague smiles on their faces until one day they're found in a Motel 6 in a Bo Peep costume harnessed to a bewildered sheep, and everyone thinks they've gone batty when in fact it's their first real step toward self-actualization . . ."

Beelzebub was tapping into an underground reservoir of vocabulary. My mind and mouth were too dry to keep up. I wished for the crickets again.

". . . God is great, God is bad, let us thank him, dear old dad, for the sweetest thing in the world, a taste of humanity without mortality, life without end, amen . . ." He was still clutching the railing and staring down at the street. His slow sway mesmerized me. ". . . So happy in my hate, in my bed of darkness, because I created it, we created it, so Lucifer, don't ever feel guilty on my account for making me lose Heaven, it was the kindest thing you ever did for me, and I only wish I could prove to you that it wasn't a mistake, that we're better off without God," his voice came faster and louder, "so you can stop pining away for the good old days, because the good old days sucked, and if he doesn't want us, then fuck him, and fuck them all is what I say!" He shook his fist at the stars. "I'm not afraid, and I won't crawl on my belly in the dust like a worm, just to feed the ego of some distant, megalomaniacal tyrant!"

Beelzebub leaped onto the balcony railing. He flailed for an instant before achieving an unsteady balance, then ripped open his shirt to the sky.

"Go ahead, God, you fat, filthy motherfucker, lightning-bolt my ass into oblivion if you're so tough."

I buried my face in my arms. My head felt like it was full of gyroscopes. *This is not happening,* I thought, or maybe I said it out loud, *this is a hallucination.* Except hash doesn't make you hallucinate—it just makes reality feel like a hallucination.

I heard Beelzebub's feet slam to the surface of the balcony, then his voice came close to my ear.

"See, Lucifer, God doesn't care. No matter what we do, he doesn't care. We could bring this planet to its knees, and he wouldn't blink."

"That's not true. He's waiting for us to fuck up, I know it, then he'll destroy us."

"No. There's nothing we can do anymore to piss him off enough to even look at us."

"Then what's the point?!" I reached up to clutch at Beelzebub's collar. The cold air hit my face and made me realize it was soaked with something salty.

"The point?" he said. "The point of what?"

"Of all this! Of all we do! Is it just evil for evil's sake?"

He scratched his chin and thought for a moment. "Yeah, whatever. I say it's just for the fun of it, the what-the-fuck factor, you know?" He wiped the cold sweat off my forehead with his sleeve. "The funny thing is, Lucifer, you're really the one who wants to be God. I'd settle for just being the Devil."

"You want the job?" I said. "Take it."

"It isn't that easy."

I tried to focus on his face.

"Sorry," he said. "It's been you since the beginning of time, and it's gonna be you forever." He stood and offered his hand to me. "Come on. It's time to eat."

When he joined me at the table, I told him, "You'd make a good Devil, Beelzebub."

"And you'd make a good God."

"You think so?"

"Yeah, definitely. You never would have let things get so fucked up. You're a good manager." He passed me the rice. "Hey, you never know when there'll be an opening. Keep an eye on the classifieds. People are always looking for God."

"Would you mind not saying his name around me from now on?"

"Sure. Hey, do you remember anything I said outside just now? 'Cuz I don't, but I have a feeling it was pretty wild."

"I might be able to reconstruct it," I said. "Have you been reading a lot of Nietzsche lately?"

"A lot of what?"

"Never mind."

I don't remember much else about dinner, only that we ate voraciously and that halfway through the meal I couldn't feel my tongue anymore.

"Let me clear the table," Beelzebub said. "You look too stoned to be carrying things that break."

"Okay. I think I'll go stare into space now."

I sat in my living room chair and faced the empty fireplace. When Beelzebub returned, he handed me another glass of whiskey and sipped a new bottle of beer.

"Want me to build a fire?" he said. I shrugged and nodded. He picked up a log. "Should I build it in here or—"

"Here's fine."

He lit the wood, then sat on the fireplace and looked at me. "I didn't mean to buy the quiet hash."

"It's really good," I said, "just to have a blank brain once in a while."

"Yeah, I guess. 'Course, my brain's blank most of the time anyway, right?" I smiled with the half of my mouth that was working. "Damn, Lou, you look so . . ."

"Peaceful?"

"Peaceful. Actually, I was gonna say 'mellow.' Peace isn't something we get a lot of."

"Peace is good, Bub. You really should try it."

"I wouldn't know where to find it." I gave him a goofy smile. "I see," he said. "I gotta find a girlfriend of my own, huh?"

"You'd be surprised what it can do for your outlook."

"There's nothing wrong with *my* outlook."

"And there's something wrong with mine?"

"Well . . ." I could see him struggle for diplomacy. "There are some things about your . . . thing with Gianna that disturb me."

"Such as?"

"Everything."

"Beginning with . . ."

"The idea of you celebrating Christmas with a cozy little Catholic family would be hilarious if it weren't true."

"What if I was spending Christmas with some Pentecostals?"

"Lou, you know what I mean." He stood and began to pace, drinking faster from the bottle. He seemed to be coming down off the high already, much sooner than I was. I envied this talent of his, the ability to toss off a buzz like it was an extra layer of clothing. At that moment he held a commanding coherence advantage.

"I know we usually go to Vegas at Christmas," I said. "But things are different this year."

"They sure are." He set his beer on the table. "Lou, to tell you the truth, this whole thing scares the shit out of me. I don't want to see you get . . . you know . . ."

"Get what?"

"Remember in the movie *Rocky*, what Rocky's trainer made him chant while he was hitting the punching bag?"

"No."

"'Women weaken legs.'"

"You'll be glad to know," I said, "my legs have never been stronger."

"I'll be the judge of that."

"You think so?"

"I'm speaking . . . you know . . . not literally, but . . ."

"Metaphorically?"

"Yeah." Beelzebub pointed at my lower extremities. "Your metaphorical legs are practically paralyzed by this woman."

"You don't know what you're talking about." My voice lacked the intensity I felt. The clouds still surrounded my head and made me an easy target for Beelzebub's lasso.

"You're not yourself lately, Lou. It's like you're possessed. What excellent revenge—the Prince of Darkness possessed by a mere human."

"It's not like that."

"If you want," he circled my chair, "I'd be happy to perform the exorcism."

My brain struggled through its bleariness like a tadpole swimming through gelatin. "No, thanks."

"No one knows you like I do. This woman doesn't even know who you are. How can you be real with her? How can you be your true self?"

I didn't answer, thinking how he had it all backward—it was with Gianna that I was real, and with Beelzebub, pretending.

"I don't want to continue this pointless argument," I said. "You've spoken your mind, and I appreciate your frankness. Let's change the subject."

"Fine." He stretched out on the floor facing me and propped his head on his hand. "Better yet, let's not talk at all." He fixed his eyes on mine and began to unbutton his shirt.

"What are you doing?"

"What does it look like?" He pushed his shirttail back to reveal a tan, taut torso. "I'm trying to get you to come hither."

"Your mind-control techniques won't work with me, remember? I'm an angel, just like you."

"Of course, of course." Beelzebub crawled towards me and knelt beside my chair. "And how long has it been since you were, you know . . ." he swept his fingers across my knee, ". . . touched by an angel?"

I closed my eyes and searched for a single fragment of strength to resist him. It cowered in a cold, abandoned recess of my mind.

"Not long enough," I said. His hand halted in its journey up my thigh.

"What?"

"Look, Beelzebub . . ." I turned to him and began to button his shirt, taking care not to be singed by his flesh. "You are my most delightful diversion, always know that. But right now I don't want any diversions, male or female, mortal or immortal."

He pulled away from me and walked back to the fireplace.

"Lou, I don't . . . I . . ." He picked up his beer and took a long swig. "I don't get it. You've never turned me down before."

"Maybe it was because you only asked when you knew I'd say yes. What happened to your intuition?"

"Nothing happened to it. You're the one who's fighting it."

"Fighting what?"

"Come on. I saw the way you've been looking at me all night."

"It's the drugs," I said.

"Bullshit."

"Okay, it's not just the drugs. It's the whole setup: the drugs and the scotch and the chicken and the conversation, and that cologne—"

"The one I only wear for you."

"Yes. It's obvious that this whole evening was a calculated seduction attempt."

In a moment he was kneeling before me, his hands on my forearms.

"I'm not known for my subtlety. So let's go fuck."

"No."

"Come on . . ."

"What did I just say?"

"I didn't hear you," he said. "You know, I learned a few new tricks at the Delta Gamma house. Actually, I didn't learn them, I invented them."

"What kind of tricks?"

"Good ones." He slid his hands under the rolled-up cuffs of my sleeves. "Or bad ones, depending how you look at it."

"Tell me."

"You think I'd give you my new secrets for free just so you could try them with your girlfriend?" His thumbs caressed the soft flesh on the inside of my arms. "I'm so bad with words, anyway, I'd never do it justice, so I'll have to demonstrate." I frowned. "Lou, come on . . . if you want . . . I'll wear the wings."

"Stop it." I pulled my arms out from under his grasp.

"But you want to, right?"

"Yes, but—"

"So what's the problem?"

"I want to," I said, "but I don't want to."

"Lou, is this some kind of game?" He cocked his head. "If it is, I kinda like it."

"No, it's not a—"

"It makes me feel like you're in control."

He gazed at me from under his thick brown lashes and parted his lips a fraction of an inch. My eyes fixed on the wet darkness between them, and I felt myself tip towards him as if drawn by gravity. Beelzebub closed his eyes and tilted his chin.

When my mouth was only an inch or two from his, I stopped, and peered into the cherubic face of sweet, aching temptation. The fire flickered warm shadows across his skin and through his hair.

I kissed him softly on the forehead and felt his brow furrow under my mouth. He pulled back a little to study my face, a tentative smile playing about his lips. I slid my fingers through his silken hair, lingering at the ends of the golden strands.

"What's up?" he said.

"Nothing. It's just . . ." I ran my fingertip along the curve of his jaw. "You are . . . so beautiful."

"You don't have to sweet-talk me. I'm right here."

"No . . . Beelzebub, you don't understand." I clasped his face between my palms and stared into his eyes. "I don't know who I am anymore."

"Then let me remind you." He moved closer, insinuating his body between my knees. "You are Lucifer, the Prince of Darkness, Emperor of the Underworld, the second most powerful and single most cool being in the Universe . . ." With every hyperbolic piece of flattery, Beelzebub unfastened one button of my shirt. "Author of All Evil, the Adversary, the Arch Fiend . . . this is how the world knows you, those who hate you and those of us who . . . don't hate you so much." He slid one hand down the front of my trousers. "You are the Infernal Serpent."

My breath escaped in a low moan of lust, and my mouth watered. "You're not nearly as stupid as you pretend to be," I whispered.

Beelzebub's fingers tightened. I gasped again and clutched the arm of the chair.

"I know what you like," he said. "But if you want, I could pretend I don't, and you could show me."

His right hand burned on my chest as it crept up to brush my shirt back. He held my gaze like a vise, unblinking. I tried not to show fear, but every muscle in my face was beginning to tremble.

"No," I said. "Please stop."

Beelzebub's eyelashes flickered. "Oh, so now you're the one to beg. An interesting twist, I must say." He pressed his body against mine.

"Don't make me push you away."

"You're going to have to." He slid his tongue along my jugular vein, sending waves of heat down my throat and into my heart. "If you can."

My hands gripped his sides, uncertain whether their task was to embrace or reject. Beelzebub writhed underneath my grasp.

Every cell in my body except one screamed, "WHY NOT?!"

Only rage could give me the strength to separate us, to counteract the heat already sealing our flesh together.

"Stop!" I hurled him to the floor, then stood to loom over him. "You do as I tell you. Remember who you are, and who I am!" Beelzebub gaped at me, every trace of smugness gone.

"You can play your cute little boy toy games with the other fools," I said, "but when I say no, it means no!" I slapped my forehead. "Listen to me, I sound like a fucking public service announcement!" I turned away from him to button my shirt.

"I'm sorry," he said. From the corner of my eye I saw him sit up slowly and run his fingers through his hair. "Do you want me to leave?"

"Not unless you want to."

"Doesn't really matter what I want, does it?" he murmured.

"What?"

"Nothing." He stared at the floor.

"I don't want to hurt you, Beelzebub."

"Hurt me?" he scoffed. "I'm not hurt, I'm just horny." He stood up and retrieved his beer, then pulled the pack of cigarettes from his jacket pocket. I said nothing. He sat in the chair opposite me and began to smoke. After a minute, he said, "Stop feeling sorry for me."

"I'm not feeling sorry for you."

"Then why else would you let me smoke in your apartment?"

I held up my hand. "Let me have one."

He smiled a little. "You only smoke when you're sexually frustrated, my friend."

"Just give me one."

He tossed the pack to me. We smoked in silence for a few minutes, then Beelzebub cleared his throat.

"I still don't get it, Lou. You always used to play along."

"That was before."

"Before Gianna."

I took a long drag before replying. "Yes. Before Gianna."

"Well, I don't understand it, but I'm sure you know what you're doing."

"Say that like you mean it." I needed to hear it.

He gazed at me for a moment, then said, "Wanna watch the hockey game?"

22

Quid Sum Miser Tunc Dicturus?

When Gianna opened the door, she was wearing a Santa hat with a jingle bell dangling from the white puff ball.

"Hey, you're early," she said.

"I know." I took her hand and led her into the apartment towards her bed. "There's something we have to do before we leave."

"What's that?"

"Fuck." I lifted her onto the bed and began to unbutton her blouse.

"On Christmas Eve?" she said. "Are you crazy?"

"What do you mean?"

"I've never had sex on Christmas Eve. It almost seems sacrilegious."

"Even better." I gave her my finest wicked grin before pressing my face into her neck.

"You are such a heathen." She laughed a little, but pushed

against my chest. "No, knock it off." I didn't. "Lou, we can't do it now. I'm all out of condoms."

"So?" I knew we didn't need them, but didn't feel like explaining why at the moment. I reached under her and unzipped her skirt.

"So you want me to tell our firstborn child that he came into existence when Daddy date-raped Mommy on Christmas Eve?"

I froze. "What?"

"I said no." She pressed her first two fingers into the base of my throat. "Now get off me."

I held up my hands and backed away. "I'm sorry, Gianna, I—I got carried away."

"Yes, you did."

"I was way out of line."

"Yes, you were."

"And I'm sorry."

"Apology accepted."

"I could run to the drugstore and—"

"No, Lou, that's not the point. Besides, we don't have time." She looked in the mirror. "Look what you've done to me already. My hair, my clothes—I can't show up at my parents' looking all post-coital like this!"

I moved next to her and gazed at her image in the mirror. "I think you look sexy. And as long as you look like we've been fooling around, why don't we—"

She pulled my hand off her waist. "Go sit on the couch and don't move."

"Okay, okay." I ran my hands through my hair and gnawed my lip. If Beelzebub could see my frustration, he'd be laughing his ass off. "I need a cigarette."

"You don't smoke," she said.

"Hardly ever." I sat on the edge of the couch cushion.

Gianna stepped to the edge of the bedroom area, a hair-brush in her hand. "Look, Lou, while we're at my parents' house, can you just follow my lead when it comes to public displays of affection?"

"You mean, don't touch you unless you touch me first?"

"Basically. I have to feel them out first, see how comfortable they are with you. Please let me handle it as I see fit."

"Fine." The walls of the next two days were already closing in. I bounced my heel against the floor.

"You don't have to come with me if you don't want to," she said. "I know you hate Christmas to begin with, and meeting my family during a holiday adds so much more pressure."

"I want to do this, Gianna."

"Are you sure? I could still take the train."

"Don't you want me to come?"

"Oh yes, I do, Lou, more than anything." She sat next to me and took my hand. "I want this, I do, but my family can be a little scary."

"Not as scary as mine, believe me."

"I just . . . I don't want to lose you."

"Gianna . . ." I caressed her cheek, then pulled her close to me. "No one will ever come between us. No one."

"I believe you," she said. "I don't know why, but I believe you." She kissed me, then examined my face. "You look like shit. What were you guys up to last night?"

"I'm not sure."

"That's not surprising. Your eyes look like candy canes. Why don't you take a nap while I pack?"

I stretched out on the couch. Antigone leapt onto my chest and burrowed into the crook of my arm. Gianna pulled a suitcase from under the bed and opened it. She stood in front of her bureau, hands on her hips, deep in thought.

"I can feel it when you stare at me," she said.

"What's it feel like?"

"Ever heard the expression 'mind fuck'?"

"It sounds nice," I said in a low voice.

Gianna looked at me and smiled a little. "Kinda . . ." She turned back to the dresser. "Stop it, Lou."

"Stop what?"

"By the way, I told my parents you're Episcopalian."

"What!?"

"It's at least marginally better than being an atheist."

"I told you, Gianna, I'm not an atheist." I sat up and brushed the cat onto the floor. "I believe in What's-His-Face, I just don't worship him."

"In any case, it'll make it a little easier, just for Christmas, if you would pretend."

"I can't pretend to be an Episcopalian when I don't know anything about them. You could have at least given me a little more warning so I could do some research."

"Episcopalians are basically like Catholics, except they don't believe in transubstantiation or the Pope. And a few other little things, but basically they're Catholic Lite."

"What's transubstantiation?"

"It's the process by which communion becomes the body and blood of Christ."

"You mean symbolically?"

"No, for real."

"Let me get this straight," I said. "At the moment of the sacrament of communion, a little cracker and a cup of port somehow magically transform into the body and blood of someone who's been dead almost two thousand years?"

"Yes."

"You believe that?"

"Yes," she said. "Sort of."

"Isn't it a little . . . macabre? Cannibalistic, even? Not to mention impossibly silly."

"It's one of the holy mysteries. You can't examine it and pull it apart like a science fair project."

"The big holy mystery is why you people believe your god still cares about you."

I was relieved to discover I hadn't actually said that last comment out loud.

"Anyway," she said, "you sound like a pretty authentic Episcopalian."

"Method acting. I have to get into the part." I crawled to the end of the couch closer to her. "So what do Episcopalians think of premarital sex and birth control?"

Gianna stopped folding the sweater in her hands, then replied without looking at me, "They're cool with it, I guess, as long as it's within the context of a loving, committed relationship."

"Uh-huh. And what's the Catholic party line on those issues?"

"You know very well what it is." She plopped the sweater in the suitcase.

"So why don't you convert? That way you won't be such a sinner."

"Stop toying with me, Louis."

"I thought you liked theological debates, or was that just naked theological debates?"

"I'm not going to convert."

"Or was it just theological debates where you know what you're talking about?"

"Where *I* know what I'm talking about?" She slammed down the lid of her suitcase. "You didn't even know what transubstantiation was."

"Yes, I did, I just wanted you to give me the chance to

make fun of it. I've forgotten more about religion than you'll ever know. As a matter of fact—"

"You're an arrogant prick."

"—it's a favorite subject of mine."

"You study religion so you can feel superior to it? So you can mock others for their beliefs?"

"No, I—"

"Or do you think you'll find God that way? You'll never find Him by going through your head."

"Then how do I find him, assuming I want to?"

"You won't," she said. "He'll find you."

"Not if I see him coming."

"You won't."

"You're giving me the creeps, Gianna."

"Good." She took her purse into the bathroom and began to fix her makeup. I picked up her suitcase and carried it to the door. While I waited I heard her singing:

God rest ye merry, gentlemen
Let nothing you dismay . . .

I had to stop her. I searched for something to throw at her, but all I saw were shoes, and none were soft enough.

Remember Christ our Savior
Was born on Christmas Day . . .

I put down the suitcase and moved toward her.

To save us all from—

I grabbed her arm, spun her around, and kissed her hard. She responded with equal force, then pulled away.

"Trying to shut me up?" she said.

"No, I just wanted to kiss you."

"I don't believe you." Gianna pushed me up against the wall and kissed me again. Before I could trap her in my embrace, she backed off and picked up her makeup case. "Let's go," she said. "We'll be late."

23

Te Decet Hymnus, Deus

"Can we listen to Christmas carols?" Gianna asked in the car.

"No," I said.

"Please?"

"No."

"I thought you loved me."

"I love you, Gianna, but not as much as I hate Christmas carols."

She didn't respond.

"That was a joke, of course," I said, "a joke that will be repeated whenever you pull that line on me again, just so you know."

She was silent for another minute, then she said, "You said no one would ever come between us. But that's not true. God comes between us all the time."

"Yes, he would."

"Why? Because He hates you?"

"That's right."

"How do you know He hates you?"

"Because he told me."

"Very funny," she said. "You know, sometimes I think you get God and your father mixed up in your head."

"You think so?"

"That's why you think God hates you, because you think your father hates you. Well, I've got news for you. God loves you and forgives you for whatever you did. And you know what? I bet your father does, too."

"If I let you play Bing Crosby, will you shut up?"

"Uh-huh." She reached in the back seat and pulled the tape from her overnight bag. "But I meant what I said. I don't know about your dad, but God definitely—"

I yanked the tape out of her hand and stuffed it under my seat, out of her reach. "Sorry, you just lost your tape privileges with that comment."

"You're a psychopath, you know that?"

When we pulled up to Marc's row home in Fells Point, he was sitting on his semicircular brick porch wearing a Santa hat. Brightly wrapped presents surrounded him on the porch steps. In a forest-green cardigan and a red vest-style windbreaker, Marc looked like a skinny, updated version of the Ghost of Christmas Present.

He stretched and began to gather up his packages. I got out of the car to help him.

"Hey, how's it going?" he said.

"Fine."

He looked at me, then at Gianna, who smiled at him tight-lipped.

"Hold on a second," Marc said. "Let me go get my chain saw to cut this tension."

"Louis hates Christmas, and he's making me hate it, too."

"Ooh, neat." Marcus grabbed his suitcase. "Can I join the debate?"

"No, it's over," Gianna said. "We're practicing being civil."

"She's practicing being civil," I said. "I'm practicing pretending I like Christmas."

"You'd better get real good at it."

※

"Yeeeeeeee!!! Merry Christmas!!"

A red-and-white blur that was most likely Gianna's mother burst out of the house before my car had rolled to a stop. She ran toward the car with her arms spread wide.

"Oh, for God's sake," Marc said, "she just saw us at Thanksgiving."

"Don't worry," Gianna said to me. "Just switch into charm mode, and she'll be putty in your hands."

I swallowed the last lump of trepidation and stepped out of the car. Mrs. O'Keefe was already smothering her two children with hugs and kisses. Their arms flailed, useless for defense against the onslaught of affection. Finally, Gianna's mother stepped back, turned to me, and fluffed her thick black hair.

"You must be Louis," she said.

"It's a pleasure to meet you, Mrs. O'Keefe." I shook her hand and softened my eyes to gaze at her face. She beamed at me.

"Oh, please, call me Rosa." She withdrew her hand reluctantly. "Come on in out of the cold. It's going to rain any second now."

The four of us headed for the porch as the front door opened. A black-and-white shepherd dog streaked across the lawn towards Gianna and Marcus, then slid to a stop as it passed me. The dog turned, looked at me, and raised its hackles. Its face became an explosion of white teeth and blood-pink gums as it snarled and crouched to attack.

"Bobo, no!" Rosa dropped the package in her hand.

My eyes met the dog's as I squatted on the ground and whispered his name. Bobo whined once, then lowered his tail and trotted to me. The others watched, jaws agape, as he licked my chin and pawed my knee.

"That was bizarre," Marc said.

"No kidding." Rosa stared at me for another moment, then picked up the package she'd dropped. "Okay, kids, let's get these gifts under the tree where they belong." She and Marcus stepped onto the porch and into the house.

I turned to Gianna, who had not moved from the driveway.

"That's exactly how Antigone reacted to you." She joined us and reached down to stroke Bobo's ears. "You have an odd way with animals, you know?"

I looked up and down the tree-lined street at Gianna's neighborhood. Not one of the charming brick colonial houses could have had fewer than five bedrooms.

"This is where you're from?" I said.

"Yeah, why?"

"With your overdeveloped sense of class consciousness, I figured your family lived in the shadow of an oil refinery or inside a series of refrigerator boxes taped together."

"Hey, where does it say that a working-class hero has to be working class?" she said. "Come on, let's go in."

Gianna's mother was still prancing with excitement in the living room.

"Yaay, it's so great to have all my babies here on Christmas Eve. Your dad and Matt and Luke went out to do some last-minute shopping, and Donna and Dara are feeding the shelter critters. Gianna, why don't you show Louis where to put his stuff so he can relax?"

Gianna led me upstairs and out of her mother's hovering range.

"And I thought *you* were effusive," I said. "Compared to your mom, you're a wallflower."

"Compared to my mom, Joan Rivers is a wallflower. Wait until you meet my grandmother." She opened a door near the top of the stairs. "Here's your room."

I rested our bags on the twin bed.

"I know it's probably a little small for you," she said. "Sorry about that."

"It's doubly small for us."

"No, this is your room. I'm sleeping down the hall, in my own room."

"You mean, we're not . . ." I gestured to the bed.

"Sleeping together? No way. My folks are too old-fashioned for that."

"You're not exactly a teenager anymore, Gianna. Has anyone told your parents?"

"Sorry. I know it's absurd, but—"

"Do they think that we don't sleep together? Do they think you're still a virgin?"

"Shhh. No, it's just that they don't want my sex life shoved in their faces, you know?"

I slid my arm around her waist. "Can you come visit me, then?"

"Maybe tomorrow night. But not tonight. I like to spend Christmas Eve night alone, contemplate the mystery and all. It's a time of peace I guard very jealously."

"I'm the one who's jealous."

"Lou, it's important to me. Don't mock, all right?"

"All right." I brushed back the edge of her bangs from her temple. "I'm sorry I've been so mean about Christmas. I promise I'll be good for your family."

"I know the holiday touches off something bitter in you, probably about your past. Ugly memories?"

I kissed her forehead and said nothing.

"Of course you won't tell me," she said. "You'll go far away inside your head and just smile at me."

I smiled at her. She laughed and took my hand. "Come on, let's go relax with Mom and Marc before you have to meet everyone else. It's best to wade into this family gradually."

As we reached the bottom of the stairs, two sets of clones, male and female, burst through the door, weighed down with shopping bags, followed by a tall, boisterous redheaded man. Gianna turned to me.

"So much for wading. Hope your swan dive is in perfect form."

Soon I was immersed in a flood of garrulous people, huge plates of snacks, and overflowing bowls of eggnog and wassail. By the time I had become acquainted with Gianna's other brothers, Matthew and Luke, their wives Donna and Dara (which man was married to which woman never became clear to me), and her father Walter, the house was barraged with cousins, aunts, uncles, neighbors, and friends. Each group would enter with a chorus of hollers and hugs, make mad revelry for about twenty minutes, then sweep out again, to be replaced with another gaggle of well-wishers. In the background blared a strangely pleasant blend of Irish Christmas carols, most of which sounded like ribald drinking songs, as long as I didn't pay close attention to the words.

Once Gianna saw that I was socially adept enough to be left unchaperoned, I saw little of her for the next two hours. At one point I joined Walter and his sons gathered around the Christmas tree.

"See, that's what I mean." Walter pointed to one of the

ornaments, emblazoned with the Coca-Cola symbol. "Proof that Christmas is getting too goddamned commercial."

"Dad," Matthew said, "that ornament is—

"—at least thirty years old," Luke finished.

"And that's about how many times we've heard this diatribe, guys," Marc said to his brothers. "And again, I'll say, Dad, commercialism is part of what makes Christmas so great."

"Don't you dare, ya little heretic." A smile crept about Walter's lips as he issued this warning.

"It's the trappings that society has laid on top of Christmas that choke me up the most," Marc said.

"For you, Dad," Luke said, "Christmas begins with the first Sunday in Advent. For us, it begins with—"

"—Santa Claus riding a Norelco razor across our TV screens," Matt concluded.

"Are you saying," I asked, "that you could strip Christmas of its religious significance, and it would still move you just as much?"

"Yeah, almost as much," Marc said. His brothers nodded.

"Why would you want to strip it of its religious significance?" Walter asked. "Then it becomes just another spiritually devoid heathen holiday, like Thanksgiving."

"So let the heathens take part in our holiday, Dad," Matt said. "What's the harm? It'll still mean the same to you. Nothing can take that away."

"If anything," I said, "it's a great public relations campaign for Christianity."

"I suppose it could use one these days." Walter sipped his wassail. "Gianna tells me you're Episcopalian."

"Hey, look, there's Sandra in the kitchen!" Marc pulled my arm. "She was my piano teacher. You really should meet her." He dragged me away from his father.

"Thanks for the rescue," I said to Marc, "but I was looking forward to faking it."

"It's hard to fool Dad. He sees right through me, though he doesn't let on. That's one conversation I'm dreading."

"Which one, when you discuss the fact that you're gay, or the fact that you're no longer Catholic?"

"Okay, two conversations," he said. "How'd you know?"

"Because of the way you look at me."

"No, I mean, how did you know I'm no longer Catholic?"

"Like I said . . ."

Marc squinted at me. "You baffle me, Louis. I like that in a man—in a guy, I mean." He winked and punched me in the arm, then glanced behind me and suddenly put on an indignant look. "No, Louis, I will not kiss you! Oh, hi, Gianna."

"Hi, dipshit," she said. "Are you enjoying yourself?" she asked me.

"This is quite a party," I said. She and Marcus laughed.

"Party?" she said. "This is just a gathering. Wait 'til later."

"What's later?"

"Over to my aunt's house for the *vigilia*."

"What's a *vigilia*?" I asked her. "It sounds religious."

"No, it's Italian. My mom's side of the family has one every year. Basically, we eat and drink more. Seven dishes, seven fishes. You've never had calamari like my aunt Loretta's calamari."

"I think I'm beginning to like this holiday."

As far as I could tell, the *vigilia* was nothing more than another Christmas Eve party, with a bit more emphasis on eating over drinking than the O'Keefe "gathering." I felt at ease and chastised myself for being so nervous about the holiday celebration.

My equanimity began to falter, however, when Gianna's

uncle Pasquale, a retired opera singer, got up to sing "Gesu Bambino." I tried to retreat to the kitchen, but Gianna stopped me.

"Lou, you've got to hear this." She dragged me back to the living room. "It's so beautiful, you'll want to run out and get baptized tomorrow morning."

"I seriously doubt that." I stood behind Gianna with my arm around her waist.

Of course it was beautiful. On an aesthetic level, I rejoiced. On a physical level, I was suffocating. A fierce itch tormented my nose. When I started to sniffle, Gianna squeezed my hand, mistaking my allergic reaction for sentimentality.

"So that was pretty moving, huh?" she said after it ended, about five minutes later than I would have liked.

"Yeah, I never knew that song had so many verses," I said.

"Gianna," her mother called, "we'd better leave now if we're going to get a seat at Midnight Mass."

"Okay, Mom, we're coming." She turned to me. "You don't have to come if you don't want to. We can drop you off at the house on the way."

I considered my options. The holy carol had produced only a slight histamine reaction, but one song in a South Philadelphia living room was nothing compared to the waves of holiness I'd receive packed into a cathedral with several hundred ecstatic worshipers. All bets were off as to what shape my head would be in by the end of the service, assuming it even managed to stay on my shoulders.

"I'll go with you to Mass," I heard myself say.

"Oh, thank you, Louis." She wrapped her arms around me. "That means so much to me."

"Yes, I thought it might."

"Will there be incense?" I asked Gianna when we had squeezed ourselves into the pew.

"Yes, why?"

"I'm allergic to incense."

"Why didn't you tell me?"

"It's not a serious allergy—usually. I just wanted you to be prepared in case I need to run out suddenly."

"How do you feel now?" she asked. "I think there's still some incense in the air from the eight o'clock Mass."

"A little stuffy, but not too bad."

I sat at the end of a pew in the middle of the church, with Gianna to my right side. The chapel was grand and intimidating. There were enough statues and frescoes and stained-glass windows to keep the most bored child occupied for an entire Mass. The fourteen stations of the cross were carved in plaster on the walls, seven on each side. I examined each one and became lost in distant bittersweet memories.

"It's beautiful, isn't it?" she said. "The chapel? They just finished renovating it last year. God only knows how many students didn't get scholarships because of the cost of the renovations, but hey, we're reaping the benefits now, right?"

"It's gorgeous." In fact, the high level of ornateness, combined with the fact that the thoughts of the humans around me were preoccupied primarily with Christmas presents, kept the atmosphere's holiness at a subemergency level.

"The music program should be starting soon," she said. "That goes on for about half an hour, then the Mass starts."

"Swell."

"You'll like the music."

A single violin began to sing behind the altar.

"Oh, cool, it's 'Un Flambeau, Jeannette, Isabella,'" Gianna said. "I love that one, and it's so rare to hear it. I hope they sing it in French."

A hammer dulcimer joined the violin. The tune was almost unbearably sweet and pretty. Gianna's face held a look of purest rapture. I gazed at it, bathed in soft white light, until she glanced at me out of the corner of her eye.

"Don't stare at me," she whispered.

"I can't help it. I've never seen anything so beautiful."

She turned to me, her eyes doe-soft, and smiled a serene, Mona Lisa smile. "You know what?"

"What?"

"This is my favorite moment ever, right now." She nodded, then turned her attention back to the music.

As the program continued, the stuffiness in my head worsened a little, then plateaued at a tolerable level. I began to relax again.

Then the nightmare began.

The organ roared to life, and everyone in the congregation stood as one. I joined them, then looked up the aisle with dread as the singing began.

In the steady hands of an altar boy, the cross approached me, triumphant. My lip curled.

I will not look away, I will not look away. I fixed my eyes on the polished wood beams and held in my heat.

"Glooooooria . . ."

Just as the cross passed by, a hand touched my back. I bit back a shriek before realizing it was Gianna.

". . . In excelsis Deo."

At last the endless procession of priests and altar boys reached the front of the church, and the music stopped. My head was already reverberating like a gong.

"Almighty God, you have caused this holy night to shine

with the brightness of the true Light: Grant that we, who have known the mystery of that Light on earth . . ."

"You look a little shaky," Gianna whispered. "Too much incense?"

"When do we get to sit down?"

"Now."

A woman with tiny glasses and a green turtleneck dress stepped to the podium and cleared her throat. "A reading from the Book of Isaiah."

"You didn't tell me there would be Bible stuff," I said to Gianna.

"Shhh." She poked me in the leg. "This is just the beginning."

"The people who walked in darkness have seen a great light; those who dwelt in a land of deep darkness, on them light has shined . . ."

"I sense a theme here," I mumbled. Gianna poked me again, harder.

". . . and his name will be called 'Wonderful Counselor, Mighty God, Everlasting Father, Prince of Peace.' His empire shall be multiplied, and there shall be no end of peace . . ."

There was more singing, and the pain inside my face began to creep around and behind my eye sockets.

An interminable psalm followed:

> . . . For who in the skies can be compared to the Lord,
> who among the heavenly beings is like the Lord,
> a God feared in the council of the holy ones,
> great and terrible above all those round about him . . .

I thought of all the caustic and witty mockery of this ceremony I'd be making if only my sinuses had not compressed my brain to the size of a seedless grape.

More singing ensued (why did all these fucking carols have four verses?), then the priest stepped in front of the altar carrying an enormous book.

"The Gospel of the Lord according to Luke."

Quick, Lucifer. Think unholy thoughts. Think unholy thoughts.

Behind the stifling congestion and shuddering pain that permeated my head lurked another sensation. In this chapel, of all places, I felt . . . safe. This feeling terrified me, and finally drove me to flee.

I indicated my intentions to Gianna, my handkerchief over my face. She nodded and moved to join me.

"No," I whispered. "Stay. I'll be all right."

"Are you sure?"

"Yes. Look, your favorite song's coming up next."

She squeezed my hand. "We won't be long."

I tried to minimize my stagger as I exited the church. A relieved stander took my vacated seat.

It was still raining. I opened my umbrella and stumbled down the marble steps to a bench near the parking lot, in view of the chapel doors. Within moments my breathing eased, and the pain in my temples had subsided enough that I could fully open my eyes.

At least I had avoided the communion issue. I had no idea what might happen were I to partake in this ritual—probably nothing, but I didn't savor the thought of revealing myself to Gianna by having my tongue burst into flames on Christmas Eve.

Yet it had been beautiful—the singing, the statues, the incense, even the prayers. I craved the sight of Gianna's bliss again, and longed to view it with a pair of clear, painless eyes.

The rain pattered on my umbrella and mixed with the faint sound of a thousand voices singing praises, mere echoes of angelic anthems that had once risen from my lips, in what seemed like another lifetime. For the first time since the Fall, I could almost hear one of the old melodies in my head. The notes floated, unjoined, searching for one another in the vast, scorched fields of my consciousness.

Then the rain fell harder and drowned out the hymn within me. I huddled alone on the bench, staring towards the light and warmth like a banished child, and sighed.

I n my dream I relived the previous night with Beelzebub as if I were watching a movie with all the frames out of order. His words trampled over my sleep like a stray dog in a flower garden:

"You are Lucifer, the Prince of Darkness . . ."

"How long has it been since you were touched by an angel?"

". . . Emperor of the Underworld, the second most powerful and single most cool being in the Universe . . ."

"If you want . . . I'll wear the wings."

". . . Author of All Evil, the Adversary, the Arch Fiend . . ."

"No matter what we do, God doesn't care."

". . . You are the Infernal Serpent."

The scene would rewind and fast-forward itself at random, until the entire sequence of events became a causeless, effectless blur.

Until the end, that is.

This time, after rejecting him and hurling him to the floor, as I stared at his face full of fear and surprise, something inside me snapped.

I pounced on him.

With one movement I tore off his shirt. Buttons clattered against the floor and table and walls, and then I was holding him, his body arched against my lips. My tongue and teeth devoured his smooth, hot chest and neck, and finally our mouths crashed together in a brutal kiss.

Fingers tore at each other's skin and clothing. We dragged ourselves to the rug in front of the fireplace. I knelt over him. His hands crawled up my bare thighs, and he peered up at me in triumph.

His mouth was hot and wet and precise, and unendurable. I pushed him away and pinned him flat to the floor with my body.

"No," I said. "Not like men, this time. Like demons."

The edges of his mouth quivered. "Are you sure?"

"Yes."

Our core temperatures soared to levels that would have killed a human being. While our hands and mouths stroked and searched, our flesh began to bubble and melt until we dissolved into one pulsing, radiating liquid body.

The walls shook with our screams. The sensations came not in waves but in one excruciating escalation of delirium. When my eyes were open, I could glimpse a strand of his hair or a corner of his face, but nothing more. The boundaries between us could no longer be seen or felt.

The heat continued to rise, and we writhed together, burning like the molten pits into which we had been flung as children. We consumed each other in a furious union of fire and flesh, until the last blaze nearly annihilated our bodies and minds.

Finally the heat subsided, and we had to separate before we cooled or risk tearing flesh from each other's bodies. But we clung together, gasping for breath and searching for strength. When we finally wrenched ourselves apart, the searing pain and cold made us wail. I collapsed onto the floor next to him and saw that the rug was scorched with the outline of our united body.

I woke, shaking and weeping, on Christmas morning.

24

Mihi Quoque Spem Didisti

"Are you feeling better today?"

I looked at Gianna over my steaming cup of coffee. My hands shook.

"Somewhat," I said. "In a way."

"I think Santa Claus came while you were sleeping."

He's not the only one, I thought, then ducked back into my coffee. "Really?" I said. "How can you tell?"

"Take a look under the tree."

I followed her into the living room. "Holy shit," I said.

Presents not only sat under the tree, but extended out from its base at least four feet in every direction, piled as high as Gianna's waist.

"Every year my dad says, 'I'm warning you kids, this is going to be a lean Christmas,' and every year it gets worse. More stuff. Part of the extreme display is due to the fact that my mom wraps every piece of every gift separately, numbered in descending order of importance, so that it might take you all morning to figure out what the hell they've given you. But that's part of the fun. You'll see."

To detail everyone's gifts to everyone else would require a three-dimensional, color-coded scorecard with blinking arrows and a live professional commentator. Gianna gave me an exquisite dark brown leather jacket (she said she was curious to see what I looked like in something other than black) and a framed photograph of us at the Grand Canyon. In the picture, taken by a passing tourist, we gazed into each other's eyes while the hungry raven perched in the background, slightly out of focus. The family oohed and aahed over the gifts I presented to her, especially the blue dress I'd bought in the boutique with the nosy, helpful lady in line behind me.

Finally, I handed her a small flat box. "This isn't as impressive as the other gifts, but I think you'll like it."

She took off the ribbon, opened the box, and began to cry.

"Gianna, what is it?" Rosa leaned forward.

"Show us, show us," Donna and Dara chimed.

"None of my presents ever made you cry," Marc said.

"That's not true, Marc," Luke said. "Remember when she turned four and you wrapped up a live cockroach?"

Gianna lifted the silver cross out of its box and looked at me as if we were the only two people in the room.

"I know how much this means," she said, "coming from you."

"No, Gianna. You have no idea."

She dropped the box on the floor and embraced me. "I love you so much."

I slowly closed my arms around her. The rest of the room was silent for a full five seconds.

"Will someone please roll the credits now so we can eat?" Marc said.

Amidst the laughter, the gift-giving party broke up in favor of a cleanup party to make way for the dinner-fixing party, which was, of course, to prepare for the Christmas dinner party itself. Each of us grabbed a separate box and poured the many components of his or her gifts inside, to be sorted out and pieced together later, perhaps in June.

Uninvited to the dinner-fixing party, Gianna and I sat on the living room couch while Marc and Walter watched the football pre-game broadcast. She fastened her pendant around her neck and admired it cross-eyed.

"I'll never take it off," she said. "I'll be like those really tough Irish Catholic boys who pray to the Holy Mother before their boxing matches. They always wear those little crosses, and you just know they wear them in the shower and in bed—"

"You're kidding, right?" I said.

"About me, yes. I'd probably strangle myself if I slept in it, and that would be a tragedy on so many levels."

The doorbell rang.

"Get the door, Gianna," Marc said.

"You get it. You're closer."

Marc got up from the floor and dashed to the other side of the room. "Not anymore."

"Oh, for God's sake," Gianna's father said, "you're turning into little brats again. No toys for you next year." He pushed past Bobo, who was leaping at the door and growling. "Hush, Bobo, you silly mutt. What's the—" He opened the door. "Oh. Well . . . Merry Christmas, Adam."

"Aw, fuck me with a kazoo," Gianna said under her breath.

Marc leaned over her shoulder. "You want I should break his legs for my baby sister?"

"I don't think so," she said.

"Seriously, I'll ask him to leave if you want."

"No, I need to handle this one on my own." She squeezed my hand. "I'm sorry, Louis. Just let me get this over with." We all stood, and Gianna moved forward towards Adam, who was entering the living room despite the best efforts of Bobo.

"Uh . . . Gianna honey, Adam's here to see you." Walter moved out of the way for a tall man with putty-colored hair and thin-framed glasses, a man who looked at Gianna as if she were the last step of a thousand-mile journey. It was the man I'd seen her with outside the House Office Building the day of her testimony.

"Hi, Gianna," Adam said. "Merry Christmas." His voice was gentle and more than a bit tremulous.

"Merry Christmas, Adam." Gianna wore a tight smile. She folded her arms across her chest.

"You're looking well."

"Thank you."

Adam cleared his throat. "Yeah, so I was talking to your dad last week, and he said you'd be here for Christmas."

Gianna gestured to her surroundings. "And I am."

"So I was in the neighborhood, and I thought I'd—" His gaze tripped past her and fixed on me. "You must be . . ."

"Adam, this is Louis Carvalho," Gianna said. "Louis, Adam Crawford."

We shook hands, and I could feel his heart wither.

"Good to meet you," he said. "Carvalho. Is that Italian or Spanish?"

"Portuguese, actually."

"Really?" Gianna said. "That's interesting. I always assumed it was Spanish."

"People make that mistake a lot," I said.

"Right. Yeah, I'm sure it's an easy mistake."

The three of us stood there, nodding and how-'bout-that-ing, until Marcus broke the strained politesse by putting his arm around Adam's shoulder.

"So, Adam," he said, "how ya been? Life treating you okay?"

"Yeah. Fine, thanks." Adam's blush deepened, and he moved away from Marc under the pretense of petting Bobo. He stretched out his hand to the dog, who almost bit it off.

"Bobo!" Walter grabbed the dog's collar. "I'm sorry, Adam, let me get him out of here. I don't know what's come over him."

"Bobo, I thought we were buddies." Adam watched the dog and Walter disappear into the basement.

"I guess he's found a new buddy . . . buddy," Marc said.

"I guess." Adam turned back to Gianna. "Anyway, so, I was . . . uh . . ."

"In the neighborhood," Marc said.

"Right."

"This neighborhood, thirty miles from your home."

"Right."

"And you thought you'd stop in and . . . what?"

"Oh, I wanted to drop off some gifts." Adam held up a red shopping bag. "Ho ho ho and all that."

"Gifts?" Gianna said.

"Yes, I brought something for your mom and dad," Adam pulled a large flat gift-wrapped box out of the bag and placed it on the coffee table, "and something for you." He held out a tiny box towards Gianna. She made no move to take the gift.

"Adam, we need to talk," she said.

Marcus and I went into the dining room on cue.

"Geez, Lou, sorry about that," he said. "I had no idea he'd show up on Christmas Day. He's got some sizable *cojones*, I'll say that much."

Walter entered from the basement. "Poor guy. I hope she sets him straight once and for all."

Gianna and Adam passed by the dining room door on their way to the study.

"Hey," Marc said. "Wanna go listen to her break his heart?"

"Marcus, have a little mercy." Walter sat at the table. "It's bad enough he's got to be rejected without you selling front row seats."

The voices from the study suddenly rose in volume, and the three of us fell silent.

"Why, Gianna, why? I still don't understand why you want to throw away nine years. We worked hard on our relationship."

"I know, I know, but I got tired of doing nothing but work," she said. "It just wasn't fun anymore."

"Fun? Is that what you're having now? Fun?"

"Technically, we're not eavesdropping," Marc said. "We're just having a conversational lull, and they—"

"Shhh." I held up my hand. "I'm eavesdropping."

"Is that his Mercedes out there?" Adam was saying. "Is that why you're with him? For his money?"

"You know me better than that, Adam. I love Louis in spite of his money, not because of it."

There was a short silence, then Adam's desperate voice rose again. "You love him? You love this guy, after what, six weeks you've been seeing him?"

"Yes."

"How can that be love? That's not love. Love is fighting the same battles together and nursing each other's scars. Love is picking up each other's socks off the living room floor and not complaining. Does he pick up your socks, Gianna?"

"He doesn't have to! I pick them up myself, the way I do everything else since I left you. I don't need you or my brothers or anyone else looking after me, okay?"

Their voices lowered again, and Marcus and I pressed forward near the study door to hear their conversation.

"I don't want to hurt you, Adam."

"Gianna, I just want you to be happy."

"I am happy. You want me to be happy with you, and I can't be."

"But—"

"I don't love you anymore," she said.

Those words carried by her voice turned my blood to ice. I suddenly felt like a voyeur to my own future. I moved back into the dining room. Marcus followed me and laid a hand on my arm.

"That's not you in there, Lou, remember," he said. "She loves you, in a way I've never seen her love anyone."

The study door swung open. Marc, Walter, and I grabbed silverware and pretended to be preoccupied with setting the table. When Adam passed the dining room doorway, he stopped. He fixed his slate blue eyes on me. The light in them was dim now, like a half-buried ember.

"If you ever hurt her, Louis, if one tear ever falls from those eyes because of something you said or did, I swear to God I'll destroy you." Adam swept out the front door without looking back.

I went into the study. Gianna was on the couch, her face in her hands. I sat next to her.

"I'm sorry," she said. "I'm sorry you had to see that."

I hooked a finger underneath one of her arms. She leaned against me and began to weep. I pulled her close to me and felt for the first time the ultimate transience of mortal emotion.

"I love you, Louis. I know you look at Adam, and you wonder if that will be you someday, and I can't promise that this will never happen to us. But you feel right in a way Adam never did."

"And he probably felt right in a way I never will," I said.

She sighed. "I hate it when you're wiser than I am."

"It's not just fools who fall in love, you know. The fools are just the ones who believe that love lasts forever."

I kissed her and knew that anything less than forever with her would be a tragic joke.

Christmas dinner provided a new flood of relatives, food, and spirits. I hadn't experienced this much revelry outside of Hell since the days of the pagan feasts.

Gianna's cousin Kathleen, a gorgeous young woman with cascades of strawberry blond hair, watched me for most of the meal. At one point, a crimson drop of lamb juice oozed onto the corner of her mouth, and she fixed her eyes on me while she curled it back in with her tongue. I sensed Gianna was watching my reaction to this display, so I kept my face impassive, though a howl of lust echoed inside my brain.

Meanwhile, Gianna's grandmother, Serafina, had been chattering like an insulted mockingbird.

"So Friday I went to Thelma's house, and you should see her great-grandson. He's riding a bike, and he's only four years old, no training wheels. And her grandson's wife is pregnant again. I tell you, I could sit and watch little children all day." She peered around the table.

Gianna held up a plate of something turkey-shaped. "Lou, want some faux turkey? Donna made it."

"Sure, I'll try anything." I took a small helping and tried a piece. "Not bad. What's it made of?"

"Seitan," Donna said.

"Satan?!" Serafina said. "It's made from Satan?!" Her shriek rasped my vertebrae against my spinal column.

"No, Grandmom, seitan," Matthew said. "It's—"

"Wheat gluten," Luke said. "Kinda like—"

"Flour. You knead it and simmer it for a couple of hours, then it gets—"

"Chewy, like meat. Try some."

"Oh, no," Serafina said. "I don't want to eat anything to do with the Devil. You know, my neighbor told me she has demons in her garage."

"Demons in her garage?" Rosa said. "What makes her think that?"

"The door keeps going up and down all day and all night, halfway up, halfway down."

"Ludicrous," Walter said. "The automatic door opener probably just short-circuited."

"Just the same," she looked over her tiny glasses at her mashed potatoes, "I'm glad I don't have a garage."

Marc nudged my elbow and pointed at the seitan. "Hard to believe it never walked and squawked, huh?"

"All the food is wonderful." Rosa nodded to her husband. "Walter, your gravy is delicious as always."

"Thanks, honey."

"It's a perfect dinner," Rosa said. We all nodded in silent agreement.

"Except there aren't any children." Serafina sighed.

"We're the children, Grandmom," Marc said.

"No, I mean little ones. When are you all going to have babies?"

"Mom, don't start," Rosa said.

"I don't understand any of it." Serafina gestured to the twins. "You four spend all your time taking care of animals nobody wants," she pointed to Gianna, "you never married that nice man who would have made a wonderful father, and now you're hooked up with some young playboy who can't possibly be serious about you—"

"Hey," I said, but Gianna squeezed my knee to silence me.

"And you," Serafina said to Marcus, "what's your excuse? You're better-looking than the rest of them put together, so why aren't you married? How come you never bring home any of your girlfriends?"

Rosa set her wine glass on the table. "Mom—"

"I don't have a girlfriend at the moment, Grandmom." Marc shifted in his chair.

"You're almost forty now, Marcus, it's time for you to get serious about women."

"Mom, stop—"

"My friend Edna has a granddaughter, about thirty years old. You should meet her, maybe go out for coffee or lunch or—"

"Mom, for God's sake, can't you see the boy's gay!?"

The word and Rosa's shrill voice hung in the silent, stuffing-scented air. Everyone had stopped in mid-chew and seemed to be trying to find an inconspicuous way to swallow.

"Gay?" Serafina whispered. "You mean . . . how do you know?"

"Isn't it obvious?" Rosa said.

"He's not gay, he's just . . . artistic." Serafina's hand flitted over her pearl necklace. "Marc, tell your mom it's not true."

Marc looked at his mother, then his father, then at the pseudo-turkey. "It's true."

Serafina stared at him, emitted a short peep, then began to cry.

"Aw, for the love of Christ, Rosa," Walter said, "why'd you have to go and do that?"

"I couldn't bear it anymore, this charade." She gestured to Marc, who was still staring at the turkey. "Walter, how long were we supposed to pretend we didn't know?"

"This is how you broach the subject?" he said to his wife. "Do you feel better now? Your mother's hysterical, your son's catatonic, and everyone else here suddenly wishes they were on Jupiter."

I had to admit, the gravity in the dining room had increased to at least half that of the giant gas planet. Gianna looked frightened.

"Grandmom, it's okay," she said. "It's nothing to cry about."

Her grandmother continued to bawl. Rosa put her hand to her mouth and rushed out of the room. I had a mad desire to stand up and shout, "He may be gay, but I'm the Devil!" at the top of my lungs.

Matthew put his hand on his grandmother's shoulder. "Can I get you anything?"

"Just take me home now," she said.

"No, please stay," Luke said.

"I think Christmas dinner is dead, at least in spirit." Walter tossed his napkin onto the table. "I'll take her home." He helped his mother-in-law out of her chair and led her to the door, where he turned and looked at Marc. "I'm sorry, son. This wasn't the way I wanted it to be."

The rest of us sat in silence until the front door shut, then Kathleen said, "You okay, Marc?"

He blinked a couple of times, then said, "I can't believe my mom just outed me over Christmas dinner."

We all pondered this reality for a few moments. I was the first to laugh. Soon the rest of the table joined me in savoring the melodramatic absurdity.

"That's one for the therapist's sofa," Gianna said.

Matthew ran his hand through his thinning brown hair. "Holy—"

"—shit," Luke said.

Matt looked at him. "Actually, I was going to say 'Holy mother of God.'"

"Really?" Luke said. "How 'bout that?"

"It must be a new era," I said.

Gianna dabbed mock tears from her eyes. "You're all growing up so big. I'm so proud of my babies."

"Shut up, Mom," Marc said.

"Does this mean you're going to stop flirting with me?" Kathleen asked him.

"It means I'll be flirting with you even more, cousin." He blew a lascivious kiss in her direction.

"I'm glad you all think this is so funny."

We turned to see Rosa in the doorway.

"Your poor grandmother is probably having a heart attack right now," she said, "and it's mostly my fault."

"Aw, Mom, look at it this way," Marc said, "if she keels over from this, that's one fewer Christmas gift we'll each have to buy next year."

Rosa hurled a small kumquat at her son's head. It bounced off his temple into the sweet potatoes.

"Ow! Come on, Mom . . ." He held out his hands to her.

"Kathleen, let's clear the table for dessert," Gianna said.

"But I'm not finished dinner," I said. She poked me in the arm. "Oh, right."

Between the seven of us, we cleared all the plates in one trip, leaving Marcus and his mother alone in the dining room.

"I can see why you like Christmas," I said to Gianna in the kitchen. "It's very entertaining."

T hat night I lay naked in my tiny temporary bed, staring at the doorknob. After two hours, it turned, and Gianna entered. She removed her nightgown, slid under the blankets next to me and kissed me long and deep. "Hi."

"What took you so long?"

"I had to wait until the house was totally quiet."

"And is it?"

"Yes, and it has to stay that way. Look, this bed is incredibly creaky, and there's a guest room right below us."

I pulled her on top of me. "We won't make a sound."

We didn't, almost. Gianna let out a little gasp at first, then bit her lip. Barely moving, we slowly brought each other to orgasm, the torture of silent ecstasy allowing us no release but locked gazes and pulled hair.

When it was over, Gianna rested her forehead on my chest. The cross around her neck fell between my ribs. I pulled the icon out where I could see it.

"Gianna?" I whispered.

"Mmm?"

"Why did you love Adam?"

She lifted her head to gape at me. "What?"

"He's so unlike me. How could you love us both in the same lifetime?"

"What do you want me to say? That I was a different person then?"

"No, I want to know the truth. I'm curious."

"He was . . ." She shook her head. "I'm not comfortable discussing this while naked. Let's go down to the kitchen where we won't have to whisper."

We got dressed and went downstairs. Gianna filled a kettle with water and set it on the stove.

"Do you want some tea?" she asked. "My throat's kind of scratchy."

"No, thanks. Are you sick?"

"No, it's probably from all the talking and laughing." She turned to me. "He was my comrade."

"Who?"

"Adam. We fought our crusade together, we had the same values, the same goals. We were united in our struggle against people like you."

"Am I going to wish I hadn't asked?"

"We were each other's heroes." She reached in a cupboard

for a mug. "Ultimately, of course, it wasn't enough for me. When I left him earlier this year to move to Washington, it was like abandoning half of what I believed in."

"Why?"

"I'm a player now, just like you. I work within the system, while Adam actually deals with the people we're trying to help. Every day he sees their misery and despair, and somehow he still believes that things can get better."

"So do you. That's one reason why I love you."

She frowned. "You don't think I'm naive? You don't laugh at my delusions behind my back?"

"No, only to your face."

"How honorable."

The kettle began to whistle softly, and Gianna grabbed it. She poured the boiling water over the teabag in her cup.

"There's something else," I said. "Marc told me a few things."

"About what?"

"About Adam."

Gianna scoffed and set the kettle down on a cold burner with a slight bang. "Marc's just being overprotective, like always. I wish he'd let me grow up."

"Has Adam sent you flowers and gifts?"

"Did you ever hear the saying, 'When all you have is a hammer, everything looks like a nail'? Marc's hammer is domestic violence, so he sees abuse wherever he looks. Even in Adam, who is one of the kindest—"

"You didn't answer my question."

"Yes, he sent me flowers and gifts."

"And?"

"And I sent them back."

"Did you ask him to stop?"

"Yes, I asked him to stop, and he stopped. Today was the last time I'll ever see him. He's finally accepted that it's over between us."

"I hope you're right."

"Trust me." Gianna came to me and wrapped her arms around my waist. "Please."

I kissed her warm forehead. "I do trust you. It's the rest of the world I don't trust."

Later, as she left me outside my bedroom, I said to her, "Maybe next year you can stay here all night."

"Yeah, right. That'll never happen in this house, not unless we were—"

Her eyes widened. I didn't blink. She stared at me for a moment, then shook her head. "Good night, Lou."

I slipped into bed and watched the snow skitter across the windowpane. A bizarre thought entered my mind and would not be banished, and I had to struggle not to erupt in gales of laughter. A squeaky, Mickey Mouse voice inside my head declared that this had been "the very best Christmas ever."

25

Quem Patronum Rogaturus

I awoke late the next morning, nine-thirty by the clock on the nightstand.

After showering and dressing, I went downstairs to find Gianna's mother sitting at the kitchen table drinking coffee and reading the newspaper.

"Good morning, Lou. I'm glad someone's finally up. I was starting to wonder if everyone had left in the middle of the night."

"I'm not usually such a sloth. I must have been really tired."

"You must have been." She looked at me directly, her playful smirk informing me that she was aware of Gianna's late-night visit to my room. "I'm glad we have a chance to talk. I wanted to apologize for Adam's appearance yesterday."

"It's not your fault." I poured myself a cup of coffee.

"He's been around a lot in the last six months, ever since Gianna left. He and Walter will sit and watch football together, and I end up inviting him to dinner because I don't know how to send him away. Adam's a good man, but . . ."

"I don't hold it against him," I said. "If anything, I feel sorry for the guy. If Gianna left me, I'd—"

"You'd what?"

I tried to think of something to say that would sound romantic but not psychotic. The last thing this family needed was another loser stalking their daughter.

"I'd be crushed."

"Lou, you seem to be just what she needs right now. You're strong, but not domineering, and you obviously adore her, but not in that needy, clingy way." She placed her coffee cup on the table and adjusted her glasses. "Of course, I worry, naturally, about the age difference and whether . . . I mean, Gianna's thirty-five years old—you knew that, right?" I nodded. "Okay, good. So of course I worry about her future."

"You hear her biological clock ticking, and you're worried that I'm too young to do anything but hit the snooze alarm."

"That's what I like about you, Lou. You cut through the bullshit so gracefully." She looked at her watch. "It's not like Gianna to sleep this late. I'll go check on her. I know you two need to be on your way."

"Thanks."

As Gianna's mother exited the kitchen, Bobo entered. He sat next to my chair and fixed his eyes on my face. I tried to ignore him, but he shuffled around so as to stay within my line of sight. Whenever I looked directly at him, his tail wagged softly two or three times, then stilled.

"Stop that," I said. Bobo turned in a circle once, then lay across the kitchen threshold and stared at me.

"Bad news." Gianna's mother stepped over the dog into the kitchen. "Gianna seems to have the flu."

"The flu? I'd better go see her."

"She doesn't want you to come up there, because she says she looks ugly. Which she does, but I think you should go, anyway."

Bobo stepped aside like a sentry and followed me up the stairs to Gianna's room. I knocked on her door.

"Gianna, it's me."

"Don't come in."

I opened the door and entered. On her bed was a human-sized lump entirely covered by a sheet. The blankets were in a heap on the floor.

"Are you deaf?" Gianna said from under the sheet. "I told you not to come in."

"Why shouldn't I?"

"Maybe because I asked you."

"Oh." I sat on the bed next to her. "Well, I'm here now, so you might as well talk to me."

"I'm miserable."

"I'm sorry."

"It's not your fault," she said. "Probably caught it from Ellen. I hate her now."

I reached for the edge of the sheet and tried to pull it back.

"No!" she croaked. "Don't look at me like this."

"You can't stay under there forever." I gave the sheet another gentle tug. "And in your weakened condition, you aren't up to fighting me."

"Okay, but don't say I didn't warn you." She pushed the sheet off her face, which was puffy and covered in sweat.

"Aaaaaaagggh!" I covered my face. "My eyes! My eyes!"

"Jerk."

"Wait, it's okay. I can work around this." I reached in my shirt pocket for my sunglasses and put them on. "There, that's better." Gianna covered her face with the sheet again. "Hey, I'm just kidding. You're getting to be as vain as I am."

"It's different for you," she said. "You're gorgeous."

"True, but look at it this way—you still have your inner beauty."

"When I get better, I'm going to punch you in the stomach."

"Okay. So when do you think you'll be ready to leave?"

"Lou, I can't even turn over in bed without feeling sick."

"It's that bad?"

"Haven't you ever had the flu before?"

"No, actually."

"That's right, I forgot you were an alien," she said. "Getting the flu is like being body-slammed by a huge invisible flaming mucus monster."

"Now that I've experienced, so I can understand."

"Good. Then go away."

"Gianna, wouldn't you rather suffer in your own bed? Come on, I'll get you home, and I'll . . . take care of you, you know, bring you stuff."

She was silent for a moment, then said, "I want my mommy."

"Fine." I stood to leave.

"No, wait." Gianna sighed and stretched a limp hand towards me. "We should go home. Help."

I took her hand. It was burning hot, and it filled me with a sudden surge of lust. I put my arms around her feverish body and helped her to her feet. She clutched my arm and stood swaying for a moment, her eyelids fluttering. My passion faded into a sensation I'd never felt before.

"Ohhh, I feel like shit, shit, shit," she said. "Make it go away."

I put my arm around her and imagined the virus inside of her, intending to burn it out. But it had taken hold of her entire head and throat and chest. There was no way to destroy it without hurting her. I had no healing powers—and until that moment had never wanted them.

"I need to wash my face," she said. I helped her to the bathroom, where she pulled her hair back with a headband and examined herself in the mirror. "Jesus God, look at me. I mean, don't look at me." Gianna put her hand out to my face. "Go away."

I placed a soft kiss on her burning temple. "You look fine," I said to her reflection.

"You're lying."

"I love you."

She looked at me in the mirror for a few moments, then began to sob.

"I'll go get Marc," I said, "and we'll leave as soon as you're ready."

"So, Lou, what did you think of your first real Christmas?" Marc asked me in the car.

"Not bad," I said. "From what I can tell, Christmas is mainly about eating and drinking and arguing."

"You bissed da poid of id." Gianna sniffled.

"The bore you talk, Giadda," Marc said, mocking her stuffy nose, "the bore we'll bake fudda you." He flailed his arms. "Hep be, I deed a decondethdud."

"Shuddup." She pointed at me. "Dode you dare laugh ad be." I smirked. "Dode smirg eeder," she said. Marc and I wailed with glee. "I hade you guys."

When we got to Gianna's apartment, I helped her up the stairs and into bed. By the time I'd brought her presents in from the car, she had tossed all the sheets onto the floor and lay whimpering on her sweat-soaked bed.

"I need to take a shower," she said. "Help me up."

I helped her drag herself to the bathroom, where she shut the door without a word. In a moment the water began to spray, and the shower door slid open and closed.

"Ow! Ohhhh, shit." The water turned off. I stood outside the bathroom door.

"Gianna, are you okay?"

"No," she sobbed. I opened the door. She stood inside the shower, huddled in a bath towel. Part of her hair was dripping wet and pasted to her face.

"What's wrong?" I said.

"It hurts. The water from the shower hurts my skin. That's how achy I am. Pathetic, huh?"

"Gianna . . ." I moved to help her.

"No, don't touch me. It hurts. Everything hurts. But I want so much to be clean, Lou." Her bloodshot eyes pleaded with me.

"Why don't you try a sponge bath?" I pulled a wash cloth from her towel rack and handed it to her.

"But what about my hair? That's the worst part."

"You could wash it in the sink . . . or I could wash it for you."

"You'd really do that for me?"

"Sure. Yes. I would. I would do that."

"Wow. Um, okay. Let me do this first."

"Just come out when you're finished." I stepped out of the bathroom and closed the door. The impulse to leave her apartment and never come back swept over me, and then it was gone, as if a ghost of my former self had passed through my body on its way to oblivion.

I found a plastic basin and a small pitcher under the kitchen sink and filled them both with hot water. I moved her gifts off the couch to make room for her to lie down. As I set the large red department store shopping bag in the corner, I noticed the horn-blowing angel printed in gold on the side of the bag. I smirked, wondering how Michael tolerated these watered-down images of him and his colleagues.

Then my stomach went cold. Michael . . . What were his words? *"Don't assume Gianna will be as lucky as Doctor Faustus was."* I turned my head towards the sound of Gianna's whimpers.

"You bastard . . . don't you dare."

The bathroom door opened. Gianna appeared with a towel around her neck and a bottle of shampoo in her hand.

"What are you doing?" she said.

I covered my paranoia with a smile. "I thought it might be more comfortable for you just to lie back on the couch and stick your head over this," I pointed to the basin, "rather than standing over the sink. You could put the pillow under your neck."

She didn't speak, only nodded and settled herself on the couch. Her limp black hair was matted and oily. I dampened it, then worked the shampoo into her scalp.

"How's that?"

"Nice, real nice." Her voice was raw and hoarse.

"Tell me, is it normal to be this sick with the flu?"

"I hear it's a nasty virus this year. Ellen was miserable from it. Maybe not this bad, though."

"So you think you caught it from her?"

"Probably. The night you were hanging out with your brother I brought her some chicken soup and Popsicles." Gianna frowned. "Maybe I should've worn a big plastic bubble to keep out the germs. But I could've caught it on the Metro or at work, or anywhere."

"So it's very contagious."

"Yeah. Why? Are you afraid you'll catch it?"

"No—I mean, yeah, a little worried. If I were sick I wouldn't be able to take care of you."

"Then we'd just take care of each other." I began to rinse her hair. She sighed. "Lou, you're so good to me."

I almost dropped the pitcher on her head. "What did you say?"

Gianna opened her eyes, bright with fever, and looked up at me. "I said you're so good to me."

I stepped back, stunned. That word had never been ascribed to me before. I'd been called a good dancer, good chess player, good nuclear strategist, sure, but never simply . . . good.

She closed her eyes again. "I don't think I ever really believed you before when you said you loved me. Now I believe you."

I rinsed her hair, dried it, then changed her sheets and tucked her into bed. Gianna accepted my kindness without embarrassment.

"Feeling better?" I asked as she settled her head into the pillow.

"Much. If only I weren't incredibly sick, I'd feel great." She stretched out her hand to grasp mine. "Thank you."

"Can I get you anything else?"

"Mmm-hmm. Please bring me . . ." she yawned ". . . everything."

"For instance?"

"Medicine. Something so strong it's barely legal to be sold over-the-counter."

"Okay." I picked up my coat.

"And some tea. Chamomile. And honey and lemon."

"Right."

"Tissues, too. A couple boxes. Soft ones."

"Got it."

"And throat lozenges," she said. "The sugar-free kind so I can eat them after I brush my teeth at night."

"Do you want to write this down for me?"

"No, thanks." She fell asleep.

When I arrived at the drugstore, Beelzebub was coming out.

"If it isn't Santa Claus himself," he said. "Did you have a merry Christmas?"

"It was interesting."

He followed me back into the store. "We had a blast in Vegas. You wouldn't believe how many little kids are there now that they're trying to turn it into a family vacation destination. Nothing like playing with the minds of little people who still believe in the Bogeyman. It wasn't the same, though, without you there."

"I'm sure." I found the cold medicine aisle.

"What are you doing here, anyway?"

"Getting something for Gianna."

"Yoko's got you running errands for her now?"

"She's very sick," I said.

"You seem a little freaked out, bro."

"'Freaked out' doesn't begin to describe it." I turned to him. "I see her suffering, and there's nothing I can do about it, nothing at all. We can't heal, we can only hurt. We can't create, we can only destroy. Doesn't that ever bother you?"

"No. Besides, it's just the flu."

"Today it's just the flu. But what happens someday when it's cancer or congestive heart disease or some virus they haven't even discovered yet?"

"She's young," Beelzebub said.

"She won't always be young."

"So what are you saying? That you're gonna stick it out with her until she dies?"

"I don't know," I said. "Why not? Her life is just half a breath compared to mine. It's hardly any time at all."

"I suppose." He twirled his bag around his finger. "Hey, if she had a tumor, you could destroy that."

"I've thought of that. But if I did, I'd destroy her in the process. I'd be worth no more than chemotherapy or radiation."

"I don't know, Lou, but death and disease sound like two good reasons not to get mixed up with mortals for more than one night."

An old man shambled into the aisle. Beelzebub moved a few feet away from me. The man searched the cough syrup shelf, picking up one bottle after another and reading it.

"Anyway, you seem to be doing all you can for her." Beelzebub gestured to the shelf in front of me.

"No more than anyone else could. Even less, actually." I opened my arms to the shelves. "There must be three hundred different cold medicines here. How is anyone supposed to know which one to take?"

"I don't know." Beelzebub scratched his head, then pointed to a blue box in front of me. "That one has a pretty cool commercial."

"Yeah." I picked it up and examined it. "But it says non-drowsy formula. Shouldn't she be getting lots of sleep?"

"But you don't want her to conk out while you're having sex."

The old man looked over at us.

"That's not an issue," I whispered to Beelzebub. "That's how bad she feels."

"Whoa. Then you definitely want the medicine that'll put her to sleep."

The old man chose a cough syrup and left the aisle shaking his head.

"I think I'll just get one of each color and let her decide," I said. "So what are you here for?"

Beelzebub held up his bag. "Condoms."

"You, buying condoms? I thought you swore you'd never do that."

"Yeah, well, humans these days, they insist. And rape isn't as much fun as it used to be."

I dropped three of the cold medicine boxes. "Look, I have

to make a couple of other stops before I go back to Gianna's, so I'll see you later, okay?" I walked toward the cash register.

"Okay. Hey, what are you doing New Year's Eve?"

"Take a wild guess."

"Right." He stuffed his bag in his jacket pocket. "I guess I'll see you around, then."

I didn't look at him. "Yes, you will."

Gianna's fever burned through the night, and my lack of need for sleep came in handy. Twice I changed her damp sheets and pillowcases for fresh, cool ones.

At 4 A.M. she awoke from another fifteen-minute bout of fitful sleep and said, "Is there anything on TV?"

"I checked already," I said to her from the couch. "Four different shades of snow and an infomercial on a new peat moss."

"I can't sleep. I need a distraction."

"Wanna have sex?"

"No," she said. "Read me something. What are you reading over there?"

"The new Ronald Reagan biography."

"Oh, Lou, that thing's just a Republican PR campaign. Reagan's not even dead yet."

"I guess they figure he's not going to do anything else memorable," I said. "Get it? Memorable?"

"You're sick, and I love you."

"You sure you don't want to have sex? You wouldn't have to do anything. I'm very self-sufficient."

"If you're so self-sufficient, then why don't you just jerk off?"

"Not in front of Reagan."

"Ow, don't make me laugh," she said. "It hurts to laugh."

"Should I make you cry?"

Gianna giggled. "Tell me a story."

"What kind of story?"

"Any kind. But not a funny one, remember."

"Okay." I dragged a chair next to her bed and sat in it. "It was a dark and stormy night . . ."

"Oh, please."

"Wait, this is going somewhere. See, the dark and stormy night is a metaphor for, uh, the psyche of our story's hero. Yeah, that's it."

"Go on."

"It was a dark and stormy night, inside the psyche of our story's hero. For he was a monster, cursed to be alone and miserable throughout his existence."

"Who cursed him?" she said.

"A sadistic, omnipotent wizard. No more interruptions, please."

"Sorry."

"No one knows why he was cursed. Perhaps it was all a big misunderstanding, but the fact was, he was cursed. He lived alone in a fabulously furnished tower, cursed and miserable, miserable and cursed, with nothing but his misery and his curse to keep him company—that and a talking iguana, but then the iguana died."

Gianna batted me with a limp hand. "No funny stuff."

"It's not funny. He really liked that iguana. Anyway, our hero missed his pre-curse days, because he wasn't always a monster. He was once a glorious prince, beautiful in both body and spirit, but his beauty had disappeared. However, somewhere it was written, although the monster didn't know about it—it was probably a footnote in the sadistic wizard's curse book—that the only way to break this curse was if a beautiful and intelligent woman would come to love him."

"This sounds an awful lot like 'Beauty and the Beast,'" she said. "And how come dumb ugly women don't count?"

"Hey, at four in the morning, don't expect originality or political correctness. So the monster meets hundreds of beautiful, intelligent women, and has some brilliant times, but none of them love him, because he's a monster, remember, and besides they don't get much of a chance to love him, because they never see him again.

"But one night he meets the smartest, most beautiful woman in the whole world, and she sees through all his monster bullshit and somehow figures out that there's a prince hiding underneath." I touched my fingertips to Gianna's. "And the marvelous thing is, she loves both the prince and the monster, so he gets to be something in between."

"And they live happily ever after?"

"Yeah. At least until they get run over by a big yellow steamroller."

26

Dies Irae

Gianna's flu receded over the next few days, and by New
Year's Eve she was able to walk without tottering. We returned
to my apartment to get ready for our all-night revelry at the
finest hotel in Washington, D.C.

As we passed through my living room, I stole a quick
glance at the rug in front of the fireplace—no scorch marks.

"I have an idea." I unbuttoned her blouse. "To save time,
let's shower together."

"Save time, right." She nudged my hands away. "We're running late as it is."

"Gianna, it's been almost a week."

"Then a few more hours of celibacy won't kill us. I don't
want to get tired before our evening even starts. I'd like to be
conscious at least through the end of the year." She hung the
dress I gave her on the back of the bedroom door. "Speaking of
which, do you have any New Year's resolutions?"

"I'm going to get a new tuxedo," I said from the closet.

"That's not very ambitious."

"I don't want to put too much pressure on myself."

"I'm going to run for office," she said.

I backed out of the forest of clothes. "What?"

"I said I'm going to run for office. I'm tired of kissing politicians' asses, throwing myself on their mercy to get changes made. They're not any better or smarter than I am, so why shouldn't I take their jobs?"

"Gianna, that's fantastic." I embraced her. "What brought you to this decision?"

"You."

"Me?"

"Indirectly, yes," she said. "Louis, since I met you, I've cared more about life, more about what I believe in, than I ever did before, even though you don't believe in the same things."

"I believe in you."

"Exactly. It brings it back to me, to what I can do, the changes I can make."

"You can, and you will." I clutched her hand. "Gianna, you are so much stronger than you realize. Your power is incomprehensibly huge. Don't ask me how I know, and don't ask where it comes from, because I don't know. I do know that if you unleashed it out there the way you do with me, the world would fall at your feet, just like I do."

"Wow. You're not just saying that to seduce me, are you?"

"If I were, would it work?"

"Probably," she said.

"Then, no, I'm not." I kissed her forehead. "Go take a shower."

While we got ready, I formulated a strategy to make her president within fifteen, twenty years at the most. I decided not to startle her by revealing it all at once.

We arrived at the New Year's Eve bash just as dinner was being served and thus decided to bring our bags up to our hotel room after midnight.

While we waited in line at the coat check, Gianna said, "I'm not going to drink tonight, except maybe champagne at midnight. I had to take an antihistamine before we left. The last thing I need is to make a drunken fool out of myself in front of the illustrious and powerful."

"Someday you'll be illustrious and powerful yourself, then you can drink all you want. Like me."

"I don't want to be—"

"Gianna? Is that you?"

We turned to see Adam Crawford standing next to the line. Beside him stood a short black woman with lively eyes and a wide smile.

"Adam." Gianna gritted her teeth. "What are you doing here?"

"You're not the only one with friends in high places." He put his arm around his companion. "Lorraine Morrison, you remember Gianna O'Keefe, and this is her . . ." He cleared his throat. "This is Louis Carvalho."

Lorraine shook my hand and grinned. "Of course, from the Carvalho consulting group. You've made quite a name for yourself on the Hill. I work for Representative Livingstone, one of the House Judiciary Committee members." Now I remembered her as the person talking with Gianna and Adam outside the Rayburn building after Gianna's testimony.

Adam took Lorraine's arm. "We'd better head into the dining room now. Good to see you both again."

"Well, that was less painful than a root canal," Gianna said when they were gone. "At least he seems to be moving on."

"You didn't see the way he looked at you. I bet this isn't the last we'll see of him tonight."

Dinner was sumptuous and productive. I procured a few new clients from the Office of Management and Budget, and Gianna managed to wrangle an appointment with a Senate committee chair's chief aide.

"You're the only person I know," I told her as I led her onto the dance floor, "who can lament the plight of the hungry while eating triple chocolate terrine."

She didn't answer me, and I noticed she was watching Adam and Lorraine dancing.

"Are you jealous?" I asked her.

"Huh? Oh, no. Not at all."

"She seems nice."

"Yes, she is. It's just weird that less than a week ago he was begging me to marry him."

"He proposed to you on Christmas? We didn't hear that part."

"You were eavesdropping?"

"Marc and I, yeah."

She shook her head and sighed. "My brother's a bad influence."

"Maybe I should go over there and defend my honor. The nerve of that guy, proposing to my girlfriend while I was in the next room. I'll get my dueling glove. Pistols at dawn, squire!"

Gianna laughed. The music changed to a slow dance. She wrapped her arms around my neck and began to sway with me. I shut my eyes and pulled her close to inhale her perfume.

Someone tapped my shoulder. It was Adam.

"Mind if I cut in?"

"As a matter of fact—"

"Where's Lorraine?" Gianna asked him.

"She went to the ladies' room. So how 'bout it? Half a dance, for old times' sake?" He did an unsteady half-spin to illustrate.

"I don't think so, Adam," Gianna said. "Not behind her back like that."

"She won't care. She's very open-minded."

"Are you okay? You don't seem like yourself tonight."

Adam stopped swaying. "I'm fine. I'm just drunk, 's all. It's New Year's Eve." He turned and headed for the bar.

"Weird." Gianna began to dance with me again. "I wonder if he knew I was going to be here."

"How would he know?"

"My parents may have told him, but I don't know if I told them where I'd be, and even if I had, I doubt they'd remember."

Over Gianna's shoulder I watched Adam down another shot. Lorraine joined him at the bar, but he barely acknowledged her on his way to the men's room.

"Excuse me," I said to Gianna. "I'll be right back."

I paid the restroom attendant to step out for five minutes, then waited for Adam to emerge from the stall. When he did, his skin was pale and sweaty. Without noticing me, he moved to the sink and splashed cold water on his face. I handed him a towel. He dried himself, put his glasses back on, and turned to thank me. He froze when he saw my face.

"Feeling a little under the weather tonight, Adam?"

"What do you want?" His voice was raw.

"Glad you asked." I leaned close to him. "I want you to leave her alone. Not just tonight, but for good. Do you think you can remember that, or do I need to tattoo it on the back of your eyelids?"

"Why should I listen to you?"

I kept my voice low and pleasant. "Because I could make your life very painful. I don't mean an annoying, think-I'll-take-an-aspirin-and-lie-down kind of pain. I mean the kind of pain that makes you look forward to your own death the way children look forward to Christmas, the way the working Joe looks forward to his annual trip to the beach, the way an addict looks forward to her next fix. You will greet the end with joy."

Adam's face twisted with nothing that resembled fear. "How dare you threaten me." He looked at me with a cold strength I hadn't seen in his eyes before. "You're not right for her, Louis. I know it, she knows it, and deep down inside, you know it." He dropped ten dollars in the tip basket and walked out.

I found Gianna chatting with a group of congressional staffers.

"There you are," she said. "I was getting worried. It's five minutes to midnight."

"Let's find a more private spot, shall we?"

I led Gianna out into the hallway, stopping to pick up two champagne glasses.

"Why are we going out here?"

"Because I don't want to kiss you in front of your ex-boyfriend. Not the kind of kiss I'm planning to give you."

"Ooh. Let's sit down, then, in case my knees turn to jelly." We sat on a small red divan in a quiet corner. "I hope Adam doesn't try to follow us."

"Would you mind not saying his name for the rest of the year?"

"Sorry." She glanced in the mirror behind me and touched her hair.

"You look perfect," I said. "As always."

"I don't look perfect."

"You look good enough."

"Good enough for what?" she said.

"You'll see."

"What? When? I'll see what when?"

"Twenty seconds to midnight, Gianna." The crowd in the ballroom began to count down.

"I don't want to wait. Kiss me now."

I did, until the count reached seven.

"I have to ask you something." I brushed the hair out of her eyes. "Just let me look at you." I reached into my pocket and as the noisemakers rattled and honked around us, I opened a tiny velvet box to reveal a diamond ring. Gianna's face froze. Her hand trembled as it reached to touch the jewel.

"Is this what I think it is?"

I pulled the ring out of the box and slipped it on her finger. "Gianna, will you—"

"Yes!" She threw her arms around my neck, then tensed. "Jesus God, shit, I can't believe I just said that." She pulled away. "Go ahead, Lou. Ask again."

"Okay . . . Gianna, will you . . . would you . . . please . . . be my wife?"

Gianna put her hand to the side of her neck. "I think I'm going to pass out." She leaned against the arm of the divan. "This is insane, Lou, insane. We haven't even known each other for two months."

"So we'll have a long engagement if you like. Anything you want. Anything." I took her hand. "I want to give you the world, Gianna."

"It seems like a lot of it is yours to give."

"I'll lay it all at your feet."

"I don't want it all. I don't want the world."

"Then just take me. If you want."

When she lifted her face to me, her eyes were full of tears. "I do want you." She kissed my hand. "For you, I'd even be a rich man's wife."

"You would?"

"Yes."

"Yes!" I shouted to the ceiling. My joy echoed up and down the hallway. I kissed her. "You've made me the happiest man who ever lived."

She lifted her hand to examine the ring. Two tear-shaped diamonds were flanked by a tiny garnet on either side.

"Do you like it?" I said.

"I love it. It's perfect. Exquisite, but not ostentatious. I know you could have bought me a rock bigger than my nose, but this shows you understand me."

"I try. Besides, I wanted to save my money for the ice sculptures."

"The what?"

"The ice sculptures. At the wedding reception." I slid my hand under her thigh. "Picture this. A sculpture of you and me in a moment of extreme passion, tastefully rendered in ice. It'll be a hit, I guarantee."

Gianna laughed. "Oh, yes, especially with my grandmother."

"I can see her now, chipping off a piece of my butt to chill her Bloody Mary." I laid my face against Gianna's neck and felt the vibrations of her laughter. She wrapped her arms around my back.

"Tell me you love me," she said.

"I love you, Gianna. I've never loved anyone before, but I know I can't ever live without it again." I kissed her deeply and pulled her tight against me.

"Good night, you guys."

It was Adam again, this time with his date. I glared at him, but he ignored me.

"Um, good night," Gianna said. "It was good to see you again, Lorraine."

They started to turn away when Adam saw the jewelry box on the coffee table next to us. He looked at Gianna's left hand.

"You got engaged?" he said, in almost a whisper.

"Oh, that's so romantic." Lorraine leaned over and examined the ring. "Gorgeous! Congratulations to you both."

"I can't believe you got engaged." Adam stared at the wall behind us as if gazing into another time, then he shook his head once. "Have a nice life." He shuffled away towards the hotel elevator. Lorraine trailed behind him.

"I will." Gianna turned back to me. "I will have a nice life."

"Perhaps 'nice' is too bland a word. But it will be interesting." I picked up our champagne glasses. "So how would you like to celebrate? Partying with the crowd? Or getting naked and sweaty with me?"

"Can I do both?"

"Not at the same time."

"Your reputation, of course." She stood up. "I'd like to finish this glass of champagne and have one more dance, please. Then we'll check out the naked thing."

While we danced, Gianna pressed her cheek against my shoulder. "I can't believe we're getting married. I never really considered it before, but as soon as I saw the ring I knew I wanted to spend my life with you."

"Maybe you just wanted to spend your life with the ring."

She slapped my chest lightly. "You know me better than that."

"Yes, I do." I kissed her temple. "And I want to know you even better."

"I'll tell you all my secrets, if you tell me yours."

If we hadn't been dancing, she wouldn't have felt my sudden tension.

"What's wrong?" she said.

"Nothing." A lifetime of lies lay ahead of us. "Can we go upstairs now?"

We said our goodbyes and made our way to the parking garage to retrieve our bags from my car. The garage was well lit but empty of people. My Mercedes was parked at the far end of a row behind a large concrete pillar.

Gianna huddled close to me. "Parking garages give me the creeps."

"You've seen too many movies."

"You're probably right. Even my dreams are cinematic."

"Mine are usually pornographic. Does that count?"

As we turned around the pillar, a man stepped out of the shadows.

"Happy New Year, Gianna."

It was, of course, Adam. My patience gave out. I moved toward him.

"Look, asshole, if you don't leave her alone, I'll—"

He pulled a gun from behind his back and pointed it at me. "You'll what?" Adam's laugh was full of glee. "Who's the asshole now, huh?"

"Adam, no!"

"Gianna, get down!" I yelled. "Get behind the car!"

"Don't move!" he said to her, the gun still trained on me. "I want her where she can see me."

Two instincts battled within me: to preserve my facade, and to preserve her life. If he turned the gun on her, it would be an easy choice, but for the moment, I wanted to find a mortal way out of this predicament.

"Don't worry, Gianna," Adam said, "this isn't for him or you. As if I had the guts to kill someone. It's for me." He pointed the gun at his own head. "I want you to be the last thing I see."

Gianna pleaded with him. "Adam, don't do this. You're drunk. You aren't thinking straight."

"I've never had a straighter thought in my life," he said.

"You don't want to do this."

Yes, he does. Though I would have welcomed his demise, for Gianna's sake I was trying every trick I knew to manipulate his mind into dropping the gun. But his will was too strong. He wanted to die, and he wanted her to watch.

"You hate guns," Gianna said. "Where did you get that?"

"From Lorraine's glove compartment." He pulled it away from his head and examined it closely. "It's a .38 Special, apparently. She has a fear of being carjacked. I guess 'cuz that's how her brother died."

"Where is Lorraine now?"

"Upstairs asleep. We didn't . . . I mean, I couldn't . . . I kept thinking of you."

"Don't you think she'd want you to—"

"How many times did I ask you to marry me?"

"I—I don't—"

"How many times, Gianna? Answer me!!"

"I don't know!"

"I'll give you a hint—it's a prime number."

"I don't remember. Seven?"

"You lost count, I guess. But I remember. It was nine. Once for every year we were together."

"Actually, nine's not a prime number," I said.

"Shut up!" He pointed the gun at me for a moment, then turned it back to his temple. "Do you know what she said to me every time I proposed?"

I shook my head.

"No, she didn't say 'no.' She said—do you know what she said? She said, 'Not yet.' First it was 'Not yet, we're too young,' then 'Not yet, I'm in grad school,' then 'Not yet, I'm in law school,' then 'Not yet, we don't have the money,' and then she gave up on good excuses and just said, 'Not yet, Adam darling, I'm not ready.' Then one day . . . one day 'Not yet' turned into never." He sank against the concrete pillar and started to cry.

"Adam, I'm sorry I hurt you."

He wiped his face. "And now here she is, and here you are, and now she's ready. And I've wasted almost ten years of my life waiting. She let me wait for nothing." I felt a dangerous shift in his mind. He lowered the gun to his side. "I've changed my mind, Gianna."

"Thank God."

"I want you to know what it's like to be alone." He pointed the gun at me and fired. I saw the muzzle flash a moment before the pain erupted in my chest. Gianna screamed. Adam fired twice more, and my abdomen felt like it was filled with flames. I fell to my knees. Hot blood soaked my shirt and scalded my skin.

Gianna lunged for Adam and tried to grab for the gun, but he stepped back and pointed it at her. It was all I needed to see. I fired.

The temperature inside Adam's skull spiked. He dropped the gun and grabbed at his head before collapsing on the pavement.

"No—" was all he said before the convulsions began. He started to flail and flop like a fish on a riverbank. Gianna stood frozen next to his thrashing body.

It was too much. I hadn't meant to . . .

I lurched to my feet and moved toward her. Adam twitched a few more times, then lay still, his eyes wide and white. A putrid smell filled the air, like a raw steak left out in the sun.

Gianna covered her mouth and nose and whimpered. She backed into me, shrieked, and whirled around.

"Oh my God . . . Louis . . ." She saw the blood covering my chest and stomach. "We have to get help."

"No, we don't."

"You shouldn't be standing up. You'll lose more blood."

"I'm all right."

"I'll call an ambulance." She pulled her phone out of her purse. Her fingers shook as they tried to dial. I grabbed the phone.

"Gianna, listen to me! I said, I'm all right. I don't have time to explain, so just look." I tore off my jacket, ripped open my shirt and smeared the blood away from the disappearing wounds. The hole in my chest closed before her eyes. She sucked in her breath.

"How did it—?" Gianna reached to touch me, then drew back her hand as if from a fire.

"I can explain everything later, but we need to get out of here."

She backed away from me, staring at my chest and shaking her head.

"Gianna, please. If anyone saw us like this, I'd have to . . . it could get crazy."

She blinked at me, then turned towards Adam. "What happened to him?"

I shook my head. "I'm sorry, Gianna."

"What do you mean?"

"I only wanted to stop him, but the pain . . ."

"What are you talking about?" Her voice started to shake. "What did you do?"

"I saved your life."

"You . . . you did this?" She pointed at Adam's still figure.

"If I hadn't killed him, he would have killed himself."

"I don't understand. How did you—"

"Understand later. Now we have to go." I picked up the gun, opened the trunk of my car, and tossed it in. I took off my bloody shirt and jacket, then pulled a clean shirt out of my duffel bag. Gianna was still standing over Adam's body, crying. I moved to the driver's side door, buttoning my shirt. "Get in the car, Gianna."

"No! Not until you tell me how you did this."

If I give her part of the truth, I thought, then maybe she'll be satisfied enough to shut up and come with me.

"I . . . I have certain powers."

"What do you mean, powers?"

"I'm . . . to start with, I'm pyrokinetic."

She stared at me. "You're what?"

"I can set things on fire by—"

"I know what pyrokinetic is, and it's not real. This is some kind of trick."

"Adam is dead. That was no trick."

"But why?"

I gripped the edge of the car door. "Gianna, please come with me now. If anyone finds us—"

"No, I can't just—"

"If anyone finds us, I'd have to kill them, too."

Her jaw dropped, and she took a step backwards.

"To protect us," I said. "To protect you."

She glanced at the garage's exit doors and started to tremble.

"Trust me, Gianna. Please, just trust me once more."

For a few moments there was only the sound of her unsteady breath. She took a last look at Adam, then dashed for the car.

27

Lacrymosa Dies Illa

Gianna stared at me from across the car like a rabbit at a not-too-distant fox. "Where are you taking me?"

"Back to my place." Her hand clutched at the car door handle. I drove faster. "Put your seat belt on. I didn't save your life so you could get creamed by a drunk driver."

"He shot you." She was staring at my chest again. "I saw him shoot you. How can you be alive?"

"It's hard to explain."

"Does this have anything to do with what you did to Adam?"

"In a way."

"In a way? In *what* way?"

"I'm not answering any more questions until we get home. Just try to calm down."

She started to take a deep breath, but it choked off into a sob. "I can't believe this is happening." She pressed her palms against her face. "I can't believe Adam's dead, and I watched you kill him."

"I had no choice."

"They'll find his body."

"Mysterious circumstances, yes, but no evidence of foul play. Hopefully they'll rule it a massive aneurysm. If anyone questions you, the last time you saw him was outside the ballroom, okay?"

"This isn't happening." She sobbed again, then wiped her eyes and looked at me. "If I made you angry, would you do that to me?"

"No! Gianna, you know I would never hurt you."

"Like the time you almost threw me into the Grand Canyon."

"You were never in any danger, I told you that."

"Why should I believe you?" she said. "You—"

"I would never lie to you—"

"—lied about everything else—"

"—about anything important—"

"—like that crime bill, you never told me—"

"—like the way I feel about you."

"—you were working on that, you kept it hidden—"

"Gianna—"

"—like all the other secrets, and now you're—"

"Gianna—"

"—someone I don't even know anymore, and you—"

"Gianna, would you put your fucking seat belt on!" I screeched to a halt in the middle of Constitution Avenue. "There are some very bad drivers in this town, and they are all out there on the icy road tonight. I don't want to lose you, so I'm not moving until you do as I ask." I turned my hazard lights on.

Without taking her eyes off me, Gianna reached across her shoulder and pulled her seat belt across her. As soon as it clicked, I put the car in gear and sped away.

In the ensuing silence, I tried to concoct a plan. What

would I do with Gianna when I had her alone in my apartment? Explain the whole story? Convince her that I'm really the Devil but that she should love me anyway?

Or turn back the clock in her mind to erase the last hour? She'd wake up tomorrow as my happy fiancée, a bit hung over but cozy in her ignorance.

I glanced at her shivering form beside me and felt tempted to peek inside her mind. I needed any advantage I could gain at this point.

But she wasn't an opponent; she was my lover. I wanted her whole and fierce, independent of my or anyone else's control. Manipulating her mind or her memory would turn her into my pet. There had to be another way.

We didn't speak any more until we got to my apartment building. Once in the elevator, Gianna said, "You told me you would explain later. I'm waiting."

I wiped my hand over my forehead, which was slick with sweat. "Can't we just drop it?"

"No!"

"Don't make me lie to you, Gianna."

"I don't want you to lie to me. I want the truth."

"I can't tell you the truth."

"Why not?"

"It would destroy us."

"I refuse to believe that." Gianna laid her hand on my arm. "Louis, when I thought you were dead back there, I didn't care whether he killed me, too. I love you, and there's nothing you could tell me that would change that."

I turned to look in her eyes. They were clear and bright and intense.

"Do you really mean that?" I said.

"Yes. I swear it."

I wanted to believe her, so I did.

"Gianna . . . I . . . I'm the Devil."

The elevator chimed and the door opened. Gianna just stared at me, blinking.

"Would you like to come inside?" I said.

"Lou, on any other day, this would be funny, but not after what just happened."

"I'm not joking." I crossed the hallway and opened my door. "Are you coming or not?"

She hesitated for a moment, then clenched her jaw and strode past me into my apartment. "I don't believe this."

I followed her in. "Will you at least admit that I'm not human?"

"Maybe you're just insane," she said. "A schizophrenic psychopath whose delusions are so intense that you've somehow acquired these unusual powers."

"Gianna, this isn't a comic book, and I'm not a superhero." I reached for her coat, but she pulled it close around her. "You can believe I'm some kind of fire-breathing mutant, but not the Devil?"

"You can't be the Devil. You're not even . . . you know . . ."

"What? I'm not even what?"

"You're not evil."

I flinched and tottered back as if she had struck me. My mouth hung open, a protest lodged between my tonsils.

"Wh—what? What do you mean, I'm not evil? Of course I'm evil!"

"You're not. You took care of me when I was sick, you took me to the Grand Canyon, you came home with me for Christmas." She pointed at me. "Aha! Christmas! You couldn't have done that if you were the Devil. Your head would explode."

"Remember that sinus attack I had during Midnight Mass?"

"You said you were allergic to incense."

"That was a lie."

"You love me. Is that a lie, too?"

"Of course not," I said. "I do love you."

"How can you love me and still be the Devil?"

"I ask myself that question every day. Look, this isn't easy for me, either. I lived ten billion years thinking that love was a sick joke played by my sadistic father, then one day discovered I was the butt of that very same joke."

"Your father . . ."

"My father. Your father. Our father, who art in Heaven, or so they claim."

"All those things you said about him, about your rebellion and him disowning you." She took a step backward. "You really do think you're the Devil, don't you?"

"I am the Devil!"

"Stop saying that! You're scaring me."

"I don't want to scare you, Gianna." I reached to touch her face. She recoiled, and I realized my hands were still bloody. "Sorry." I gestured down the hall. "Let's go in so I can clean up, okay?"

Gianna slunk into the living room and looked around her as if she were there for the first time.

"Let me get you a drink," I said.

"I'll get it myself."

I went into the hallway bathroom and closed the door. When I looked in the mirror, I saw that blood had smeared onto my new shirt. I removed it and scrubbed my skin until it was clean.

When I entered the living room, Gianna was sitting in the armchair on the edge of the seat. She turned her head to look at me, then jumped at the sight of my bare chest.

"What's wrong?" I said.

"Your body . . . it's so perfect," she whispered. "Is that why?"

"Is what why?"

"And the scratches I left on your back that night . . ." A ter-

rible truth had finally poked its way through to her consciousness. She stood slowly. "Prove it."

"Prove what?"

"Prove to me that you're the Devil."

"Do you think I have a license hanging on my wall? A
board-certified demon? There's nothing here to prove who I
am. There can't be. If I had to leave everything behind and
move away for any reason, no one would suspect. That's the
way we have to live."

"We?"

Uh-oh.

"We who?" she said.

"We . . . uh . . . my fellow . . . my associates and I."

"Who?"

"It's not important."

"Your brother? Is Bob in on this hallucination, too?"

"Please don't make me go into it." She didn't move. I sank
onto the couch and took a deep breath. "If you must know . . .
Bob is actually Beelzebub, Malcolm is Mephistopheles, and Bill
is Belial. We're all what you might call . . . Hell's angels." It
sounded so stupid.

She stared at me for a second, then hurled her glass at the
fireplace. It shattered and scattered its pieces across the floor.

"No!" Her hands curled into fists. "Are you kidding me?
Are you fucking kidding me?"

"No, I—"

"Don't lie to me, Louis!" She advanced on me with tears of
fury coursing down her cheeks. "Tell me who you really are,
and don't tell me you're Satan!"

I rose to my full height and glared at her.

"My name is Lucifer," I said in a low, tense voice. "Never
call me by that other name. It's a name of disgrace . . . Satan."
The word hissed through my teeth.

"You're insane, you know that?" She shoved me in the chest. "You're a fucking maniac!"

I grabbed her shoulders. "Look at me, Gianna! Look into my eyes and tell me I'm crazy, that I'm not who I say I am."

Gianna stared for a few moments. "I can't. I can't see into your eyes. There's nothing there." She pushed herself out of my grip and stood trembling with her back to me. "I always knew there was something about you that wasn't quite right. A voice inside of me kept hinting at it, even that first night, in your bedroom. There was always something strange . . ." She lifted her head, then spun to face me. "That feather . . ."

I sprung to my feet. "The feather! Yes!" I raced into my bedroom, retrieved the feather, and presented her with it. "From my wings. Scorched during the fall from Heaven."

She took it with quivering hands and held it at arm's length. "I don't understand," she whispered.

"You don't understand . . . what?"

She stared at the feather in her hands. "Why would this make me believe you?"

My heart slammed against my ribs. "Does it . . . make you believe me?"

She looked up at me and nodded.

"Now what?" I whispered.

"I don't know."

I started to move toward her.

"Gianna . . ."

She jumped back a few feet and dropped the feather.

"Please don't be afraid of me," I said.

"I'm not." Her eyes darted toward the door.

"You can go if you want. I won't stop you." I didn't realize it was a lie until after it had left my mouth.

"When were you planning to tell me?" she said.

"Never."

"Never? You would have carried this lie the rest of our lives?"

"The rest of *your* life, you mean. Gianna, there's nothing about my life with you that's a lie. I am who I am, in my work, and with the others. But with you, I'm just a man."

"A man who corrupts and defiles everything he touches." She gasped and put her hands to her chest. "Including me . . ."

"No . . . I never—"

"What have you done to *me*?" She bolted for my hallway. Before she could reach the door, I threw myself in front of it.

"Don't go."

"You said I could leave if I—"

"Just listen to me—"

"Lou, please let me go."

"No."

She stepped towards me. "I'm not afraid of you."

"I know you're not. That's why I—"

"Don't say it."

"I—"

"Don't," she said. "You only love yourself. That's a fact."

"It was a fact, until I met you."

"I know how you work. You tell lies, and you seduce the weak for your own pleasure and to spite God."

"Yes, but you—"

"I'm an exception, of course. That's probably what you tell all your victims."

"Gianna, listen to me!"

"No, I won't listen to you. Your words mean nothing."

"Then watch." I sank to my knees before her. My body howled at the unnatural posture, but I forced myself to remain there, my eyes fixed upon her feet. "Never, in my entire existence—and I am very, very old—have I knelt before anyone, even my Creator."

My pulse pounded in my ears as I waited for her to speak.

"Lou, why are you doing this? What do you want with me?"

"Nothing." I shook my head. "Everything."

"No." She gasped. "You spent Christmas with me. Even though . . . it made you sick, didn't it?"

"You might say I'm allergic to all things holy. Usually I spend Christmas in Vegas."

"But why did you do that to yourself? You even gave me this cross. I don't understand. Why would you do all this for me?"

"You know why, Gianna." I took her hand, drew it to my lips, and lifted my eyes to hers.

"Don't do this," she said.

"Do what?"

"Don't prostrate yourself. It's not who you are."

"Then you'd better come down here," I said, "because I'm not getting up." I pulled gently on her hand. "You said you weren't afraid."

"Not of you."

"Then come here." I pulled her hand again until she knelt in front of me. Gianna touched my face, my hair, tentatively, thoroughly, as a blind person would. Her hands were cold, and they faltered when they reached my bare shoulders.

Slowly I moved my face toward hers. She leaned away from me, her eyes full of fear and fascination. My left hand touched her cheek and seemed to soothe her. I slipped my other arm around her back and pulled her to kiss me.

Gianna succumbed to my passion for a moment, then I felt her shudder. She cried out and shoved herself away from me.

"No!" She backed up until she hit the wall. "I can't. I can't do that."

I crawled to her. "Gianna, I'm still the same man I was three hours ago. I haven't changed. It's only the way you look at me, your feelings about me, that have changed."

"But my feelings haven't changed, and that's the problem." Fresh tears flowed down her cheeks. "I still love you. I know what you are, and I still love you. What does that make me?"

I reached for her, but she lurched to her feet toward the door. I followed.

"Gianna . . ." I placed my hand on her arm. "I'm afraid that if you walk out that door, you'll never return."

"I will."

"Don't lie to me."

"Lie?!" She yanked her arm out of my grip. "You want to talk about lies? You would have let me marry you. You would have let me have your children, not knowing what they were. You would have gladly let me live that lie, would have let me be as damned as you are. Wouldn't you?"

"Can you blame me for pretending to be something I'm not, when what I am is the worst thing in the world?"

Her eyes filled with cold despair. "I've spent my life trying to serve God's will. I know I haven't been perfect, but I've tried to be good. Now that's all for nothing, thanks to you."

Gianna opened the door and slammed it behind her. When I heard the elevator doors open and close again, I turned away.

The snow outside was changing to rain. Its silent slaps against the wide window became soft patters. There was no other sound. The upper edges of the city gleamed against a sodden sky.

I went to the sliding door of the balcony and pressed my right temple and cheek against the cold smooth window. My palm slid down the glass, leaving a wet trail in the condensation.

"Gianna . . ."

Her name had escaped my lips without my consent. The heat in my blood rose. I touched my finger to the glass and watched the water sizzle and steam.

How dare she. I saved her life, and she had fled from me in horror, as if I were the monster.

I am a monster. But before tonight I had never seen that monstrosity reflected in her eyes.

My stomach flipped. The possibility that Gianna might never return, that I would never feel her eyes, her hands, upon me again, struck me so hard that I sank to the floor with an incoherent oath. How had I fallen so far that a mere human could skewer me like this?

My fingers itched to regain control. I crawled to the piano. At my touch, it spewed forth a thunderous rant that shook the floor under my feet.

After perhaps half an hour of maniacal musical raving, I stopped. The last notes bounced off the ceiling and walls and faded as I sat there panting. I curled my trembling hands into fists, raised them above my head, and slammed the keys with a final punch. A string snapped. It wobbled in the air, twanging a single strangled note.

There was no way to release this torment. I needed to erase myself.

I went to the bar and grabbed the first bottle I could reach. In less than a minute, it was empty. Another bottle of pale brown liquid found its way down my throat as the rain slammed harder against the window. The third bottle's seal was unbroken. I took it with me to the sofa and held it between my knees while my nearly numb fingers struggled with the cap.

Finally I smashed the neck of the bottle against the coffee table. Glass and whiskey spilled onto the floor before I raised the broken neck to my mouth and drank. I could barely feel the glass slice my lips and tongue, but I tasted the blood mingling with the scotch as it flowed into me.

When I stopped to breathe for a moment, I looked around my apartment and had an overwhelming urge to set everything on fire.

Fortunately, this was when I passed out.

28

Cor Contritum Quasi Cinis

My day was filled with distorted dreams. I was plagued with a recurring sensation of falling back into my body as I half woke.

I was flat on my face when I heard the sounds. I opened my eyes to see nothing but black, the leather of my sofa. My head screamed when I shifted it to hear better. There was someone in the kitchen. A cupboard door closed with a click of its magnet.

I lurched off the couch towards the noise. My legs shook, but I forced them to keep moving. At the kitchen threshold, I spoke her name in meekest hope.

"Gianna . . ."

"Sorry. It's only me."

I gaped at Beelzebub for a bleary moment, felt brief shame at my pathetic desperation, then looked over my shoulder towards the front door.

"She's not here," he said.

I turned away from him with a grunt and staggered back to the sofa where my (somehow) still upright bottle of scotch waited for me. Beelzebub followed me and handed me a glass. I tried to hold the bottle in one shaky hand and the glass in the other, but they refused to make contact, so I set the glass on the table and aimed the jagged mouth of the bottle towards it. As a result of intense concentration, the glass became full, at least until I reached for it and knocked it off the table.

"Damn."

"Here, let me." Beelzebub poured the drink and handed it to me. He regarded the broken neck of the bottle before setting it back on the table.

"Thanks. You're a real pal." I crossed my legs and sipped the drink with exaggerated propriety. "So, my good man, what brings you out on this ghastly morning?"

"Dude, it's six-thirty at night."

"Is it still January first?"

"Yeah."

"Then Happy New Year. Have a drink with me, won't you? Celebrate new beginnings."

"Nah, I had enough last night to last me a week," he said.

"And when did you become the patron saint of moderation?" I lifted my glass towards him. "My New Year's resolution: never to be sober again. It's just not worth it." I downed the rest of the glass and tossed it at him. "Fill 'er up, won't you?" He poured me another drink. "How did you know I was alone? How did you know she wasn't here?"

"Why, Lucifer, I can feel it. I can sense when you're alone, when you're in agony, from all the way uptown."

"Really?"

"No." He handed me the glass of whiskey. "I saw Gianna at the grocery store with that redheaded friend of hers. She looked like she'd been crying. I figured it had something to do with you."

"Yes, I would imagine. What with her boyfriend being the Devil and all."

He stared at me. "She knows?"

"She knows." I gave him a brief account of the previous evening's events. "Call me paranoid," I said, "but I have this feeling that You-Know-Who was behind it."

"You mean her ex-boyfriend is some kind of angelic hit man?"

"No, nothing that blatant. Our father is more subtle than that, working inside people's hearts. I don't think he wanted Gianna dead, but he knew I'd have to reveal myself if her life were threatened."

"I think it's a stretch, but believe what you wanna believe. What I can't get over is the fact that she knows you're the Devil, and you didn't kill her."

"Of course not."

"You could have wiped her memory." He stood and began to pace. "She would have thought she just blacked out from drinking too much. Lucifer, why didn't you do that?"

"You know that's not completely harmless, especially when they're awake."

"It is when you're good at it, like I am. You want me to do it for you? I'll go over there right now."

"No! It's too late to do it without hurting her."

"I'll be gentle, I promise. You want her back or not?"

I considered his question. Her absence was already slicing larger and larger voids within me. Maybe we could start over . . .

"No," I said finally. "I don't want her like that."

"You want to do it the hard way, suit yourself. I'd have to say the odds are pretty bad, though, right down there with the Cubs winning the World Series."

"But I thought . . . I thought maybe who I was wouldn't matter to her."

"Wouldn't matter?" Beelzebub cackled. "These are humans we're talking about here. Stupid creatures scared pantless of what might be lurking under their beds and in their closets. You think any of them wouldn't mind if they were sleeping with the Devil?"

I slouched further down on the couch and put my fingers to my temple. "Please stop shouting at me. Get me something to eat, would you?"

"What do you want?"

"Toast. Dry toast."

He walked back into the kitchen. I got up and searched his coat pocket for his cigarettes, lit one, and returned to the couch.

When Beelzebub reentered with a plate of toast, he snickered at the cigarette. "You're smoking. Does that mean you—?"

"Not since Christmas night."

"Whoa. A week without sex? I'm surprised you're not setting things on fire by now." He handed me the plate and sat down in the chair again. "I could fix that for you, if you need me to."

I shot him as withering a look as I could muster with a faceful of crumbs. "That won't be necessary."

"I was just joking." He watched me inhale his offering of food. "So I disgust you now, is that it?"

"No." I set the empty plate on the coffee table and took another drag off the cigarette. "I disgust me."

"But when you look at me, you see everything you hate about yourself."

I didn't reply, only finished my cigarette and dropped it in the now-empty bottle of scotch. "Okay," I said. "Come here, and I'll show you how much you don't disgust me."

"Now you're really drunk."

"My thoughts are very clear. And you know what I'm thinking right now?" I licked my lips and stroked his body with my eyes.

Beelzebub hesitated, then shook his head. "I changed my mind, Lucifer. I won't be your consolation prize."

"Oh, really?" I chuckled a little, then turned serious. "Yes, you will." I placed my hand on the sofa next to me. "Now come here."

He winced a little, then slowly stood and crossed the room toward me. When he was within reach, I grabbed him and shoved him face down on the couch.

"Hey!" he yelped as I pounced on him and pressed my weight on his back.

"What's wrong, Beelzebub? This is what you wanted all along, isn't it? Gianna out of the picture and me on top of you again?"

"It's not like that! This isn't some sick love triangle."

"Oh, yes it is," I said. "It is, because I love Gianna, and because I love you."

"No!" He squirmed to cover his ears. With one hand I seized his arm and held it to his side; my other hand grabbed his hair and twisted his face so that I could reach it with my mouth.

"I don't love you the way I love Gianna. I wouldn't kill for you, or die for you, or even bare my true soul to you. But Beelzebub, my darling little cherub . . . I do love you." I planted a soft, sweet kiss on his cheek to finalize the insult.

"How dare you?!" His shrieks rippled through our bodies. "How dare you say that to me, you pervert!"

I leapt off of him and stood laughing the deep, throaty cackle usually reserved for my most fiendish acts against What's-His-Face. Beelzebub sat up slowly, then rubbed his arms.

"There." I collapsed in the chair facing him. "Now I disgust you, too."

Without a word he stood and put on his jacket. He stopped when he reached my chair.

"Why did you let me go just now?" he said.

"Like you said the other day, rape isn't as much fun as it used to be."

He lowered his eyes and moved on behind me towards the door.

"Don't leave," I said.

"Fuck you."

"I mean it. I'd rather you . . . I'd rather you stay."

He stopped. "What if she comes back?"

The possibility of Gianna's return, perhaps even tonight, hadn't occurred to me. In the depths of my wallowing I had forgotten to be prepared for that event.

"Okay, leave."

Before the front door had slammed behind him, I was in my bedroom, stripping off the pants and socks I'd been wearing for over twenty-four hours. With some trepidation, I entered the bathroom and looked in the mirror.

The bright light stung my bloodshot eyes, and when I was finally able to focus on my own image, I had to laugh. Even if I were included in a lineup of gangsters, dictators, and politicians, anyone could easily finger me as the Author of All Evil. The two vertical creases between my eyebrows had become entrenched in my skin. I tried to massage them into obscurity, to no avail. A thick shadow of stubble and a mangled mop of hair completed the beastly picture. I looked as if I should be crawling on all fours through the forest, biting the heads off baby bunnies.

Ahhh . . . baby bunny heads. Maybe another wilderness sabbatical was in order.

Or perhaps a hot shower would be more appropriate.

Once clean, I got dressed and sat in my living room to wait. She'd be back. Soon.

29

Benedictus Qui Venit in Nomine Domini

A week later I sat in my office, still waiting. I had spent the first days of the new year moving stacks of paper from one side of my desk to another, canceling appointments, and staring out the window. My nights had consisted of moving furniture from one side of my living room to another, canceling social activities, and staring out the window.

This particular morning I was sorting my pen collection in alphabetical order according to their color name in Swedish when someone knocked on my door.

"Just a second." I crushed out my half-smoked cigarette and hid the ashtray in my desk drawer, then ran a comb through my hair. "Come in."

Beelzebub entered.

"Oh," I said.

"Again, only me."

"Did we have an appointment?" I buried my face in my calendar to avoid looking at him.

"It's been more than two weeks since we met. In your office, at least." He sat in the chair across from my desk and held up a brown paper bag. "Bagel?"

"Not hungry." I pulled out the ashtray and lit another cigarette. "Go ahead. What do you have for me?"

Beelzebub opened his briefcase and handed me a stack of clipped articles. "Things are looking pretty gnarly in the Middle East," he said in a voice that lacked enthusiasm. "We've hardly had to lift a finger there to make them scream for each other's blood." While he spoke, I let my gaze travel over his hands, his hair, and finally his face. "Forget the Oslo accords, forget any peace talks over the last—what are you looking at, Lou?"

I blinked slowly, then sighed and lowered my eyes to stare through the papers in front of me again.

"I know you've always liked to brood," he said, "but I haven't seen you this depressed since Waterloo." He shut his briefcase. "She'll be back, okay? I'm sure you're the best lay she's ever had."

"Humans care about more than sex, Beelzebub."

"Of course they do. They also care about money. And since you've got that going for you, too, I wouldn't worry." He pulled a bagel out of the paper bag. "Anyway, if that's what it takes to get you functioning again, then I hope she comes back. You're starting to depress me, and that's not an easy thing to do."

"I know." I pushed the papers to the side of my desk. "Look, Bub, I'm sorry about the other night. What I said to you . . ."

"Hey, it's cool," he said, though he turned away from me slightly. "You were piss drunk, and in a foul mood. I've forgotten it already. I know you didn't mean it."

I wanted to tell him that I did mean it, that I did love him, that the only thing scarier than loving one is loving two, because it could grow from there, and where would I ever draw the line?

"I had a dream about you and me Christmas morning," I said.

"Yeah, what happened?"

"We fucked."

"Yeah, I have that dream a lot." He picked a sesame seed off the bagel and popped it into his mouth. "That's all it is anymore, just a dream, since you—"

"Like demons, Bub. We fucked like demons."

He froze. A lock of hair dropped onto his forehead. "Really?"

"Really."

"You mean . . . full body penetration and everything?"

I swallowed hard. "Uh-huh."

"Wow." He sat back in his chair. "How long has it been since we did that?"

"Maybe a hundred years."

"I think maybe ninety-eight years, two months, and three days," he said.

"And at least twice as long since the time before that."

"When we accidentally set that one city on fire."

"London."

"Right."

We stared at each other in silence.

"When did you say you had that dream?" he said.

"Christmas. Two weeks ago today."

Beelzebub peered toward the ceiling as if he were calculating something in his head. Suddenly his eyes widened.

"What is it?" I said.

"Nothing. I'd better go." He shoved his uneaten bagel back in the bag and stood up.

"You had the same dream the same morning, didn't you?"

He moved toward the door. "This is some weird shit, Lou."

"You did, didn't you?"

"Not that I don't like weird shit." He rested his hand on the doorknob. "But this is just too . . . I don't know what to do with all this. I'll see you around, okay?"

Beelzebub left me covered in a fresh sheen of sweat.

Later that day I sat by the Reflecting Pool, on the bench where I first found Gianna reading *The Nation*. It was the first time since she left me that I'd ventured out of my apartment other than to go to work.

I stared at the half-frozen water through the clouds of my breath, thick with steam and smoke. A deepening pile of cigarette butts lay at my feet. I removed my gloves to open a new pack.

Out of nowhere a man appeared to my left, careening toward me. He tripped over my outstretched feet and fell to the sidewalk screaming.

"I've fallen, and I can't get up!" He turned to me and said, "Quick, who am I? Too slow. I'm you! Get it? I've fallen . . . and I can't get up!"

"You forgot your banana peel and rubber chicken, Raphael."

"Hey, I thought you quit smoking." Raphael sat up and laughed. "But then again, you never really do quit smoking, do you?" He touched my knee and made a sizzling noise.

"What do you want?"

"I don't want anything. Although I could go for a cheeseburger." He sat next to me on the bench. "I thought you could use a friendly face."

I looked at the angel's soft cheeks and round brown eyes. "Yours is one of the few truly friendly faces I've ever known. It's good to see you." We shook hands. "So how's life in Heaven?"

"Oh, it's . . . you know . . ." Raphael nodded.

"You can't say, of course."

"Of course."

"Is he dead yet?"

"Now you're the funny one. No, last time I checked, the universe was still humming along, pleased as punch with itself."

"Who sent you?"

"No one," he said. "This is an unofficial visit. They don't even know I'm here. Well, I'm sure the Creator knows, being omniscient and all. So technically, I suppose God wants me to be here, otherwise I probably would have been sucked into a black hole or something. I hate when that happens. It takes forever, literally, to find myself again." He put his arm around my shoulder. His touch was cool and light, like a spring breeze. "Wanna grab some lunch?"

"I haven't eaten in a week."

"You're lucky. I haven't eaten in thirty years." He reached in the pocket of his ratty brown coat and pulled out a quarter and a clump of lint. "What's a burger cost these days?"

"I'll treat," I said. "On one condition."

"With you, always conditions. You're not getting my soul."

"Tone down the holiness vibes. You heavenly entities give me splitting headaches."

"No problem. I would ask you to do the same with your evil, but you already have."

"No, I haven't."

"Right," Raphael said.

"So Jesus is hanging on the cross, and he whispers, 'Peterrrrr,' and Peter steps forward and says, 'What is it, Rabbi?,' and Jesus says, 'Come closer.' So Peter steps a little closer and says, 'Speak to me, master,' and Jesus says, 'Peter . . . come closer.' Peter gets right to the foot of the cross, and Jesus says, 'Peter . . .', and Peter says, 'I'm here, what is it you wish to tell me?' and Jesus says, 'Peter . . . I can see your house from here.'"

The angel giggled and spread a knifeful of horseradish sauce on his cheeseburger.

"That's a real knee-slapper, Raphael," I said. "So what are you doing here?"

"I want to help you."

"No, you don't."

"Okay, not really. But I am curious."

"Curious about what?"

"I heard about the woman," he said, "the one that you're in love with."

"I wish you would all stop spying on me. Besides, you're reading yesterday's news. She left me. I'm starting to think she's not coming back."

"So what are you doing here?"

"I'm waiting."

"Waiting. Uh-huh." He wiped his chin with a paper napkin. "Man, they don't make cheeseburgers like this in Heaven. Corporeality has its advantages, as I'm sure you're aware." He put his burger down. "Of course, it has its disadvantages, too. Excuse me." He got up and headed for the men's room.

I looked out the diner window through the ghost of my reflection in the glass. Somewhere, amidst the teeming throngs of people, Gianna was out there. I could find her if I wanted to, pick up her trail and track her down like a bloodhound after a criminal. She could make it easy or difficult for me to find her, based on her feelings toward me and the energy she sent out.

"Have you seen those automatic faucets?" Raphael said as he sat down again. "Of course you have. You live here. And the hand dryers, too. I can't wait until they make a machine that'll take a pee for you. Think of the increase in productivity."

"Did you know that Michael paid me a visit last month?"

"He told me. He went on and on about having to resterilize himself after being mired in so much filth."

"He seemed pretty sterile to me," I said.

"I know. As totally buff as Michael is, he can be such a priss." Raphael licked the ketchup from his thumb. "You've no need to fear him, though. He can't touch you. None of us can."

"What do you mean?"

"You're protected. We're under strict orders never to harm you personally. Kind of like the mark of Cain."

"Why?"

"I don't know," he said. "I guess He's saving you for something really nasty, wants to have the pleasure of direct punishment. I've learned not to question."

"Why are you telling me this?"

"Because I like you."

"Thanks."

"Don't get excited. I like everybody." He sipped his iced tea. "What I said before only applies to you, though. Everyone around you, everyone you care about, is fair game."

"Fair game for what?"

"You saw what happened to Belial."

"Belial?" I slammed my fork down. "I knew it. It was you. You tricked him."

"Not a trick. He was beckoned."

"Then why is he sitting in an asylum right now instead of rehearsing in the heavenly choir?"

Raphael fidgeted with his straw. "We haven't received orders yet as to what to do with him."

"So you'll just let him rot until then?"

"Look, I know it's not ideal," he said, "but it's out of my hands. Like I said, I've learned not to—"

"Not to question, of course." I passed him the dessert menu, covered with photos of luscious sweets. "You know, if you came to work for me, you could have a say in how things are run."

He laughed. "You never change, do you?"

"I try not to. Come on, Raph. I'll buy you a piece of Dutch apple pie à la mode."

"As always, your offer is tempting, but no thanks." He handed me the menu, and his face turned serious. "I meant what I said before, though. You should be careful."

"You're starting to sound like Michael."

Raphael held up his hands. "Hey, these aren't threats. More like warnings. Like I said, I like you, and I don't want to see anyone get hurt."

"Like who?"

"I should get going." He crumpled his napkin and dropped it on his empty plate. "I've already said more than I should have."

"Just like that? No hints? No advice? What good are you, then, coming here and letting me buy you lunch so you could fuck with my head?"

"You want advice?" Raphael glanced around, then skimmed his gentle brown eyes over my face. "I'll tell you a secret." He curled his finger at me, and I leaned closer. "If you follow love, you can't go wrong, even if it leads to disaster. Trust it."

He slid out of the booth and stood up. "I'll get in big trouble for that one, but what are they gonna do, fire me? I've got tenure." He touched my shoulder. "Thanks for lunch. I'll see you around."

Raphael grabbed several toothpicks and breath mints on his way out of the diner. When I looked at him through the window, he was standing on the curb watching the pedestrians. He helped an old man with a walker board a bus. As the man's legs passed in front of him, Raphael's hands hovered behind the rickety knees. I knew the healing would come gradually over the next few months—remarkable from a medical standpoint, but not quite miraculous. Raphael was never one to grandstand.

He waved to the grateful gentleman, then looked directly at me. With a casual salute, Raphael turned and meandered down the street.

30

Quidquid Latet Apparebit

O n a tree-lined avenue near Woodley Park, Gianna's scent became stronger. I quickened my pace.

Warmer. Warmer. Warmer—shit, colder. I turned and followed an almost hidden alleyway. All at once the tips of my fingers began to tingle and burn. She was here. I looked up.

She's clever, I thought. Faithless, but clever.

I forced my legs to carry me up the wooden stairs, then placed my hand on the church door. It creaked open.

Gianna was kneeling behind the front left pew, her head bowed. I crept down the aisle until I could see the edge of her face.

"I could feel you looking for me," she said.

"You could have lost me if you'd kept moving."

She said nothing.

"But you wanted me to find you here," I said.

"How dare you enter a house of God."

"I'd follow you into much worse."

She looked up then. Her eyes were red. They made my knees weak.

"Come here," she said. I sat on the bench next to her. "No, here, next to me."

"I am next to you," I said.

"No. Down here. Kneel."

"You're joking."

"Do I look like I'm joking?"

In fact, she did not. I stole a glance at the altar.

"You don't know what you're asking," I said.

Her eyes were steel. I stared at the wooden floor. Another test. She must stay in my life at all costs.

I reached out one hand, then the other, to grasp the back of the pew, then pulled myself forward slowly, carefully. The kneeler, though cushioned in vinyl, bit into my bones. I waited until I was sure I would not pass out, then looked at Gianna. Her eyes were wide.

"What else would you do for me?" she whispered.

"I will not claim Jesus as my personal savior," I said through gritted teeth.

"I don't understand you."

"Then stay with me until you do."

"I'm afraid," she said.

"So am I."

She glanced at the crucifix at the front of the church. "I don't want to be alone with you."

"Then let's find a crowd. I have many things to tell you."

"Now before we start," I said, "promise me that even if you don't believe a word I'm saying, you won't accuse me of lying. That could get very tedious and frustrating, and you don't want me to get upset around all these animals."

"So that's why we're here." She gestured to the sleeping panda in front of us. "Zoological diplomacy tools." There were only half a dozen other zoo visitors—a Norwegian couple and a Japanese family—milling about the panda house. They all looked disappointed at the natural sluggishness of the famous panda.

Gianna sat at the other end of my bench. "The most mind-boggling part of your existence is that it means that God exists, too."

"Did you ever doubt it?"

"Sure. I went through an existentialist-atheistic phase as a teenager. Even after I returned to Catholicism, my intellect raised doubts, but I always shut it up with a heaping dose of faith. Somehow I always felt like my faith was a form of denial." She pulled her feet up on the bench and rested her chin on her knees. "But if you're real, and if God's real, then the Bible has it right. We have the correct version of the story, and not just another take on the myth."

"Let's not get carried away. The creator of the universe has many names and forms, as do I, some male, some female, some many ages extinct. All the myths are true."

"How can that be?"

"The truth is much huger than anyone, even we angels, can comprehend. But whenever the mythmakers—writers, artists, thinkers—seek the truth with a passionate mind, they'll find it, or a piece of it, anyway." I slid closer to her. "That's why humans are so special. You're always seeking, always trying to find or invent bigger and bigger pieces of this truth. You'll never grasp even a fraction of it, but you keep trying, and that's what we all find so charming, so compelling. I think it's why he loves you all so much, not because you're more precious in his eyes than pandas, because you're not. What makes you different from pandas is that you're never happy."

"And that's a good thing?"

"Maybe not good, but it's beautiful." I stood and gestured to the panda. "He's having panda dreams right now. You know what pandas dream about? They don't dream about lounging in a bamboo field, or a fight they had with their mate, and they don't dream about their own deaths. Right now that panda's mind is full of soothing abstract shapes in shades of gray, pieced together from images he saw during the last two hours before his nap. A child's face becomes a drifting oval next to the cylinder of a bamboo stalk and the odd shape of his keeper's hat. It's nice, if you like that sort of thing, but it's not beautiful."

"How do you know this?"

"I'm telepathic, of course."

"Of course." Gianna covered her face. "I should have guessed."

I sat beside her. "I swear to you, Gianna, I've never probed your mind, not even once. Okay, once."

"When?"

"When we first met," I said. "I had to convince you to go out with me, so I gave you a little push."

"A little push?"

"Aren't you glad I did?"

"No!"

The eager expression melted from my face as her declaration sank in.

"I'm sorry." I stood and walked out of the panda house.

"Lou, I didn't mean . . . Lou . . ." Gianna caught up to me.

"You wish you'd never met me."

"I didn't say that."

"You're happy you met me, then? You thank your lucky stars every day that you fell in love with the Devil?"

"No, I—"

"Which is it, Gianna? Are you happy or not?"

"I'm human, aren't I?" Her voice tightened. "According to you, I'm never happy." She glared at me. "What about you? Are you happy?"

"Since I met you, yes. Closer to happiness than I've been since I was in Heaven. Right now, though, I'm not happy, because I don't know if in twenty minutes, you'll still be in my life or not. And I don't think you know either, do you?"

Her face contorted, and she took a deep breath. "I need more time."

"Time. I've got plenty of that. I'm twelve billion years old, and unless I do something colossally stupid I may be permitted to exist another twelve billion years." I touched her arm and felt her flinch. "But Gianna, nothing would make me happier than spending the next forty or fifty of those years with you."

She began to cry. "Don't say that. I can't be responsible for your happiness."

"Sorry. I guess that was a pretty codependent remark. How about this: if you leave me, I'll set all these animals on fire, one by one."

"What?!" She shoved my hand off her arm. "Don't you dare!"

"I was only kidding."

"How am I supposed to know that?"

"Because you know me," I said.

"No, I don't. Not anymore."

"Yes, you do. Gianna, forget everything you think you know about the Devil, and remember what you know about me. You love me. Remember that." I moved towards her again, helpless to stop myself. "You do still love me, don't you?"

Her tear-filled eyes answered me. I bent to kiss her. When my mouth was an inch away from hers, she said, "Where were you during the Holocaust?"

"What?"

"You heard me. Tell me the truth. I need to know."

"I wasn't where you think I was," I said.

"Where were you?"

"I wasn't working with the Nazis. Germany produced Hitler all by itself. I never even met the guy—not while he was alive, anyway."

"Then where were you?"

"I was . . . uh . . . setting up a gulag in Siberia."

"Oh, that's much better," she said. "No shame in that at all."

"What did you expect? That I was planting victory gardens and running the local USO?"

"Did you know what was happening, what the Nazis were doing?"

"Of course I knew. I've always had informants around the world. I knew from the moment the genocide began."

"And you didn't do anything to stop it?" she said.

"*I* didn't do anything to stop it?" I wanted to shake her. "Gianna, I may be the second most powerful being in the universe, but I'm a very distant second. What about the great and merciful What's-His-Face?"

"You mean God?"

"Yes! Where was he during the Holocaust? I'll tell you where he was. He was there. He was there, because he's everywhere. But he turned away, like he always does in the face of suffering."

"That's not true," she said, "and besides, who are you to accuse God? I know humans who have done more to alleviate suffering in a few years than you've done in your whole life."

"You're absolutely right, Gianna. I don't alleviate suffering. In fact, I increase it. But that's my job. That's why I'm the Devil, and he's not. And you're not. And all the very nice people you know, they're not the Devil, either."

"What if you did something good for a change? Would you still be you?"

"What do you mean?"

"What if you did something that wasn't in your job description? Like taking care of the one you love when she's sick, or risking your professional reputation to save hers, or sacrificing your own well-being to make her and her family happy? Would you suddenly cease to exist?"

"Obviously not," I said.

"Suppose for a moment that you did something good that was really big, something that was within your power to change, an enormous act of generosity or kindness, or even thwarting an act of evil. Would you still be the Devil?"

"I am who I am."

"You'll always be Lucifer. But what if someday the name of the Devil wasn't Lucifer? What if there were no Devil at all?"

"You'll have to excuse me," I put my hand to my forehead, "I'm having an existential aneurysm."

"Think about it. I bet you've already thought of something you can do, something that will make a difference. Why don't you try it, just for kicks, and see how it feels?"

"But Gianna—"

"How can you expect me to love you, to look at you without disgust, when you've resigned yourself to this role you play?"

"It's not just a role, it's my fate. It's who I am."

"It's who you've been."

"Yes, for ten billion years."

"It doesn't matter how long. Anyone can change." She wrapped her scarf around her neck. "Look, I'm not asking you to be a saint. I'm only asking you to perform one righteous act, for its own sake. Then try to tell yourself about fate."

She walked away, and a dull ache was born in my stomach, as I realized what I had to do.

31

Libera Eas de Ore Leonis

*T*his is just for kicks, I told myself as I broke into Mephistopheles's office. *Just to see what it feels like.*

He'd be out of town until that afternoon, performing an urgent errand I'd assigned to him in Richmond, Virginia. It was a legitimate request, so that if I lost my nerve and didn't do what I came to do, he'd return unsuspecting, and our lives would go on as usual.

I stood in front of his inner chamber office door in front of the keypad. I knew that if I missed any of the entrance codes by one digit, I'd spend days reattaching my severed limbs. My photographic memory served me well, though, and a minute later I booted up his main computer.

Just for kicks. Using Mephistopheles's passwords, observed and cached in my own memory over six weeks ago, I found his elaborate file directory.

I'm not doing this for the good of humanity. Ignoring the expanding pit of pain in my gut, I deleted the basic program, then the related files for the Million Man Massacre. His strategies, maps, statistics, formulas—I zapped his years of toil into nonexistence.

Fuck humanity. I accessed the first of three backup files and deleted it. In another two minutes the second one was gone. I found the third one and wondered if it was in fact the last remaining reproduction of his work, or if he had lied to me about how many copies he'd made.

But Mephistopheles trusted me.

For nearly ten minutes I stared at the screen, at his last hope for the American future he'd envisioned: flames and blood and rebellion and oppression and murder and chaos. Then, with one steady and deliberate finger, I pressed the Delete key.

Kicks, kicks, kicks. Whee. I set his computer to do a complete backup of his new, Massacre-free hard drive. In his outer office, I inserted a blank four-millimeter tape into his main server to hold the new backup. Finally, I collected the offsite copies from his and Beelzebub's apartments, as well as Belial's house, and returned to my office, where the fifth copy remained. From any of these tapes he could have restored at least a large fragment of his masterpiece.

I melted them all, lit a cigarette, and waited. At quarter past three, he came.

"LUCIFER!!"

"Mr. Mephistopheles, how are—"

"Where is he, Daphne?! I'll tear his fucking—"

"Do you have an appointment?"

I stood. He threw open my door and glared at me, black eyes blazing, nostrils trembling with fury. I stared back at him with simple, cold supremacy.

"Lucifer, what the fuck were you thinking? Why did you—what were you . . . how dare you . . ." Mephistopheles pointed

at me, but his wrath was already subsiding under my gaze.
"Why?"

"I don't have to explain myself to you," I said.

He clutched at the back of the chair facing me. "If it wasn't
good enough . . . if it wasn't evil enough, why didn't you tell
me?" He crammed his forehead into his palms. "You didn't
have to destroy it. You took all the backups, too, didn't you?"

I nodded at the small pile of melted plastic on my conference table. Mephistopheles sucked in his breath and staggered
over to the remnants of his would-be legacy.

"No . . ." He cradled the disintegrated bits of data storage.
"It's still in my head, you know—parts of it, anyway. I could
reconstruct it." He looked up at me. "But if you don't want it
to happen, I guess I could find something else . . . Lou, this was
so random. I don't understand." My stern silence pressed him
back towards the door. He put his hand on the knob and
stopped.

"Lucifer, that Massacre . . . that Massacre was like a fuckin'
baby to me." Mephistopheles stepped back through the doorway. "And you killed it."

When he was gone, my knees gave way. I sank into my chair
and laid my forehead on the desk to keep from passing out.

"Mr. Lucifer . . ." Daphne's voice was at the door. "What's
going on?" I said nothing, didn't even look at her. In a few
moments, her footsteps retreated, and the door closed.

W hen I reached my apartment that evening, Beelzebub
was waiting for me outside the front door.

"What did you do to Mephistopheles?" he hissed.

"Why don't you ask him?" I brushed past him into the lobby.

"I did ask him, and in between all his blubbering, I got a

pretty good idea of what happened. Why did you do it, Lou? You didn't consult with any of us." Beelzebub followed me into the elevator. "What the hell is wrong with you? Are you trying to destroy us? What are we supposed to do?"

"You said yourself there was no point to all of it, so who cares what we do or don't do anymore?"

"You betrayed him, Lucifer. He trusted you, and you betrayed him. Why?" The elevator door opened, and I crossed the hallway to my apartment. "Is it because of her?" he said. "Did you do this just to impress a girl?"

"She doesn't even know about it. I don't need approval from her or you or Mephistopheles. I just want to be left alone."

"Okay, Greta Garbo, I'll leave you alone. You go in there and wallow in your misery and play with your piano and think about how much you hate your poor little self. Meanwhile, the rest of us will be out here trying to accomplish something, or at least have fun trying." He got back in the elevator. "If this is the way you're going to be, then we don't need you. Think about that."

For the first hour, I sat on my sofa and played with the snow globe Gianna had given me. I tipped it, watched the little white paint flecks drift and fall through the baby oil sky, then shook it so that all the snow fell off the branches of the Christmas tree in the center. Finally, I put it down, picked up the phone and dialed the leader of my armed forces.

"Moloch, it's Lucifer."

"Sir!"

"Colonel, I'm sorry I've been putting you off for so long. I'd like to take a look at those plans."

The following morning I drove north into the central Maryland hills, on the outskirts of Camp David, to Moloch's underground military headquarters.

As I entered the war room, a wave of nostalgia swept over me. Around this long, oval table I had plotted hundreds of revolutions and counterrevolutions. Dozens of maps covered with colored pins lined the walls, remnants of the days before we simulated our wars on a computer screen.

"I want to see that map," I told Moloch.

"Which one, sir?"

"The one you tried to show me a couple of months ago. The back door to Heaven you said you found."

"Ah, that one." Moloch's stiff face couldn't restrain a smile. He reached into a drawer at the end of the table and pulled out a large rolled-up sheet of paper.

"Here you are, sir. Since I last spoke with you, we've been able to narrow it down to within a few meters."

He unrolled the map in front of me and secured its corners with paperweights. My eyes were drawn to the star in the center indicating the alleged portal. I scanned the area around it, then spied the name of the nearby river. I looked at Moloch.

"This is a fucking joke, right?"

"I've never been known for my sense of humor, sir."

"But how can this be?" I wrapped my fingers around one of the paperweights. "You'd better be damn sure about this."

"General, I assure you, we've never been this certain about anything."

"But why there? I don't get it."

"Perhaps we're not meant to get it, if you know what I mean."

"Moloch, don't hand me any of that 'mysterious ways' bull-shit. This just doesn't make sense." I grabbed the map and shook it at him. "I want answers, Colonel. I want to know why."

"Sir, perhaps the answer is simply, because." He spread his hands. "What does it matter, why? It just is. Be grateful we know that much."

"I suppose. I just . . . I just always imagined it would be in the Himalayas." I rolled up the map. "I'll take this copy."

"Certainly, sir. Did you want to hear about my invasion strategies?"

"Put them in a report. Right now, I want you to think defensively. Put all the troops on alert."

"Sir, is everything all right?"

"I'm not sure." I clutched the map in my hands. "There's a storm coming, Moloch. Maybe it just wants me, but we should all be careful."

"Lucifer, you know we'd fight to the death to protect you."

Moloch seemed so determined and small, like a terrier ready to wrestle a hurricane.

"I know," I said. "Thank you. I may need you soon."

"It would be an honor, General."

I returned his salute and left before I could tell him the truth: that nothing was an honor anymore.

32

Ingemisco Tanquam Reus

I drove back to my office, determined to do some serious work, to prove to myself and the others that I hadn't become a soft-hearted, ineffectual slug, that I had not only plenty of evil left in me, but also directions in which to send it.

The map bothered me, though, and in between phone calls and advisory meetings I would unfurl it and scrutinize the red star and its surroundings, trying to apprehend the meaning behind the apparent absurdity. I flipped through my address book and collection of business cards for someone I could trust, someone who could give me a piece of the puzzle.

Gianna.

Yes, this map pointed to a truth that she grasped, a truth I hadn't even begun to reach for. I called her office.

"Gianna, it's me."

"What do you want?"

"I need some advice," I said.

"Legal advice? I thought you had your own team of sharks."

"No, not that. I need . . . spiritual advice . . . sort of."

"Is this a trick?"

"No. Gianna, I need answers, and you're the only one who can help me. There's something I want to show you."

The phone was silent for several seconds. "All right. I'll come by later."

✳

"This had better be good."

I stood aside to let Gianna step into my apartment. "Would you like a drink?"

"What did you want to show me?"

"So much for formalities." I led her into the living room, where the map lay spread on a coffee table.

We sat on the couch, and Gianna examined the map. She pointed to the red star. "What's that?"

"It's a back door, a portal. To Heaven."

Gianna huffed and started to stand up. "I didn't come here so you could play with my mind, Lou."

"I'm not kidding," I said. "Believe me, I wish I were. If I were lying, do you think I'd invent that as a location?"

"Sure, why not? It makes sense."

I almost fell off the couch. "It does?!"

"If it is what you say it is."

"Explain it to me. Why there? I expected it to be in a cave on a two-mile-high mountain, or maybe in the Amazon rain forest."

"No." She sat down and gestured at the star. "This place is about people. It's about suffering, and compassion, and death. Seems like an appropriate place to me."

"But isn't it a bit . . . lowly? A bit wretched?"

"You can't buy your way into Heaven," she said. "Remember? 'The last shall be first, and the first shall be last.'"

"How could I forget?"

"What I want to know is, how does this exist at all?"

"Physics isn't exactly my strong suit," I said, "but the best way to explain it is that there's this stuff that humans have named exotic matter. It's got a negative energy density and therefore negative mass and even negative gravity. So it actually repels material and creates a sort of hole. Now a hole big enough to fit an actual human body would create a rip in the space-time fabric and literally cause all Hell to break loose. But anything whose essence is spirit, like a human soul, or an angel, can pop in and out of these entrances—that is, if they vibrate at the right frequencies."

"What are the right frequencies?"

"It depends on who you are. You need a different quantum password, so to speak, to get into Hell or Heaven. They can't visit us, we can't visit them. We can't even detect each other's entrances."

"But you found one of theirs," she said. "Lou, what if this door was meant for you?"

"You mean as a trap? I've thought of that."

"No, not a trap. An invitation."

"That's impossible," I said.

"Why is it impossible?"

"Unforgiven means unforgiven. Forever. Even if it were possible, I wouldn't go."

"Why not?"

"Because you'd be here."

"What if this is your only chance? What if this offer expires if you don't accept it?"

"I don't care," I said. "I want to be with you."

"Lou . . ." She bent her head forward. A lock of hair fell onto her face. I brushed it back and rested my hand on her cheek.

"I love you, Gianna. I'd give up everything to be with you, so please let me be with you."

I kissed her softly, and felt her wilt beneath my lips. She put her hand against mine. It trembled like an injured bird.

"Marry me, Gianna."

She jerked back, stifled a choke, then began to laugh.

"What's so funny?" I said.

"Marry you? You're kidding, right?"

"No, I'm not kidding. You didn't think it was funny before, on New Year's Eve."

"But then you weren't—I mean, I didn't know who you were."

"And now?"

"Come on, Lou, you can't expect—"

"Can't expect what?" I lurched off the sofa. "You already said yes once. I know things are different now, but you said you still love me."

"I do, but—"

"Then marry me, Gianna."

"Why?" She stood and faced me. "Why would you want to get married? It's a sacrament."

"Because I want to have a normal life with you, in the eyes of society, in the eyes of your family. Because I want to have children with you."

She recoiled. "Children? You want me to have your children?"

"I've never had any. Contrary to legend, I don't run around impregnating every woman I see. You think I like the idea of a bunch of little me's lurking around the planet? I couldn't stand the competition." I moved toward her. "But with you, I think I could create something beautiful."

"No! I won't bring more evil into this world."

"Gianna, listen—"

"No!" She held out her hand to keep me away. "I would have married Louis Carvalho in a second. But I'll die before I give birth to the spawn of Satan!"

The word stopped my breath on its way out. My lip curled into a snarl.

"I told you NEVER to call me that!" I grabbed the snow globe from the table at my side and hurled it to the floor at her feet. I stepped over the broken glass towards her. The smell of baby oil and paint flecks filled the air between us.

Her face crumpled in fury. "I am not afraid of you!"

"You should be!" I grasped her chin with one hand and burned my eyes into hers. "I sure as hell am."

"Then let go of me before you do something we'll both hate you for."

"As if we don't both hate me already." I jerked my hand from her head.

Gianna choked back a sob "What have I done? I should have stayed with Adam. He was a real angel."

"Stop speaking every thought that enters your head. You might accidentally reveal stupidity."

She slapped me. I didn't flinch. She slapped me again and again. Finally I restrained her arms.

"Stop that," I said. She kicked me in the shin. "Ow!!" I let go of her and bent over in pain.

"Don't ever call me stupid," she said.

"I didn't say you were stupid. What you said was stupid, though."

"I meant it."

"No, you didn't. You have no regrets. If you did, you wouldn't be here right now." She was silent. "I'm tired of you running in and out on me, Gianna." I sat on the floor and rubbed my shin. "Do you think you can't hurt me? If you do, then you are stupid, and cruel. So either stay or leave, but whatever you do, it has to be for good. If you try to leave . . ."

She took a step backward.

"If you try to leave," I said, "I'll let you go. No more arguments. It's time for the jury to retire." I got to my feet. "Speaking of retiring, I'm going to bed now. When I wake up, if I sleep, you'll either be lying beside me or gone forever. It's your choice. It's always been your choice." I limped to the bedroom door and turned to face her. "I love you, Gianna, but you can't save me. If you stay, it has to be for you, not for me. Look at your life and decide if I belong there."

I left her standing in the center of my living room. Once I had slipped under the sheets and lay in silence, I could hear her sobs float through the door. The sound compressed the blood vessels in my chest and throat until I could barely breathe. I stared at the doorknob for hours, but it never turned.

I must have fallen asleep, for it was light when my eyes opened again. Afraid to see my solitude, I reached out a hand behind me. Cold sheets met my touch. I closed my eyes and wondered if I could sleep another century until the pain faded.

A sound came from the living room. I leapt out of bed and opened the door. Gianna was lying on the sofa.

"I'm sorry," she said. Her eyes were red and swollen. "The jury's still out. Forgive me."

33

Nil Inultum Remanebit

To distract myself from my emotional crisis, I spent the morning brain-deep in the latest astrophysics research. In the last few years, I had become so preoccupied with mundane economic and political "realities" that I had neglected to track human awareness of the largest and smallest questions.

I was so engrossed in this study that I jumped when Gianna burst through my office door.

"Hi," I said. "It's good to see—"

"Have you seen this atrocity?" She slapped the morning's *Washington Post* onto my desk. The main headline read "Senator Kills Foreign Aid Bill."

"Redskins are out of the playoffs. Shame about that."

"No, this." She pointed to the center of the page. A bloated, balding man—Gianna's "Senator Scrooge"—stood before Congress, caught in midrant. "Those people are starving, and that monster won't send food because they're Communists. As if Communists can't feel hunger."

"He knows they feel hunger," I said. "He's glad they feel hunger. If people are hungry enough, they'll start killing each other for resources, and the next thing you know, they'll be capitalists."

"Can't you do something about this?"

"You mean stop the famine? That would involve creation, not destruction. Sorry." I scanned the article. "However, maybe I could do something about the senator."

"Is he one of yours?"

"One of mine?" I snickered. "Oh, that's a good one. No, he's just some guy."

"Oh."

"Some guy with a wife, two kids and a dog. Visits his mother every Sunday. No, wait . . . two dogs now. They just got a new puppy." I set the paper aside and took another sip of coffee. "But I can have him killed for you. Just say the word."

"No!"

"That's not the word, Gianna. The word is 'yes.'"

"I don't want you to kill him!"

"Don't you?" I stood and leaned over my desk to face her at eye level. "Don't you hate this man?"

"Yes, but—"

"And don't you think the world would be a better place without him?"

"I—"

"He stands in the way of so much good, doesn't he? It isn't fair that someone so despicable, so small-minded, should have so much power."

She took a half-step backwards, but kept staring at me. "Think about it," I said. "All the lives that could be saved, the anguish avoided." I reached out and touched her cheek. "Gianna, let me help you in the only way I know how."

"Lou, it's not right." She took my hand from her face but did not let go of it. "It's not right."

"What he does isn't right, either." I picked up the phone. "All it takes is one call. Seven little digits." I began to dial. "1-2-3-" I looked at her. "What's it gonna be?"

"Don't."

"4-5-6." I drew her finger towards the last button. "It could all be fixed."

She pulled her hand out of mine and placed it on the phone line's glowing light. The dial tone rose from the receiver.

"You've made your point," she said.

"Good. Wanna have lunch?"

"No, I should go."

"Why? Do you have a meeting?"

"No." She backed away. "I just think . . . I need to be away from you for a while."

"Again? What now?"

"I don't like what you're doing to me, Lou." She pointed to the phone. "I really wanted you to make that call. I still do."

"And?"

"And I don't like the part of me that wants that. I don't know where that came from."

"And you think it's my fault?" I moved toward her and saw that, for the first time, she was afraid of me.

"I—I don't know." She put her hand on the doorknob. "But if I can just get away from you, maybe it'll go away."

She opened the door. I pushed it shut and glared down at her.

"No, Gianna, it won't go away."

"Let me go."

"No."

"Please, you're scaring me."

"I'm not scaring you, Gianna. You're scaring you." I grabbed her arm and dragged her to the mirror. "Look." I

clutched her chin. "Look at this self-righteous little face. Look
in your own eyes and tell yourself that you are innocent, that it
was I who planted these dark impulses in your heart."

"Lou—"

"Don't look at me. Look at yourself, because in the end,
that's all you have, and you have to accept everything that you
are, the beautiful and the ugly, the noble and the depraved. If
you don't face your sins, they will consume you as they have
consumed me."

"No!" She slipped out of my grip, backed away and pointed
at me. "I am not like you!"

"You're not?" I advanced towards her again, and this time
she did not even flinch. "Who are you like, then?" She didn't
answer. I laughed. "Oh, yes, made in his image. You are truly
one of his children if you condemn those whose ways you do
not understand." I picked up the newspaper. "Smite the
Canaanites, smite the Babylonians . . ." I threw the paper at
her feet. "Why not smite the Republicans?"

"Your twisted logic won't convince me to sentence another
human being to death."

"You don't need my logic to convince you. You've got the
facts, the history of this man's life, a life devoted to bigotry and
ignorance, a life that's better off ended before he does any
more damage. Right?"

"No," she said. "It's not up to me to decide who dies, no
matter how tempting that power may be."

I realized then that I would not win this argument with
words. I took a deep breath.

"You're right," I said. "I forget sometimes that we're not in
the same boat."

"We're not even floating on the same sea, Lou." She turned
to leave, then stopped. "Just give me some more time, okay?"

"All right. Whatever you need."

"Thank you." When Gianna reached the door, she looked back at me for a moment, then left.

I picked the newspaper off the floor and carried it to my desk. I punched the redial button on my phone, then finished the number with a final digit. Rimmon, my personal physician and most stealthy assassin, answered on the first ring.

"Good morning, boss. May I take your order?"

"Good morning, Rimmon. I've got a high-priority job for you today."

He listened to my demand. "Ooh, I love the public ones," he said. "Nothing like watching your handiwork on the evening news, is there? I don't suppose I can ask what prompted this request?"

"No."

"Just checking. Whether it's all part of the master plan, or just a passing whim, I'm here to serve. I'll get right on it."

"You're a gem, Rimmon. Have fun."

34

Ne Perenni Cremer Igne

I decided to spend the evening at one of my usual haunts, Capitol Hill's hippest political watering hole, a favorite hangout of bright-eyed congressional staffers and lobbyist flacks. I had insinuated myself into one of the prettier groups and was debating Keynesian versus neoclassical economics with a couple of energetic young professionals when one member of the group darted up to the table, his pitcher of beer sloshing onto his tie.

"Guys, you won't believe this. Check out the news!"

The bartender turned up the television, and the pub quieted to hear about the sudden death of a senior senator, who had been stricken with a brain aneurysm in the congressional men's room.

When the main broadcast was over, the news team began a brief retrospective of the senator's career and mentioned that a more in-depth look at the man's life would appear on the ten o'clock news magazine.

"Holy shit," said the Milton Friedman devotee sitting next to me. "I can't believe he's dead."

"Yeah, and me without my tap shoes," muttered the woman next to him. The other people at the table gaped at her. "Come on, let's not be hypocrites," she said. "He's done a lot to make our lives miserable the last few years. We're all better off, whether we'd like to admit it or not."

"I think the man deserves a toast," I said, "no matter how we felt about him."

This gesture seemed to unite the group, and we all raised our glasses. Before I tilted my head back to drink, however, I saw a figure in the doorway of the bar. She stared at me with cold fury.

"Excuse me." I rose from the table.

"See you later?" the senator-hating woman asked. I didn't answer as I passed her chair on the way to the door.

"Hi," I said to Gianna. She did not return my ingratiating smile. "I guess you heard." She didn't reply, but fixed her eyes upon mine until I looked away. "You want me to get a table?"

"I hate you."

"Or we could sit at the bar."

"Did you hear me?" Her voice was low and rumbling, like a Rottweiler's growl. "I said I hate you. You're an evil, wretched creature, and I curse the moment I met you. I should have stayed in bed that day, I should have slit my own throat, rather than let you touch my life."

"I thought you'd be happy."

"No, you didn't. You knew I'd be angry, but you had something to prove. You've proven what a despicable, loathsome being you are and always will be." She turned and walked out of the bar. I followed her.

"I did this for you, Gianna. It was what you wanted."

"You don't get it, do you? All you understand is power and

desire. You want something, and you just take it, because you can. But a man is dead now, and it's my fault."

"No, it's not. You didn't do this, I did. You wanted him to disappear, but you didn't want it on your conscience. You didn't have the courage to let your soul take the fall."

"Courage?! Courage to ask my boyfriend the Devil to kill someone for me?" She threw up her arms. "That doesn't take courage. It was harder for me to tell you *not* to kill him."

"But I gave you what you wanted without you having to be responsible. It's a win-win situation."

"Not for him. He's still dead."

"So?"

"'So?' How can you think that a person's life is so insignificant?"

"Listen." I turned her to face me. "You are alive. You are mortal. You don't realize how small a life is compared to what lies beyond. Many people say they believe in an afterlife, but no one knows for sure if there's anything other than the darkness and silence of a corpse. For you there is no fate worse than death, because you cannot begin to comprehend the unbearable beauty of Heaven."

"Whatever lies beyond, life is still precious." She began to walk away again. I stayed a few paces behind her. We covered almost a half a mile before she slowed to walk next to me.

"Can you forgive me?" I said. She didn't answer. "I was trying to help. Besides, I needed to show you that I still am who I am, and you can't change that. But I feel like I'm evolving into something else. That terrifies me.

"Being evil is all I've ever known, Gianna. With all my power, it's so easy to just say 'fuck it,' and do whatever I feel like. There are no consequences for me—until now, that is."

"So I'm the superego you never had," she said. "That's fun."

"Gianna, I need you. You may be my only chance."

"Chance at what? World domination?"

"No."

"Then what?" She stopped and turned to me. "What other goal could you possibly have?"

"I—" I lowered my eyes, afraid to voice my deepest hope.

She waited for me to speak, then whispered, "You told me that I can't save you. You've shown me that you can't be saved. But do you really believe it yourself?"

"I don't know what I believe anymore."

I sensed that if I touched her then, I would either keep her or lose her forever. The tips of my fingers brushed against hers. She winced but did not move away.

"I wish I could see what you've seen," she said. "Maybe then I could understand why you're so awful."

"No, you still wouldn't understand, and it would probably drive you mad."

"Can you show me? Just a glimpse?"

"No, I can't do that."

"You'd kill for me, but you won't let me inside your own mind?"

"That's right," I said, "because that vision could hurt you."

"So be careful, then."

I sighed. "You're a real Pandora, aren't you?"

"Yes. I want to know. I want to see."

"Your thirst for knowledge is too much like mine."

"Then you'll do it?"

I looked around at the busy street. "Not here."

We entered my living room. I went to the bar and pulled out a bottle of brandy and a small glass.

"You should probably have a drink first," I said. "It'll help you relax." I poured her a shot, hesitated, then added another one. She downed it in two gulps.

"Okay, let's get started."

We sat on the couch, and I grasped her wrist to feel her pulse.

"Now just relax and look into my eyes, Gianna. Tell me if you feel like you're going to die." She nodded and blinked with anticipation. I closed my eyes. When I opened them again, they had become unlocked windows to my memory.

Her pupils grew wider and wider as she was drawn into the darkness. I let her push her way through at her own pace, and hid only the most gruesome portions of my existence. I carried her back through time and shared with her my few triumphs and countless defeats. Tears rolled down her cheeks, and her teeth began to chatter.

"Do you want to keep going?" I said.

"Y—yes. Don't stop." Her whole body was shivering now, and her forehead was wet with icy sweat. I fought to control my own emotions as I relived the first days after the Fall—the despair, the rage, the brief moments of repentance. The solitude.

"Show me . . . before," she said.

I gripped her hand so tightly I feared I would crush her slender fingers in my palm. At her first glimpse of Heaven, my original home, she drew in a sharp breath, as if she had been stabbed.

"So . . . beautiful." In the next instant, Gianna's pupils constricted to pinpoints. She screamed.

I squeezed my eyes shut and felt her collapse in my arms. Her heart flailed against her chest. She panted and heaved like a resuscitated drowning victim.

"W—was that . . . was that . . . ?"

"Yes," I said, "it was."

She let out one last sigh, then fainted. I laid her body back on the couch and stroked her hair until she entered a deep, dreamless sleep. I fetched a stack of blankets and covered her with them. When she had stopped shivering, I sat in the chair opposite the couch and watched her sleep.

Gianna did not stir until the first red light of dawn bled onto the walls of the room. She coughed once, turned on her back, then sat straight up. I jumped.

"Are you all right?" I said.

She turned to look at me, then with an unwavering gaze upon my face, rose from the sofa, came to me and crawled into my lap. Her eyes, which seemed to reflect a faraway light, devoured mine.

"Do it again," she said.

"What? Are you crazy?"

"I want to see again."

"Gianna, you practically went into cardiac arrest the first time. No, it's not safe. I shouldn't have even done it once."

"Oh, but you have to. Please."

"I said no."

She slumped to the floor at my feet and clutched at my shirt. "Yes!" The tears began to fall again. "Please, Lou, you've got to show me—"

"Why?"

"I have to see Him again!"

I gaped at her. "*Him?* You have to see *him* again?" I shoved her hands away from me and stood up. "You'll see him soon enough."

She covered her face and moaned.

"I don't understand." I moved away from her. "I'm with you every day and night, I show you how much I adore you, I lay the fucking world at your feet, and you still love him more than me?"

"How could I not?" She lifted her palms. "If I loved you more than God, I'd be as doomed as you are."

"Then why are you even here, Gianna? Why don't you just run along and let What's-His-Face keep you warm at night?"

She lurched to her feet. "Why can't you just say His name? Why can't you call Him God?"

"Because I am forbidden!" Her glare dissipated, and her jaw dropped. "Yes, forbidden," I said. "Forbidden to speak to him, forbidden to invoke him, forbidden to utter even his stupid little name. That's how cut off I am."

Gianna sank back onto the chair and hung her head. "I didn't know. I'm sorry. I always thought you were just . . ."

"What? That I was just being obnoxious?" She nodded. "I was being obnoxious," I said. "We all mock what we can't have."

She pulled her knees to her chin. "When I was . . . inside of you last night, I saw . . ." She was shivering again. "I saw it all . . . what you went through . . . and felt it with you." She gazed up at me. "How did you endure? The rejection, the hopelessness . . ."

"I found comfort in evil, in whatever small acts of defiance I could accomplish, and in the camaraderie of my fellow rebels. I grew accustomed to the despair, because it was all I knew. Until I met you."

"When we first made love," I said, "really made love, I mean—not that act of pure carnality in my library—I saw something . . . something that had been beyond my reach for as long as I could remember. It was more than a memory, more than a vision. It was like being . . . there again." Tears chased each other down my face. "Gianna, this love between us could . . . it could change everything."

I knelt in front of her, wrapped my arms around her legs and pressed my cheek against her knee. "I need you, Gianna, but I fear I'll destroy you. I fear he'll come between us, that he'll punish me for being so happy. He's a jealous god, and if you ever loved me more than him—"

"Shhh." She wove her fingers through my hair and kissed the top of my head. "Lucifer, if God sees into people's hearts, and I think He does, then He already knows."

"Knows what?"

"He already knows that I love you more than anything."

She pressed her cheek against mine so that our tears became one smooth, wet smear. Then she kissed me, a kiss that burned with the desperation known only to those on the border of salvation and damnation. At that moment, I wasn't sure on which side of this boundary either of us stood.

She rose to her feet and took my hand to lead me to the bedroom.

"Are you sure?" I said.

"Yes. Only . . . let me . . ."

I closed my eyes and didn't move while she undressed me and covered my body with the tenderest of kisses and caresses, searching out the ribbons of pain and despair that still dwelled in every cell. Gianna made love to me all morning, in the soft glow of the winter sun.

We didn't speak the rest of the day, only remained near one another, united by a silent wonder. Inside of me, stirring near the back of my rib cage, was a scrawny little scrap of a feeling I'd heard humans call hope.

❋

"Gianna, wake up."

I shook her shoulder in the dark. She stirred and stretched, then fell back to sleep. I jostled her again.

"Gianna, wake up, I have to tell you something."

"Wha—?" She rolled over to face me. "What is it?"

"I've decided to quit."

"Huh? Quit what?"

"Quit being the Devil."

She rubbed her nose. "And do what instead? Sell insurance?"

"Anything. I want us to have a normal life."

"I can't believe I'm hearing this."

"I just want to be Louis Carvalho, the man you fell in love with."

"But that's not who you really are."

"I can reinvent myself," I said. "Humans do it all the time, why can't I? All I do is play a role, like you said, an increasingly obsolete one. I can't play that role anymore. Not as long as you're in my life, which I hope will be as long as you live."

"What about afterwards?" She sat up. "What about after I die, what will you do then?"

"I haven't thought that far ahead."

"What if it's not that long?"

"It will be," I said.

"How do you know?"

"I've dreamed it, your death, more than once." I reached up and touched her chin. "You're very old, in this dream, and still very beautiful. There are young people there, and it feels like they're our children."

"Are your dreams premonitions? Do they always come true?"

"Not always. But this one feels true."

She leaned back on the headboard. The city lights sneaking through the window glinted in her eyes. "So you spend the next fifty years playing house until I croak, and then what will you do for the rest of eternity?"

"Grieve," I said.

"Won't that get tiresome?"

"I don't know." I sat up. "Look, Gianna, I don't know what I'll do for the rest of eternity. I may pick up where I left off the day after your funeral. But for right now I don't want to come home to you and not be able to talk about what I did at the office." I touched her arm. "Can you really expect to keep loving me if you knew that every day I was working to increase suffering? Wouldn't you rather I do something good, or at least something neutral for a while?"

"Only if it's your choice," she said. "I don't want you to sacrifice too much for me. You'll only hate me later."

"I can't hate you." I rested my head in her lap and wrapped my arm around her hip. "Especially since I'll be sponging off you until I break into the music business, which shouldn't be too long, since I have lots of contacts there."

"Would you promise me something, Louis?"

"Anything."

"Promise me that after I die, you'll consider using that door? The one to Heaven?"

I squeezed her. "Ever the lawyer, even in the middle of the night. Sure, I promise I'll consider it. What the hell."

"You're going to have to tell me all of this again in the morning, because I still believe I'm dreaming."

"Okay."

"I mean it," she said. "If you change your mind between now and then, just don't say anything. I'll think it was a dream."

"Okay."

In the morning, I rose early, set the alarm for Gianna, then left for the office by daybreak. Next to the coffee pot I left her a note that read, "Had to leave early to clean out my desk and check the want ads. Love, Louis."

35

Mors Stupebit et Natura

"You wanted to see me?"

Beelzebub stood in my office doorway, his arms folded across his chest.

I stood and reached for my coat. "Let's take a walk."

We bought a cup of coffee at a shop off Constitution Avenue, then strolled down the street. The impotent January sun couldn't take the edge off the bitter wind. We were the only ones on the sidewalk not hurrying for shelter from the cold.

"I thought about what you said, Bub, about you and the others not needing me anymore."

"Lou, I didn't mean that, you know. I was just pissed off."

"You were right. You were right to be pissed off, and you were right about my job performance. I'm no good to you in this condition, so I've decided to take a sabbatical."

"A sabbatical?"

"A few years off to pursue other interests."

"I know what a sabbatical is," he said. "How many years?"

"Just forty or fifty."

He halted. "Forty or fifty years?! Are you nuts?"

"It's nothing I haven't done before. Remember a few cen-turies ago, after What's-His-Face shut up for good, I took time off for my music? I'm doing that again. My music suffers when I only know evil, when I don't experience the full spectrum of—"

"This isn't about your music, is it?" he said. "Forty or fifty years—for the rest of Gianna's life, right?"

"That's right."

He threw his half-full coffee cup on the sidewalk. It splat-tered across my shoes and against the trunk of a small tree.

"I don't fucking believe this!" he said. "It's not enough that we never see you anymore, it's not enough that you go off cele-brating Christmas and ruining our plans for world terror. Now you're quitting to be with her?"

"I'm not quitting. This is only temporary. Fifty years is nothing to you and me."

"And when you come back, everything will be the same, huh?"

"I—"

"It won't be." He shook his finger at me. "Don't lie to me and tell me you'll pop back into your seat at the helm of the evil machine and act like you've just been on a little vacation."

"Bub—"

"This is crappy timing, you know? I've been talking to Moloch, and I know we're headed for another showdown with Heaven."

"All the more reason for me to step aside. It's me they want, not you. Maybe things will cool down a bit if I take myself out of the picture."

"Oh, so now I'm supposed to believe you're doing this out of concern for us? That's so sweet, it breaks my—"

"You don't have to like what I'm doing," I said. "You just have to accept it."

"You think you can change who you are just by saying it?"

"Yes. This is America."

"Lucifer, when are you gonna realize that being you isn't just a job? You can't strip off your destiny and hang it in the closet like a uniform."

"There's no such thing as destiny."

"There's definitely such a thing as nature, and what you're doing goes against your nature." He grabbed my coat sleeve. "She's trying to turn you into something you're not."

"No!" I shook off his hand. "You're the one doing that, Beelzebub. You're trying to make me into your image of me, of pure evil. But I'm not pure evil, and if you'd let go of your own fear for one moment, you'd realize that you're not, either."

I caught his fist just before it reached my jaw. Our eyes clashed in a stream of fury.

"You did not just say that," he growled.

"You want me to say it again? Or should I write it down for you so you won't forget?"

"No." Beelzebub pulled his fist out of my hand and stepped back. He straightened his coat. "So is this one of those 'we can still be friends' moments?"

"I'd still like to hang out with you."

"Yeah, I'll come over for Christmas dinner." He spat on the sidewalk. "Afterwards we'll have a couple beers, watch the game, worship Jesus. It'll be fun."

I moved toward him. "Bub—"

"No." He stepped aside and held up his hand, waist-high. "Hey, it's cool, okay?" He glanced at his watch. "Look, I've got a meeting at the World Bank in half an hour. We'll get together before you leave. We'll have business to discuss, you and me and Mephistopheles, work out who takes over each of your projects, that kind of thing. Maybe we'll even throw you a goodbye party."

"You mean a 'see-you-later' party," I said.

"Right." Beelzebub's pale blue eyes met mine, then shifted away. "I'll see you around."

When I returned to my office, I called Gianna.

"Hey," she said, "speak of the Devil."

"You've been waiting to use that one, haven't you?" I said. "What are you doing tonight?"

"There's this concert I really want to go to. They're doing Verdi's *Requiem* at St. Matthew's."

"Would you like a date?"

"It's in a church, Lou."

"I love Verdi. Maybe that would offset my allergies."

"Are you sure?"

"If my head starts to blow up, I'll leave and meet you afterwards, like I did on Christmas Eve."

"Okay, then. Pick me up here at six."

That night will never leave me.

From the mournful, haunting strains of the "Requiem/Kyrie," to the terrifying, nerve-stretching throbs of the "Dies Irae," Verdi's *Requiem* made me want to weep with fury, fear, and sorrow. Gianna gripped my hand throughout the ninety-minute performance. Her wistful rapture of Christmas Eve Mass paled before the wide-eyed fervor that captured her face that night.

Afterward, we sat speechless in the pew. Finally, she turned to me and said, "How do you feel?"

"I feel everything."

"No, I mean, your . . . allergies."

"That's odd. There's no sign of them. I didn't even think about it once the music started."

"That was an incredible performance," she said. "I'd never heard it sung live before. I think I actually got a fever during the 'Dies Irae.'"

"That was my favorite section."

"Naturally. That's the nasty part with all the fire."

"Nah, I just like the drums. They kick ass."

She picked up her coat. "Ready to go?"

"Yes. I'm getting a little stuffy now that this place has turned back into a church."

We stepped out into the chill evening. Gianna threaded her arm through mine as we strolled down the sidewalk.

"I've been pondering a couple of things," she said.

"For instance?"

"Like running for office. I've decided to run for city council first. Maybe after a few years of that, I'll move out to Maryland and run for Congress, unless they see fit to give D.C. proper representation before then."

"Let me be your campaign manager," I said. "You can't lose. You want to be president? I can get that for you, too."

"No, I—"

"You wouldn't be the first."

"Why doesn't that surprise me? Nixon, right?"

"No, I'm kidding, of course," I said. "My specialty was always Third World dictators. More emphasis on weapons, less on mass hypnosis. So what else were you pondering?"

"Oh, that other thing." Her grip on my arm tightened for a second. "I was thinking that . . . I'd like to marry you."

My feet stopped of their own will, and I almost tripped. "Wh—?"

"Will you marry me, Louis?"

My mouth fell open. Cold air rushed in and made it too dry to form words.

"I still have the ring." She fished in her pocket and pulled out the diamond ring. "Louis, say something."

I couldn't. I grabbed the ring, dropped it, crawled after it down the sidewalk, and retrieved it just before it fell into the sewer. Gianna laughed and knelt down beside me on the concrete. I slipped the ring on her finger and kissed her as if it were the first and last kiss on earth.

My voice still didn't work, so I just mouthed the words that stretched from my soul.

"I love you, too, Louis." She pulled me to my feet with her. "You know what? This is my new favorite moment ever, right now."

"For the wages of sin is death," a voice close behind her said, "but the gift of God is eternal life in Christ."

I looked over her shoulder to see a tall, freckle-faced man reach inside his jacket.

"Gianna—"

She began to turn her head as the muzzle of a gun pressed against it. Then the sky cracked, and someone screamed.

Gianna's eyes met mine for a moment before they went dim. I caught her lifeless body and sank to my knees. Distant shouts clamored from what seemed like another world, but in my arms was the unbearable, stifling quiet of instant death. I clutched at Gianna's back and stared into the darkness, the darkness into which I could never follow her.

She was gone. Gone forever, with no poignant deathbed scene, no lingering goodbyes, no trembling last kisses.

Gone.

From within the orb of silence that surrounded us, I heard a cry of anguish that contained the sorrow of ten billion years of solitude. The cries of all my precious damned souls, together in a chorus of wretchedness, sounded like mere whimpers next to the sound that crawled out of my throat. If it did not blow apart the gates of Heaven and wake the fat, sleeping giants who dwelled within, nothing ever would.

The people who were beginning to gather around us recoiled and covered their ears. Some ducked behind cars as if bullets were still flying.

The man who killed Gianna, the man who will sit before the mother of all grand juries, was already at the next corner, scampering down another alley. I let him go.

Gianna's blood steamed in the cold air. I buried my face in her hair, singed from the gun blast, and breathed in the last of her life.

Red lights and sirens surrounded me. A paramedic was shouting at me to let go of Gianna.

"It's too late," I said.

"We have to try." He tugged at my sleeve. "Please, sir, let her go."

I unwrapped my arms from Gianna's body. There was nothing left of her there now, only the cold, beautiful shell she once inhabited. Now she was . . . somewhere else, I couldn't quite sense where, only that she was . . . waiting?

I saw her face, unmarred and astonished.

"She's dead," I said to them. "It was a .22, point blank."

The paramedics pushed me aside and began resuscitation attempts.

"Don't take her away from me," I said.

From the corner of my eye I saw a homeless man leaning against a nearby building, watching the scene. Then I saw nothing, as my eyes iced over with tears, and I collapsed at her feet.

What seemed like hours later, someone shook my shoulder.

"Sir, can you step away from the body, please?"

I did not move or speak.

"Sir, this is Detective Frank Brunner, from the homicide department. I need to ask you a few questions about the shooting, if I may. We've gotta tape off the crime scene, so if you'll come with me for a moment . . ."

I clutched at her shoe, a brown suede boot, and had an insane compulsion to take it with me.

"Sir, please come with me."

I commanded each of my fingers to let go of her, one by one, then without looking at her, I turned away and followed the cop to his squad car. He poured me some thick coffee from his thermos bottle and said, "Look, I know this is tough for you, but the sooner we get some kind of ID, the more likely it is we'll get your girlfriend's murderer. Did you get a good look at the shooter?"

"Fiancée." My voice was hoarse.

"Sorry?"

"Fiancée. We were engaged. Just a few minutes ago." I looked out the car window. The paramedics were boarding the ambulance, leaving Gianna on the sidewalk. A uniformed police officer was winding police tape around a lamppost.

"I'm sorry, sir." He took off his hat and examined the brim. "That's about as tragic as it gets."

Numbness was beginning to creep over me, starting at my fingertips. "What were you saying?" I asked him.

"I asked if you got a good look at the shooter."

I stared into the murky coffee. *Yes, a good look inside his mind.* I was not going to let anyone, including the police, take from me the justice I deserved.

"I don't remember," I said.

"You don't remember what he looked like?"

"I'm sorry. I can't think right now. Maybe in the morning I'll be a better help to you. Right now, I'm just . . . I'm . . ."

"You're still in shock, I understand, but the sooner we can get better information, the more chance we have of catching this guy." I remained silent. Brunner sighed. "Well, we have some descriptions from the other eyewitnesses. We'll try to get at least some photos for you to look at tomorrow morning, if not a lineup."

"Okay."

"Can you tell me about the victim, sir? Her name, someone in her family who we can call?"

"Her name was Gianna O'Keefe." Her name made my voice stumble. "She . . . she has a brother Marcus who lives in Baltimore. If I were you, I'd call him first." My wandering gaze returned to the homeless man, who was still hovering outside the crime scene.

"Do you have any idea who might have wanted to kill her?" he said. "Did she have enemies?" I shook my head and said nothing. The detective sighed again. "Mr. Carvalho, is there somewhere I can reach you in the morning?"

I gave him my card and slipped out into the cold, declining his offer of a ride home. The coroner's van pulled up to the curb, and a medical examiner got out to speak with the detective's partner. I pressed as close as I could to the scene. Gianna's body was already covered. My internal organs shrank together. I turned away and began to stumble home to await Marc's inevitable call.

Outside the church, someone grabbed my sleeve. It was the homeless guy.

"Get the fuck off me." I yanked my arm back. Then I saw his face. "No . . ."

Not here, not now. Underneath the knit cap shone eyes of crystal gray. Michael reached for me again.

"Lucifer—"

"What are you doing here? Why now, why—" I looked up

the street towards the murder scene, then back at Michael. "'The wages of sin is death.' You did this. You had her killed."

"No, I —"

I lunged for his throat. Michael used my own fury and momentum to hurl me to the ground with barely a touch. My head knocked against the edge of the church's lowest marble stair.

"Lucifer, get a hold of yourself."

"Bring her back."

"I can't do that."

"You can do miracles. He'll give you the power. Bring her back."

"There's nothing I can do."

"Nothing?" I sneered at him and tried to rise, my head still swimming from the jolt. "Nothing, of course! Every day you do nothing. You stand there, and you watch!" I pointed at him with a quaking finger. "People's suffering is a spectator sport for you. You and your fucking father!"

Michael shook his head. "Our Father hears when the sparrow falls."

I spat a shower of sparks. "Yeah? Well, Gianna was no sparrow. She was a person, with more courage and beauty than all you simpering little angels combined, and now she's gone." I turned my eyes to the church door. "It's like falling all over again."

"I know."

"No!" I stood and faced him, my fingers curled into fists. "You do not know. You have no idea what it feels like never to hope, and then to have that hope for a few moments, only to be ripped away again. You didn't know her, and you didn't love her."

I backed away before I could give in to the desire to throttle him, to tear the pity off his perfect face.

"You are too much of this world, Lucifer," he said. "Now you rage against death like a mortal, mourn and fear the transience of life when you know there is so much more beyond."

"I'm not afraid of my own death, if there is such a thing." A spark of hope flamed. "Wait, is that why you're here, to destroy me, too?"

"No, I'm—"

"Would you?"

"Would I what?"

"Please . . ." I seized him by the lapels of his overcoat. "If you have any compassion in that insufferable soul of yours—"

"Get your hands off me."

"—you'll kill me now."

"You know I—"

"Come on, Michael, chance of a lifetime."

"—can't kill you."

"Just try!"

"No!"

"Please, Michael—"

"I can't!" He wrenched my hands off him and pushed me away.

"Do it!!" I tore open my shirt. "What are you waiting for, huh? Afraid you don't have the power? Afraid Daddy will get mad? Kill me now, or I'll send you back to Heaven in an ashtray!"

"Stop it," he said.

"It's not a trick, Michael, I just want to die." My tears came, unbeckoned. "Please . . . don't make me beg . . ." He stood silent, with his arms folded. I sank down onto the church steps and buried my face in my hands. "I hate you so much. I know you hate me, too. Can't you just end it all right here? I'm sure he'd understand."

"I don't hate you, Lucifer."

"You're an abominable liar."

"I'm not here to hurt you. I'm here to give you a choice."

I looked up. "A choice?"

"Yes. I'll let you decide Gianna's eternal fate. She can come with me, or . . ."

"Or what?"

"You can take her home with you."

Slowly I rose to my feet. "Home?"

"Home. And I don't mean your Foggy Bottom penthouse."

The cold night air seeped into my chest. I pulled my coat around me and turned away. "Oh. That home."

Gianna O'Keefe, Queen of Hell. We could rule together, play together among the demons and sorrows. She would bring a light fueled by something other than despair to that darkest of realms. With her at my side, I could transform the place into a paradise that would rival Heaven. The perfect balance of the cosmos would teeter.

And always there, her face, her hair. Gianna. I remembered the nights we lay together, pressed in heat, and I felt in my throat a longing so thick I felt I would choke.

I turned to Michael.

"What does she want?"

"She is beyond all desire, Lucifer. She now lies in the palm of yours."

My decision. I pictured her two paths, one in glory, the other in chains, and the two possibilities flickered back and forth like a choppy newsreel, until I wasn't sure which was Heaven and which was Hell.

"Don't do this," I said. "Don't tempt me with this choice." My breath came heavy, and I leaned against the staircase's iron railing. "Gianna . . ." I gripped the cold steel and half-turned to Michael. "I won't play your game, with her soul as the pawn. I won't choose."

"Then I can't promise what will happen to her. She's a borderline case—cared for the poor, but was full of wrath and lust."

"I can't believe I'm hearing this. Gianna, a borderline case?"

"Loving you will either damn her or save her, but I can't say what His final judgment will be. It depends."

"It depends?" I advanced on him. "On what? On whether he's in an Old Testament or New Testament kind of mood?"

"Do you want her or not?" Michael said.

"I don't know!" I turned back to the church and stared up at the stained-glass window, now dark. "I need time to think about it."

"There's no time. She's in limbo as it is. Soon she'll become aware she's dead and begin to feel alone and afraid. One of us has to be there for her."

I closed my eyes. How could I exist after this, no matter what my decision?

"Take her," I said. "She's better off with you. I mean, you're . . . who you are, and I'm . . . who I am."

"Are you sure? You can't ever get her back, not even part-time."

"I know, and no, I'm not sure. So go now, and take her, before I change my mind."

"Suit yourself." I heard Michael take a few steps away, then stop. "You did the right thing, Lucifer. I'm surprised. There may be hope for you yet."

"What?" I lifted my head slowly and turned it to face him. "You mean it?"

He gave me a long, level look and said, "No." Then he was gone.

I stared at the place where Michael had stood, his last word echoing in my ears. A rumbling began at the bottom of my chest. Smoke filled my brain and seeped out of my pores.

Enough.

In one leap, I mounted the staircase. I slammed open the church doors and stalked down the aisle toward the altar.

"Wake up, God, it's me—Satan! Yes, I'm talking to you. No more minions, no more messengers, just you and me."

I vaulted onto the altar. "You're going to listen to me, you chicken-shit murderer! You didn't pull the trigger, but you let her die. She believed in you, trusted you. She loved you, and you betrayed her! I want you to come down here and explain it to me. NOW!" I snatched the wooden crucifix off the wall and hurled it to the floor. The cross split down the middle, and Jesus's disembodied head spun off into the corner.

I leaped to the floor. "You like human sacrifices, right?" I ripped open the cabinet on the side wall and pulled out a plate of communion wafers. "Transubstantiation: not just a good idea—it's the law!" The plate now oozed with warm pieces of human flesh. I plopped it on the altar.

"And let's not forget the refreshments." I pulled out the decanter of wine and shattered it against the choir box. The walls of the church began to bleed—at first seeping, then pulsing red like slit arteries.

"You eat, drink, and shit misery, and then your people blame it all on me!" I strode to the top of the stairs next to the pulpit, my boots squelching in the cascades of blood. "Okay, Daddy, it's time for you to see the monster you created." The flames started at my feet and shot forward and sideways in both directions. I listened, felt, for any connection, any anger directed at me.

Nothing.

"Listen to me! Listen to me, Goddammit! Keep ignoring me, and the whole world will look like this. Your precious humans will drown in blood and fire. And you'll do nothing! You'll sit there on your big God couch, a beer in one hand and a remote control in the other, and when their weeping bores you, you'll yawn and change the channel. Or maybe you'll smack me around before letting a few of them live. And they'll praise your mercy and feel lucky to be chosen, never daring to question your wisdom—your infinite, ineffable insanity!"

There was still no sound under or above the roar of the flames and the rush of blood. I thought of Gianna's face, by now blank and serene, full of light and empty of life. By now she would not even remember me.

I yanked loose the altar gate and smashed it against the pulpit. A shower of sparks rained around me.

"You bastard, you could have had anyone, everyone else, why did it have to be her?" I sank to the floor. My fingers tore at the flaming, blood-soaked carpet. "Why Gianna? Why now? Why?!"

There was still no answer. Pieces of blazing ceiling fell around me. I tried to speak one last plea, but the smoke and the screaming had scorched my throat. When I heard the fire engine howl outside, I slunk out of the church into the shadows.

I stood on my balcony and burned. Cathedrals, synagogues, mosques—ravished by flames. The night sky was orange with the glow of my vengeance. Sirens wailed as an overtaxed fire department tried in vain to keep up with me. Soon fire trucks from Maryland and Virginia would flow in to assist—just in time for their own churches to burn, unrescued.

Even if it took months, I would destroy them all, all over the world, or be destroyed in the process. So far I'd reduced to rubble all the houses of worship in the Northwest and Southwest quadrants of the District. As they got farther away, I had to concentrate more deeply, and I barely heard the phone ringing on several different occasions.

After two hours and ninety-eight churches, my legs weakened, and my extremities began to chill. I sank to my knees on the balcony floor, clutched the bars, and thought of Gianna's face in her last moment of life. Three distant churches exploded at once.

I gasped for breath and pushed on. My teeth chattered so hard I bit my tongue and tasted my own blood. If only it had been my blood on the sidewalk instead of hers . . .

Another four churches vaporized.

"Lou!"

Beelzebub was at my side. I gazed up at him, bleary-eyed.

"Lou, I saw on the news about the churches, and I figured it had to be you. What the hell are you doing?"

"They killed her, Bub."

"What? Killed who?"

"They killed Gianna." I hiccuped on a clump of swallowed tears and incinerated a seminary. "Help me, Beelzebub. I want to burn them all. Help me."

"My aim's not so good, remember?"

"I don't care!" I clutched at his shirt. "Burn everything. Please, I'm so tired now. Just burn it all."

He nodded. As Beelzebub raised his eyes to the crimson horizon, I collapsed against him and slipped into unconsciousness.

36

Solvet Saeclum in Favilla

"Lucifer, make him stop crying."

Beelzebub's violent shaking shattered my dreamless sleep. I jerked to a sitting position in my bed.

"What?!"

"There's someone on the phone for you. Marc something-or-other."

Marc . . . Marc . . . who's Marc . . . Where was I . . . What year was it? I picked up the extension on the nightstand.

"Hello?"

"Louis . . ." Marcus's voice was choked with tears. Reality slammed through my bleariness and crushed my chest. Gianna was dead. I had watched her die.

"Marc . . ." I couldn't speak. Beelzebub left the room and closed the door.

"Lou . . . I've been trying to call all night. They came to my house . . ."

"Who?" I pictured an angel of God, a twisted grin on his face, delivering the news.

"The police here, and a social worker. The detective in D.C. thought I should hear in person. I spoke to him . . . he said you were there."

"I'm sorry." Tears cascaded down my cheeks. "Marc, I couldn't do anything to save her. I wish it had been me. I'd give anything if—"

"Lou, it's not your fault. Please . . . I have to come down to identify the . . . to identify her." His voice disintegrated, then recovered. "Will you come with me?"

"I can do it for you. I've already seen her."

"It has to be a family member. It's cruel, but it's the law. Meet me there in an hour, okay?"

"All right. Marc . . . be careful."

I hung up the phone and placed my hand on the cold pillow where Gianna had last laid her head. I wanted to crawl under the bed and waste away, to die swamped in my sorrow. But I'd promised my comfort, or at least my presence, to her family.

When I shambled out of the bedroom, Beelzebub was setting the table.

"I made you an omelet," he said.

"I'm not hungry."

"You should eat something. You've hardly got any strength left after last night."

Last night . . . flames and fury. I crossed to the balcony window.

"It's all over the news this morning, worldwide," he said. "The mayor's practically declared martial law, rounding up every gang member off the streets and questioning them about the biggest arson ring in history." He placed two cups of coffee on the table. "They're going after the Satanists, too."

"Good." The morning sky was dim with soot and smoke. My stomach wrenched. "How many people died?"

"None, so far as they know."

"None?"

"Lots of minor injuries, nothing life-threatening. Weird, huh? They're calling it a miracle."

"A miracle." I leaned my forehead against the glass. "I guess that proves your theory wrong, that God doesn't care. He does care. He just doesn't care about us. If he did, Gianna would still be alive."

"I guess." Beelzebub sat at the table. "Come on, Lou, you've got to eat."

"This is what you wanted, right?"

"What?"

I opened the sliding door and went out onto the balcony. "This is what you wanted, isn't it, my ever-patient father? To break me, to crush me into nothingness. You gave Gianna to me just so you could take her away." I faced the sun, my tears freezing on my cheeks. "You treated her like a toy, handing her to me so I could finally love something, so I'd finally have a chink in my armor. But she was more than a toy to me, and she should have been more than that to you. You used her to shatter me."

I sank down onto one of the chairs, for the first time feeling as old as I really was.

"Are you happy now? I'm broken and empty. I've nothing left but a tiny ember of hatred for you. But it's dense, like a neutron star, and it will never stop burning until the day you put me out of my misery. If you're as merciful as they say, you'll end me right now."

I let my face drop into my hands, and sobbed without tears. Beelzebub touched my shoulder softly, then placed his hand on my head.

"I'm sorry," he said.

B eelzebub accompanied me to the police station, where I made him wait outside. The place was swarming with reporters clamoring for news on the church-burning story.

"Which way to the morgue?" I asked the officer at the front desk. She pointed down.

As the elevator doors opened on the bottom floor, I saw Marcus sitting on a bench outside a door marked "Morgue." He raised his red eyes to meet mine.

"Lou . . ." He collapsed into my arms. We sobbed together and held each other up.

A medical examiner came out of the door and asked if we were ready. Marc wiped his nose and nodded. As we passed through the doorway, he gripped my arm.

"I can't do this, Lou. I can't."

"Then let's call one of your brothers."

"No." Marc ran his hand through his uncombed black hair. "I've got to be the one. I'm the oldest. I've got to be the strong . . ." He took a deep breath. "Thank you for coming with me."

We followed the medical examiner around a corner to a stretcher. Under a bright white fluorescent light, the doctor pulled the sheet back from Gianna's face.

Marcus stared at her for a long moment, then suddenly became calm. "She looks . . . so peaceful."

"She is peaceful," I said.

He reached to touch her face, then stopped. He looked at the medical examiner. "It's her," he said. "It's Gia—" his voice choked ". . . it's her."

The doctor nodded, then covered Gianna's face again. She handed Marcus a small paper bag.

"Here's your sister's jewelry," she said. "Her clothing is being kept for evidence right now."

"Thank you," he whispered.

"Have your funeral director give me a call as soon as you've made arrangements." She handed him her card. "I'm sorry, Mr. O'Keefe, for your loss."

We left the morgue and stood in the hallway.

"I guess I'd better call Mom and Dad now," Marc said.

"You haven't told them yet?"

"I wanted to . . . I guess I wanted to make sure. I just need a minute first." He sank onto the bench, opened the paper bag and peered inside. "Oh, God." Marc reached in and pulled out a topaz earring. "I gave her these for Christmas." He made no attempt to hold back his tears as he poured the rest of the contents into his left hand. "What's this?" He held up the engagement ring. "Were you—?"

"Yes." My throat began to close.

"I didn't know." Marc looked at the ring. "Why didn't she tell me?"

"Because it just happened . . . last night . . . right before . . ." My breath cut off, and my head fell against his shoulder.

"Why?" he cried. "Why did this have to happen to her?" He clutched at my back. "How are we supposed to go on?"

My phone rang inside my jacket. I steadied my breath in gulps before answering.

"Mr. Carvalho, this is Detective Brunner. We've got a few photos for you to look at, to see if you can identify the suspect. Can you come down to the station?"

"Actually, I'm down—" I looked at Marc. He was staring at the jewelry lying in his palm, his face a swamp of tears. "I'll be there as soon as I can." I hung up. "Marc, I've got some business to attend to with the police. Will you be okay for a couple of hours?"

He sniffled. "You do what you have to do. I'll be all right."

I gave him my card. "Meet me at my place in three hours. If you need anything before then, call me."

"Okay," he said. I stood to leave. "Louis?"

"Yes?"

"Don't let this guy get away with it. Do whatever you have to do, but make him pay."

I nodded, then walked down the hall and left the building through the back exit.

I knocked on the door of James Benson's shabby row house, then stood aside to hide myself. There was no answer. I knocked again, this time less urgently. In a few moments, the door opened an inch.

"Hello?"

I jerked open the door and shoved Gianna's assassin inside the house. His eyes grew huge, and he emitted a strangled yelp before my hand closed around his throat.

"You . . ."

"Do you recognize me, Mr. Benson?" I pushed him onto his back on the staircase. "Do you know me for who I really am?"

He gagged and writhed. I turned his chin to force him to look at me. He stared into my eyes for a moment, then jolted like he'd been electrocuted.

"N—nooo! Oh, God, no!!"

"Shut up!!" The back of my left hand slammed across his face, spraying blood onto the worn wooden banister. I filled my other hand with his scraggly red hair.

"Listen to me, Mr. Benson. Are you listening?" He whimpered and tried to nod. "Good. "Now I have two options. I can pluck out your eyelashes, teeth, and nails one by one before boiling your heart in your own blood, or I can snap your neck like a twig. My preference would be to kill you slowly, to watch you bleed and vomit and cry and beg for death to rescue you. But never let it be said that I am entirely without mercy."

"W—what do you want from me?!"

"I want the truth. Who sent you to kill her? Tell me, and your death will be quick."

"I don't know who it was! I don't know!"

"Fine, then. Slow it is." I reached for his mouth.

"I mean, I don't remember!"

"We'll see about that." I forced open his yellow eyes and shoved my way into his mind. He screamed.

"Auugggggh! It hurts!!"

"Good," I said. "Hold still." He squirmed under my grip. I bent his neck back as far as it would go without snapping. "I said, hold still."

Again I plunged my consciousness into his brain, bulldozing his neurons and ganglia. His eyes rolled up into his head, so I slowed my search. I needed him alive until I had the truth.

It took over five minutes to comb every cranny of Benson's mind. I even checked his brain's distal lobes where memories never reside. Nothing.

By not finding my answer, I had found my answer.

I let go of him, sank down onto the stairs and covered my face with my hands.

It was true.

"I'm sorry," Benson said. He coughed again, then began to sob. "I'm sorry. I didn't mean to do it, man. I didn't want to do it."

"Be quiet."

"They made me. Someone made me. I swear, I've never killed anyone before."

"I said, be quiet."

"I don't know how it happened. I don't remember, just

standing there with the gun is all I remember, you gotta believe me. And she was just dead there, and I—"

"I said, BE QUIET!!!" I pounced on him and seized his head between my hands.

"Oh, God, no! Don't hurt me anymore, please!!"

"No, no more pain, only death. Like her death, painless and quick. Like Gianna's." My grip on his skull tightened.

I prepared to sever his spine with a swift twist. Benson opened his eyes, and I stared into his frightened, bloodshot gaze. He trembled like a mouse in a cat's clutches.

"You know what you are?" I whispered. "You're a pawn. You may have captured my queen, but you're still nothing but a pathetic little pawn."

I let go of him, stood up, and shuffled toward the door. When my hand touched the doorknob, I stopped. Her family needed justice.

I retrieved the dirty yellow telephone from the end table and carried it to where Benson still lay supine on the staircase. I handed him the receiver.

"I'm calling the police." I dialed the number. "You'll confess to Gianna's murder or I'll melt all your fingers together into two useless paws."

He drew the receiver to his ear. "H—hello?"

"Ask for Detective Brunner in Homicide," I said.

Benson did as he was told. When the call was over, I replaced the telephone on the table and turned to him.

"I'll watch this house until they come for you. Don't think of leaving."

"I won't." He wiped the blood from his nose. "I am sorry, really. Like I said, I didn't—"

"Shh." I held up my hand. "I know. I'm sorry, too. I'm sorry you were dragged into this. I'm sorry you ever existed. But if it weren't you, someone else would have pulled the trigger."

"I don't understand."

I opened the front door and said without looking at him, "Neither do I."

When I returned to the police station, I found Beelzebub still sitting on the steps. He saw me and leapt to his feet.

"I thought you were in there." He jerked his thumb towards the building. "I've been waiting out here in the freezing cold for two hours. Where the hell were you?"

"I went to visit Mr. Benson."

"Who?"

"Gianna's murderer."

"Oh."

"At least the man directly responsible, the man who pulled the trigger." I began to walk down the street away from the police station. Beelzebub followed me.

"Did he tell you why he did it, who was behind it?"

"No."

"How did you kill him?"

"I didn't."

Beelzebub stopped. "What? You didn't kill him? How come?"

"He was only an instrument. Killing him would have meant no more than if I had destroyed the gun that held the bullet." I turned down a narrow alleyway. "I wanted to kill him. I thought it would make me feel better. But nothing can do that. Nothing will ever do that." We walked in silence for a few moments.

"Hey, Lou?"

"What?"

"Are you gonna be okay?"

I stopped and faced him. He squinted up at me, his tiny nose crinkled like a rabbit's.

"I mean," he said, "you seem, like, I don't know, dead or something. I've never seen you like—"

"Why?" I whispered.

"Huh?"

"Why, Beelzebub? Why did you do it?"

He stopped squinting. "What?" He took half a step back. "Do what, Lou?"

"You didn't have to go so far. Look at me now. You've destroyed me."

"I don't know what—"

"Is this what you wanted?"

"—you're talking about. I never did anything to—"

"DON'T LIE TO ME!!" I rushed at him and hurled him to the ground. In half a second, my boot was at his throat. He squeaked in protest, but could not struggle.

"No, Lou! I never—"

"Don't you dare lie to me, Beelzebub. After what you've done, I won't let you tell me it wasn't you. No one else could have wiped Benson's brain so clean, no one else is as good as you at making them forget."

"Lou—"

"You killed her! You killed her, and I want to know why. Tell me!"

Beelzebub choked and flailed. I removed my boot from his neck and kneeled on his chest. He gasped and wheezed for a moment.

"I had to . . . I had to do it, to save you."

"Save me?!" I grabbed his collar and shook him. "You killed the only one who was capable of saving me. How could you do that to me?"

"That's—that's just it. She would have saved you." He emitted a strangled cough. "Couldn't take that chance."

"What are you talking about?"

"Of you, making it to the other side, without us. We need you."

"You think I would have left you behind, sought redemption only for myself?"

"For her . . . yeah."

I stared into my brother's strange blue eyes and knew he was right. I let go of him and stood up. "Then you knew how much she meant to me."

"I knew." Beelzebub rolled on his side and coughed again, several times. "I knew, but I didn't know." He lay his forehead on the pavement. "So what are you going to do to me?"

"I don't know. How can I punish you when you're as damned as I am? Hell is already your home." As soon as I said this, I knew what I had to do, and that I'd have to do it quickly. I turned my back on him.

"You're fired." I began to walk away.

"What?"

"You heard me."

He scrambled to his feet and ran to catch up to me. "What's that supposed to mean?"

"It means what I said." I did not look at him, wanted never to look at him again.

"You're cutting me off? Banishing me?"

"Yes."

"Lucifer, you can't mean this. Wh—where'll I go? What'll I do?"

"Frankly—"

"I wasn't the only one, you know." He pulled on my sleeve. "I'll give the others up if you just don't send me away. Please."

"I know you didn't act alone, Beelzebub."

"Don't you want to know who it was? Hey, it—it wasn't even my idea!"

"I don't care."

"But that's not fair!"

"I don't care about the others," I said. "I only ever cared about you."

"Lucifer, this is me you're talking to—your old buddy. I was the one who believed in you first. I was the one who pulled you out of the fire after the Fall. I've always been there for you!"

"Then why betray me now, after all this time?"

"Why? Because I'm evil! And I thought you were evil, too. If anything, you're the one who betrayed all of us. Falling in love, like some weak, stupid human. How can we ever trust you again after that?"

"'How can *we* trust you?'" I said. "Beelzebub, there is no more 'we' for you. You can never come back, and 'we' can no longer know you."

"Why? Because you said so? Maybe you're the one who should be banished."

I grabbed him and covered his face with my hand so that I could hold him in place without seeing his eyes.

"Leave me now, Beelzebub. Live out your measly existence on this earth however you please, but never approach me or our brothers. If I ever see you again, I will end you, do you understand? I will end you."

His voice was muffled under my palm. "You don't have that power."

I leaned close to his face and whispered, "Maybe I do, and maybe I don't. I do know that it will hurt us both a great deal for me to try, and I *will* try."

He stopped struggling and placed his hand on my wrist. I slowly let go of his face. He was crying. I felt sick.

"You can't forgive me?"

"No. Not for this."

"Everything I ever did," he said, "was always for you."

I took his other hand. "Then do this one last thing for me. Leave me."

Beelzebub looked away, then nodded. He moved to embrace me. I stepped back, out of his reach. He shoved his hands in his pockets and shuffled down the street, not looking back. I stared after him until he disappeared into a crowd of shoppers.

37

Requiem Aeternam Dona Eis, Domine

Gianna's funeral was three days later, in Pennsylvania. I spent those three days with her family, who were as inconsolable as I. Rosa wept constantly, awake and asleep. Valium had no effect on her. Walter spent most of his time taking Bobo for walks. Even the wake was a somber affair. The enormous quantities of alcohol we all consumed at it made us even more morose.

I would often go out alone, to run errands for the O'Keefes or just to get away. One day I sat in my car outside a supermarket and watched the people go in and out, occupied with their lives.

How can the rest of the world carry on and on and on without her? They breathe and move and eat and walk and shop and laugh. Everything still lives on. Everything lives.

But not her. And not me.

The sobs that racked my ribs would have split a human in half. I had not even death to look forward to, just an endless fall into nothingness.

The morning of her funeral was cruelly sunny and cold. Outside the church, Marcus handed me an opened envelope marked "To be opened when I buy the farm."

"I found it in my sister's safe deposit box. It was the only thing in there." I slid out the piece of paper inside. "Check out the date," he said. "She wrote this on the day she died."

Dear Marcus
(or Matthew or Luke, if Marc has gotten himself dead already),

I know this sounds really morbid, okay, but I've come up with a list of Bible readings for my funeral. It occurred to me this morning that this was really important, and I figured I'd better get on it, in case I got hit by a bus or a meteorite or something. Don't laugh. Those things happen to people, you know.

Anyway, here they are:

Song of Solomon 5:9—16
Psalm 31
1 John 4:7—19
Luke 15:1—7

They're a bit unorthodox, but don't let Mom talk you out of them, because they mean a lot to me, and hopefully a lot to someone else. Thanks.

Ciao Bello,
Your little sister Gianna

P.S.: Tell Louis I love him, and that I'm waiting for him (at least until I find a foxier angel).

"I don't know what this is all about," Marc said, "but we'll do as she asks."

"May I keep this?" I asked.

"Sure." He stared at the envelope in my hand. "Sometimes I can't believe . . . it's like it hasn't really hit me yet. I feel like I'm outside my body somewhere watching myself mourn, and I . . ." He passed a hand through his hair. "I'm scared of what'll happen when I come back inside myself. When I have to be me again and figure out how to . . ." Marc turned away. I touched his arm, but he moved it out of my reach. "No, I can't cry, I'm a god-damned pall bearer!"

He kicked a stone into the parking lot. "I'm tired of this already," he said. "I want her to come back."

I stood silent while he kicked another rock, then another. Then he looked up and said, "Check it out. Adam's mom."

An elderly woman dressed in black slowly crossed the parking lot. She approached us and held out her hand to Marc, who took it in both his own.

"Marcus, I'm so sorry. I just don't know what to say."

"Me neither. Thank you for coming." He squeezed her hand. "Mrs. Crawford, this is Louis Carvalho. He was—"

"I know who you are." She accused me with large, sorrowful eyes. I looked away. I heard her pat Marc's shoulder and say, "I'll go in and see your parents now."

As Adam's mother walked towards the church, Marc pulled out a pack of cigarettes and offered me one. I shook my head.

"I didn't know you smoked," I said.

"Only when I'm in mourning." His face hardened with the first drag. "In the last ten years, I've been a nonsmoker for a total of fourteen months. I'm thinking of giving it up entirely."

"Smoking?"

"Not smoking." Marc looked at his cigarette. "Everyone should have something in their lives that doesn't go away." He let out a deep, harsh breath. "I feel so fucking old today."

I said nothing.

He glanced at me, then said, "Why don't you go inside and sit down with Mom and Dad and Grandmom? The mass should be starting any minute."

I entered the church and moved down to the front pew, my eyes on the floor as I walked. Rosa moved over so I could sit on the aisle. She gripped my hand for a moment, then grabbed her enormous pile of tissues again. Her sniffles were deafening in the silence.

The procession began while a small choir sang the "Lacrymosa" from Verdi's *Requiem*, at my request. Its melancholy notes chilled my heart as I thought of Gianna's tearful reaction to it on the night of her death. Her brothers, along with some cousins, accompanied the coffin down the aisle, then joined Donna and Dara in the pew behind me. After the introductory rites, Marcus stood and climbed the stairs to reach the lectern.

"A reading from the book of songs:

'How does your lover differ from any other, O most beautiful among women?...'
'His head is pure gold;
his locks are palm fronds,
black as the raven...'"

Afterwards Matthew rose and took Marc's place to read the psalm.

Have pity on me, O Lord, for I am in distress;
with sorrow my eye is consumed;
my soul also, and my body.
For my life is spent with grief
and my years with sighing...
Once I said in my anguish,

'I am cut off from your sight';
Yet you heard the sound of my pleading
when I cried out to you.

Then it was Luke's turn to be Gianna's mouthpiece:

Beloved, let us love one another because love is of God . . . The man
without love has known nothing of God, for God is love . . .

Our final theological debate, and I don't get to talk back to her. I almost smiled.

The priest stepped forward with the Books of the Gospel. "The Gospel of the Lord according to Luke: 'He addressed this parable to them: Who among you, if he has a hundred sheep and loses one of them, does not leave the ninety-nine in the wasteland and follow the lost one until he finds it? And when he finds it, he puts it on his shoulders in jubilation. Once arrived home, he invites friends and neighbors in and says to them, "Rejoice with me because I have found my lost sheep." I tell you, there will likewise be more joy in Heaven over one repentant sinner than over ninety-nine righteous people who have no need to repent.'"

I saw what she had planned with this choice of scripture. She lulled me with the love poem, played to my fears with the psalm, made me wonder with John's letter, then sent the Gospel in to bat cleanup. I gazed at her coffin.

You're amazing, I told her. *Yes, I understand. I miss you.*

Her fantasy about my return to Heaven clearly included a reunion between us. I wished that were possible, even in the unlikely event that I would ever get there. By now she was no longer Gianna O'Keefe but a mere essence with no recollection of her earthly life, no memory of any existence other than perfect bliss. If I could be with her in Heaven, I would have busted down the door the night she died.

The priest gave a short homily, then the prayers began. As soon as I knelt, my tears began to flow again. I struggled to keep from shrieking my grief against the walls and rafters of the church.

I did not partake of communion, though part of me longed for a taste of comfort. I remained on my knees until it was over.

The men came forward to accompany the casket out of the church. Luke stumbled, his eyes blinded with tears. Matthew laid his hand on his twin's shoulder. The choir began to sing "Amazing Grace." By the end of the first verse, only the choir was still singing; everyone else was either choked with sobs or wailing outright. Rosa, silent, walked between me and her mother. Either denial or Valium had finally taken hold of her.

For the first time, I was part of one of those highway funeral processions I'd always mocked. I sat in the front passenger seat of the main limo, with Marc and his parents in the back.

"You okay, Mom?" he said when we were on the road. "You look like you're not completely with us."

She said nothing.

Minutes later, we arrived at the enormous Catholic cemetery and wound our way through an elaborate maze of headstones to get to the grave site. The pallbearers set Gianna's coffin over the grave, where it was surrounded by so many flowers it was barely visible.

"In sure and certain hope of the resurrection to eternal life . . ."

My hands covered my face as the priest crumbled the soil over the coffin.

". . . ashes to ashes, dust to dust . . ."

The others recited the Lord's Prayer through chattering teeth while I stared at the grave site and knew I'd forever hate the smell of flowers.

"Rest eternal grant to her, O Lord."

"And let light perpetual shine upon her," we said.

When it was over, and the others had driven away, Gianna's family and I stood next to the grave in silence. One by one, they too retreated to the warmth of the limousines, until I was left alone by her side.

I drew a red-and-white rose from inside my coat and laid it on top of the casket.

"Gianna, I'm sorry I let you down." I gripped the smooth side of the coffin. "All I ever wanted . . . was to be worthy of you." My knees gave way, and I sank to the ground. "May God have mercy on me." I hung my head to soak the frozen soil with my tears.

All at once a warmth enveloped me, as if a blanket had been wrapped around my body and held snug by an unseen force. I drew in my breath so sharply I almost choked.

There was a presence. I looked over at the others to see if they had noticed it, too. Marcus and the limo driver were smoking cigarettes and chatting across the hood of the car. Everyone else was hidden within the limousines.

I was alone with my Father for the first time in ten billion years.

"Hello," I said. He spoke to me not in words, but in a wave of comfort and peace. "I missed you," I blurted out before my pride could stop me. I covered my mouth with my sleeve to hold back a sob.

"So this is what it takes," I said, "to bring us together again. You're a sad, sadistic son-of-a-bitch. I guess that's where I get it from. But such a cost, so much sorrow, to bring me to the point where I'd cry out for you. All the people who loved her, and all the people she could have helped. If anything I ever did has led to this, then I'm sorry. I'm not sorry to you, or to me. I'm sorry to her.

"I'll come to you, like I promised her, and you can accept

me back into your realm, if it is your will. But I won't obey you, and I won't serve you. We've been apart too long for that. I'll just be near you. If your love is as unconditional as she said it was, you won't ask for more." I lowered my head. "I know I won't ask for more."

The warmth lingered for a moment, then swept through me and away. I shivered.

"Goodbye, Gianna." I stood and touched her casket with my fingertips. "Thank you."

Marcus approached me. "Ready?" he said. I nodded, and we walked back toward the limo together. "Who were you talking to back there?"

"God."

"Oh. Sorry to interrupt."

"It's okay," I said. "He's gone now."

"Well, that's a comforting thought."

38

Et Lux Perpetua Luceat Eis

Dear Marcus,

Don't panic. I haven't killed myself, though sometimes I wish I could. I must go away, and you will probably never see me again. If only I could be there for you and your family to share our grief, but there's somewhere I need to be. Please understand, although that's impossible.

I have enclosed several important items:

The first is a list of numbers and passwords for all my Swiss bank accounts. The money is now yours. All the legal arrangements have been made. I chose you because I knew you'd only keep the first few million dollars for yourself. Please give the rest to whatever causes or charities Gianna supported. I am ashamed to admit that while she was alive I never cared to find out what they were.

The rest of the package consists of my musical compositions.

If you like, you may claim them as your own. Just make sure
they're heard.

I think I will miss you a great deal. There is a piece of Gianna
that dwells within you. Keep it alive.

Your friend,
Louis

I thought about adding "P.S.: Beware of my brother," but
didn't want to end the letter on an ominous note.

After mailing the package to Marcus, I made a direct
deposit of fifteen million dollars (after taxes) in Daphne's
checking account and sent her a telegram that read:
"Congratulations! You're fired. Have a good life."

I couldn't bring myself to meet with my former comrades,
knowing that some of them had conspired to end Gianna's life.
But I sent a general proclamation officially transferring all infernal authority to Mephistopheles. He would make an efficient
and occasionally brilliant Devil. I had Belial transferred to a private psychiatric hospital and secured enough money for him to
live there in peace until he was finally called to Heaven, which I
hoped wouldn't be long.

So went my preparations for ending my time on Earth.
Now I sit here in my library enjoying my last glass of fine
scotch. I will leave this manuscript, my own *Requiem*, here next
to the feather from my scorched wings. I wonder what my new
wings will feel like, or if I'll even get that far. Perhaps I will be
annihilated the moment I enter the doorway, disintegrated
like a leaf at ground zero. Either way, it will be a quieter
Armageddon than any poet or preacher could have imagined.

It's too much to ask to be remembered for anything other
than terror and despair and cold-blooded chaos, for anything
other than evil. I can only beg the muse of history to include

this among my legacies—that I loved Gianna as well as I could.

Without knowing it, she gave me in return a glimpse of a forgotten paradise. If Heaven is the sun, then Gianna was the moon for me—a pale, brilliant reflection of God's love in the midnight of my long, dark existence.

Epilogue

At twilight, on a dark street in the depths of Anacostia, a young boy in a gray hooded sweatshirt loitered outside a liquor store. A blue sport utility vehicle pulled up to the curb a few feet away from him. Money and vials changed hands.

The night grew darker. The neighborhood's only functioning streetlight burned across the street, outside the AIDS hospice. A little girl in pigtail braids approached the boy.

"Luther, Mama says come home for dinner."

"Get back, bitch. Can't you see I'm workin'?"

"I'm tellin' her you called me that!" The little girl ran down the sidewalk, then stopped and stared at the approaching figure.

Walking up the other side of the street was a tall, well-dressed white man with black hair. He carried a large rolled-up piece of paper.

"That one of your customers, Luther?" the girl said.

"I hope so." The boy began to saunter across the street, then saw the man pause in front of the hospice. "Naw, he's just a doctor or a priest or somethin'. Shit."

The man examined the piece of paper in his hands under the pale orange streetlight, then looked at the building again, his head cocked. He stuffed the paper in his back pocket and took a step toward the brick facade. Without looking around, he stripped off his clothing until he was naked.

"What the fuck?" Luther said under his breath. "Don't look, Mia." The little girl gawked at the naked man and tugged on her green mitten string.

The man hesitated only a moment before moving his hand towards the hospice building, on the brick next to the door. Instead of touching the wall, his hand moved through it, and as it did, the bricks transformed into light one by one, until they created a luminous doorway.

"Holy shit!" Luther ran to his little sister and swept her into his arms. He backed away from the street until he bumped into the side of the liquor store.

The man stepped through the doorway of light. As he did, his body seemed to dissipate until it too was made of light. There was no sound.

Suddenly, the doorway vanished, and the bricks became bricks again.

Mia whimpered in Luther's arms. He looked at her tear-drenched face, then back at the building, then at his sister again.

"Let's go home, okay?" he said.

Luther turned and walked down the sidewalk, Mia's arms around his neck.

"Mama made tater tots," she said.

"Yeah?"

"Uh-huh."

"Good. I like tater tots."

Appendix: Requiem

I. Requiem & Kyrie

Requiem aeternam dona eis, Domine,
et lux perpetua luceat eis.
Te decet hymnus, Deus, in Sion,
et tibi reddetur votum in Jerusalem.
Exaudi orationem meam,
ad te omnis caro veniet.
Kyrie eleison, Christe eleison.

Eternal rest grant unto them, O Lord,
and let perpetual light shine upon them.
There shall be singing unto Thee in Sion,
and prayer shall go up to Thee in Jerusalem.
Hear my prayer,
unto Thee all flesh shall come.
Lord have mercy, Christ have mercy.

II. Dies Irae

Dies irae, dies illa,
solvet saeclum in favilla,
teste David cum Sibylla.
Quantus tremor est futurus,
quando Judex est venturus,
cuncta stricte discussurus!
Tuba mirum spargens sonum,
per sepulchra regionum,
coget omnes ante thronum.

Day of wrath, day of mourning,
earth in smouldering ashes lying,
so spake David and the Sibyl.
How great the trembling shall be
when the Judge shall come,
by whose sentence all shall be bound!
The trumpet, sending its wondrous sound
through the tombs in every land,
shall bring all before the throne.

Mors stupebit et natura,
cum resurget creatura,
Judicanti responsura.

Death shall stun and nature quake
when all creatures rise again
to answer to the Judge.

Liber scriptus proferetur,
in quo totum continetur,
unde mundus judicetur.
Judex ergo cum sedebit,
quidquid latet apparebit,
nil inultum remanebit.

The written book shall be brought forth
in which all is recorded,
whence the world shall be judged.
Therefore, when the Judge shall be seated
nothing shall be hidden any longer,
no wrong shall remain unpunished.

Quid sum miser tunc dicturus?
Quem patronum rogaturus,
cum vix justus sit securus?

What shall I, a poor sinner, say?
What patron shall I entreat
when even the just need mercy?

Rex tremendae majestatis,
qui salvandos salvas gratis,
salva me, fons pietatis.

King of tremendous majesty,
who sends us free salvation,
save me, fount of mercy.

Recordare, Jesu pie,
quod sum causa tuae viae,
ne me perdas illa die.
Quaerens me, sedisti lassus,
redemisti crucem passus;
tantus labor non sit cassus.
Juste Judex ultionis,
donum fac remissionis
ante diem rationis.
Ingemisco tamquam reus,
culpa rubet vultus meus,
supplicanti parce, Deus.
Qui Mariam absolvisti,
et latronem exaudisti,
mihi quoque spem dedisti.
Preces meae non sunt dignae,
sed tu bonus fac benigne,
ne perenni cremer igne.

Remember, kind Jesus,
that I caused thy earthly course.
Do not forget me on that day.
Seeking me, Thou sat down weary,
redeemed me on the cross of suffering;
such labor should not be in vain.
Righteous Judge of retribution,
grant the gift of absolution
before the day of reckoning.
I groan, as one who is accused;
guilt reddens my cheek;
spare thy supplicant, O God.
Thou who absolved Mary,
and harkened to the thief,
hast given hope to me.
My prayers are worthless,
but Thou, who art good and kind,
rescue me from everlasting fire.

Inter oves locum praesta,	With thy sheep give me a place,
et ab hoedis me sequestra,	and from the goats keep me separate,
statuens in parte dextra.	placing me at thy right hand.

Confutatis maledictis,	When the wicked have been confounded,
flammis acribus addictis,	doomed to the devouring flames,
voca me cum benedictis.	call me with the blessed.
Oro supplex et acclinis,	I pray, supplicant and kneeling,
cor contritum quasi cinis,	my heart crushed almost to ashes;
gere curam mei finis.	watch o'er me in my final hour.

Lacrymosa dies illa,	Tearful shall that day be
qua resurget ex favilla,	when from the ashes shall arise
judicandus homo reus.	guilty man to be judged.
Huic ergo parce, Deus,	Spare him then, O God;
pie Jesu Domine,	gentle Lord Jesus,
dona eis requiem. Amen.	grant him eternal rest. Amen.

III. Offertorio

Domine Jesu Christe, Rex gloriae,	Lord Jesus Christ, King of glory,
libera animas omnium fidelium defunctorum	free the souls of all the faithful departed
de poenis inferni et de profundo lacu.	from the pains of hell and from the deep pit.
Libera eas de ore leonis,	Free them from the lion's mouth,
ne absorbeat eas tartarus,	lest hell devour them
ne cadant in obscurum;	or they fall into darkness;
sed signifer sanctus Michael	let the standard-bearer, St. Michael,
repraesentet eas in lucem sanctam,	lead them into the holy light,
quam olim Abrahae promisisti et semini ejus.	as you promised Abraham and his seed.

Hostias et preces tibi, Domine,
laudis offerimus.
Tu suscipe pro animabus illis,
quarum hodie memoriam facimus.
Fac eas, Domine, de morte transire ad vitam,
quam olim Abrahae promisisti et semini ejus.

A sacrifice of praise and prayer, O Lord,
we offer Thee.
Accept it on behalf of those souls
we commemorate this day;
let them, O Lord, pass from death to life,
as you promised Abraham and his seed.

IV. Sanctus

Sanctus, sanctus, sanctus,
Dominus Deus Sabaoth!
Pleni sunt coeli et terra gloria tua.
Hosanna in excelsis.
Benedictus qui venit in nomine
  Domini.
Hosanna in excelsis.

Holy, holy, holy,
Lord God of Hosts!
Heaven and earth are full of thy glory.
Hosanna in the highest.
Blessed is he who cometh in the name
  of the Lord.
Hosanna in the highest.

V. Agnus Dei

Agnus Dei,
qui tollis peccata mundi,
dona eis requiem sempiternam.

Lamb of God,
who taketh away the sins of the world,
grant them eternal rest.

VI. Lux Aeterna

Lux aeterna luceat eis, Domine,
cum sanctis tuis in aeternum,
quia pius es.
Requiem aeternam dona eis, Domine,
et lux perpetua luceat eis.

Let eternal light shine upon them, O Lord,
with thy saints forever,
for Thou art merciful.
Eternal rest grant unto them, O Lord,
and let perpetual light shine upon them.

VII. *Libera Me*

Libera me, Domine, de morte aeterna,	Deliver me, O Lord, from eternal death
in die illa tremenda,	on that dreadful day,
quando coeli movendi sunt et terra,	when the heavens and earth shall be moved,
dum veneris judicare	when Thou shalt come to judge
saeculum per ignem.	the world by fire.
Tremens factus sum ego et timeo,	I am full of fear and I tremble,
dum discussio venerit atque ventura ira.	awaiting the day of account and wrath to come.
Dies irae, dies illa,	Day of wrath, day of mourning,
calamitatis et miseriae,	day of calamity and misery,
dies magna et amara valde.	that day great and most bitter.
Requiem aeternam dona eis, Domine,	Eternal rest grant unto them, O Lord,
et lux perpetua luceat eis.	and let perpetual light shine upon them.

About the Author

Jeri has been telling stories in her head since she was five but waited twenty years to start writing them down. She has a master's degree in public policy. *Requiem for the Devil* has won numerous awards, including First Place, National Writers Association Novel Contest 2000; Third Place, PublishingOnline.com's Great North American Fiction Awards; Semifinalist, Warner Aspect First Novel Contest; and Honorary Mention, Santa Fe Writers Project Literary Awards.

Jeri lives in Maryland with her husband and three cats. She can be reached at jeri@jerismithready.com or on the Web at www.jerismithready.com.

Printed in the United States
203286BV00012B/4-6/A